She shrugged. "When someone returns to town after a dozen years, people are bound to talk."

"No doubt," Luke admitted, his tone grim.

"All good stuff," she told him.

He lifted his mug, swallowed a mouthful of coffee. "It seems that you have me at a disadvantage."

"How so?"

"You obviously know my name—and apparently a lot more—but I don't know yours."

She touched a hand to the bib of her apron. "Oh. I forgot my name tag today," she realized. "Eva Rose Armstrong."

He set down his mug and proffered his hand. "It's a pleasure to meet you, Eva Rose Armstrong."

She felt a tingle through her veins as her palm slid against his. His hand was wide and strong, with calluses that attested to a familiarity with manual labor. It was a man's hand, and every womanly part of her responded to the contact.

"Eva," she said. "My friends call me Eva."

"Are we going to be friends, Eva?"

"I think so," she said, not daring to admit that she already hoped "friends" was only the beginning of what they would be to one another.

"I could probably use a friend," he admitted, releasing her hand to pick up his fork again. "I don't think I have any left in this town."

* * *

Montana Mavericks:
The Great Family Roundup—
Real cowboys and real love in Rust Creek Falls!

THE MAVERICK'S MIDNIGHT PROPOSAL

BY
BRENDA HARLEN

MILLS & BOON

Brenda Harlen is a former attorney who once had the privilege of appearing before the Supreme Court of Canada. The practice of law taught her a lot about the world and reinforced her determination to become a writer—because in fiction, she could promise a happy ending! Now she is an award-winning, national best-selling author of more than thirty titles for Mills & Boon. You can keep up-to-date with Brenda on Facebook and Twitter or through her website, www.brendaharlen.com.

For my parents,
who exemplify the joys and blessings of home—
not just at the holidays but always.

Prologue

Lee Stanton paused as he entered the room, his gaze caught by the blinking light on his phone indicating that he had a message. He picked it up to check the call history. The same number had shown up on his display more than a dozen times in the past four days, though the caller, who'd identified himself as David Bradford, had only left two messages previously. This would be the third.

He pressed the button to connect to voice mail, then punched in his access code.

"This is David Bradford again, the private investigator from Tulsa, hired by Hudson Jones to track down Luke Stockton from Rust Creek Falls, Montana. Please call me back at 539-555-6234."

Lee hit the erase button.

The investigator was nothing if not persistent, and the client—Hudson Jones—was obviously getting his money's worth. Unfortunately, his perseverance wasn't going to pay off this time, because it wasn't possible to find someone who didn't exist, and Luke Stockton had disappeared twelve years earlier on his way to Cheyenne, Wyoming.

Lee tried to put the call out of his mind as he rummaged through the refrigerator, looking for something—anything—to throw together for dinner. After seven hours on horseback feeding cattle and checking perimeter fence, he was cold and tired and hungry. And apparently long overdue for a trip to the grocery store.

He pulled a bottle of beer out of the fridge and twisted off the cap. He tipped the bottle to his lips as he picked up the phone again, dialing from memory the number for Peppe's Pizza.

While he waited for his dinner to be delivered, he turned on the television and flipped through the twelve channels that were included with basic cable as part of his rent. But nothing on the screen held his attention for long.

For the past dozen years, he'd walked the right side of the law, working from sunup to sundown, falling into bed exhausted at the end of the day. But no matter how fatigued his body was, he couldn't escape the memories that continued to haunt his dreams. Memories of a past he'd wanted only to leave behind. Now he couldn't help but wonder if that past had caught up with him.

...hired by Hudson Jones to track down Luke Stockton...

He opened the laptop he'd picked up secondhand and kept plugged in because the battery didn't hold much of a charge. He opened a browser, then started a search for Hudson Jones.

The results were numerous and instantaneous, and a quick skim of the headlines revealed that Hudson Jones was a millionaire cowboy originally from Oklahoma. Since he knew that Luke Stockton had never been to Oklahoma and hadn't rubbed elbows with any millionaires in his past, he figured the PI had taken a wrong turn somewhere. He was about to close the browser when a headline announcing Hudson Jones's marriage caught his eye. The name of the man's wife: Bella Stockton.

Bella? Married?

Stunned, he clicked on the link and found himself looking at a photo of the millionaire cowboy and his beautiful bride. The caption indicated that the couple had exchanged vows early in June—almost six months earlier.

Lee's heart hammered against his ribs as he leaned toward the screen for a closer look. The stunning young woman in the white gown didn't bear much resemblance to the awkward teen he remembered. Except for the eyes. Even in an online photograph, even after so much time had passed, there was no mistaking those big brown eyes.

He blinked away the moisture that blurred his vision and finally acknowledged the truth that was staring back at him: Hudson Jones's bride was indeed Luke's little sister.

And if her new husband had hired a PI to find Luke, then Bella must have told him about losing touch with her siblings. Maybe she'd even asked Hudson to help her find them.

Lee shook his head and tipped the bottle to his mouth again. He was only speculating about her thoughts and motives. He had no way of knowing if Bella wanted to find Luke, but the possibility tugged at him.

Half an hour later, after he'd finished another beer and half of his pizza, he finally picked up the phone and dialed the PI's number.

Chapter One

Anticipation and trepidation wore on Luke with every mile on his tires throughout the drive to Rust Creek Falls. The scenery outside his window was a blur as memories of his first twenty-one years played through his mind like an old movie—and not one with a happy ending.

He'd traveled from Cheyenne to Butte the day before and crashed in a cheap motel. Though his body had craved sleep, his mind wouldn't let him rest and he'd stared at the ceiling for a long time, questioning the impulse that had brought him on this journey.

When he woke in the morning, his first thought had been to turn around and go back to Wyoming.

Because he was a coward.

But apparently the fierceness with which he missed his family was stronger than his cowardice, because instead of turning back, he pushed forward.

After fueling himself with an extra large coffee, he'd started back on the road to Rust Creek Falls. Three and a half hours later, he was almost there.

His gaze searched for the familiar sign that welcomed visitors to town. Twelve years earlier the sign had been old and worn, so it was possible that the marker was no longer standing or—if it was—it might be faded so much that the paint was impossible to read. It didn't matter. Luke didn't need a marker to let him know he'd arrived. Even if he hadn't recognized the terrain, he would have known it in his gut.

But twelve years was a long time, and people changed more quickly than the towns they lived in. Bella hadn't even been a teenager when he left; now she was a woman—and a wife.

Mrs. Bella Jones.

He shook his head, still unable to believe that his little sister was all grown up, still struggling to come to terms with the time he'd lost with his family. And the staggering weight of guilt, because he knew it was his fault.

Of course, Bella didn't know that. Because if she did, she would never have made the effort to find him. More likely, she would have been grateful that he'd left town, and happy he'd stayed away. But she deserved to know the truth—all of his brothers and sisters deserved the truth. A truth that Luke had been too ashamed to tell them, and the grief and remorse weighed on him still.

Although a dozen years had passed since he left Montana, in all that time, he'd never forgotten—or stopped missing—the family he used to have. Since he left Rust Creek Falls, not a single day passed without him thinking about the family he'd walked away from. Bailey and Daniel had gone with him, and the three oldest brothers had stuck close together—at least for a while.

Over the years, he'd lost count of the number of times he'd thought about going home—only to remember all the reasons he'd left. For Luke, "you can't go home again" was more than a catchphrase—it was the reality of his life.

So why was he trying to change that reality now?

Because Bella wanted to see him.

He'd finally called her from the motel the night before to tell her that he was on his way. Partly because he was desperate to hear her voice and partly because he knew that if she was expecting him, he'd be less inclined to turn around and head back to Wyoming.

He'd let her down once, but he wouldn't do it again.

Now he was finally going home—a prospect that filled him with anticipation and more than a little bit of trepidation. As a result of one foolish, youthful error in judgment, he'd lost them all: his parents—Rob and Lauren, and his six siblings—Bailey, Danny, Jamie, Bella, Dana and Liza.

His error.

He tried to push the painful memories aside, because he knew that there was no way to go back in time and do things differently. But sometimes, late at night and deep in dreams, he allowed himself to make a different choice. A smarter choice. And in those dreams, he woke up in the same house he'd lived in for the first twenty-one years of his life, his mother making breakfast in the kitchen while he crawled out of bed, grumbling about the early hour as he dressed in the dark and headed out to the barn to help his father and brothers with the chores.

And every time he dreamed about them, he awakened with such a huge, heavy weight on his chest, he wondered how it was possible that his broken heart was still beating. Then he'd grab a granola bar or pour himself a bowl of cereal and head out to the barn at whatever ranch he was currently working and throw himself into the physical labor, as if successfully wrestling bales of hay would somehow help him overcome the grief and guilt.

His foot eased off the accelerator as he approached the town limits, doubts again battering at him from all directions. Was he really going to do this? Was he, finally, after so many years, going to see his sisters and brothers again?

He'd programmed his GPS to take him to Just Us Kids—the day care facility owned by Hudson Jones's family and where Bella was employed as a manager. The day care hadn't existed twelve years ago, which made him wonder how many other businesses had come and gone in that period of time. Was Crawford's General Store still the only place in town to buy a quart of milk? Did the Ace in the Hole still have the flickering neon sign that beckoned local cowboys with the promise of cold beer and pretty girls? Was the coffee at Daisy's Donut Shop still always hot and fresh?

He could use some of that coffee now. Especially when he glanced at the display on his GPS and saw that his ETA was less than fifteen minutes.

Less than fifteen minutes after more than twelve years.

His fingers tightened on the steering wheel as he drove down Cedar Street, the winter finery on display reminding him that Christmas was less than three weeks away. Garlands and twinkling lights festooned all the storefronts, and a dusting of fresh snow on the sidewalks added to the holiday atmosphere.

Even in Wyoming, he'd heard about the flood that had devastated Rust Creek Falls a few years back, but the community had obviously come together to rebuild.

He'd expected—maybe even hoped—that the town had changed, but everything looked very much the same.

He impulsively turned the corner toward Daisy's Donut Shop, desperate not just for a quick cup of coffee but also a few extra minutes to regain control of his emotions before facing his sister.

He pushed the door open and joined the line at the counter. An elderly man, headed to a table with a mug of steaming coffee in his hand, nodded in his direction.

Just a friendly resident greeting a stranger in town— or so Luke believed until the man said, "Nice to see you, Luke."

The gruff voice was as familiar as Old Gene's face. "Good morning, Mr. Strickland."

"You home for the holidays?" the old man asked.

Home.

The word tugged at something inside him.

Was this his home? He'd been wandering for so long, never setting down roots in any one place, that the word was almost unfamiliar to him.

Unfamiliar and yet oh-so-inviting.

"Just here to visit my sister," he said.

Gene nodded. "She'll be glad to see you."

Luke hoped he was right.

The old man carried his coffee to a booth, where a group of his contemporaries was already seated and waiting for him.

A middle-aged man with graying hair and a much younger blonde woman stepped up to the counter next to place their order. Luke recognized the man as Ben Dalton—the only attorney in town. Ben spotted Luke when he turned to speak to his companion and his eyes widened in obvious surprise. After shaking Luke's hand, Ben introduced his female companion.

"This is my law partner, Maggie Crawford." Ben winked. "I stole her away from a big firm in Los Angeles."

"Then you're a long way from home," Luke said to the woman.

She shook her head. "This is my home now."

"Maggie's married to Jesse Crawford," Ben told him.

"Jesse went to school with my brother Bailey," Luke explained the connection to Maggie. And he'd gone to school with Ben's daughter, Paige.

"Small world," she murmured.

"So it would seem," Luke agreed. "Although Rust Creek Falls has grown even more than I realized if it's able to support two lawyers now."

"Four," Ben corrected. "My daughter, Lindsay, has been working with us since she passed the bar last year. And Maggie's brother, Ryan Roarke, hung up a shingle after he married Kristen Dalton."

"Good to know there are options if I find myself in need of legal services," Luke said.

"Speaking of legal services," Maggie said. "We've got to get to Kalispell for a settlement conference."

Ben nodded. "It was good to see you again, Luke."

"You, too," Luke said. "And nice to meet you, Maggie."

As the two attorneys turned and walked away, he stepped up to the counter.

"Can I help you?"

He glanced from the tempting variety of sweets in the glass-fronted display case to the even more tempting woman behind the counter, and awareness hummed in his veins. Or maybe he'd just imagined the sensation. Maybe what he'd felt was simply relief that here, finally, was someone who didn't know him or his history. Because the gorgeous blonde with wide blue eyes wasn't anyone from his past. If he'd met her before, he was certain he would have remembered.

She followed up the question with a smile, drawing his gaze to the curve of her glossy pink lips. Yeah, her mouth looked a lot sweeter than the glazed donuts for sale, but he'd come back to Rust Creek Falls for one reason and it wasn't to enjoy the local sights—no matter how pretty they might be.

"Coffee," he suddenly remembered. "Large. Black."

Those beautiful blue eyes sparkled with humor. "For here or to go?"

"To go."

She selected a tall paper cup, filled it from the pot then snapped on a lid.

"Thanks." He passed her his money in exchange for the beverage.

She smiled at him again. "You're welcome."

"Large café mocha with extra whipped cream."

Eva Armstrong regretfully shifted her attention from the backside of the handsome cowboy making his way to the door to her next customer. Ellie Traub was a regular who always ordered an old-fashioned glazed along with her large mocha and carried both to a table where she'd sit with Mary and Rita Dalton—sisters-in-law by marriage—and chat about all the comings and goings in town.

"That Luke Stockton sure grew up to be a handsome man," Ellie commented.

Eva mentally assigned the name to the cowboy, satisfied that it fit—even if it didn't answer any of the questions racing through her brain.

"Of course, they were all good-looking boys," Ellie continued.

"Who?" Eva asked.

"Luke, Bailey and Daniel. And Jamie, too, of course." She used the tongs to select a donut from the case and set it on a plate. "I didn't remember that Jamie had so many brothers."

The older woman nodded. "Rob and Lauren had seven kids altogether—four boys and three girls."

Eva punched the order into the cash register.

"And then, when they died in that accident…" Ellie let the words trail off as she shook her head. "Of course, you were probably too young to remember that. It was close to a dozen years ago now."

Twelve years meant that Eva would have been thirteen when they died. And now that she had the reference of a timeline, she did vaguely recall hearing about a car accident that resulted in the deaths of a local rancher and his wife and orphaned their children. In fact, one of the daughters, Bella, had been a year behind Eva in school.

She handed the customer's change across the counter. "Have a good day, Mrs. Traub."

"Thanks," Ellie said, and carried her mug and plate away from the counter.

Eva turned with a smile to the next customer in line but was admittedly distracted by thoughts of Luke Stockton. In fact, she felt a little dazed after the brief encounter with the handsome cowboy, as if she'd been hit over the head with a sack of flour.

Of course, she had a habit of falling hard and fast—

and always for the wrong men. But no matter how many times her heart ended up bruised, she refused to give up hope. Just like the fairy-tale princess who believed that someday her prince would come, Eva believed that her soul mate was out there somewhere.

Or maybe, just maybe, he was right here in Rust Creek Falls now.

The rest of the morning passed in a blur. The donut shop did a brisk business, which kept her hands busy but didn't prevent her mind from speculating about the new man in town.

"You trying to rub the Formica right off that table?" asked a voice behind her.

Eva glanced back at Tracie, the cook who worked the lunch shift. "I guess my mind was wandering," she admitted as she dropped the cloth onto the tray filled with plates and cups that she'd already cleared away.

"Maybe it could wander back to the kitchen and get started making a lemon meringue pie."

"I thought apple and coconut were on the menu today."

Tracie nodded. "But I got a call-in order for a lemon meringue." She looked at the slip where she'd written the customer's name and number. "Lydia Grant. She's making dinner for her fiancé tonight and apparently lemon meringue pie is his favorite."

Eva knew that, of course. Because Lydia's fiancé was Zach Dalton, a rancher who had recently moved to Rust Creek Falls with his father and siblings after the devastating loss of his mother in a house fire.

Unlike so many men, Zach was a traditional kind of guy who wanted to get married and have children. In fact, he was so determined that he'd even advertised in the *Gazette* for a woman who was an excellent cook and homemaker and loved kids, dogs and horses.

Eva had gone on a few dates with Zach before he'd fallen in love with Lydia—who didn't have any of the traits that he'd claimed to be looking for in a wife. Now Eva, who had fulfilled all of his requirements—at least on paper—was being enlisted to make Zach's favorite pie for his future wife to serve to him.

As she carried the tray of dirty dishes to the kitchen, she acknowledged that this was only the most recent in a string of romantic disappointments.

But her heart wasn't heavy as she began to measure the ingredients for the pastry. Because she wasn't thinking about Zach and Lydia's engagement—she was thinking about the return to Rust Creek Falls of sexy cowboy Luke Stockton.

Luke sat in his truck in the parking lot outside Just Us Kids Day Care Center. Somewhere inside the brick building with the colorful sign that looked as if it had been written in thick crayon by a first grader, his sister was waiting for him. He took another minute to finish his coffee as he continued to sit and stare at the double doors that would take him from the present to his past.

He lifted the cup to his lips and let his gaze shift to the fenced-in play area where a group of kids, bundled up in thick snowsuits, hats, mittens and boots, were playing in the deep snow. Despite the frigid temperatures, they were laughing and giggling and having a great time. He didn't know how old they were—three? four?—but watching them reminded him of Bella when she'd been a similar age.

As a child, she'd had seemingly endless energy and

enthusiasm, and she'd found joy in every aspect of life. Of course, that was a lot of years before their parents were killed, sucking all the joy out of all their lives.

Before he could go too far down that dark path, he stepped out of the truck and made his way toward the entrance. He lifted his arm to reach for the handle, then hesitated again. Over the past dozen years, he'd never let himself think about a potential reunion with his siblings because he never believed he would come back to Rust Creek Falls. Now that the moment was here, he was paralyzed by his own doubts and fears.

Apparently his sister felt differently, because the door he was staring at suddenly flung open.

"You're here!"

Those two words were the only warning Luke got before Bella launched herself into his arms. He caught her—a reflex action—and she pressed her cheek to his, covering his face with kisses and tears.

The unexpected outpouring of affection made his heart swell inside his chest, so much that his ribs actually ached.

"You're really here," she said again.

"I'm *really* here," he confirmed.

"I know you said you were coming," she acknowledged, "but I've been waiting for so long that it feels like forever."

His arms tightened around her. It felt like forever to him, too. And though he'd had more than a few reservations about returning to Rust Creek Falls, right now, with Bella in his arms, he was certain that he'd made the right decision.

All too soon, she was drawing away again. "Come on," she said, tugging on his arm. "I want you to meet my husband." Her eyes sparkled as her lips curved. "We've been married for almost six months, and I still get such a thrill every time I say that."

"I feel a shock to hear you say it," Luke confessed. But he was eager to meet Hudson Jones—and to thank him for hiring the PI who had tracked him down.

When he stepped into the building, he was immediately enveloped by warmth—a welcome reprieve from the bitter winds blowing outside—and assailed by various sounds and scents: crying and cooing and singing; baby powder and Play-Doh and fresh gingerbread.

"We're baking cookies for the toddlers to decorate today," she explained. "And to eat, during snack time."

"I guess day care isn't all about story time and building blocks," he mused.

She laughed. "You have no idea."

He took a minute to catch his breath and survey the space. The tiles beneath his boots were multicolored, the walls were painted sunshine yellow and decorated with artwork that he suspected had been done by children who attended the day care. "How did you end up working here?"

"The facility was opening at a time when I was desperate for a job," she admitted. "Jamie's wife died after giving birth to their three babies, so I came home from college to help him with Henry, Jared and Katie."

He'd thought nothing could surprise him more than discovering that Bella was married, and now she was telling him that his youngest brother had also married—and been widowed—and was a father. "Triplets?"

She nodded.

"And you left school to be his babysitter?"

"He's family," she said simply, as if that explained

everything. "And the only brother I had left after you, Bailey and Danny took off."

"Bella—"

"We'll talk about that later," she interjected, hooking one arm through Luke's and raising her other hand to knock on a partially open door beside the main reception desk.

"Come in."

She pushed the door open the rest of the way. "Hudson, there's someone here that I want you to meet."

The man behind the desk slid his chair back and stood up. The smile that lit his eyes when he looked at his wife assured Luke that he was just as much in love with Bella as she obviously was with him.

Then his gaze shifted, and cooled noticeably. "You must be Luke."

He nodded and shook the proffered hand. "It's nice to meet the man who won my sister's heart."

"She won mine first," Hudson said. "And I'd do anything for my beautiful bride, so I was pleased to hear that David Bradford was successful in tracking you down in Wyoming."

"I'm grateful for your efforts," Luke said sincerely.

"I just want Bella to be happy," Hudson said.

Luke understood what the man was saying—and what he wasn't. Hudson had hired the private investigator to find Bella's siblings because it was what she wanted, but he wouldn't tolerate anyone—even her family—hurting his wife. Although Hudson's demeanor made him a little wary, Luke couldn't help but respect his new brother-in-law for wanting to protect his bride.

"I *am* happy," Bella assured him. "And I know this is going to be the best Christmas ever, not just because it's my first as Mrs. Hudson Jones—" she sent an ador-ing look toward her husband "—but because Luke is fi-nally home and Danny is planning his Christmas Eve wedding."

Luke opened his mouth, intending to tell her that he wouldn't be staying in Rust Creek Falls for Christmas, but the last part of her statement pushed everything else from his mind.

"Our Danny?"

Bella nodded.

"He's here—in Rust Creek Falls?"

"You didn't know?"

Luke shook his head. "We kind of lost touch a few years back," he admitted.

"He's been here since October," Bella told him now. "After he saw an interview with Jamie on *The Great Roundup*, he realized he missed his family and finally decided to come back."

"What's *The Great Roundup*?"

His sister seemed surprised by the question. "Don't you watch TV?"

"Not a lot," he admitted.

"*The Great Roundup* is a reality show, similar to *The Amazing Race* but with a Western theme," Hudson ex-plained. "There are various challenges of skill and sur-vival, and the winner gets a million dollars."

"And you watch this?" Luke asked, his tone dubious.

"Travis Dalton and Brenna O'Reilly are on the show," his brother-in-law explained.

"And they're engaged!" Bella exclaimed.

Although Luke didn't know Travis or Brenna, he knew the Daltons and O'Reillys were longtime residents of Rust Creek Falls. But he was more interested in what she'd said about their brother than the details of a reality show. "And you said Danny's engaged, too?"

"To Annie Lattimore," she said, naming their brother's high school sweetheart.

"I should have known," he realized. "Danny never wanted to leave Rust Creek Falls—or Annie."

"Then why did he?" Bella wondered. "Why did *you*?"

He answered with the truth—or at least part of it. "Because we couldn't stay. The grandparents made it clear they didn't want us hanging around, that even four kids were too much of a burden."

"Not long after you left, they sent Dana and Liz away, too," Bella told him.

Hudson slid an arm across her shoulders—a wordless gesture of support and comfort—while Luke just looked on helplessly.

"I'm so sorry," he told her. "We—*I*—honestly thought it was the best decision at the time."

"Well, you're here now," she said again, blinking away the tears that had filled her eyes. "And Dana's been found, too—she lives with her adoptive family in Portland—so I'm confident that we'll all be together again soon."

Luke shifted his gaze to his brother-in-law. "Has your PI succeeded in tracking down everyone else?"

"Not yet," Hudson admitted. "But he's got some leads and I'm sure we'll see results soon." He glanced down as his cell phone buzzed. "Sorry—that's a business call I need to take."

"Of course," Bella acknowledged, nudging Luke back toward the door, then closing it softly after she'd followed him out. "I need to get back to work, too," she said apologetically.

Luke nodded. "Maybe we can catch up some more later."

"We'll definitely catch up later," she immediately responded. "But now you're probably exhausted after your long drive, so why don't you go back to our house, put your feet up and relax? Even have a nap if you want."

"A nap?" he echoed.

"Nap time isn't just for preschoolers," she assured him, pressing something into his palm.

He stared at the key, wondering how it was so easy for her to not only accept his sudden reappearance in her life but even open up her home to him after so much time had passed. "I don't want to impose," he told her.

"It's not an imposition," she insisted. "We're happy to have you."

He believed that *she* was happy, but he didn't think her husband was overjoyed.

"You and Hudson are still newlyweds," he protested. "I should get a room at the boarding house so you aren't tripping over me."

She laughed. "Obviously you haven't yet seen the house. When you do, you'll realize that there's plenty of room and no reason to worry about anyone tripping over anyone else."

Still, he wasn't entirely comfortable with the idea of staying with the sister he'd had no contact with for more than a decade. Or maybe it was the prospect of staying in Rust Creek Falls at all that made him uneasy.

"Please," she added, and with that single word, the last of his resistance melted away.

"Okay," he relented. "I'll stay for a couple of days."

"That's a good start," she agreed.

Chapter Two

Luke was smiling and shaking his head as he walked out of the day care and headed back to his truck. He'd forgotten how sneaky his sister could be—and how he'd never been able to refuse anything she asked. But he was grateful for her invitation and looking forward to the opportunity to catch up with her and Jamie and Danny.

He was also curious to check out Bella and Hudson's house, but he wasn't quite ready to put his feet up. What he was, his growling stomach pointed out, was hungry.

Earlier, his gut had been so twisted up in knots over the impending reunion with his sister that he hadn't been able to eat anything. Now that the initial meeting was over, he realized he was famished.

He hadn't forgotten about the Ace in the Hole—or the thick, juicy burgers that were served with a mountain of crispy fries. In fact, the memory alone was enough to make his mouth water and, when his stomach rumbled again, he steered his truck toward Sawmill Street.

But for reasons he couldn't fathom, he abruptly turned off Sawmill onto North Broomtail and pulled up in front of Daisy's Donut Shop again.

* * *

After graduating from high school, Eva had wanted to follow her passion and pursue a diploma in baking and pastry arts. But following her heart had led to heartache more times than she could count, so she'd listened to the urging of her parents and opted to study accounting instead. She'd just completed her first year when her father was diagnosed with lymphoma, so she'd returned to Rust Creek Falls to support her family and postponed the rest of her studies.

She'd been fortunate to get a job at Daisy's Donut Shop. The part-time hours had allowed her to earn a little bit of income while also providing the flexibility she'd needed to take her father to his various doctors' appointments and therapies. When Ray Armstrong had finished his treatments, she'd been able to increase her hours and now she was working full-time. Since the doctors had officially declared her dad to be in remission, he'd been pressuring his daughter to return to school and complete her degree. In the spirit of compromise, she'd been taking some online courses and was now only a few courses shy of completion, but she was still happier baking than studying.

Her friends liked to tease that she would be the perfect wife and homemaker, but she hadn't yet met a man who agreed with their assessment.

Maybe having her heart stomped on time and time again should have taught her to be wary, but there wasn't anything she wanted more than to fall in love, get married, fill her home with babies and her kitchen with the sweet scents of baking, so she was trusting fate to put the right man in her path.

In the meantime, she kept busy filling Daisy's display case with mouthwatering goodies. Since the morning rush had passed and it was still early for lunch, Eva took advantage of the lull to brew a fresh pot of coffee, then sipped a cup while she took inventory of the goodies that remained. The white chocolate cranberry cookies had sold out, which made her feel pretty good. Her boss had protested that there was no need to expand their offerings beyond the tried-and-true muffins and donuts, but Eva had been playing around with some of her grandmother's recipes, tweaking here and there, and the residents of Rust Creek Falls—most of them creatures of habit—had overcome their reluctance and started to look forward to daily specials.

Today's pumpkin spice muffins had been gone within the first two hours of the shop's opening, the sticky buns had sold out shortly after and there were only two eggnog biscotti remaining in the jar on the counter. She pulled an empty tray out of the case—the cheesecake-stuffed snickerdoodles had also been decimated by the morning crowd—replaced the liner and set out neatly decorated gingerbread boy and girl cookies.

She glanced up when the bell over the door chimed, and her heart immediately skipped a beat.

He was back.

The handsome cowboy with the sexy voice and troubled eyes.

She'd hoped to see him again, but she hadn't expected that her wish would come true so quickly.

"You're back," she said, because her brain couldn't seem to focus on anything else.

He seemed surprised that she'd remembered him from earlier—or maybe he thought he should remember her from years ago—but he only said, "I'm hungry."

"Then you've come to the right place." She smiled, wanting him to feel welcome, and wishing she could ease the tension that was evident in the line of his jaw and the set of his shoulders. "Breakfast or lunch hungry?"

"Huh?" He looked at her blankly.

She didn't know where he'd gone after he'd left the donut shop earlier, but it was apparent that his mind wasn't occupying the same physical space as his body.

"Are you hungry for breakfast or lunch?" she asked again.

"I don't even know what time it is," he admitted, glancing at the watch on his wrist.

"It's definitely time to get you some food," she decided. "How does a roast beef sandwich with steak-cut fries sound?"

"Delicious."

She smiled again as she filled a mug with coffee and set it on the counter, then gestured to the chair. "Sit."

He sat, then lifted his eyes to meet her gaze. "Are you always this bossy?"

She winked at him. "Only when the occasion warrants."

She left him with his coffee while she slipped into the kitchen to get his food, pausing first to pull out her lip gloss and quickly swipe the wand over her lips.

"He's back," she told Tracie, tucking the tube into her pocket again.

"Who's back?" the cook asked.

"Luke Stockton."

"That's old news," Tracie said, continuing to chop cabbage for the coleslaw she was making. "Half the town saw him in here this morning."

"I don't mean he's back in town," Eva told her, piling

thinly sliced beef onto bread to make his sandwich. "I mean he's back *here*. Sitting at the counter."

"Is that why you're loading up that plate?"

"He said he's hungry."

The cook chuckled. "And the way to a man's heart is through his stomach," she agreed.

Eva felt her cheeks flush. "I'm not interested in his heart."

"Just his body?" Tracie teased. "Can't blame you for that—the man is spectacularly well built."

Eva's cheeks burned hotter. He certainly was that, but that wasn't why she wanted to feed him. Or not entirely.

"He looks a little...lost," she said, adding fries to the plate.

"He hasn't been home to Rust Creek Falls in twelve years," the cook reminded her. "He's probably feeling a little lost."

Twelve years.

Eva couldn't imagine being apart from her family and friends for more than a decade. Even the few months that had passed between visits when she was in college had seemed like an eternity. "I wonder why he stayed away for so long."

"There was a lot of speculation about that," Tracie mused. "But if you want the truth, you'd better ask the man himself."

"I just might do that," she decided.

"Wait," the cook said when she started out of the kitchen.

Eva held back a smile as the other woman added a couple of sprigs of parsley to the plate.

"Presentation matters," Tracie reminded her. "You

know it, or you wouldn't have retouched the gloss on your lips."

Unable to deny that she had done just that, Eva silently took the plate and returned to the counter.

"Thanks," Luke said when she set the meal in front of him.

"Enjoy," she said, and busied herself tidying up the arrangement of mugs as he picked up his fork.

She was glad that he was early for lunch, so that he was the only customer in the donut shop and she was able to focus exclusively on him. Although she suspected that even if she'd had a line all the way to the door, she would have found her attention solely on the handsome stranger.

"Do you want to talk about it?" she asked when he'd polished off the sandwich.

He looked up, obviously surprised by the question, but immediately shook his head.

She gave him another minute before she asked, "Where did you go when you left here this morning?"

He dipped a fry into the ketchup he'd squirted on his plate. "To see my sister."

"I can only imagine how excited Bella must have been when you showed up."

Thick brows drew together over his dark blue eyes. "How'd you know Bella is my sister?" he asked warily.

"I heard Ben Dalton call you Luke," she confided.

"It's quite a jump from my first name to my family connections," he pointed out.

She shrugged. "When someone returns to town after a dozen years, people are bound to talk."

"No doubt," he admitted, his tone grim.

"All good stuff," she told him.

He lifted his mug, swallowed a mouthful of coffee. "It seems that you have me at a disadvantage."

"How so?"

"You obviously know my name—and apparently a lot more—but I don't know yours."

She touched a hand to the bib of her apron. "Oh. I forgot my name tag today," she realized. "Eva Rose Armstrong."

He set down his mug and proffered his hand. "It's a pleasure to meet you, Eva Rose Armstrong."

She felt a tingle through her veins as her palm slid against his. His hand was wide and strong, with calluses that attested to a familiarity with manual labor. It was a man's hand, and every womanly part of her responded to the contact.

"Eva," she said. "My friends call me Eva."

"Are we going to be friends, Eva?" he asked, releasing her hand.

"I think so," she said, not daring to admit that she already hoped *friends* was only the beginning of what they would be to one another.

"I could probably use a friend," he admitted, dredging another fry through ketchup. "I don't think I have any left in this town."

"You haven't stayed in touch with anyone here?"

He shook his head and shoved the fry into his mouth.

"I have to admit that piques my curiosity," she told him.

"You know what they say about curiosity."

She ignored the warning. "Twelve years is a long time to stay away from your family."

"I was working."

The abrupt response and clipped tone cautioned her

to back off, but she pressed on anyway. "You didn't get any time off?"

"Ranching is a full-time job."

She nodded an acknowledgment of the fact. Though her parents both worked in education, no one who lived in Rust Creek Falls was oblivious to the arduous demands of working the land. "No time to make a phone call?"

"How do you know I didn't?" he challenged.

"Did you?"

He pushed his now-empty plate aside. "No."

"Well, you're here now," she said. "That's a start."

"Maybe," he allowed, lifting his mug again, only to discover it was empty.

"More coffee?" Eva offered, wanting to give him an excuse to linger at the counter awhile longer.

Although the lunch crowd would soon fill up the tables, she didn't want to watch Luke Stockton walk out the door because she didn't know when—or even if—she would see him again. And maybe it was unreasonable and irrational, but she couldn't help feeling that the man sitting in front of her was going to change her life—but only if she could get him to stick around long enough to do so.

"No, thanks," he said. "Just the check."

"How about dessert?" she offered as an alternative. "I made the pies fresh this morning, and the coconut cream is a favorite of many customers."

"Actually, I'm more of an apple pie kind of guy."

"We have apple, too."

He rubbed a hand over his flat belly and shook his head. "That sandwich was more than enough to fill the hole in my stomach."

She reluctantly wrote up his check and slid it across the counter.

His fingers brushed hers as he reached for the slip of paper, sending little sparks dancing up her arm and making her wonder how she would respond if he ever really touched her.

Unfortunately, he seemed completely unaffected by the brief contact.

"Thanks," he said. "For the meal and the company."

"My pleasure," she told him.

He retrieved his wallet from the inside pocket of his sheepskin-lined leather jacket, then selected some bills and tucked them under the check before he slid off the stool and rose to his feet.

Her heart sighed as her gaze skimmed over him again. She guessed that he was at least four inches taller than her own five-foot-eight-inch frame, with broad shoulders that tapered to a narrow waist and long legs encased in well-worn denim.

She wanted to tell him that everything was going to be okay, that whatever had caused him to stay away for so long was water under the bridge, that his siblings were all going to welcome him back—because Rust Creek Falls was where he belonged. And she wanted to tell him that she was glad he was home—because she'd been waiting for him her whole life.

But mindful of the brevity of their acquaintance, she wisely kept those thoughts to herself.

Instead, she reached for his check again and impulsively scribbled her cell number on the back of it. "In case you ever need pie...or donuts...or...anything."

Luke looked at the hastily scrawled digits, then at Eva. *Pie...or donuts...or...anything.*
Anything?

Was she hitting on him?

As if she could somehow read the thoughts that circled in his mind, her cheeks flushed, the pink color adding a natural blush to her creamy skin.

Eva Rose Armstrong really was a beautiful woman and maybe, under different circumstances, he might consider what she was offering. Hell, there was no *might* about it. If he'd come to town for any reason other than to reconnect with the family he hadn't seen in a dozen years, he would already have asked when her shift ended and made plans to meet her later.

But he *was* in town to reconnect with his family and he had no time—and even less inclination—for anything else. He'd proven adept enough at messing up his own life; he wasn't going to mess with a pretty young thing who wasn't smart enough to be wary of strangers.

But she'd been kind to him, so he carefully folded the check in half, then tucked it into the inside pocket of his jacket with his wallet. "See ya."

"I hope so," she replied, her lips curving into another sweet smile before he turned away and headed to the exit.

Because that sweet smile seemed to promise all kinds of things that he wasn't sure she meant—and that he couldn't accept even if she did.

Still, as he turned his truck toward Bella and Hudson's house, it was Eva's pretty eyes and warm smile that lingered in his mind.

Luke's first impression of Bella and Hudson's home was that it looked like a million dollars. Of course, his sister's husband was a multimillionaire so it was entirely possible the house they'd purchased from Clive Bickler was worth that much—or more. It was certainly a lot bigger and grander than the home the seven Stockton siblings had shared with their parents, and the newlyweds lived there alone.

He unlocked the door with the spare key, then punched in the code that Bella had given him to disarm the alarm system. A man with Hudson Jones's wealth would want to protect what was his, and Luke appreciated that the protection extended to his sister.

Curious about the house and whatever insights it might give to the couple who lived there, Luke decided to wander around. The home was constructed with high-end materials and included all the latest conveniences, but it wasn't ostentatious. As he made his way from room to room, he couldn't deny that it had a warm and homey feel, and he was pleased to know that his sister had been lucky enough to fall in love with a man who could provide her with all the love and luxuries she deserved.

When he stepped into the family room, his gaze was immediately drawn to the river-rock fireplace and the assortment of photos displayed on the mantel. He crossed the glossy hardwood floor for a closer look. The first picture that caught his eye was of his youngest brother, Jamie, standing next to a woman he thought he recognized as Fallon O'Reilly, with three adorable toddlers at their feet. The next frame contained a wedding photo, and the groom looked enough like Hudson that Luke guessed the man was his brother, but the bride looked vaguely familiar to him, too. Beside that picture was one of Danny, cheek-to-cheek with his high school sweetheart, Annie; beside it was a photo of Dana, all grown-up and proud at her high school graduation.

The smile that tugged at his own lips faded when his gaze shifted to the next photo—an older picture of all the Stockton siblings together with their parents, Rob and Lauren. A reflection of the happy family they'd once been. Before he ruined everything.

Suddenly Luke couldn't bear the thought of facing his sisters and brothers again. He couldn't face the condemnation he was certain he would see in their eyes when they learned the truth about the events of twelve years ago. It would be better for him—for everyone—if he went back to Cheyenne and forgot any ideas about a happy reunion that could never happen.

He retraced his steps to the door, eager to escape the house, the whole town and especially the memories and regrets that assailed him. He yanked his coat off the hanger and was reaching for the door when the sound of the bell stopped him in his tracks.

What was he supposed to do now?

He felt weird answering the door at a house he was only visiting, so he peeked out the window instead.

Almost eight years had passed since he'd last seen his second youngest brother, and his heart gave a hard kick against his ribs when he recognized him on the doorstep now.

He opened the door. "Danny."

"I almost didn't believe Bella when she called to tell me that you were in town," his brother said.

"So you stopped by to see for yourself?"

"Nah, I stopped by because Bella was afraid you might have been spooked by her emotional outburst and decide to take off again before she got home." He looked pointedly at the jacket in Luke's hand. "Was she right?"

"I guess I can't blame her for thinking I'd run...again," he admitted, sliding his jacket back onto the hanger. "There are a lot of memories in this town."

"More good than bad," Danny said.

"The bad are more powerful," he argued.

"Maybe more recent," his brother acknowledged. "Because you've been away for so long."

Danny stepped across the threshold and pulled him in for a man hug. "It's good to see you, Luke."

Luke slapped him on the back as he attempted to swallow the lump in his throat. "You, too, Danny."

His brother cleared his own as he stepped away and moved down the hall toward the kitchen, obviously familiar with the layout of their sister's house. "Bella also said that there were snacks and drinks in the fridge, and to make sure that you didn't go hungry."

"No worries there," Luke said. "I grabbed a bite at Daisy's before I came here."

"Well, I could use some coffee," Danny announced. "You want a cup?"

"Sure." Luke warily eyed the programmable machine that could brew individual cups or full carafes. "If you can figure out how to use that thing."

"It's not as complicated as it looks. The harder task might be finding the coffee."

But it turned out that Bella kept the coffee pods conveniently located in the cupboard directly above the coffee maker. When the coffee was brewed, they took their mugs to the table where Danny told his brother about his reunion with Annie and finally meeting Janie—his daughter.

"And the surprises keep coming," Luke murmured.

"How do you think I felt?" Danny asked. "When I first discovered that Annie had a child, I assumed her husband—ex-husband now—was the father."

"A reasonable assumption," he agreed.

"When we left… I never even considered the possibility that Annie could be pregnant," Danny admitted.

"You were eighteen," Luke reminded him. "Most guys that age are only thinking about sex—not the potential repercussions of it."

"And then I ran away, and I missed the first eleven years of my daughter's life."

Luke stared into his mug. "You didn't run away," he denied. "*I* ran away—and you and Bailey came with me." And the fact that Danny had missed those eleven years with his daughter was one more thing Luke was responsible for. One more wrong he could never make right.

"But now you're home," Danny said, sounding genuinely pleased. As if he'd already forgiven Luke for everything he'd done.

But Danny didn't know the half of it.

Chapter Three

"This isn't my home," Luke said, regretting that it was true. "Not anymore."

"Then why are you here?"

He lifted his cup to his lips as he considered his brother's question. It was the same question he'd asked himself countless times since he'd tossed his duffel bag into his truck and turned it in the direction of Rust Creek Falls.

He still wasn't sure he knew the answer, so he responded with a simple if incomplete truth. "I got a call from Hudson's PI."

"Good to know the guy's finally earned some of the big bucks our brother-in-law is paying him."

"It looks like Hudson has a few bucks to spare," Luke noted, turning his head to encompass the whole room.

"That he does," Danny agreed. "Although it was actually Jamie's wife who started the search last year. Fallon tracked down Dana in Oregon, but she hit a lot of dead ends after that and Hudson offered to take the lead."

It was obvious to both of them that Bella's husband had a lot more resources to throw at the task—and more success as a result.

"Over the years, I'd given a lot of thought to reaching out to our siblings, but I'm not sure I ever would have found the courage to come back if Bradford hadn't made contact."

"We've all been carrying a lot of baggage for a lot of years," Danny noted. "Maybe it's time to let it go and make a fresh start."

It sounded like a good idea to Luke, but he wasn't sure it was possible. "Was it that easy for you?" he asked.

"It wasn't easy at all," his brother said. "But it was necessary."

Luke swallowed another mouthful of coffee.

"So how long are you planning to stay?" Danny asked.

"I haven't thought that far ahead," he admitted.

"There's no specific date that you're expected back in Wyoming?"

He shook his head. "My boss told me to take as much time as I needed."

"Then you can stay for my wedding."

He recalled Bella mentioning plans for a Christmas Eve wedding. "December twenty-fourth is still two-and-a-half weeks away."

"Two-and-a-half weeks isn't a lot of time after so many years," his brother pointed out.

But if he was there for Danny's Christmas Eve wedding, Luke suspected that Bella would insist he stay for Christmas and he wasn't accustomed to celebrating the holidays. In fact, he hadn't celebrated anything in a very long time.

Sensing his hesitation, Danny said, "It would mean a lot to me to have you there."

"Bella and Hudson might not want me hanging around that long," he warned.

"In this house, Bella and Hudson won't even know you're here," Danny said.

"I'll think about it," he decided.

"Or maybe there's another reason you don't want to stay," his brother allowed. "Maybe it's not just cattle and chores waiting for you back in Wyoming."

Luke looked at him blankly.

"Maybe there's a special lady anxiously awaiting your return?" Danny suggested.

He immediately shook his head. "No, there's no one in Wyoming."

But as soon as the words were out of his mouth, an image of the pretty blonde from the donut shop popped into his mind. *Eva.* As pretty and sweet and tempting as the biblical figure for which she was named.

"No one in Wyoming," Danny echoed curiously. "Does that mean there's someone waiting for you somewhere else?"

Luke shook his head again, attempting to shake the image loose. "No," he denied. "There's no one at all."

"That's too bad."

"I like being on my own, with no one to depend on me but me."

"And no one to rely on but you, too," Danny pointed out as he pushed away from the table and went to the refrigerator.

"It works for me," he insisted.

"I thought it worked for me, too, but I was only kidding myself." He pulled out the tray of snacks Bella had prepared and set it in the middle of the table. "I missed a lot of years with Annie and Janie, but I'm determined to make up for that now."

"I'm still trying to get my head around the fact that you're a father—to an eleven-year-old."

"It's been an adjustment for everyone," Danny admitted. "And as much as I want to hate Hank—Annie's ex—because he got to be there when Janie was born, to hold her as a baby, soothe her when she was crying, witness her first steps and take her to school on her first day, I can't. The truth is, I'm grateful that he was there for them, because I wasn't."

"You didn't know," Luke reminded him.

His brother nodded, though he didn't seem reassured by the fact. "Anyway, I can't wait for you to meet her," he said, the pride in his voice unmistakable. "She's smart and funny and absolutely beautiful."

"She must look like her mom, then," Luke teased.

"That she does," Danny agreed. "But the shape of her eyes and the stubborn tilt of her chin are just like our mom."

Luke reached for a cube of cheese.

"Mom and Dad's first grandchild."

His brother nodded. "When I found out that Janie was my daughter, when I got over the shock, I couldn't help but think of Mom and Dad—how they would have responded to the news that they were grandparents."

"They would have been thrilled," he said and popped the cheese into his mouth.

"Yeah," Danny said. "But only after Dad kicked my ass into next week for getting Annie pregnant."

"He would have done exactly that," Bella said from the doorway.

Both Luke and Danny turned. "We didn't hear you come in."

"You were preoccupied with your journey down memory lane—without me," she said, sounding just a little piqued.

"It's a long road," Danny pointed out. "And we only just got started."

"I don't really mind." She settled into the empty chair between them. "I'm just so glad that you're both finally home again."

Luke felt something inside twist painfully. "Rust Creek Falls isn't my home, Bella. Not anymore."

She tipped her chin up and met his gaze squarely. "Of course it is," she insisted. "And after you've spent some time here, you'll realize it's true."

"Bella." He touched a hand to her arm, hoping the contact might ease the harshness of the truth she needed to hear. "I've been living in Wyoming for twelve years—that's my home now."

"But you've never stayed in any one place for more than two years," she pointed out.

He frowned. "How do you know that?"

"It's one of the reasons it took Hudson's PI so long to track you down. The other reason—" she pinned him with a look "—is that Luke Stockton somehow became Lee Stanton."

He picked up a cherry tomato and popped it into his mouth, but his sister wasn't letting him off the hook.

"Why?" she demanded.

Before he could respond, Danny's cell phone buzzed. "That's my cue to run," he said. "Annie went to Kalispell this afternoon for a dress fitting, so I have to pick Janie up from her study group at school."

Luke pushed away from the table and stood up, offering his hand to his brother. Danny shook his hand, then pulled him in for another hug.

"Stop by anytime," he urged his brother. "I know Annie will be happy to see you, and I'm eager for you to meet my daughter."

"I will," Luke promised.

Then Danny gave Bella a quick hug, too, before he disappeared down the hall.

"Now," Bella said, turning her focus back to Luke, "answer my question."

"What question was that?" he hedged, selecting a broccoli spear from the plate.

She snatched it out of his hand before he could lift it to his mouth and held it away from him. "Why were you living in Wyoming as Lee Stanton?"

"It wasn't intentional," Luke told her. "At least, not at first. The bookkeeper at the ranch we were working put me on the payroll as 'Stanton' by mistake and it just seemed like too much effort to try to correct it. When I moved on, I continued to use Stanton so that I could reference my work history under that name. And, in some ways, it was easier to start a new life with a new name."

"But why did you want a new life?" she pressed. "Why did you leave?"

He heard the confusion in her question—and the hurt. "It wasn't an easy decision to make," he admitted, wanting to explain the past and soothe his sister. "But what choice did we have? The ranch was going to be taken by the bank, and the grandparents didn't have room to take us all in—and no interest in doing so. As Gramps said, we were legal adults and they had no obligation to provide us with food or shelter."

Bella's dark brown eyes filled with tears. "I always suspected that they made you leave."

"They didn't make us leave, but they didn't give us

any reason to stay, either. And we thought Jamie, you, Liza and Dana would all be together."

"After they sent Liza and Dana away—" she swiped at a tear that spilled onto her cheek "—there were times I wish they'd sent me and Jamie away, too."

"Was it really so bad?" Luke asked.

"Probably not. We had a roof over our heads and meals on the table. But there was no affection. There was rarely even any warmth or kindness."

"I'm so sorry, Bella."

She shrugged. "It's water under the bridge now. Or mostly, anyway. Because it turns out that you were wrong about the ranch."

"What do you mean?"

"Sunshine Farm doesn't belong to the bank—it belongs to us."

"To you and Hudson?" he guessed, because it seemed a reasonable assumption. Bella's husband obviously had a ton of money, and it was just as obvious he would spend it all to make his wife happy. If the property had been for sale, Luke could imagine Hudson buying it for her without blinking an eye.

But she shook her head. "To you, Bailey, Danny, Jamie, me, Liza and Dana."

He stared at her, uncomprehending. "But…how?"

"When Dad remortgaged the property to fix the barn and buy the new equipment, he also bought mortgage insurance."

Luke was stunned. Even at twenty-one, he'd had a pretty good picture of the tight financial situation at Sunshine Farm. He'd heard his parents talking about it in hushed and worried tones when they thought their children were asleep. He'd recognized the strain in his father's voice, seen it in the lines that furrowed his mother's brow. He'd listened to them argue about the purchase of secondhand equipment that they couldn't afford but desperately needed to keep the ranch operating, and he knew that they'd had to remortgage the property. He hadn't known they'd also arranged for insurance on that mortgage.

He and Bailey and Danny had left because they hadn't believed that there was any other option. For the past twelve years, they'd worked for other people when they could have been working at Sunshine Farm. Or maybe it was naive to think that they might have been able to keep the ranch going—a difficult enough task when Rob Stockton had been around to oversee the operation. More likely, Luke and his brothers would have run the ranch into the ground and been forced to sell anyway.

"We just discovered that the property had been transferred into all of our names, pursuant to the terms of Mom and Dad's will, a few months ago when Zach Dalton approached Jamie to see if we were interested in selling," Bella explained.

"Are you going to sell?" he asked.

"That's a decision we have to make together," she said. "*All* of us."

"I guess that explains why you're so eager for a family reunion," he noted.

"We only found out about the property a few months ago," she said again. "We've been looking for you a lot longer than that." She smiled again. "And now you're finally here."

"Are you sure Hudson doesn't mind me crashing here? Because I can call Melba Strickland to—"

"No," Bella interjected firmly. "Hudson doesn't mind,

and no, you're not staying at Strickland's Boarding House when you've got family here."

He turned his hand over and linked his fingers with hers. "I missed you," he confessed, his voice quiet. "All of you."

"Then why didn't you ever come home?"

He could understand her confusion. She had no way of knowing that his leaving had been prompted not just by grief over the loss of their parents but by guilt—because he was responsible for their being out on the road that night. In addition to all the other factors, that truth was what had compelled him to leave Rust Creek Falls—a futile effort to escape the daily reminders of the mistakes he'd made.

He owed Bella the truth. After all this time, she deserved to know the real reason he went away. But she seemed so happy to see him, and it felt so good to be welcome. The happy light in her eyes warmed the deepest, darkest places in his soul, and Luke didn't want to dim that light.

Not yet.

"You know what? It doesn't matter," she decided when he remained silent. "It only matters that you're here now. And—fingers crossed—Bailey and Liza will soon be, too."

"I don't know if this helps at all, but the last time I saw Bailey, he was heading to New Mexico with his fiancée," Luke said.

"Then Hudson's PI will be heading to New Mexico next," she decided.

"What's in New Mexico?" her husband asked, walking in with a couple of flat boxes in hand.

"Not *what* but *who*," Bella said, lifting her face for his kiss. "And, fingers crossed, the *who* is Bailey."

"New Mexico is a pretty big state," Hudson noted, glancing at Luke. "Any chance you can help narrow down the search?"

Luke shook his head. "Sorry. At the time, I was so baffled by his decision that I didn't ask many questions."

"No worries," Hudson said. "If he's still there, Bradford will find him."

He set the boxes on the table.

Luke sniffed. "Is that…pizza?"

"And wings," Bella told him.

"There's a pizza and wings place in Rust Creek Falls?"

"Wings To Go recently expanded their menu to include pizza." She pushed away from the table and moved to the cupboard to retrieve plates.

"And Daisy's Donut Shop is more than donuts now, too," he noted.

"You've been to Daisy's?" She grabbed a handful of napkins and set them on top of the plates.

"Twice," he admitted. "For coffee on my way to the day care this morning, then for lunch afterward."

"Did you have dessert?"

He shook his head. "The huge roast beef sandwich and mountain of fries filled me up."

"You should have had dessert," Bella said, setting the plates and napkins on the table.

"The woman behind the counter did say that the coconut cream pie was popular," he told her.

"All of the pies, cakes, cookies and pastries are popular," his sister said. "Especially if Eva did the baking."

"Eva?" he echoed, surprised. "The waitress?"

"She sometimes serves customers," Bella confirmed.

"But she does most of the baking at Daisy's. I don't know if she has any formal training, but no one who's tasted any of her creations would question her qualifications as a baker."

"Now I'm sorry I skipped the pie."

"But you got to meet Eva," she noted.

"I guess I did," he agreed.

"She's very pretty, don't you think?"

"I think you need to work on your subtlety," Hudson said to his wife, opening the lid of the pizza box.

"I wasn't trying to be subtle. I was trying to ensure Luke appreciates everything that Rust Creek Falls has to offer."

"I'm not looking for any kind of romantic entanglements while I'm in town," Luke said firmly.

Hudson grinned. "That's what I thought, too, when I first came to Rust Creek Falls."

Chapter Four

Eva had just hung up her apron when the bell above the door jingled. She glanced at Karen, a single mother who worked part-time at the donut shop while her kids were in school. "I have to take off," she told her coworker. "I've got my final exam tonight and I want to review my notes."

"Yeah, I just need a sec," Karen said, not looking up from her phone as her thumbs tapped the keypad. "Sally's at my mom's today, home from school with a fever."

Eva looked longingly toward the promised escape of the back door but, unable to fault the woman's concern for her child, she returned to the front counter.

Her forced smile widened naturally and her heart gave a happy bump inside her chest when it recognized the customer: Luke Stockton.

"Are you here for food or just coffee today?"

"Coffee," he said. "And… I was hoping to see you."

Her heart bumped against her ribs again. "You wanted to see me?"

"Hudson and Bella are both at work today, leaving me alone with my thoughts for the past few hours, and they're really not the best company."

"What were you thinking about?" she asked, filling a ceramic mug from the pot.

"Everything. And nothing." He picked up the mug she set on the counter. "Any chance you can take a break and have a cup of coffee with me?"

"Since I just finished my shift, there's a very good chance," she told him, reaching for a second mug.

Luke carried their beverages to a booth near the window.

Eva slid into the seat across from him. "Do you want to talk about the everything or the nothing?"

He smiled, just a little. "The one very big thing."

"Which is?" she prompted.

"My sister—and my brother, Danny—have asked me to stay in town until his wedding," he confided.

Eva knew—because there were very few secrets in Rust Creek Falls and because the bride had asked her to make the wedding cake—that Danny Stockton and Annie Lattimore were getting married on December twenty-fourth. "It makes sense that he'd want his family to share the occasion," she noted.

"But Christmas Eve is still three weeks away."

"And you have to be back in Wyoming before then?" she guessed.

He shook his head. "No. For the past couple of years, I've been working on a huge spread outside Cheyenne—there are plenty of hands to cover the work, especially this time of year."

"So you could stay...but you don't want to?" she asked, seeking clarification.

"I'm not sure what I want," he admitted. "Bella and Hudson have gone out of their way to make me feel welcome, but it still feels strange to be back after so many years. And I haven't even seen my brother Jamie yet."

Eva remained silent. Though she had a thousand questions she wanted to ask, it was obvious that he needed someone to listen—and not judge.

"He was only fifteen when I left," Luke continued. "Now he's married—for the second time—and the father of three toddlers."

"Henry, Jared and Katie." She opened a packet of sugar and dumped it into her cup, stirred. "They're adorable."

"I guess I'll see for myself this weekend. The invitation to their house came to me through Bella, from Jamie's wife. I'm not even sure if my brother knows that I've been invited."

She lifted her mug and sipped.

"You're not saying much," he noted.

"You haven't actually asked for my opinion on anything," she pointed out.

"Maybe I just needed an ear," he acknowledged. "And a caffeine fix."

"We do have the best coffee in town," she assured him.

"And the best desserts, or so I've heard."

She smiled. "Your sister is a big fan of my brownie bottom cookie dough cheesecake."

"That's probably a little too sweet for my taste, but maybe I will try your apple pie," he decided.

"Sorry," she said sincerely. "It's not on the menu today. But we have key lime and pecan pies, and cherry tarts."

"In that case, I'll try the pecan."

"With salted caramel ice cream or bourbon whipped cream?"

"Bourbon whipped cream sounds interesting," he said.

She slid out of the booth. "Coming right up."

He reached across the table and touched her arm to halt her retreat. It was a casual touch, but the moment his hand brushed her forearm, she felt a jolt of awareness arrow straight to her core. Luke drew his hand away quickly, making her suspect that the shock that had reverberated through her system might have been felt by him, too.

"I thought your shift was finished."

"It is, but—" she glanced toward the counter, where her coworker was unloading a tray of cups with one hand and continuing to text with the other "—Karen's got a lot on her mind right now."

The other woman didn't even look up when Eva moved past her to remove the pie from the case. "How's Sally doing?" she asked as she cut a generous slice and slid it onto a plate.

"Better," Karen said, relief evident in her tone. "The acetaminophen has brought her temperature down, and my mom said she's sipping ginger ale and watching cartoons now."

Eva found the bowl of whipped cream in the refrigerator and added a dollop to Luke's pie.

"Do you want me to deliver that?" her coworker asked. "I thought you said something about needing to study."

"I want to do a final review before the exam, but that shouldn't take too long."

"Well, don't look now," Karen said, "but the handsome cowboy in that booth is studying *you*."

She felt her cheeks flush. "He's just waiting for his dessert."

"He looks like he's got an appetite for something sweet, that's for sure."

Karen was chuckling as Eva hurried away with Luke's

pie. She was pleased that she'd managed to distract the other woman from her worries about her sick child, but she didn't want Luke to be scared off by any speculation or gossip about their personal relationship. Especially when they didn't have a personal relationship—at least not yet. But his admission that he'd come to Daisy's looking for Eva gave her hope.

"Wow," Luke said when she set the plate in front of him. "That's a big slab of pie."

"There are a lot of ranchers in this town," she reminded him. "We're accustomed to serving big appetites."

"Aside from shoveling the driveway—because I didn't know that Hudson had a snowblower—I haven't done much of anything today."

"If the short-term forecast is accurate, you'll be able to shovel again tonight."

"More snow in Montana in December? I'm shocked."

She smiled at that. "Is the weather much different in Wyoming?"

"Not much," he confirmed, sliding a forkful of pie into his mouth, then chewing slowly. "My sister did not exaggerate," he said after he'd swallowed. "This is…damn fine pie."

Eva smiled again, pleased by his reaction. Maybe accounting was a more marketable skill, but she doubted she would ever get as much joy from balancing a ledger as she did from watching a customer enjoy one of her desserts.

And when that customer was as handsome as Luke Stockton, her joy was indescribable.

For the next few minutes he focused his attention on the pie, and Eva sipped her coffee while she pretended not to watch him. Only when his pie was half-eaten, did he speak again.

"One of the other things I've been thinking about is the surprising news I got last night."

"What was that?" she asked him.

"The farm where we grew up—that we assumed would be taken by the bank that held the mortgage—belongs to me and my siblings now."

"And you didn't know?"

He shook his head. "We—at least me and Bailey and Danny—knew that my parents had added to the mortgage to buy some new equipment, so we figured the bank would have taken the property. We didn't know that they'd also added mortgage insurance, and when they were killed, the insurance paid off the money that was owing."

"What about the property taxes?" she wondered.

"Yeah, that's still a big question mark," he admitted.

"You don't know how much is owing?"

"No, we don't know who's been paying them for the past dozen years, but someone has."

"Then there would be a record of the payments at town hall," she pointed out.

"You'd think so," he agreed. "But when Hudson inquired, he was told there's no documentation. No copies of the checks or bank drafts because the payments were cash."

"Cash?" she echoed, surprised.

He nodded. "The taxes aren't small change, either."

"And you have no idea who might have made the payments?"

"None," he confirmed, nudging his plate toward her.

Eva held up a hand, declining his silent offer.

"You know what they say about a chef who doesn't eat her own cooking?" he asked.

"No, I don't. What do they say?"

"I'm not sure," he admitted. "But I think the refusal raises questions about the food."

"So you have questions about my pie?"

Luke chuckled at the indignation in her tone. "Of course not. I'm just asking for help to finish what's left of it."

Sharing his dessert seemed, to Eva, like an intimate act. Was it a sign that he liked her? Or was she reading too much into an innocent offer?

She wanted to believe that his return to Daisy's today was another sign that he was the one, but she was trying not to let her imagination run away with her heart—again. Still, she picked up the spoon she'd used to stir sugar into her coffee and scooped up some of the pie.

"What about your grandfather?" she ventured to ask. "Is it possible that he paid the taxes?"

Luke snorted derisively. "He's the last person who would do anything for us."

"Why would you say that?"

"Matthew and Agnes Baldwin made no secret of the fact that they felt overwhelmed by the responsibility of their grandchildren and decided that me, Bailey and Danny—as legal adults—were on our own. That's why we left Rust Creek Falls. What we didn't know then—what I only found out when I came back—was that even four kids were too much for them, and they sent Dana and Liza, our two youngest sisters, away to be adopted."

"I'm so sorry," Eva said sincerely. "I can't imagine how awful that must have been. Not only did you lose your parents, but only weeks later, your family was essentially torn apart, too."

He nodded. "And now Bella has some idealistic notion about putting the pieces back together, and I'm not sure that's even possible. Not after so many years have passed and so many life experiences have separated us."

He scooped up the last bite of pie and offered it to her.

She shook her head. "If you want to make it work, you'll find a way."

"Are you always a glass half-full kind of person?"

"I try to be," she admitted. "So…have you decided whether or not you're going to stay for your brother's wedding?"

"No, but I'm thinking about it," he said.

Karen approached with a fresh pot of coffee in hand. "Refill?"

Luke slid his mug toward her. "Sure. Thanks."

"Eva? An extra kick of caffeine to keep you awake while you're studying?"

She shook her head. "No, thanks. A pot a day is my absolute limit."

Her coworker smiled as she moved away.

Luke sipped his coffee. "What are you studying?"

"I'm taking some online courses toward my accounting degree," she confided.

"You're not really a baker?"

"That's my job—and my passion," she admitted. "But I went to college to study accounting. I'd just finished my first year when my dad got sick." Even now, five years later, she felt the chill right down to her bones to recall the doctor saying the word. "Lymphoma."

"That sucks," Luke said.

She nodded in response to his simple but apt comment.

"The diagnosis was devastating, for all of us. I couldn't imagine going back to school and leaving my mom to deal with all of the doctor appointments and treatment schedules on her own."

"You're an only child?" he guessed.

"No, I've got two older sisters, but they're both married and live out of town."

"So you quit school to help out?"

"I took a leave of absence from my program," she clarified. "But my dad is doing great now—and nagging me to finish my degree. So I've been trying to complete at least one course a term online, and I'm only four courses short now—three, after this term, assuming I pass my final exam."

"And I'm taking you away from your studies."

"I've been studying for the past two weeks."

"Still." He pulled out his wallet and tucked some bills under his plate. "Thanks for your time."

"Thanks for sharing your pie."

He smiled, and she thought that maybe, just maybe, his gaze dropped to her mouth when he said, "Technically it was your pie, but it was my pleasure."

Eva watched him walk toward the door and found herself hoping that she would share a lot more pleasure with the sexy cowboy while he was in town.

Luke had never had any trouble walking away from a woman.

But it was more difficult than he'd expected to slide out of the booth where Eva was still seated and walk out of the donut shop without glancing back.

Maybe it had been a mistake to seek her out, because there was no denying that was exactly what he'd done.

With Bella and Hudson both at the day care, their house had seemed too big and empty, and he'd had no idea what he would do to occupy his time. Then Eva Rose Armstrong's face had popped into his mind, beckoning him with her beautiful blue eyes and welcoming smile.

Not that he was going to "do" the pretty baker, but stopping by Daisy's for a cup of coffee at least gave him an excuse to get out of the house for a while. And to see Eva again.

He couldn't deny that he was drawn to her, and while he wouldn't have said that he had a particular type when it came to the women who caught his eye, he would have said that Eva was definitely *not* his type. She was far too sweet for a man like him. But it was her sweetness that somehow called to him. As if everything that was light and good and whole in her might somehow fix everything that was dark and bad and broken in him.

As if anything could.

Determined to put her out of his mind, he got in his truck and drove. He didn't think he had any particular destination in mind, but a short while later he turned down the familiar gravel drive of what had once been the Sunshine Farm and parked behind Danny's vehicle.

He climbed out of his truck and glanced toward the house but made no move in that direction. While he couldn't deny that he'd been drawn back to the property that had once been his home, he wasn't quite ready to face the memories that waited for him inside the house. Instead, he shifted his attention to the barn—and the Dumpster beside it half-full of old wood and garbage.

Tucking his chin into the collar of his jacket as a defense against the wind, he moved toward the barn, his boots crunching in the snow. There were lights—and heat—inside the barn, and Luke quickly closed the door behind him to keep the cold out and the warmth in.

He found his brother wrestling apart some boards that he recognized as part of a stall enclosure.

"What are you doing?" Luke asked.

Danny paused to wipe the perspiration off his brow with his sleeve. "Building an igloo."

Luke nodded, silently acknowledging the poor wording of his question. "Okay, maybe what I should have asked was 'why are you gutting the barn'?"

"I'm not gutting the whole barn," his brother denied. "Just taking down some of the stall dividers to make room for the chairs."

"Chairs?" he echoed, uncomprehending.

"Annie's got it in her head that this would be the perfect venue for our Christmas Eve wedding."

Luke looked around the dim and undoubtedly aged structure. "Your fiancée wants to get married in a barn?"

"Yep." Danny picked up a sledgehammer again, and another wall partition came down.

"Why?"

"She thinks it will be romantic."

Luke kept his opinion of that to himself as he walked out of the barn and back to his truck to retrieve the heavy-duty work gloves he kept tucked behind the seat with his toolbox.

Danny looked up when he returned. "I thought the mention of romance had scared you off."

Luke began to load up his arms with broken pieces of wood. "I haven't been to a lot of weddings," he acknowledged. "But generally the decor runs to flowers and bows, not cobwebs and dirt."

His brother set down the hammer and bent to pick up

some of the accumulated debris. "I'm getting rid of the cobwebs and dirt to make way for the flowers and bows," he said, following him to the Dumpster.

Luke tossed the wood into the receptacle. "It would be easier to rent the community center."

"I've put a deposit on it," Danny admitted. "Just in case."

"You've done a lot of work already," he noted.

"I can't take credit for all of it. Jamie's been here a few times, Bella and Hudson have also pitched in and Annie's here as much as possible—although I suspect that's as much to ensure I'm following her grand design as to lend a hand."

Luke chuckled. "Spoken like a man who understands his woman."

"I've loved Annie forever, but we could have a hundred years together and I don't think I'd ever pretend to understand her."

"I hope you have a hundred years together to try," he said sincerely.

"You know, that almost sounded like a wedding toast," Danny mused. "Maybe you can repeat it on the twenty-fourth with a glass in your hand."

"I haven't decided if I'm going to stay that long," he reminded his brother.

"I know," Danny acknowledged. "But even if you don't stay, you could come back for the wedding. I'd really like you to be there."

"Then I will be," he decided. "Even if I don't stay, I'll be here on the big day."

"Of course, if you stay, you could help me turn this place into a wedding venue."

"I'm a ranch hand, bro, not a miracle worker."

Danny chuckled as they both got back to work.

But while Luke continued to ferry broken boards and debris to the Dumpster, he thought that maybe he would stay.

And maybe he would spend some time with Eva Armstrong while he was in town.

Chapter Five

A day off from the donut shop usually meant sleeping in for Eva, but she was awake early Saturday morning. She had too many things on her mind to be able to linger in bed. Or maybe it was too much of one thing on her mind—Luke Stockton.

She hadn't stopped thinking about the man since he stepped up to the counter at Daisy's on his first day back in town and ordered his coffee. Large. Black. To go. It wasn't really the way he drank his coffee that stuck in her mind—it was the low, rumbling tone of his voice, the intensity in his deep blue eyes, the sexy curve of his unsmiling lips, the strong line of his jaw, the breadth of his shoulders and—

She shook her head.

And she was pathetically infatuated with a man she'd only crossed paths with a few times.

But in her heart, she was sure that Luke's return to Rust Creek Falls now, after a dozen years away, was destiny. And after more failed relationships than she wanted to acknowledge, she believed that fate had deliberately put him in her path.

Of course, fate had given her signals before—inaccurate

and unreliable ones. But Eva refused to give up. She believed in true love and happily-ever-after, and she trusted—with all of her heart—that she would find hers.

After a quick shower, she went downstairs for a cup of the coffee she knew her mother would have left on the warmer. Since her father's cancer diagnosis, her parents had vowed to live every minute to the fullest. As a result, it was rare for them to spend time just hanging out around the house. Today they'd planned to leave early for Kalispell to browse the antiques shops; then they were having dinner with friends in the city, which meant that Eva had most of the day and the house all to herself.

As she sipped her first cup of coffee, she gathered the ingredients for her not-quite-famous, melt-in-your-mouth pie crust. Because a day off from the donut shop didn't mean a day away from the kitchen. In fact, she was never happier than when she was mixing and measuring.

From an early age, she'd been fascinated by the process of putting together various dry and wet ingredients. Maybe they didn't look like much of anything before they were put in the oven, but somehow, as she watched through the glass window, magic happened, turning unappealing pans of goop and lumps of batter into the most delicious cakes and cookies that brought smiles to the faces of her family and friends. By the time she was old enough to understand that it wasn't magic but heat that caused the transformation, it didn't matter—she was hooked.

As she cut the butter into the flour, the bowl of glossy red apples on the table snagged her attention. Well, that made the decision easy. She would make an apple pie. Not because Luke happened to mention that he was "an apple pie kind of guy" but because she had the necessary ingredients on hand.

She peeled and sliced the apples—enough for two pies, so that her mother could serve one for dessert after Sunday dinner.

Then she squeezed lemon juice over the fruit, sprinkled on some cinnamon and a light dusting of flour, then tossed the apples to ensure they were evenly coated.

Setting that bowl aside, she floured her work surface and rolled out the pastry she'd mixed earlier. She divided the filling between two dishes, then cut strips of rolled-out pastry to make the basket-weave crust, laid it over the apples, trimmed and pinched the edges, then sprinkled the top with sugar and slid the glass pie plates into the oven.

She tidied up the kitchen and sat down at the table with a second cup of coffee to wonder what she was going to do with the rest of her day. Of course, her thoughts then wandered to wondering what Luke Stockton was doing.

When the scent of baking apples began to permeate the air, she looked up Hudson Jones's phone number and impulsively dialed. As she listened to the ring, she felt butterflies fluttering in her belly. Maybe this was a mistake. It was certainly presumptuous. The man had simply made a throwaway comment about apple pie and—

"Hello?"

She immediately recognized Luke's sister's voice. "Hi, Bella, it's Eva Armstrong—from Daisy's Donut Shop."

"Hi, Eva." The other woman's tone was friendly enough, but Eva could hear the unspoken question in her response.

"I hope I'm not interrupting anything, but I'm trying to reach your brother, Luke."

"Luke?" Bella echoed, sounding even more surprised now.

"When he was at the donut shop the other day, he mentioned that he liked apple pie and I baked one this morning that I could drop off for him."

"He does like apple pie," Bella confirmed.

"Should I bring it over, then?"

"I wish I could say yes and maybe steal a slice for myself," his sister said, "but Luke's actually at Short Hills Ranch visiting Jamie and Fallon and the kids today."

"Oh." Eva felt her spirits sink along with the possibility of crossing paths with the handsome cowboy.

"Of course, Jamie has a sweet tooth, too," Bella told her. "If you wanted to take a drive over to the ranch, I'm sure your pie would be devoured and appreciated there."

"I don't want to intrude on their reunion," she protested.

"I'm sure Luke would be happy to see you. Maybe even relieved."

"Relieved?" she echoed.

"I know Jamie's glad that Luke came home," Bella explained. "But I'm not sure he's quite ready to forgive him for leaving in the first place."

"He must have had his reasons," Eva ventured, recalling what he'd told her about the situation after their parents were killed.

"Do you know where Short Hills Ranch is?" Bella asked her now.

"I do," Eva confirmed. "But—"

"Good." The other woman cut off her objection. "It would be a shame for that pie to go to waste."

And Eva let Luke's sister's words convince her.

Luke might have grown up with six younger siblings, but he'd had little-to-no contact with kids in recent years.

And while he'd been looking forward to seeing Jamie again and meeting his brother's little ones, he couldn't deny that he was feeling a little overwhelmed.

The toddlers were so active and boisterous, it was hard to believe that they'd been preemies. Maybe Henry, Jared and Katie were still small for twenty-two months—since he had no idea what was the average height or weight of an almost two-year-old, he'd take Fallon's word for that—but they were undoubtedly healthy and happy. And loud. Very loud.

Which wasn't entirely a bad thing as their non-stop chatter filled the long gaps and uncomfortable silences that punctuated his attempts at conversation with his youngest brother. Fallon tried to help, introducing topics that she thought might establish some common ground. But it was obvious to Luke that his brother was still angry—and maybe even hurt—by what he considered the abandonment by his three older siblings almost a dozen years earlier.

And though Jamie had apparently welcomed Daniel with open arms when he'd returned to Rust Creek Falls, Luke understood why his youngest brother might harbor more resentment toward him. As the oldest, Luke was the one who could have—and maybe should have—taken the initiative to look after his siblings and keep them all together. Instead, he'd failed them all.

The dogs provided another welcome distraction from the awkwardness between the brothers. In addition to three babies, Jamie had two retriever-shepherd mix puppies that were just over a year old. And the adorable mutts, like the kids, held nothing back.

According to Fallon, Jamie had found the pups the previous winter. The mother had been hit by a car and

Jamie had rounded up her babies—seven in total—and taken them to the vet to be checked over and placed in good homes. Jamie hadn't intended to keep even one for himself, but he'd somehow ended up bringing two of them home.

Andy and Molly had barked like crazy when Luke showed up at the door, jumping all over one another in their efforts to be the first to greet the visitor. A quick word from Jamie, however, and they'd immediately dropped their butts to the floor, although their bodies had continued to quiver with repressed excitement.

There was nothing repressed about them now as they tumbled on the floor with the kids, rewarding tugs on their ears and tails with sloppy, wet kisses. Growing up on Sunshine Farm, there had always been at least one dog around, but over the years, Luke had forgotten how much comfort and companionship an animal could provide. Maybe when he got back to Cheyenne he could drop by the shelter and pick out a dog. The idea was incredibly appealing to him, but he suspected a dog wouldn't be happy confined in a tiny apartment while his human companion was gone from sunup to sundown every day.

"Are you getting hungry, Luke?" Fallon's question drew him back to the present.

"*I'm* hungry," her husband interjected.

"You're always hungry," she said, but she softened the reproach with a smile that was filled with love and affection.

Luke looked away, deliberately refocusing his attention on the babies so that he didn't feel like a voyeur.

Maybe he shouldn't stay in Rust Creek Falls too long. Both of his siblings who had remained in town—and the one who had returned—had fallen in love, and he had no desire to walk down the same path. He'd already experienced enough heartache to last a lifetime.

Sure, it warmed his heart to see Bella with Hudson, and to witness the way her millionaire husband doted on her. And yeah, he could appreciate the obvious connection between Jamie and Fallon—and no doubt Jamie appreciated having not just an extra set of hands to help with his three babies but the partnership of a woman who clearly loved Henry, Jared and Katie as if they were her own.

The engagement of Danny and Annie was less surprising to Luke, because he remembered how deeply in love his brother had been before they left town. In fact, Danny was the only one who had balked about the decision to leave Rust Creek Falls, and Luke had always suspected that Annie was the reason.

"I'm just going to check on the bread that's in the oven," Fallon said at the same time the doorbell rang. "Were you expecting more company?" she asked her husband.

Jamie shook his head.

"Bella?" Luke guessed as Henry climbed up onto the sofa and then onto his uncle's shoulders from there. He instinctively reached up to hold the boy steady, not wanting to be responsible for the little guy tumbling off and crashing to the ground.

"She lived here with me and the triplets for more than fifteen months—she rarely remembers to knock before walking in," Jamie responded, but there was affection rather than disapproval in his tone.

Jared—eager to do everything his brother did—was attempting to crawl up Luke's front. "I'm glad you and

Bella stayed close," Luke said as he steadied the second toddler.

"We had to," Jamie said pointedly. "We were all that we each had left."

Luke didn't know how to respond to that. No matter how many times he apologized, it wouldn't change what had happened when he'd left Rust Creek Falls—or the reasons he'd felt compelled to go. Nothing could change the past, so he'd learned to put one foot in front of the other and move forward, though the weight of the guilt and regrets made the progress painfully slow.

He was grateful when Fallon came back into the family room, and even more so when he realized that she wasn't alone.

"Look who dropped by," she said.

Luke did look, and he felt an immediate pull low in his belly when he saw Eva Armstrong. He recognized the pull as basic physical attraction, and while he was willing to acknowledge that his blood hummed in his veins whenever he was near the pretty baker, he was also determined to ignore the hormones clamoring for him to stop looking and start moving.

"Bella told me that you'd be here," Eva explained before anyone could ask. "I didn't want to interrupt but—"

"You're not interrupting anything," Luke interjected, inexplicably grateful for her presence.

"Eva brought pie," Fallon said. "Still-warm-from-the-oven apple pie."

"My favorite," Luke noted.

Eva's cheeks flushed with pretty color. "Yes, you mentioned that when you were at Daisy's the other day."

"You made the pie for me?" he asked, surprised and pleased by the gesture.

She shrugged. "I like to bake, and I had apples on hand."

"If only we had ice cream," Jamie lamented as his daughter toddled over to their new guest and lifted her arms in a silent plea to be picked up.

Eva, without any hesitation, did so, propping the toddler on her hip with a natural ease that Luke couldn't help but envy. "I brought some of that, too," she said.

"Then I say it's time for pie," Jamie said.

Luke, his mouth already watering in anticipation—for Eva as much as her pie—nodded his agreement.

But Fallon shook her head. "We can have pie for dessert *after* lunch, which I am going to dish up now."

"That's my cue to go," Eva said, but Katie was winding a strand of Eva's long blond hair around her hand, effectively entangling her.

The neat braid she'd worn when she was working behind the counter at Daisy's was pretty enough and undoubtedly practical for work, but Luke liked the way she looked now, with her hair tumbling over her shoulders—and captured in his adorable niece's fist.

"But you just got here," Luke protested.

"And it's lunchtime," she pointed out.

"You can stay and eat with us," Fallon said. "There's plenty to go around."

"Oh, no, I couldn't," Eva said.

"Do you have other plans?" Jamie's wife asked her.

"No," she admitted. "But I really don't want to intrude."

"You're really not," Fallon assured her. "I'll just go set another place at the table."

"Are you sure you don't mind?" Eva asked, her gaze sliding to Luke as if gauging his reaction.

"Of course not," Fallon insisted.

"My wife always cooks enough for several extra people," Jamie said. "And her beef stew is exceptional."

"Beef stew sounds like the perfect meal to warm the blood on a cold day," Eva said.

Luke was pretty sure he knew at least a dozen more interesting ways to warm her blood, but he quickly slammed the door on that wayward thought.

"Then let's get HJK rounded up and settled into their high chairs for lunch," Jamie said, lifting Jared off his brother's chest and into the air, making the little guy giggle.

"Up! Up!" Henry demanded.

Fallon deftly took Jared from her husband so that he could treat Henry to the same high ride.

Since Eva already had Katie on her hip, she carried the little girl to the kitchen.

Luke followed, appreciating the subtle sway of her hips beneath the long, loose skirt. Most of the women he knew lived in jeans and flannel, but Eva seemed to prefer softer fabrics and styles. Rather than downplay her femininity, she embraced it. And Luke found himself wanting to embrace it, too, and every other part of her.

Eva felt a little self-conscious about sitting down with the Stocktons for what was obviously a family meal, but everyone else seemed to take her presence in stride. Fallon directed her to the empty chair beside Luke, but first, Eva set Katie in her high chair, buckling the belt around her middle to ensure the active toddler wouldn't be able to wriggle out of it.

Jamie dampened a cloth under the faucet, then made his way from one high chair to the next, thoroughly scrubbing all the little hands in what was obviously a pre-dining ritual. Although Fallon had only been married to the triplets' father for about seven months, Eva knew that Jamie's bride had been involved in caring for Henry, Jared and Katie since they were born.

After the babies' biological mother died from complications of childbirth, several residents of Rust Creek Falls had volunteered to form a "baby chain" to help the new father care for his three premature infants. As a result of Fallon's participation in the baby chain, she and her new husband already had well-established routines for the care of their little ones. And although the toddlers had only just met their uncle, Eva could tell that they had immediately taken a liking to Luke.

No doubt he would be a good father to his own children someday—a thought that brought to mind an image of chubby-cheeked babies with Luke's deep blue eyes and dark blond hair. Or maybe lighter hair, more like her own.

Eva pushed the tantalizing picture to the back of her mind, ruefully acknowledging that it was a little premature to be thinking about having babies with a man who hadn't even kissed her.

But it was going to happen.

The kiss, at least—she was sure of it.

Not that her recent dating history had given her any reason for such optimism. In fact, just the opposite was true. While it seemed as if everyone she knew was falling in love, getting married and having babies—although not always in that order—Eva was still alone.

In the past few years, she'd gone out with a few different guys—and two that seemed to have real potential. She'd dated Bobby Ray Ellis for a few months before she realized that he was still in love with his high school sweetheart—even years after she'd moved out of town and married someone else. Then Zach Dalton moved to Rust Creek Falls, and Eva had been certain that he was the one. Unfortunately, as much as she wanted the relationship to work, she had to admit there'd been zero chemistry between them. Which didn't make it hurt any less when she was dumped—again.

But she continued to trust that she would know her soul mate when she found him—as had happened for her parents and her sisters. Her dad, a young history teacher losing a battle with the school photocopier, had been rescued by the new office administrator. According to Ray Armstrong, Marion Barr had simultaneously saved his test papers and stolen his heart. Six months later, they were married.

Both of Eva's sisters had also been lucky in love. Calla met her husband, Patrick, when she was seventeen years old and on a high school ski trip in Thunder Canyon. Delphine met her husband, Harrison, at college.

Eva only wanted the same thing both of her sisters had—a husband, a family. But she was a twenty-five-year-old single woman who hadn't had a date since she'd been jilted by Zach Dalton. Still, the flutters that tickled her belly whenever she saw Luke Stockton gave her hope that might change.

"Bread?" the object of her musings asked, offering the basket that Fallon had set on the table.

"Thanks." She selected a slice and passed the basket to Jamie.

She felt something rub against her ankle and, for a moment, thought it might be Luke's foot. Then she felt the weight of a paw on her toes and realized the dogs were under the table, no doubt hoping that someone would drop—accidentally or on purpose—scraps for them.

She wasn't the only one aware of their presence, either, because Fallon tipped her head to peer under the table. "Andy, Molly—go lie down."

The dogs obediently followed her command, their ears and tails drooping in response to the scolding. Henry dropped a piece of bread as the animals moved past his high chair, which one of the pups snatched up before any of the humans could do so.

"I almost forgot to ask," Luke said to her. "How was your exam?"

"I think it went pretty well," she said cautiously.

"Now only three more courses to go and you'll be an accountant," he noted.

She was surprised that he'd remembered the details of their conversation about her studies, even if he was jumping the gun a little. "I'll have a degree," she clarified. "There are more exams after that before I'll actually be certified."

"I didn't know you wanted to be an accountant," Fallon chimed in.

"Truthfully, I'd rather bake cookies than crunch numbers, but I've been told that accounting is a more marketable skill."

"If you become a CPA, who will fill the pastry case at Daisy's?" Luke wondered.

She shrugged. "Anyone who can read can follow a recipe."

"*Almost* anyone," Jamie said, his lips twitching as he shared a look with his wife.

"It happened *once*," she said, then turned to explain to Eva. "*One time* I mixed up teaspoons and tablespoons."

"What were you measuring?"

"Baking powder," Fallon admitted.

Eva winced.

The other woman sighed. "Yeah, it was pretty bad."

"But this stew is delicious," Eva told her, dipping her spoon into the bowl again.

"I've learned to stick with what I know," Fallon said.

For the next few minutes everyone showed their appreciation for the meal by focusing on eating.

Although there wasn't a lot of conversation at the table, Eva did notice that Luke's occasional questions to his brother were met by sharp and succinct responses followed by silence. She didn't know Jamie Stockton well enough to know if he was always a man of few words or if he didn't have much to say to his brother, but his wife's obvious efforts to fill in the gaps made Eva suspect that it was the latter.

Maybe it wasn't surprising that, after so many years apart, there would be some residual tension between the siblings, but she hoped they could work it out because she suspected there was little chance of Luke deciding to stay in Rust Creek Falls if they didn't.

Chapter Six

By the time lunch was finished—including Eva's apple pie for dessert—the little ones were practically falling asleep in their high chairs. Fallon and Jamie excused themselves to get Henry, Jared and Katie washed up and settled down for their naps, and Eva and Luke tidied the kitchen.

"Was that as awkward for you as it was for me?" Luke asked as he carried a stack of bowls from the table to the counter.

"There were a few awkward moments," Eva acknowledged.

"At least I learned something about my youngest brother today that I didn't know before."

"What's that?" she wondered, dividing the cutlery between the basket compartments in the dishwasher.

"He sure does know how to hold on to a grudge."

"You've been gone for twelve years," Eva reminded him. "You can't expect to pick up right where you left off."

"I didn't have any expectations." He squirted dish soap into the sink and began to fill it with hot water.

"Are you sure about that?" she asked, slotting the bowls on the bottom rack.

He frowned. "What do you mean?"

"It just seems, at least to this outside observer, that you expected a less-than-warm welcome, and that's exactly what you got."

"A self-fulfilling prophecy?"

"Maybe," she allowed, closing the dishwasher.

He slid the pots and pans into the soapy water. "Well, I'm glad you were here—and not just because you brought dessert, although that was a definite bonus."

"I'm glad, too," she said. "I like your family."

"Tell me about yours," he suggested. "You mentioned that you have two sisters—where do they live?"

"Calla lives in Thunder Canyon, where she helps her husband, Patrick, run his hardware store. They have two kids—Fiona, who is almost ten, and Noah, who just turned seven.

"Delphine lives a little farther away, in Billings. She's a middle school teacher, married to a financial adviser. She and Harrison have three boys—eight-year-old Tommy, six-year-old Charlie and four-year-old Freddy."

"So you have a lot of experience with kids," he noted.

She shook her head. "Not nearly as much as I would like. Aside from major holidays, I rarely get to see my niece and nephews."

"But I bet you spoil them rotten when you do."

"Absolutely," she agreed. "Their Christmas presents are stacked almost floor to ceiling in my room."

"You've started your Christmas shopping already?"

"Haven't you?"

He shook his head. "I still haven't decided if I'm going to be here for Christmas."

"What does that have to do with your shopping?" she asked.

"If I'm not here, I won't need to buy any presents," he said logically.

Eva was taken aback. Not just by the statement but by his matter-of-fact tone. "There's no one else you celebrate the holidays with?"

"No."

She frowned at that. "So what do you usually do on December twenty-fifth?"

"The same thing I do on the twenty-fourth and the twenty-sixth."

"For the past twelve years, you haven't done anything to celebrate Christmas?"

"Well, some of the bigger spreads put out a fancy meal for their hands," he told her.

She was silent for a moment, not knowing what to say. Her heart ached for him, but she knew he would balk at any expression of sympathy.

"If you decide to stay, I could help you with your shopping," she finally said.

"I appreciate the offer, but I'm not sure even your company would make up for having to set foot in a mall."

"I love Christmas shopping. And wrapping presents, and trimming the tree. And holiday baking, of course."

"How is holiday baking different from regular baking?" he wondered aloud.

She smiled. "There's a lot more of it. Cookies and squares and bars. And, of course, Christmas goodies don't have any calories."

"No calories, huh?"

"Nope. Not even my absolutely decadent chocolate

almond macaroon bars, which means that I'm free to indulge."

"If your chocolate almond macaroon bars are half as good as your pies, I'd want to indulge, too," he told her. "In fact, I'm seriously considering taking a fork and eating what's left of that apple pie directly from the dish before my brother and sister-in-law come back down."

"I'm sure they'll let you take the leftovers with you."

"Then I'd have to share with Bella and Hudson," he grumbled as he wiped off the trays of the high chairs, which had been liberally smeared with beef gravy and vanilla ice cream by toddler hands.

Eva chuckled as she picked up a towel to dry the trays after he'd finished cleaning them. "I could probably bake another one sometime."

He returned to the sink to rinse the cloth, then began to tackle the pots and pans. "I would think, on your day off, you'd want to stay out of the kitchen."

She shrugged. "I like baking. The rhythm of measuring and mixing is relaxing to me."

"Do you cook, too?" he asked her, scrubbing the inside of the stew pot.

"Of course," she said, then glanced at him over her shoulder as she slid the high chairs back against the wall. "Are you angling for a meal?"

"No," he said quickly. Then he reconsidered, lifting one shoulder and offering her a half smile. "Maybe."

She chuckled. "How about dinner on Tuesday?"

"Really? You would cook dinner for me?"

"Sure."

He set the clean pot in the dish drainer and turned to face her. "I don't have any specific plans this week, so

Tuesday works for me," he finally said. "But I have to admit that I'm curious."

"About what?"

"Why you'd offer to feed a man you barely know."

"Because sharing a meal will give us the opportunity to get to know one another better," she pointed out.

"That it would," he agreed cautiously.

"How's six o'clock?" she suggested.

"Six is fine, but…"

She looked up, waiting for him to complete what was obviously an unfinished thought.

"But?" she prompted when he remained silent.

"I'm not looking for any kind of romantic entanglement while I'm in town," he finally responded. "And I feel really stupid even saying that because maybe your offer to cook dinner is nothing more than that, but I just want to be sure there's no misunderstanding."

"I appreciate that," she said, picking up the pot to dry it. "Are you involved with somebody in Cheyenne?"

He shook his head. "No."

"Somewhere else?"

"No," he said again. "I don't do relationships."

She took a minute to consider that response before she said, "I have just one more question."

"What's that?" he asked warily.

"Do you like pot roast?"

He grinned. "Does a cowboy wear a hat?"

She smiled back. "Then I'll see you at six on Tuesday."

As Luke stood at the door, hand poised to knock, it belatedly occurred to him that he should have brought something. Flowers or a bottle of wine, maybe. As he honestly couldn't remember the last time a woman had offered to cook a meal for him, he was unfamiliar with the usual procedures and protocols. And if he'd brought flowers or wine, it might have seemed too much like a date, and it wasn't. He was looking forward to sharing a meal with Eva, but he wasn't looking for anything more than that.

That conviction flew right out of his head when she greeted him with a genuine and warm smile on her face, and he suddenly realized that he wanted to kiss her more than he'd wanted anything else in a very long time.

"Good—you're on time," she said.

"You said six," he reminded her, his gaze lingering on the sweet curve of her mouth.

"And you heard," she noted, stepping back from the door so that he could enter.

He barely had a moment to look at her—the long, flowing skirt that swirled around her calves and soft pink sweater that hugged her feminine curves—before she was moving away again.

"Hang up your coat there—" she gestured to a row of hooks on the wall beside the door "—then come on into the kitchen. I was just about to start slicing the beef."

He inhaled the scent of savory roasted meat and his stomach immediately rumbled. He unzipped his jacket and hung it on one of the empty hooks on the wall, then put his Stetson on top of it. There was a bench seat beneath the row of hooks, and he sat down to remove his snowy boots before following the path Eva had taken through the foyer and into the kitchen.

He would have guessed—based on the design and the neighborhood—that the house was close to forty years old, but this room had recently been updated. With white shaker-style cabinets, dark gray granite countertops and stainless-steel appliances, it was sleek and modern and spotlessly clean.

The farmhouse table was already set with dark blue placemats and linen napkins that contrasted against simple white dinnerware. There was a bottle of wine on the table, already open, and two glasses waiting.

Not a date, he reminded himself, though the setting suggested otherwise. The only things missing were candles and flowers. Or maybe he was reading too much into her preparations.

"This is your place?" he asked, surprised that a young, single woman would choose to rent a house rather than an apartment—and that she could afford such accommodations.

Eva shook her head. "It's my parents' house."

"Where do they live?" he wondered.

"Here."

"You still live with your parents?"

Her gaze dropped away and her cheeks flushed. "For now."

"I didn't mean to imply that there's anything wrong with that," he said.

"I moved out a few years ago, when I went to college," she confided.

"But you came back when your dad was diagnosed," he remembered. Which was almost the same thing Bella had done, putting her education on hold to help Jamie with his triplets after the death of his first wife.

Eva nodded.

"I'm sorry," he said, feeling as if he'd stuck one of his enormous feet into his mouth. And despite the two place settings on the table, he had to ask, "Is this a… family dinner?"

She laughed softly. "No. I wouldn't do that to you—to anyone," she assured him.

He exhaled, immeasurably relieved by her response. A homemade meal with a pretty woman was one thing—meeting the parents of a girl he wasn't even dating was something entirely different.

"My parents are out tonight. In fact, they're out every Tuesday and Thursday night."

Which, he suspected, was why she'd chosen to invite him for dinner tonight.

"Since my dad finished his treatments, he and my mom decided they weren't going to take anything for granted or put off doing something they wanted to do for another day, because there are no guarantees of other days."

That was a lesson Luke had learned, too, the night his parents were killed.

He pushed the past aside to focus on the present.

"So they joined a couples' bowling league in Kalispell, they take ballroom dance lessons at the community center and they have regular date nights. Tonight is one of those dates, and they've gone to Kalispell for dinner and a movie."

"Still no movie theater in Rust Creek Falls?" he guessed.

"Just the high school gym on Friday and Saturday nights—and only so long as none of the varsity teams is playing."

"Go Wildcats," he said, and made her laugh again.

"So what do your parents think about you having a man in the house while they're away?" he teased.

She carried the platter of meat to the table. "I didn't tell them I was having company for dinner," she admitted.

"Why not?" he asked, following with the bowls of mashed potatoes and mixed vegetables.

"Because my parents tend to be a little…overprotective," she said as she poured gravy into a ceramic pitcher.

He lifted the bottle of merlot—a silent question. She nodded, and he poured the wine into their glasses.

"Probably because you don't have any older brothers to look out for you."

"Did you look out for your younger sisters?"

It was an innocent question—and one that flowed naturally from their topic of conversation—but it brought the harsh realities rushing back to him. "Not as much as I should have in the early years," he acknowledged. "And then I lost the chance to do so."

She touched a hand to his arm. "I'm sorry. I didn't mean to bring up unhappy memories."

He pulled away from her touch, not wanting or deserving her comfort, and picked up his fork, slicing easily through the beef on his plate. "Wow. This is so tender I barely need the knife." He took a taste and savored the bite. "Mmm. And juicy."

She acknowledged his compliment—and the change of topic—with a slight nod. "I hope Bella doesn't mind that you're not there for dinner tonight."

"Are you kidding? She decided it was a good excuse not to cook so Hudson was taking her out to eat."

"Maverick Manor?" she guessed.

"I didn't ask," he admitted, then frowned. "Is that the fancy new hotel on the highway headed toward Kalispell?"

She nodded.

"Good food there?"

"That's the rumor," she told him. "Although I couldn't say for sure, because I've never been."

"Why not?" Noting that her glass was almost empty, he lifted the bottle to top up her drink but didn't add to his own because he had a hard and fast rule about never consuming more than a single alcoholic beverage when he was driving.

"It's not exactly the type of place where a woman would go on her own—even if she could afford it," Eva said in response to his question.

He shook his head as he swallowed the last bite of his meal. "What's wrong with the guys in this town that none of them has offered to take you?"

"That's a question you'd have to ask them," she said.

Though the smile remained on her face, her tone was a little stiff, and Luke mentally cursed himself for his insensitivity. She was a gorgeous woman who worked magic in the kitchen, so he'd naturally assumed her un-married status was a matter of choice. Apparently, he was wrong.

"Did you leave room for dessert?" Eva pushed away from the table and carried their plates to the counter. "I made gingerbread and white chocolate mousse trifle."

"I would have said I couldn't eat another bite, but that sounds too delicious to resist," he told her.

"Do you want coffee with dessert?"

"I always want coffee—if it's not too much trouble," he said.

"No trouble at all," she assured him, reaching for the carafe. Then as he opened the dishwasher, she asked, "What are you doing?"

He started to load the dishes she had cleared from

the table. "Helping with the cleanup," he said, in case it wasn't obvious.

"You're not supposed to do that," she protested.

"Why not?"

"Because you're a guest."

"You were a guest at Jamie and Fallon's, but you insisted on helping."

"I was an *uninvited* guest," she pointed out. "And Jamie and Fallon had their hands full with the kids."

"My mom always said that a man could best show his appreciation for a meal by helping with the cleanup afterward."

"In that case, I will stop protesting and say thank you."

"Thank *you*," Luke said. "That was truly the best meal I've had in a long time. Of course, if you tell my sister or sister-in-law I said that, I'll deny it till the cows come home."

"I would never," she promised.

He closed the dishwasher. "Trifle?"

"Coming right up."

As much as Eva enjoyed being in the kitchen, she got even more pleasure watching others enjoy her creations, so she was thrilled when Luke finished off two servings of trifle. Except that when he set his spoon inside the empty bowl, it was a definite signal that dinner was over.

"More coffee?" she offered.

He shook his head as he glanced at the clock over the sink. "No, thanks. I should probably be heading back."

He pushed away from the table, gathered her bowl along with his own and carried them to the dishwasher. Eva followed with their empty coffee mugs.

Luke turned as she approached the dishwasher, so she

stepped to the side—and he did the same. She moved to the other side—and he did the same again.

"Dinner *and* dancing," he noted.

She smiled as she shifted again.

This time he tried to get out of her way by moving forward and she bumped into him. Or rather the mugs she carried bumped into his chest. His broad, solid, warm chest.

"You really need to stop trying to lead," he teased.

"It's the music," she bantered back.

He took the mugs from her hands and turned to set them in the top rack of the machine, then closed the door.

Eva didn't move. She was too preoccupied with the alluring view of well-worn denim stretching across his nicely curved backside.

Then he turned again and straightened, so that her gaze was now fixed on that strong chest. She lifted her eyes to his broad shoulders, the shadow of stubble on his jaw, the sensual curve of his lips.

Those lips were moving now, so she made an effort to focus on his words rather than speculate about how his mouth would feel against hers.

"It was kind of you to invite me for dinner tonight. Thank you," he said.

"You're very welcome."

Neither of them moved.

His gaze dropped to her mouth, for just a second, then jerked away. Almost as if he'd been thinking about kissing her before he remembered that he didn't want to get involved. But there had been so much intensity in that brief moment, Eva's breath backed up in her lungs and her knees actually quivered.

She moistened her lips with the tip of her tongue. "Luke."

She didn't say anything other than his name, but she suspected that single syllable told him everything she was thinking and feeling. His response confirmed it.

"Don't look at me like that," he warned.

"Like what?"

"Like you're wishing I would kiss you."

Was it the wine that made her brave? Or was it not knowing how long he was going to be in town that made her reluctant to waste any time playing games?

"Maybe I am wishing you would kiss me," she told him.

He shook his head, sincerely regretful. "It's not going to happen, Eva."

Her hopes fizzled like a balloon leaking air. "You don't want to kiss me?"

"It's not about what I want. It's about what's smart," he said.

"And kissing me wouldn't be smart?" she guessed.

"I have no business getting involved with you—with anyone—when I'm only going to be in Rust Creek Falls for a few weeks."

"So you've said," she noted.

"I just want to be clear. I came back because Bella was looking for me, but I'm not planning to stay."

"I don't think that's the only reason you came back," she said. "I think you wanted to see your siblings as much as they wanted to see you."

"Maybe I did," he acknowledged. "That doesn't change the fact that my life is in Wyoming now."

"Okay," she said agreeably.

Then she took another half step forward so that she

was standing even closer to him now, and tipped her chin up to meet his gaze.

"What are you doing?" he asked a little warily.

"Since you've made it clear that you have no intention of kissing me, I'm going to have to take matters into my own hands."

Then she lifted those hands to his shoulders, rose up onto her toes and touched her mouth to his.

Chapter Seven

It was a casual kiss. Barely a brush of her lips against his, but the effect was like touching a lit match to dry tinder, and desire flamed hot and bright inside her. Maybe inside him, too. Because before she could draw away, his arm was at her back, hauling her against him.

And then *he* was kissing *her*.

She might have initiated the contact, but Luke quickly took over. Eva was happy to relinquish control because, wow, did he know how to kiss.

His lips were warm and firm and moved over hers with just the right amount of pressure. When his tongue traced the seam of her lips, she parted willingly to let him inside.

For a man who claimed that he had no business getting involved, he was definitely involved in the kiss. And when his hands slid up her back, urging her even closer, she linked her hands behind his neck and held on while the world shifted beneath her feet.

She didn't know how long the kiss went on, except that it was long enough to melt all the bones in her body and completely blank her mind. She could think of nothing but Luke, want nothing but Luke. And even when her brain registered a quiet chime somewhere in the distance, it was several seconds later before she recognized the sound.

Luke eased his lips from hers and exhaled slowly. "That must be yours."

"My what?"

"Phone," he said.

"Oh. Right."

Eva drew an unsteady breath and tried to remember where she'd left her phone. She found it in the pocket of her coat.

"My parents," she explained, after she'd unlocked the screen and read the message. "They always send a quick text to let me know when they're on their way home."

"I guess that's my cue to be heading out."

"There's no need to rush off," she protested.

He moved toward the door and sat on the bench to stuff his feet into his boots again.

"Thanks. I really enjoyed dinner." His gaze dropped to her mouth, and his own lips curved. "And dessert."

Eva's cheeks turned pink but she seemed to accept his words at face value. "I'll get the rest of the trifle for you to take with you."

"I should tell you not to bother, but it was really good."

She laughed softly as she went to retrieve the leftover dessert from the refrigerator.

And yeah, he watched her cross the kitchen floor, admiring the nicely rounded curve of her butt as she moved.

There was no point in denying that he was attracted to her. And why wouldn't he be? She was pretty and spunky, and the sweet, seductive flavor of her lips made him want a lot more.

It had been a while since he'd enjoyed intimate female companionship. He couldn't remember how long exactly—three months? Four? Longer?

There was a woman who worked as a bartender at his favorite watering hole in Cheyenne. A curvy brunette who was amenable to hooking up when they were both in the mood. He hadn't been in the mood in a while. Truthfully, he hadn't even thought about her in months. And he suspected that, if asked, she would say the same about him.

Which was probably why he was so strongly attracted to Eva. She was a beautiful woman and he was a red-blooded man who had been sleeping alone for a long time. If the pretty baker was willing to help him end that period of self-imposed celibacy, he would be crazy to turn her down. Especially when he wanted nothing more than to peel away her clothes as if they were one of those paper cupcake liners, then lick her all over as if her body was covered in buttercream icing.

"I'm glad you enjoyed it," Eva said as she walked back to him.

It took his brain a minute to shake off the fantasy and recall the topic of their conversation. "I did," he said, accepting the bowl she offered.

Then, almost of its own volition, his free hand lifted to cup her cheek, his thumb brushing lightly over the curve of her bottom lip.

"You're a tempting woman, Eva Armstrong." And though he couldn't deny that he wanted her, he forced his hand to drop away. "But I can't afford to give in to temptation."

Once again, she surprised him. Instead of accepting the boundary he was attempting to establish, she asked, "Why?" as if she sincerely couldn't understand the reason he was determined to ignore the chemistry between them.

He wasn't sure that he understood it, either, but he knew that it was necessary. "Because I don't even know how long I'm going to be in Rust Creek Falls, but I know it's not going to be forever," he reminded her.

"I'm not looking for a ring on my finger," she told him.

He lifted his brows, silently challenging the veracity of her claim, and her cheeks flushed again.

"Sure, I want to get married someday," she acknowledged, perhaps a little defensively. "But I didn't kiss you because I want to spend the rest of my life with you."

"Why did you kiss me?" he asked, though he suspected the answer could lead down a path he didn't want to follow.

She shrugged. "It seemed like a good idea at the time. But you don't have to worry," she hastened to assure him. "I'm not in the habit of throwing myself at men who don't want me."

It would be easy to let her believe that was true. That they'd shared a kiss, and the kiss hadn't done anything for him. But after the passionate embrace they'd shared, how could she possibly think he didn't want her?

He'd practically pounced on her like a starving man at a buffet, and that first taste had failed to sate him. Even now, a primitive hunger continued to gnaw at his belly. Of course, admitting that truth might be more dangerous than allowing her to believe a lie. But he knew it hurt to be rejected, and the last thing he wanted to do was hurt her—which was why he needed to keep a safe and careful distance from the appealingly sweet Eva Armstrong.

"If you believe I don't want you, then you haven't been paying attention," he chided gently.

A spark of something flared in those beautiful blue eyes and the corners of her mouth tipped up, just a little. "You do want me?"

Only more than he wanted to draw his next breath, but there was no way in hell he would admit it—especially when he couldn't do anything about it.

"I know you're planning to go back to Wyoming in a few weeks," she assured him. "I just don't understand why, if we enjoy spending time together, we can't occasionally hang out while you're here."

Though he was still wary, it seemed like a reasonable compromise. "I guess there's no harm in that," he said cautiously. "So long as you understand that there won't be any more kissing."

"Growing up with three sisters should have taught you that telling a woman she can't do something is a surefire way to make her try," she warned.

"It wasn't a challenge, Eva," he assured her.

"Okay," she said agreeably.

But there was a twinkle in her eye that warned Luke she had taken it as such. And he suspected that keeping his hands off the pretty baker was going to be more of a challenge than he could handle. More than he wanted to handle.

Because despite his assertion that it shouldn't happen again, now that he'd kissed her once, he wanted to do it over and over. He wanted to savor her intoxicating flavor; he wanted to feel the yield of those sweet lips; he wanted to revel in the press of those soft, feminine curves against his hard, aching body.

Yeah, he wanted all kinds of things he had no business wanting. "Good night, Eva."

"Good night, Luke."

Bella and Hudson were still out when Luke got back to their place, so he put the bowl of trifle in the refrigerator and settled himself on the sofa in front of the television. Scrolling through the channels, he found highlights of recent football games, but the replays on the screen failed to hold his attention. Instead, he was thinking about a certain sexy baker and the kiss that never should have happened.

Luke was generally pretty good at reading people, and it wasn't often someone said or did anything that surprised him. But when Eva moved in and kissed him, the bold action had caught him off guard.

It shouldn't have, because she'd given him fair warning. She'd outright told him that she was going to kiss him, so it wasn't really the move that surprised him so much as his own response to the overture.

He'd kissed her back, because while he still believed that getting romantically involved with anyone in Rust Creek Falls was a bad idea, he wasn't going to refuse the sweet offering. And because he couldn't help himself.

Because that first taste of her lips had made him want more.

A lot more.

"I didn't expect that you'd be home already."

The sound of his sister's voice jerked him back to the present.

"What?" He pressed the mute button on the remote so that he could focus on what she was saying. Not that he'd actually been watching the sports update, but he'd wanted to at least preserve the illusion that he was doing something other than thinking about Eva Rose Armstrong and the delicious flavor of her kiss.

"I said that I didn't expect you'd be home already," Bella repeated.

"It doesn't take a lot of time to eat a meal."

"Maybe not." She dropped onto the opposite end of the sofa, with her back against the arm so that she was facing him. "But I thought you might linger over coffee and dessert—because I know Eva would have made something fabulous for dessert or—" she drew the word out, then let it hang for a moment "—the good-night kiss."

He refused to let his sister goad him into saying anything about the kiss that he was desperately trying not to think about.

"Trifle," he said instead. "And yes, it was fabulous."

"And the kiss?" she prompted.

"Bella," he said, his tone admonishing.

"Oh, come on," she said, refusing to be admonished. "You can't expect me to believe that you shared a romantic dinner with a beautiful woman then went on your way without even a kiss good-night."

"It was a *friendly* dinner."

She rolled her eyes at that. "A woman doesn't usually offer to cook for a man because she wants to be friends."

"Eva knows that I'm not looking for any kind of relationship."

"So there was no wine? No candlelight?"

"No candlelight," he confirmed.

"No kiss?"

He ignored her question to ask his own instead. "How was your dinner?"

The speculative gleam in her eye warned that she was

aware of his redirection—and his refusal to deny that there was a kiss—but she seemed willing to let it slide, at least for now.

"Spectacular," she said. "We had chateaubriand with a peppercorn glaze, roasted new potatoes, sautéed julienned vegetables and the most amazing caramel pecan cheesecake for dessert."

"Good," he said. "If you've already had dessert, then you won't expect me to share my trifle."

"You didn't say what kind of trifle," she noted.

"*My* trifle," he said again.

Bella laughed softly. "Okay, *your* trifle."

"Where's Hudson?" he asked, because his sister's husband never seemed to be too far away from her when he was home.

"Not digging into your trifle," she promised. "He's in the office—he had some calls to make."

"At—" Luke glanced at the clock "—ten thirty-seven p.m.?"

"It's already tomorrow afternoon in Sydney."

"He works hard, doesn't he?"

"Harder than his brother ever gave him credit for," she said. "But he plays hard, too. He believes balance is important."

"Smart man."

Bella offered him a cheeky smile. "Smart enough to marry me anyway."

"Smart *and* lucky," he noted.

"Actually, I'm the lucky one," she said. "After everything that happened in the past, I never thought I'd find anyone who would love me. And I never dreamed that someone could love me the way that he does."

It was possible that nothing would have been different for Bella if he'd stayed, but that didn't prevent Luke from wishing he'd made different choices twelve years earlier. Not just after the funeral, but before their parents were killed.

"Have you ever been in love?"

He blinked, caught off guard—again—by the abrupt shift in the conversation. "Where did that come from?"

She shrugged. "You've been gone for almost twelve years—I'm curious about where you've been, what you've been doing, who you've been with."

"I've been in Wyoming," he reminded her. "Working on various ranches here and there."

"Who you've been with," she said again.

"I've dated some, had a few relationships, nothing serious."

"Not yet," she teased.

But he suspected the issue was something more than timing. "I'm not sure I'm capable of falling in love," he confided.

"Why would you say something like that?" she asked.

"I'm thirty-three years old," he reminded her. "If it was going to happen, don't you think it would have happened by now?"

"Not necessarily," she argued. "Maybe your heart needed a chance to finish grieving before it could start loving again."

He frowned at that.

"I was so hurt when you left," she admitted. "I didn't think about the fact that you were hurting, too."

"It was a long time ago."

She nodded. "But I still remember the emptiness I felt inside when you and Bailey and Danny disappeared from my life. I didn't think anything could be worse than losing Mom and Dad, but then I lost three of my brothers, too. And, only a few weeks later, both of my sisters."

"At least you and Jamie got to stay together," he said, because he had nothing else to offer. She'd been dealt a crappy hand—there was no disputing that fact.

"I would have been so lost without him," Bella said softly. "And then, when he went away to school, I really was lost—desperate for attention and affection. And I found it…in all the wrong places."

"What are you talking about?" he asked uneasily.

"I got pregnant, Luke."

Pregnant?

He was certain his jaw had dropped, but even when he closed it again, he couldn't find any words.

"I was fifteen—still a kid myself and facing the prospect of having a kid," she told him.

"Did you…have the baby?"

She shook her head. "I miscarried in the first trimester, but not before I'd told the grandparents about my pregnancy. A few months after my baby died, Grandma died, too, and Gramps blamed me."

"Oh, Bella, I'm so sorry."

"It wasn't your fault."

But it was. He'd abandoned his siblings. Yeah, he'd thought it was the right thing to do at the time—the only thing he could do. Discovering what had happened after that, how his family had fallen apart and scattered, he couldn't help but wish he'd made different choices.

"I wish I'd been here for you," he said.

"You're here now," she said.

"You're too forgiving."

"I carried a lot of hurt and anger for a lot of years,"

she admitted. "But it wasn't your fault. None of what happened was your fault."

"Ah, Bella, you were twelve years old." He scrubbed his hands over his face. "What do you remember about what happened?"

"More than you would think," she told him.

But she couldn't remember what she'd never known—that he was responsible for tearing their family apart.

The long pause across the telephone line had Eva wishing she'd ignored the instinct to share the excitement of her evening with her sister. But when she'd watched the lights of Luke's truck disappear down the road, she'd been bursting to tell someone about the kiss they'd shared. And the someone who was her usual confidante was also her sister and best friend.

Delphine was five years older than Eva—and infinitely wiser. Married for nine years to the man she'd fallen head over heels in love with in her first year at college and the mother of three adorable boys, Del was living Eva's dream.

Of course, Eva hadn't been at college long enough to fall in love. She'd decided to take her first year to focus on her studies, adjust to living away from home and being independent, and then her father's diagnosis had prevented her from returning for a second year.

She had no regrets about the choices she'd made, but she did sometimes wonder if changing course had completely derailed all her dreams. But tonight, after dinner with Luke, she was confident that her life would soon be back on track again.

Her sister was much less optimistic.

"Honey, when a guy says that he doesn't want to get

involved, you'd be smart to listen to him," Del said to her now. "Ignoring that kind of blatant warning is a tried-and-true recipe for heartache."

"I know you're right," she acknowledged.

"So why do I get the feeling that you're not going to heed my advice?"

She didn't deny it. "Because despite what he said, the way he kissed me—" Eva couldn't help but sigh, because her lips were still tingling and her blood still humming with the aftereffects of that incredibly delicious lip-lock. "I've never been kissed like that before."

"I'm sure it was a fabulous kiss," her sister said kindly. "But you can't spin dreams of a future on the basis of a single kiss."

"He's the one, Del. I know it."

"And a few months ago, Zach Dalton was the one. You were certain of it then, too."

Another truth she couldn't deny. Because Zach had been honest and up-front about what he wanted, and when he described his perfect woman, Eva met all of his criteria. Unfortunately, his heart wasn't in sync with his head, and he'd fallen in love with Lydia Grant instead.

"This time is different," she insisted.

Del's silence spoke volumes. She didn't need to point out that Eva had said those words before, too. Not just about Zach, but about Bobby Ray before Zach, and Jason before Bobby Ray. But the truth was, as much as Eva had wanted each of those men to be "the one" at the time she was with them, none of them had made her feel the way she felt when she was with Luke.

"You have such a warm and generous heart," Del finally said. "But if you keep giving pieces of it away, you're not going to have anything left for the man who truly does love you."

"How long am I supposed to wait for him?" Eva asked, not bothering to hide her frustration. "You were already married to Harrison for four years by the time you were my age."

"Love doesn't happen on any particular schedule, but when the right man comes along, you'll know it," Del promised.

But Luke *was* the right man, and Eva *did* know it.

She also knew better than to say so to her sister when Delphine was only trying to protect her from herself.

"In the meantime," she said instead, "is there any harm in spending time with a handsome cowboy?"

"That depends on whether you can spend time with him without falling in love," her sister cautioned.

"I can kiss a guy without expecting it to lead to a ring on my finger," she insisted.

"Without expecting it maybe," Del acknowledged. "But I don't think you can stop yourself from hoping for it."

"It's hard being single when everyone else I know is falling in love," she confided.

"Not everyone," her sister denied. "Amy is still single, and she's older than you."

In fact, Amy Wainwright was the same age as Delphine and, when they were growing up, she'd spent so much time at the Armstrong house that Eva had sometimes felt as if she had three sisters. Eva had always liked and admired her sister's friend, who was pretty and smart and seemed to excel at everything she did.

"How is Amy?" Eva asked now. "She hasn't been back to Rust Creek Falls for a long time."

Del sighed. "She's busy—too busy to make the trip home."

"And probably too busy to worry about pairing off," Eva guessed.

"Speaking of pears, with an e-a-r-s," her sister said in a deliberate effort to shift the topic of their conversation. "Harrison's mom gave me a recipe for cranberry sauce with plums that I was thinking I'd make for Christmas dinner."

"What's the connection between pears and plums?" she wondered aloud.

"They both grow on trees."

Eva laughed, her mood immediately lighter. "Well, don't tell Dad about the plums. You know he's particular about his cranberry sauce."

"I know," Del confirmed.

They talked for a while longer about the upcoming holiday.

Her sister confided that the kids' wish lists to Santa had been getting longer and longer every day until their parents had instructed them to pare—"p-a-r-e," Del clarified—them down to three things.

As Eva listened to her sister and laughed over her nephews' antics, she knew there was only one thing she wanted to find under the tree on Christmas morning: Luke Stockton.

Paper and bow optional.

Chapter Eight

Despite tossing and turning for a long time the previous night, Luke was up before the sun on Wednesday. Years of early morning responsibilities had created an internal alarm that invariably woke him before his clock ever did. And although he was technically on vacation and there was nowhere he had to be this morning, he resisted the urge to pull the covers over his head and go back to sleep, because slumber failed to provide any escape from the grief and guilt that continued to plague him.

He'd anticipated that being back in Rust Creek Falls would force him to confront the demons of his past. What he hadn't anticipated was his preoccupation with a certain sexy baker who, although not part of his past, kept slipping into his dreams. Tempting and teasing him.

He'd meant what he'd said to his sister the night before—he didn't know if he was capable of falling in love. He did know that he wasn't bothered by the prospect of spending his life alone. In fact, he preferred it that way.

Sure, he'd enjoyed spending time with Eva. She was good company and a definite pleasure to look at. And as delicious as her culinary creations were, her pies—and even her trifle—didn't begin to compare to the intoxicating flavor of her lips.

Everything about her was a feast for the senses. She smelled good—a temptingly sweet combination of vanilla and sugar—and she felt even better when she was in his arms. She was slender but with curves in all the right places, and even now his blood rushed hotly through his veins at the memory of those sweet curves pressed against him.

Muttering a curse under his breath, he shoved back the covers and headed into the bathroom for a shower.

A very cold shower.

"You're up early," Hudson noted when Luke wandered down to the kitchen a short while later.

"Old habits," he said. "What's your excuse?"

"Conference call with London."

He nodded. "Not so early in the UK."

"The joys of doing business in other time zones," Hudson noted, refilling his mug with coffee, then pouring another cup for his brother-in-law.

"Thanks."

Hudson nodded. "So what are your plans today?"

"I thought I might head over to Jamie's ranch, give him a hand with the morning chores."

"Mucking out stalls your idea of a good time?"

He shook his head. "Just another old habit."

"No doubt your brother could use the help. Whether or not he'll accept it is a whole other issue," Hudson warned.

Luke mulled over those words as he drove out to the Short Hills Ranch.

Jamie had always been determined to prove himself to his big brothers—eager to do everything they did and angry whenever they left him behind. And while Luke wanted to believe that Jamie's apparent refusal to accept help was just another example of this, he suspected that his youngest brother's stubbornness was rooted in something else. After Luke, Bailey and Danny left, Jamie had been forced to do everything on his own because there was no one around to help him.

With that thought weighing heavily on his mind, he stepped out of his truck. His boots crunched in the snow as he made his way toward the barn. Another set of prints led from the house to the same place, suggesting that his brother was already inside.

The Short Hills Ranch wasn't half as big as some of the spreads he'd worked in Wyoming. On the other hand, Jamie managed all the responsibilities of this land mostly on his own, with only occasional help from a neighbor's kid. Luke had surveyed the property on his first visit, and though everything had been—and still was—covered in snow, he'd noted that the perimeter fence was in good repair and the barn sported a new roof and recent paint. The horses were in the paddock now, wearing light blankets as added protection against the frigid temperatures, which suggested to Luke that his brother was likely mucking out their stalls.

He muscled open the heavy door, then stepped inside and closed it quickly behind him again so the heat wouldn't escape. He walked down the center aisle, breathing in the scents of fresh hay and old leather. The familiar and welcoming fragrance helped ease some of the knots in his belly.

"What are you doing here?" Jamie asked, the sharp edge in his voice tightening those knots again.

"I thought I could lend a hand around here while I'm in town," Luke offered.

His brother continued to mix fresh bedding with the unsoiled straw that he'd tossed aside while he cleaned out the stall. "You think a few hours' labor will make me forget that you abandoned us twelve years ago?" Jamie challenged.

"No," Luke said, his tone heavy with guilt and regret. "I just figured that I'm a ranch hand without work right now, and you've got a ranch that could use an extra hand."

"I manage okay."

"You've done more than manage okay," he said. "You've succeeded in building up a herd and providing for your family."

Jamie finished spreading the straw so that it covered the floor, then stepped out of the stall and turned to look at his brother. "You gonna stand there talking all day or muck out some stalls?"

"I'm gonna muck out some stalls," Luke told him.

Jamie nodded and let him get to work.

Luke had only been in Rust Creek Falls for a week but, in that time, he'd missed the physical labor that ranching entailed. Within a few hours, however, his unused muscles were feeling the effects of exertion. When he dumped the last of the soiled bedding, he was more than ready to be done.

He returned the wheelbarrow and shovel to the barn just as Jamie was coming out of his office.

"I appreciate the help," his brother said only a little begrudgingly. "Especially since I promised Danny that I'd squeeze out some time to give him a hand at Sunshine Farm this afternoon."

"I'm heading over there myself in a little while," Luke

told him, having promised the groom-to-be the same thing.

"Well, you might as well come in for lunch first," Jamie said. "You've earned a meal."

Luke had planned to head into town and grab a bite at Daisy's Donut Shop. Not that he was deliberately trying to cross paths with Eva, but he did have the empty trifle bowl in his truck to return to her. The unexpected offer from his brother, though, was one that he couldn't refuse.

Three days after she'd cooked dinner for Luke—three days after he'd kissed her until her head was spinning so that she could barely remember her own name—Eva acknowledged that maybe her sister was right to be worried.

She was aware that she had a tendency to fall hard and fast and, as a result, she'd had her heart broken more times than she wanted to count. But after the kiss they'd shared, she'd let herself believe that he wouldn't break her heart. That this time, she wouldn't be the only one to fall—and she wouldn't end up alone.

But after three days with only a few words exchanged between them when he came into Daisy's to grab a cup of coffee to go—and once to return the bowl he'd taken home with the leftover trifle—she'd started to doubt her own convictions. And then finally, late on Saturday afternoon, Luke stopped by the donut shop and settled into an empty seat at the counter.

"This is a surprise," Eva said.

"I thought I should get out for a while and give the newlyweds some space."

"I'd guess that they have plenty of space in that big house."

"They do," he agreed. "But I'm sure they're aware

that they aren't alone, so I told them I was going to be out for a few hours."

"And what do you plan on doing for those few hours?"

"That depends on you," he told her.

"Me?" she asked, pleased and surprised that he'd sought her out.

"Do you have any plans tonight?"

"None," she said quickly.

Maybe too quickly.

Did she sound too eager? Too desperate?

Maybe she should have pretended to have a social life—or at least feigned the possibility by checking the calendar on her phone.

But she had no plans—no social life at all, in fact. And if Luke wanted to spend time with her, then she was more than happy to do so.

"What did you have in mind?"

"A flyer posted on the community board at Crawford's advertised *Elf* as tonight's feature movie at the high school," he told her.

"Who doesn't love Will Ferrell?"

He smiled. "Is that a yes?"

"If you're asking if I want to go with you…sure," she decided.

He nodded. "The movie starts at eight—what time do you finish here?"

"I'm not actually working," Eva said, untying the apron she'd wrapped around her waist to protect her clothes while she was in the kitchen. "I just came in to assemble and decorate the cake for a seventy-fifth birthday."

"Then why don't we make it dinner and a movie?" he suggested.

Dinner and a movie sounded a lot like a date to Eva, and she felt a giddy rush of anticipation through her veins. But she knew that Luke was wary about any romantic involvement, and just because it sounded like a date to her didn't mean that it was a date to him, so she tried to play it cool.

"We've got meatloaf with mushroom gravy and mashed potatoes on the menu tonight," she told him.

He shook his head. "I had something else in mind."

She frowned at his quick response. "You don't like meatloaf?"

"I don't think you'd be able to sit here and enjoy a meal without rushing into the kitchen to check on one thing or another," he said.

"You've been away for a lot of years," she reminded him. "Perhaps you've forgotten that there aren't a lot of dining options in this town."

"I haven't forgotten," he assured her. "In fact, I've been craving a bacon cheeseburger from the Ace in the Hole since I passed the 'Welcome to Rust Creek Falls' sign."

"They do make a good burger," she acknowledged. And although the local bar and grill was a little rough around the edges and frequently the site of fisticuffs between cowboys who liked to work hard and party harder, the food was usually decent and the beer was always cold.

"I know the crowd there can get a little rowdy on weekends," he noted, anticipating her objection. "But we should be in and out before any of the local ranch hands get too drunk and stupid."

"I'm not worried," she said. "But I do want to go home to freshen up and change my clothes first."

His gaze skimmed over her from the top of her head

to the toes of her cowboy boots and back again. The slow appraisal made her skin tingle and her heart pound. Then he spoke—

"Why?" he asked. "You look fine to me."

—and the bubble burst.

"Because I'm a girl," she said with just a hint of exasperation in her voice. "And I'd like to elevate my appearance to something more than *fine*."

"What's wrong with fine?" he asked, clearly baffled by her response.

She just shook her head. "Fine is—" she searched for an explanation that would make sense to him. "It's the equivalent of satisfactory or adequate."

"You'd rather be unsatisfactory or inadequate?"

"I'd rather look nice," she told him. "Maybe even pretty."

His brows drew together. "Why would you aim for nice or pretty when you're already beautiful?"

His matter-of-fact tone stunned her as much as his words. "If you think I'm beautiful, why did you say I looked fine?" she demanded, full-on exasperation in her tone now.

"Because I figured you didn't need to be told and I didn't want you to worry that I was hitting on you."

She only *wished* he was hitting on her, but he'd been clear that wasn't going to happen—which didn't mean she couldn't attempt to change his mind.

"I'd still like to change before we go out," she told him.

Luke shrugged. "How much time do you need?"

"I'll be ready in half an hour."

And she would use every one of those thirty minutes to ensure that when he looked at her, he wouldn't be thinking that she looked *fine*.

* * *

There were a lot of reasons that Eva loved her job at Daisy's—one of which was the proximity of the donut shop to her parents' house. Less than five minutes after she left Luke sitting with his coffee, she was climbing the steps to the front porch of her childhood home.

She was surprised that her dad's SUV wasn't in the driveway, which meant that one or both of her parents was out. If it was both, she would be saved from having to explain her own plans. Marion was already worried about the time Eva was spending with Luke, and she didn't want maternal concern to put a damper on her excitement about the evening ahead.

She'd just opened the door when her cell phone chimed to indicate a text message.

Gone out for dinner. There's leftover chicken and rice in the fridge if you want it.

Love Mom & Dad

Eva keyed in her reply:

OK. I'm going to the movie at the high school tonight. See you later. XO

Then she hurried upstairs to survey the contents of her closet, trying to decide what to wear for a date that wasn't really a date.

She didn't usually bother with much makeup because the heat from the ovens caused it to melt off her face. Since she didn't have to worry about that tonight, she darkened her lashes with mascara, colored her cheeks with powder and slicked her lips with gloss. Then she unbraided her hair and brushed it out so it hung in loose waves to her shoulders. She wrinkled her nose at the reflection in the mirror, glanced at the time and plugged in her straightening iron.

While the appliance was heating, she stripped out of her clothes and rifled through her closet, looking for her favorite wrap-style skirt. It was navy with tiny flowers embroidered all over it, and it paired nicely with the slim-fitting V-neck cashmere top in the same pale shade of blue as the flowers. She found what she was looking for and tossed both garments on top of her bed while she wriggled into a pair of wool tights. They weren't sexy but they were necessary in December, and they wouldn't be visible beneath the long skirt anyway.

After dressing, she straightened her hair, then added hoop earrings, a trio of bangle bracelets and a teardrop-style pendant on a long chain that hung between her breasts. Maybe it wasn't very subtle, but if Luke still intended to leave town after the holidays, she didn't have time for subtlety. A light spritz of perfume and she was ready to go.

And just in time, she realized, as the doorbell chimed.

She stuffed her feet into her boots, grabbed her jacket from the hook and opened the door.

Luke had decided to hang out at Daisy's for the half hour Eva had said she needed, though he was skeptical of that claim. If she could truly be ready in thirty minutes, she was more efficient than any other woman he'd ever dated.

Not that this was a date—not really. He'd left his sister's house with the intention of grabbing a bite and catching a movie, and since he enjoyed Eva's company, he'd asked her to join him. And even if a man and woman sharing a meal and enjoying entertainment together might technically fit the definition of a date, he'd made it clear to Eva that he wasn't looking to get involved.

But that was before she opened the door in response to his knock and he discovered that she had, indeed, elevated her appearance from beautiful to breathtaking.

His gaze skimmed over her, from the top of her head to the toes of her boots and back again. The heat in his eyes as they made their slow perusal warmed every part of her—including some parts that had been cold for a very long time.

"You look like champagne and caviar, not beer and burgers," he told her.

Eva ignored the way her heart was bumping against her ribs and replied lightly, "I'm flattered you think so, but my champagne and caviar outfit is at the dry cleaners."

"I didn't think Rust Creek Falls had a dry cleaner."

"It doesn't," she said. "I had to take it into Kalispell."

He chuckled as he offered his arm and led her to his truck.

It was a testament to the quality of the food even more than the limited dining options in Rust Creek Falls that the Ace was always packed on Friday and Saturday nights. Luke took her hand to help her up the rough-hewn wooden steps, then opened the door beneath the oversize ace of hearts playing card that blinked in red neon. They stepped inside the dimly lit bar just as a waitress moved past with a tray full of drinks.

"Grab a seat anywhere," she told them. "If you can find one."

Luke took a moment to glance around, then steered her toward a booth that had just been vacated, staking claim to it while the busboy was still clearing away the dirty dishes.

"Do you know what you want or do you need to look at a menu?" he asked as the waitress approached.

Though what she really wanted wasn't something she would find on the menu, Eva smiled at the server and said, "I'll have the bacon cheeseburger."

"With fries?"

"Sure," she agreed, because no one went to the Ace for a salad.

"Anything to drink?"

"Diet cola."

The waitress jotted the order down on her pad then turned to Luke.

"I'll have the same," he said. "But real cola."

After she'd gone, Luke leaned back in his seat and looked around the room. "Does that ancient Wurlitzer still work?"

"It does," Eva confirmed. "And it still plays three songs for a quarter."

"What's with the giant-screen TV on the stage?"

"Rosey had that brought in so her customers can watch *The Great Roundup* on Friday nights."

"People actually come to a bar to watch a reality show?" he asked.

"They do," she confirmed. "Because Rust Creek Falls has two residents—Travis Dalton and Brenna O'Reilly—competing for the prize money and, of course, we're all rooting for one of them to win."

"Yeah, my sister told me." But he still looked skeptical.

"You should be here on a Friday night," she told him. "It's standing room only. Once I heard a customer grumble about the number of people packed into the place, but his threat to report the establishment to the fire chief was overheard by the fire chief, who promised to look into the situation as soon as the final credits rolled."

Luke chuckled at that, then did a double take. "Wow—there's a man over there who looks just like my high school history teacher."

Eva didn't need to follow the direction of his gaze. "Did you have Mr. Armstrong for history?"

He nodded. "You, too?"

"No, but I know him very well. He's actually the principal of the high school now. And my father."

Chapter Nine

Eva held her breath as she waited for Luke to respond to her confession.

"That would explain the glare," he noted.

"He's not really glaring," she hastened to assure him. "He's just trying to figure out who you are because he's not wearing his glasses."

Luke shook his head. "I can't believe I didn't make the connection between Eva Armstrong and Mr. Armstrong in the history department."

"Armstrong isn't an uncommon name," she said. "And a lot of people try to forget about high school history."

"It wasn't so bad," he said.

She just lifted a brow, making him laugh.

"Okay, it was awful," he admitted. "But the truth is, I didn't enjoy any of my subjects because the whole time that I was stuck inside a classroom, I only wanted to be helping my dad out on the ranch."

"A cowboy through and through," she noted.

"I guess so," he acknowledged.

Thankfully, her parents had finished their meals and, after they'd paid their check, stood up to leave. But of course, they didn't go without stopping by their daughter's table first.

Luke automatically rose to his feet.

Ray Armstrong shook his hand. "Luke Stockton— I heard that you were back in town. From Wyoming?"

Luke confirmed with a nod.

"You plan on moving back to Rust Creek Falls?" his former teacher asked.

"No, sir. Just visiting for a while."

"Obviously you know my dad," Eva said, eager to cut off her father's interrogation. "And this is my mom, Marion."

Luke inclined his head. "It's a pleasure to meet you, ma'am."

"And it's nice to finally put a face to the name Eva has been—"

"Your message didn't say where you'd gone for dinner," Eva interjected before her mother could complete her sentence.

"I was hoping to talk your father into going somewhere else," Marion confided. "He knows this isn't one of my favorite places."

"But nowhere else does a burger like the Ace," Ray pointed out.

"Actually, the burgers you cook on the backyard grill are even better," his wife noted.

"The backyard grill that's currently under eighteen inches of snow?"

Marion sighed. "Which is why we're here."

"But now we're going," Ray said, and Eva sent him a quick smile of thanks.

Her father didn't smile back, and Eva suspected that

he would be watching the clock as he waited for her to return home after the movie.

"Was that as uncomfortable for you as it was for me?" she asked Luke when her parents had gone.

"Actually, it wasn't as uncomfortable as I'd feared," he said.

"At least that brief conversation confirmed that I hit the jackpot with their Christmas present," she noted.

"What did you get them?" Luke asked after the waitress had delivered their drinks.

"An indoor grill."

He studied her across the table. "Did you know that you get a sparkle in your eye whenever you talk about the holidays?"

"I love Christmas," she said simply.

He picked up his glass and sipped.

"And you don't," she guessed, feeling disappointed for him that he wasn't looking forward to the holiday.

"I don't dislike it," he denied. "I just don't get all excited about it, like..."

"Like a kid at Christmas?" she finished for him.

The corner of his mouth turned up in a half smile. "Yeah, like that."

"Why not?"

He shrugged. "I have a lot of happy memories of Christmases from my childhood, but when my parents died, everything changed."

She touched a hand to his arm. "I'm sorry."

"It was a long time ago," he said.

She knew it was true, but she also knew that he was still feeling raw. Twelve years had passed since he'd left Rust Creek Falls, but coming home now, for the first time, it was understandable that all of the memories—good and bad—would come back to him in a flood.

"And I know I promised to stay in town for Danny and Annie's wedding, but I have reservations about being here Christmas morning," he confided.

"Why's that?"

"Because Bella and Hudson are still newlyweds and I'm sure they'd prefer to spend their first Christmas together alone."

"And I'm sure that, after twelve years, there's nothing your sister wants more than to celebrate the holidays with her family—her whole family," Eva pointed out to him.

"Except that the whole family won't be together," he pointed out.

Eva knew that Hudson's investigator hadn't yet managed to track down Bailey or Liza, but she suspected that he wasn't referring to a sibling reunion, but the loss of his parents.

"Tell me how you spend your Christmas morning," he suggested, as if to distract from his own thoughts and memories.

"With my parents and sisters and their husbands and kids. We gather around the tree early—because the kids don't let us sleep past six—and we drink hot cider or Irish coffee, nibble on fresh fruit and sticky buns and open presents."

"Your sisters come home every Christmas?"

"Every Christmas," she confirmed. "Calla and Patrick will celebrate with his family in Thunder Canyon on Christmas Eve before they come here. Delphine's in-laws retired to Arizona a couple years back, so they usually head south on the twenty-sixth."

"Do you have a big meal later?"

She nodded. "A huge roast turkey with all of the trimmings."

"And pie for dessert?" he guessed.

"Pie for dessert," she confirmed.

"Apple?"

She chuckled. "Apple and lemon and pumpkin."

"I thought pumpkin pie was a Thanksgiving tradition."

"Not exclusively," she said. "And I thought apple was your favorite."

"It is," he acknowledged. "But I've recently discovered that I have more of a sweet tooth than I ever knew."

But he declined the offer of dessert when the waitress came around to clear away their empty plates, expressing a desire to save room for popcorn at the movie.

The high school was only a couple blocks from the Ace—a pleasant walk in the warmer months but an inadvisable one in December, so after settling their bill, they drove over. Tickets were sold at a table set up in the main foyer and only cash payment was accepted. Eva knew to ensure that she had small bills whenever she attended because it wasn't unusual for the cash box to be short on change.

Tonight Luke paid for their admission, then led the way to the concession area and joined the end of the line.

"Popcorn?" he offered.

"I couldn't even finish the fries that came with my burger," she reminded him.

"I'm guessing that's a no?"

"That's a no," she confirmed.

"Soda?"

"No, thanks."

Eva shook her head as he came away with a large bag

of popcorn and a cola in hand. "You can't honestly still be hungry."

"It has nothing to do with hunger and everything to do with enhancing the movie-watching experience," he told her.

"I'll take your word for it," she said dubiously.

There was a pretty good crowd gathered tonight. Of course, there weren't a lot of entertainment options in town, and the high school gym was a favorite weekend destination for those who didn't want to hang with the sometimes rowdy crowd at the Ace.

Eva and Luke found seats near the back of the gymnasium, leaving the rows closer to the front for families with children. There weren't any previews or commercials—the only warning that the movie was about to start, apart from the lights being switched off, was Mr. Hendricks—the caretaker—standing at the front of the room and shouting out a reminder for everyone to turn off their cell phones.

Elf was one of Eva's favorite Christmas movies, but about halfway through, she realized that she hadn't been paying attention to the feature. But how was she supposed to concentrate on the screen when the man beside her was so distracting? Especially when, every time Luke leaned close to say something to her, his breath tickled her ear and sent shivers down her spine. And despite her insistence that she didn't want any popcorn, he kept jiggling the bag in front of her, silently encouraging her to share. She finally succumbed to temptation—at least with respect to the popcorn. But it was the man she really wanted.

When the credits finally began to roll, she was grateful that she no longer had to pretend to be watching the movie but also disappointed that her time with Luke was coming to an end.

Maybe he was disappointed, too, because after helping with her coat, he said, "How does hot chocolate and a jelly donut sound?"

"The sound would be my stomach exploding," she told him.

"Just hot chocolate?" he suggested as an alternative.

"If you want hot chocolate, we can go for hot chocolate," she agreed.

"I'm not sure that I really want hot chocolate," he admitted. "But I am sure that I don't want to take you home yet."

"Oh," she said as happy butterflies swooped and twirled in her belly.

"I guess that wasn't very subtle, was it?"

"I prefer honesty to subtlety," she told him.

"Then it would be okay to admit that, every time I look at you, you take my breath away?"

"Well…that's a distinct improvement over 'you look fine,'" she noted.

He winced. "You must have realized by now that males have a tendency to fumble when they're in the company of a female they want to impress."

"Careful," she warned, "or I might start to think you're flirting with me."

"I shouldn't be," he admitted. "But I can't seem to help myself."

Her lips curved as he pushed open the door for her to exit, her smile widening even more when she stepped outside. "Look—it's snowing."

And it was—the sky was filled with great big fluffy

flakes that seemed to dance rather than fall in the dark night.

"Christmas snow," she said softly, reverently.

"What's Christmas snow?"

She threw her arms out to her sides, tipped her face up to the sky and turned in a slow circle. "This," she told him.

He held out a hand, watched a fat flake land on the palm of his leather glove and slowly melt away. "It looks like regular snow to me."

Eva shook her head. "Christmas snow is magic."

"Magic, huh?"

She nodded.

"And is this magic snow capable of creating some kind of enchantment?" he wondered aloud.

"Of course," she agreed.

"Is that why I suddenly find myself wanting to kiss you despite promising that it wouldn't happen again?"

"It might be the snow…or it might be that you're wildly attracted to me," she said.

Though her tone projected confidence, he could see the uncertainty in her eyes. But Luke, looking at her now—her cheeks pink from the cold, her eyes sparkling, her lips tipped up at the corners—wasn't uncertain at all.

"You might be right," he acknowledged.

She took a step toward him. "About the snow—or the attraction?"

His gaze lingered on the temptingly sweet curve of her mouth. "Either way, didn't we agree that any kind of romantic involvement would be a bad idea?"

"Who said anything about a romantic involvement?" she challenged. "Sometimes a kiss is just a kiss."

"Sometimes it is," he agreed just before his lips brushed against hers.

With a soft sigh, Eva's eyelids fluttered and her lips yielded. Luke's mouth was warm and firm and masterful, causing ribbons of desire to unfurl in her belly and spread slowly through her veins. His hands slid up her back, then down again. Even through the bulky coat she wore, she felt the heat of his touch, and she wanted more.

She lifted her arms to his shoulders, slid her hands into the silky ends of his hair and held on while the world spun around her. She felt the gentle brush of snowflakes on her face, but not even the biting wind could chill the heat in her veins.

His tongue skimmed across the seam of her lips, and they parted willingly, eagerly, so that he could deepen the kiss. She didn't know how long they stood there, in the shadows of the trees, under the falling snow. She lost complete track of time, all sense of purpose. There was only Luke and this moment. Nothing else mattered.

"I don't think that kiss was just a kiss," he said when he finally eased his mouth from hers and had given them each a moment to catch their breath.

But his arms stayed around her, holding her close, and she wondered if he could hear the pounding of her heart, or even feel it against his chest.

"What was it?" she asked, wanting to know what he was thinking and feeling, desperate for some hint that she wasn't the only one who was starting to fall.

"It felt to me like the start of something bigger," he admitted, but he didn't sound happy about it.

"And you don't want to start anything," she remembered.

"It wouldn't be fair to start something that I'm not going to be in town long enough to finish."

She knew that she should be grateful he'd put on the brakes, but it was difficult to be grateful when her body was still aching for more. And why was he so certain that anything they started had to finish? Was it really so impossible to believe that he might fall in love and want to build a life with her? But of course she didn't ask any of those questions.

"What about that hot chocolate?" she said instead. "Do you still want that?"

"If you're not in any hurry to get home," he said.

"Is my carriage going to turn into a pumpkin?"

He smiled. "It's not even close to midnight."

"Then I think I've got time."

Eva wasn't surprised to find that her mom was still up when Luke dropped her off. She was surprised that her dad wasn't in his recliner beside her, flipping through the channels on TV and grumbling that there was nothing worth watching while his wife knitted tiny hats and booties and baby blankets for the Tree of Hope at Crawford's.

She settled on the opposite end of the sofa from her mother, tucking her feet under her skirt. "Where's Dad?"

Marion's needles clicked in a familiar rhythm. "In bed."

"Is everything okay?" Eva asked, immediately worried, because when someone you loved had battled cancer— even successfully—the worry never quite went away.

"Everything's fine," her mother hastened to reassure her. "But we had an early morning and a busy day, and we drew straws to determine who could go to bed and who should wait up until you got home."

"You don't usually wait up for me," she noted.

"No," her mother agreed. "But I wanted to know how your evening was."

"Good," she said cautiously.

"Luke seems like a nice man. He's certainly a handsome one."

"He is," she agreed.

"Has he said how long he's planning to stay in Rust Creek Falls?"

"At least until his brother's Christmas Eve wedding," Eva said.

"And then he's going back to Wyoming?"

"That seems to be the plan," she acknowledged.

"You know why I'm asking, don't you?" her mother asked.

"You want to know if you need to set another place at the table for dinner on Christmas?"

Marion sighed as she tugged on the yarn. "I'm worried about you."

"There's no reason for you to worry," Eva told her.

"You're falling in love with him."

"Maybe," she admitted.

Her mother continued to knit. After another minute she said, "And when he leaves, he's going to break your heart."

"Maybe," she said again.

She understood her mother's concerns; she knew they were valid. She did have a habit of giving her heart too quickly—and having it broken easily and frequently.

"Or maybe he'll fall in love with me, too, and decide to stay in Rust Creek Falls," she suggested as an alternative.

"Maybe he will," her mother acknowledged, though the doubtful tone warned Eva that she didn't believe it was a real possibility. "Has he told you why he and his brothers left town?"

She picked a piece of fluff off the arm of the sofa. "Not really."

"Maybe you should ask him," Marion suggested.

"I figure if he wanted me to know, he would tell me."

"But don't *you* want to know?"

Of course, she did. Especially if his reasons for leaving twelve years ago were unchanged, because then it was likely that he would be leaving again. But watching him with his family, she'd seen the longing in his eyes, and she knew that he wanted to stay, even if he wasn't ready to admit it to himself.

"It's not really any of my business," she finally said in response to her mother's question.

"It is if you're thinking of a future with this man."

"Right now, I'm just enjoying being with him."

Her mother set her knitting aside and reached over to rest a hand on Eva's knee. "You deserve to fall in love with a man who will love you as much as you love him," she said. "I'm just not sure that Luke Stockton is that man."

"You've got some pretty strong opinions about a man you just met tonight," she noted.

"You're right. But I'm less concerned about misjudging him than I am about him hurting you."

"Do you remember what you said to me before I went away to college?" Eva asked.

"Probably some brilliant words of wisdom that you're going to toss back in my face now," her mother guessed.

"You said that I shouldn't ever let fear of what might happen prevent me from following my heart."

Marion sighed. "It seemed like good advice at the time."

"It was," Eva agreed. "And it's the advice I'm going to follow now, too."

Chapter Ten

Bella had encouraged Luke to come and go as he pleased, reminding him that he had a key and the alarm code and didn't need to worry about what anyone else was doing. It had taken him a few days before he felt comfortable enough to do so, but until he pulled into the driveway and discovered the house illuminated by hundreds—no, thousands—of Christmas lights, he didn't realize that this was the first time he'd been out after dark.

He kicked off his boots and hung his coat in the closet, then headed toward the stairs and his guest room on the second level. As he approached the family room, he heard the murmur of voices from within. Obviously his sister and brother-in-law were still up—a realization that tempted him to tiptoe past the doorway because he knew that if Bella knew he'd been out with Eva, his sister would commence round two of her interrogation.

On the other hand, maybe he should solicit her opinion because he obviously didn't have a clue about what he was doing—telling Eva in one breath that he didn't want to get involved and then kissing her breathless in the next.

Eva had claimed that the snow was magic, but he suspected it was the woman herself who had cast some kind of spell on him. He'd been attracted to his share of women and had been fortunate that his feelings were usually reciprocated, but he couldn't ever remember being so captivated so quickly by anyone else.

"Luke—is that you?" Bella's voice called out.

"It's me," he confirmed, stepping through the doorway and into the room to find his sister snuggled in her husband's arms, her back to his front.

Flames crackled in the fireplace, and a bottle of wine was open on the table, two half-full glasses beside it. There were more holiday decorations in here, including an enormous tree that stretched floor to ceiling and was wrapped in lights, garland and decorated with baubles and balls.

"There are glasses in the hutch," Hudson said, nodding his head toward the dining room. "If you want a glass of wine."

Luke shook his head. "I'm not sure that would mix well with the hot chocolate I just had."

"You've been hanging out at Daisy's again," Bella guessed.

"Not hanging out," he denied. "But we did go there after the movie."

"We?" she prompted, a speculative gleam in her eyes.

"Me and Eva," he admitted.

"You've been spending a lot of time with her lately," his sister noted.

"Which is nobody's business but your own," Hudson said, surprising Luke with the unexpected defense.

"Is it wrong to want to know about the woman my brother's dating?" she challenged.

"We're not dating," Luke told her. "We've just been… hanging out."

"Is that all it is?"

He wanted to answer yes—firmly and definitively—but the taste of Eva still lingered on his lips; want for her still pulsed in his blood.

"Eva knows that I'm not in any position to get involved right now," he pointed out to his sister, and reminded himself.

"Why not?" she pressed, the expression on her face matching the disappointment in her tone.

"Because my life is in Wyoming," he reminded her.

"It doesn't have to be. You could come home, Luke, to be near your family again."

After less than two weeks in Rust Creek Falls, he was more tempted by her entreaty than he'd ever thought he would be. But his sister wouldn't want him to move back to Rust Creek Falls if she knew the truth about why he'd left. If she knew that he was responsible for tearing their family apart.

He'd always thought the self-imposed exile was his punishment for being responsible for the loss of their parents. He hadn't known that the deaths of Lauren and Rob were only the beginning. He'd chosen to walk away—confident that Jamie, Bella, Liza and Dana would be taken care of by their grandparents. He hadn't known that their family had been further torn apart, that Liza and Dana had been put up for adoption, that Jamie and Bella had been given a roof over their heads but not much more.

His heart ached for all of them, but for Bella most of all. He couldn't fathom everything she'd been through—a teenage pregnancy and miscarriage followed by the death of their grandmother. Yet, by some miracle of fate, she'd gotten through all of that. And looking at her now, snuggled in the loving arms of her husband, Luke was both grateful and relieved to know that she'd found a partner who loved and appreciated the wonderful woman she was.

Jamie had traveled an equally rocky path to get where he was, including the death of his first wife only hours after the birth of their three babies. But he had worked hard to make his ranch a success for himself and his children, and he'd even found love again with his longtime friend and confidante.

Danny had been miserable when he left Rust Creek Falls with Luke and Bailey, but he'd eventually found his way home again to reconnect with his high school sweetheart and discover that he was the father of an eleven-year-old daughter he never knew existed. And while Luke suspected their reunion had been more painful and complicated than he knew, they were now planning a wedding and future together.

He was sincerely happy for each of them, genuinely grateful that they'd managed—seemingly against all odds—to find happiness and contentment in their lives. Although he'd lost touch with Bailey years earlier when his brother had headed to New Mexico, he drew comfort from the knowledge that Bailey was with the woman he loved—likely married and possibly even a father now, too.

He didn't know anything about what his two youngest sisters had been doing for the past twelve years, but he was looking forward to seeing Dana at the wedding. According to Bella, their twenty-year-old sister had been adopted by a wonderful couple and raised in a loving home. He could only hope that Liza had fared as well—

and that Hudson's private investigator would track her and Bailey down soon so that their reunion might be as complete as possible.

"Luke?"

He looked down at the hand on his arm, then up into his sister's concerned face.

"Are you okay?" Bella asked gently.

"Sorry," he said. "My mind just wandered for a minute."

"And we should wander up to bed," Hudson suggested to his wife.

"All right," Bella agreed. Then to Luke, "He thinks if I pressure you, you're going to hightail it back to Wyoming, but I just want you to know how much I want you to stay."

"I do know, Bella," he said, sincerely touched by her entreaty.

"And you're thinking about it, right?"

"Bella," Hudson said, shaking his head.

"I'm thinking about it," he said, if only to appease her.

But after her husband had dragged her out of the room and he was alone with his thoughts, he was surprised to realize that it was true.

Sunday brunch had been a tradition in the Armstrong house for as long as Eva could remember, and it was the sound and scent of sizzling bacon that lured her downstairs the following morning.

Her father was already at the table, with a mug of coffee in one hand and the *Gazette* in the other.

"What can I do to help?" Eva asked, as she always did.

"Everything's under control," her mother said, as she always did.

So Eva poured herself a mug of coffee and took her usual seat at the table.

Ray finished with his paper, folded it in half and set it aside just as his wife carried a platter loaded with crisp bacon, creamy eggs and fluffy pancakes to the table.

"Breakfast looks almost as good as you," he said with a lascivious wink for his wife.

"Flattery won't get you out of helping with the cleanup," Marion told him.

It was another common exchange—a comfortable routine they'd established over the years. And though Ray would, predictably, grumble when his wife handed him a tea towel, he never actually balked at doing his share of kitchen duty.

Her parents were the reason why Eva had so much faith in the power of love. For all of her twenty-five years, they'd been an example to her, and it never failed to warm her heart to see that, after thirty-seven years of marriage, three kids and countless crises—the worst of which had been her father's bout with cancer five years before—they were still head over heels in love.

When she was a teenager, their overt displays of affection had sometimes made her squirm. Now that she was older, she could appreciate how fortunate they were to have found one another. As were each of her sisters.

That was what Eva wanted, too. A partner in life. Someone to stand with her through the good times and not-so-good times. Someone she could count on to always be there for her.

She wanted Luke Stockton to be that man. And maybe she did have a tendency to fall hard and fast, but when she was with Luke, she forgot about every other man she'd ever dated. When she was with Luke, she forgot about everything but how much she wanted to be with Luke—forever.

Maybe she was jumping the gun a little. After all, she'd known him for less than two weeks and they'd only shared two kisses. But she felt as if she'd known him a lot longer, and those kisses made her believe they were but a prelude to something more.

Her cell phone buzzed as she was nibbling on the last bite of her bacon. She glanced apologetically at her mother, conscious of the "no cell phones at the table" rule.

"Go ahead," Marion relented. "Everyone's finished eating."

Eva pushed away from the table to retrieve the device from the windowsill above the sink. She felt a flutter in her belly as she wondered if—and hoped that—it might be a message from Luke.

But it wasn't. It was her boss, asking if she could cover Karen's shift that afternoon. Eva hesitated. Although it was only a four-hour commitment, it would mean four fewer hours that she could spend with Luke.

On the other hand, Luke hadn't asked her to spend any time with him today. In fact, when he'd dropped her off the night before, he hadn't made any mention of when he might see her again. Besides, she'd had a life before he came to town and she would have a life again when he left. But she really hoped he would change his mind about going back to Wyoming and decide to stay in Rust Creek Falls instead.

In the meantime, Daisy had given her a job when she desperately needed one—not just for the income to help her parents out but to give her a reason to stay home during her dad's treatments. So she could text back only one reply:

Happy to help.

When Eva agreed to work Sunday afternoon, she'd resigned herself to the fact that she wouldn't see Luke that day. It was after four o'clock and halfway through her shift when the bell over the door jangled and he walked in.

"Hey," he said, obviously surprised to see her. "I thought you were supposed to be off all weekend."

Which confirmed, to her profound disappointment, that he hadn't come in looking for her but had another reason for being there. "I was—but Karen's in bed with the flu." She held up a mug, a silent question.

Luke glanced at his watch, then nodded and took a seat at the counter. "Have you ever said no when someone asks for a favor?"

"Of course I have," she responded.

"Really?" he challenged, accepting the mug she passed across the counter. "Tell me when."

"Well, I can't remember offhand," she admitted. "But I'm sure that I have."

"I'll bet you haven't," he said. "You're the type of person who just can't turn away from someone in need… which is kind of what I'm counting on."

She eyed him warily. "What do you mean?"

"I need help."

"What can I do?" she immediately offered.

Luke smiled. "See? You didn't even ask what—you just said yes."

"I said, 'what can I do?'" she clarified.

"And the answer is, help me with my Christmas shopping."

"I'd be happy to," she agreed. "I love shopping, especially this time of year when the stores are all decked out for the holidays."

"I was hoping you'd say that," he said. "But that's not actually why I'm here."

"So tell me why you are here," she suggested.

"I've been invited to dinner tonight and I realized, when I was at your door emptyhanded, that I probably shouldn't have shown up emptyhanded, so I offered to take something for dessert."

"Excuse me for a second," she said, grabbing the pot of coffee and moving to the other end of the counter to top up Homer Gilmore's cup.

Not because he'd asked for a refill, but because she needed an excuse to turn away so that Luke wouldn't see how much his casual admission of a date with another woman had hurt her.

And not only was he going on a date with another woman, but he'd come into Daisy's to pick up something for dessert—likely something Eva had made. It was just like Lydia Grant's request for lemon meringue pie all over again.

She chatted with the old man for a minute, until she was fairly confident that she could return to her conversation with Luke without crying. She set the pot back on the warmer and forced a smile. "We've got a small six-layer German chocolate cake that a customer ordered for his girlfriend's birthday before he found out she was allergic to nuts."

"I don't think nuts are a problem," he said.

She took the cake out of the case to show him.

"That looks yummy—and the perfect size for four people."

"A double date?"

"What?" He seemed sincerely baffled by the question, then he laughed. "No, it's not a date at all."

"It's not?"

"No," he said again. "I'm having dinner with Danny, Annie and Janie."

"Oh," she said, feeling foolish.

"Did you really think I would come in here to get dessert for a date with another woman?"

"Well, you admitted that you didn't expect to find me working today," she reminded him.

"I didn't," he confirmed. "But I was happy to see you."

She pulled a flat piece of cardboard out from under the counter and began forming a box for the cake.

"Is this the first time you're meeting your niece?" she asked, eager to change the topic of conversation and forget that she'd jumped to embarrassing and erroneous conclusions.

"It is," he confirmed.

"While you're having dinner tonight, you should listen for any hints about what Janie might want for Christmas," Eva suggested as she set the cake in the box and closed the lid. "Preteen girls are notoriously picky and it would be good to have a starting point before you go shopping."

"Before *we* go shopping," he reminded her.

She punched the price of his cake and coffee into the register, and he passed some bills across the counter. "When are we going shopping?"

"Whatever day works best for you."

"Wednesday?"

He picked up the cake box and winked at her. "It's a date."

Luke was glad he'd stopped by Daisy's Donut Shop to pick up something for dessert—not just because the cake scored big points for him with his niece and future sister-in-law, but also because talking to Eva helped him forget, at least momentarily, that he was nervous about the family dinner.

By the time Janie got up to clear the dessert dishes from the table, Luke was surprised to realize that they'd been sitting around the table for almost three hours. Even more surprising was how much he'd enjoyed the time he'd spent getting reacquainted with his brother's fiancée and finally meeting his niece. A few weeks earlier, he wouldn't have believed it was possible for love to endure through so many life events and so much time apart, but Danny and Annie proved him wrong.

After Janie excused herself to go do homework, Annie began the washing up. Danny and Luke offered to help, but she shooed them out of the kitchen.

"She doesn't seem like one of those bridezillas you hear horror stories about," Luke noted.

"Annie's not the type to sweat the small stuff," Danny agreed. "The only thing she was really worried about was the venue."

"And it's all ready to go."

His brother snorted. "Hardly."

"Well, I know it probably needs some flowers and stuff," Luke acknowledged, sipping the beer his future sister-in-law had offered him after the meal.

"We have to pick up chairs from the community center and set them up, then decorate the whole building with miles of pine garland and twinkling lights and big red bows."

"When you say *we*, you mean you and Annie, right?"

"Actually it was intended as a collective *we*," his

brother admitted. "As in, anyone I can convince to lend a hand."

"I can haul chairs," Luke decided. "But I'm not sure I'd have the first clue what to do with twinkling lights and bows."

"Me, neither," Danny admitted. Then, when Luke put his almost empty bottle on the table, he asked, "Do you want another beer?"

He shook his head. "I've had my limit."

"You've had one," his brother noted.

"That's my limit when I'm driving," he said.

Danny's brows lifted. "Since when?"

"Since the night that I got wasted and Mom and Dad were killed." He hadn't planned to blurt it out like that, but it was time—past time—for him to tell his brother the truth.

Danny rubbed his thumb through the condensation beaded on his can of soda. "Everything changed that night, didn't it?"

He nodded grimly. "And it was all my fault."

"What are you talking about?"

"The accident." Luke swallowed. "I think Mom and Dad were out that night because…because of me."

"Why would you think that?" his brother asked cautiously.

"Because it was late, and we were drunk. Well, I was drunk, and I'm pretty sure Bailey was, too. But not you. You weren't drinking."

"I was only eighteen," Danny reminded him.

"And always a rule follower. You wanted us to leave the bar," he suddenly remembered. "But we weren't ready to go. There were girls, and they were so friendly and pretty…and I was a drunken fool."

"It wasn't your fault," his brother said.

"Where the accident happened…" Even after a dozen years, remembering brought back all of the pain. Sure, he'd gone on with his life without his parents and without the rest of his family, but everything had changed that fateful night, and he knew that there would forever be an emptiness inside him because of it.

Danny waited for him to finish his thought, though he looked as uneasy as Luke felt about where this conversation was going.

"Where the accident happened," he began again. "I always figured they were so far away from home, so late at night, because they were looking for us." He scrubbed his hands over his face. "If I'd just listened to you, given you the keys and let you drive us home, that night might have ended differently. Everything might have ended differently."

His brother, eyes suspiciously bright, shook his head. "It wasn't your fault, Luke."

"How can you know that?"

"Because it was mine." Danny set his soda can down and stood up to pace restlessly across the room. "You're right about the fact that they were looking for us—because *I* called them. *I'm* the reason they were out on the road that night. It was my fault."

Luke was stunned by his brother's revelation—and not entirely sure he'd heard him correctly. "You called them?"

Danny nodded miserably.

He took a moment to absorb the implications of this admission, then realized it didn't change anything. He didn't believe for a minute that anything that happened was his brother's fault. Luke was the one who was responsible. He was the oldest and the undisputed leader whenever the three of them were out. If he'd made better choices, Danny would never have been put in the position of having to make such a call.

"But Annie's helped me to believe that maybe it wasn't my fault," Danny said when Luke remained silent. "That the fault lies with the driver of the vehicle that slammed into Dad's truck. Maybe my phone call was the reason they were on the road that night, but I'm not responsible for what happened to them."

"You're not," Luke agreed, eager to reassure his brother. "It wasn't your fault."

"And if it wasn't mine, then it wasn't yours, either," Danny said.

"Maybe," Luke allowed, desperate to trust that his brother was right but still unable—or unwilling—to let go of the guilt that he'd carried with him for so many years.

Because if he truly let himself believe that he wasn't responsible, then he'd simply be trading one set of regrets for another—namely that he'd stayed away from Rust Creek Falls and his family for all these years.

Chapter Eleven

Given a choice, Luke would choose to muck out stalls rather than battle crowds of holiday shoppers any day of the week. But since he'd decided to stay in Rust Creek Falls for Christmas—now less than a week away—he didn't really have that option.

Thankfully, he had Eva to keep him company and guide him through the labyrinth of stores. And though she'd insisted that they hit the road early in order to be at the mall in Kalispell when it opened on Wednesday, she had two large coffees and a bag of bear claws ready to go when he picked her up at the donut shop.

Fueled up on sugar and caffeine, they'd tackled his list with purpose and determination. A few hours later, when their arms were already weighed down with too many bags, he accepted yet another along with a cheery "Merry Christmas" from the sales clerk and fell into step behind Eva as they exited the store.

"That's it," she said as they carefully merged with the crowd of shoppers stampeding down the corridor.

"What's it?"

"You're finished," she told him. "Your list is done."

"I am? It is?"

She held up the list of names he'd written out and showed him the check marks she'd put beside each name as he'd purchased gifts.

"That's great," he said, and meant it. "Now we can tackle your list. You've done a lot of looking but you haven't bought anything."

"That's because I'm finished my Christmas shopping," she told him.

"You're finished already?"

"Christmas is in five days," she pointed out. "I would guess that most of the people here are finishing up, not just getting started."

"It's been a long time since I've had anyone to buy presents for—and celebrate the holidays with—and I was feeling a little overwhelmed by the task."

"I think you came up with some really great ideas," she said encouragingly.

"Well, from what I've learned about the triplets, I suspect they'll be just as happy with the boxes as whatever is inside them."

"That's probably true," she acknowledged. "But I still think the toddler sports center was a good choice."

"And the box is big enough that Henry, Jared *and* Katie will all fit inside."

She laughed, easily picturing the scene he described. "It's a good thing you already took it out to your truck, or we wouldn't have been able to carry all of these other bags."

"Did I overdo it?" he asked.

"I don't think so. But now you have to wrap them."

"I never thought about that," he admitted.

"Which means that you need to get paper and tape and bows."

"Or I could take my gifts to that wrapping station at the center of the mall," he suggested as an alternative.

She shook her head. "That's not very personal—and it will cost you a fortune."

"But it will save me hours of wrangling with paper and tape and bows. Unless..." He deliberately left the rest of the thought unspoken.

"You're right—you don't know how to be subtle," Eva noted dryly. "But yes, I'll help with your wrapping."

Before Luke was willing to tackle that project, however, he told Eva that he needed food. So they picked up pizza and wings on their way back to his sister's house because as much as she appreciated his offer to buy dinner anywhere she wanted to go, what she really wanted was just to sit down and put her feet up for a while.

When the pizza box was empty and the wings were decimated to the bone, he cleared away the remnants of their dinner while Eva set up a wrapping station on Bella's enormous dining room table.

"I said I would help you with the wrapping—not that I would do it all," she pointed out to Luke a few hours later as he sat across from her, watching.

"Sorry," he said, not sounding sorry at all. "I'm too dazzled by your skill to concentrate on my task."

"Wrapping presents is hardly a skill. Besides, the only thing I asked you to do was measure and cut the paper."

"And I even screwed that up," he muttered.

She nodded and, unable to resist teasing him a little, remarked, "Impulsive penetration."

"Excuse me?"

"There's no need to apologize," she said soothingly. "It's a common rookie mistake."

His gaze narrowed. "Are we still talking about gift wrapping?"

She chuckled. "Yes, we're talking about gift wrapping—and the fact that you kept rushing to cut the paper without ensuring that it fit around the box."

"And that's...impulsive penetration?"

"Of course," she said with feigned innocence. "What did you think I was talking about?"

"I didn't want to imagine," he said dryly. "And now I've been demoted to bows."

"Bows *and* tags," she said, handing him the last box so that he could add those final touches. "Those tasks seem more in line with your experience."

"Where did you acquire your obviously vast experience?" he wondered aloud.

"Years of practice, including Presents for Patriots at the community center every Christmas."

"What's Presents for Patriots?" he asked.

"I keep forgetting that you've been gone for almost a dozen years," she admitted, loading up an armful of presents to add to the growing pile already under the Christmas tree in the family room. "It's a gift drive for our troops that started in Thunder Canyon and was adopted by Rust Creek Falls a few years back. Local individuals and businesses donate the presents and a few weeks before Christmas, volunteers gather at the community center to wrap them."

"And somehow, even with all the other demands on your time, you manage to participate in that, too."

"It's a good cause," she said.

"No doubt," he agreed, as he arranged the wrapped

packages beneath the tree. "But that doesn't add more hours to your day."

She shrugged. "Well, sleep is mostly overrated."

"You're an amazing woman, Eva Rose Armstrong."

"I'm not really."

He touched a finger to her lips, silencing her protest. "You are," he insisted. "Amazing…and irresistible."

Then his finger dropped away and his mouth covered hers.

His kiss was amazing and irresistible.

Not that Eva made any attempt to resist. Why would she when this was exactly what she wanted? *He* was exactly what she wanted.

And, finally, it seemed as if she was what he wanted, too.

Her lips parted willingly for him, and their tongues began to dance together in a sensual rhythm that made her heart pound and her knees tremble.

"Do you want to know the real reason that I offered to help wrap your presents?" she asked when he eased his lips from hers.

"Because you never say no when someone asks a favor?" he teased.

"Because I know you still have mixed feelings about being in Rust Creek Falls for Christmas and I wanted to help make some new and happy memories for you."

"Since we're sharing confessions, I have to admit that spending time with you has already made this holiday better than the last dozen."

The simple sincerity of his words filled her heart with joy and hope.

"Let's make it even better," she suggested, pulling his mouth down to hers again.

He didn't resist. The heat that had been simmering between them since the beginning had intensified over the past week. That heat spread through her veins now, so hot and fierce she melted against him.

As their tongues tangled together, his hands stroked leisurely up her back, then slowly down again. She shivered against him, an action that caused her already hardened nipples to brush the solid wall of his chest. A groan rumbled low in his throat as he clamped an arm behind her back and hauled her tight against him.

The unmistakable evidence of his arousal against her belly increased her own, and she rubbed wantonly against him. She had no interest in pretending that she didn't want to get naked with Luke. Right now she had no interest in anything but tearing his clothes off.

But when she reached for the top button of his shirt, he caught her wrists in his hands and held them. "As much as I want you, Eva, this isn't a good idea."

"Why not?"

"Because my time in Rust Creek Falls is limited," he reminded her gently.

"I know, and two weeks are already gone, so why are we wasting the time we have left?"

"You'd really be okay with a short-term relationship?"

"It wouldn't be my first choice," she admitted. "But if that's all you're willing to give me—"

"It's all I *can* give you."

"Then it's better than nothing."

He looked as if he was tempted to take what she was offering, but then he shook his head. "There's still so much you don't know about me, that if you did know, would make you understand why getting involved with me is a bad idea."

"So tell me."

* * *

For a lot of years, Luke had tried to not even think about what happened the night his parents were killed. He'd certainly never talked about it. That was, until a few days earlier when he'd finally confided in Danny—only to discover that his brother had never blamed Luke but had, instead, put the whole responsibility on his own shoulders.

It had been a little easier after that to tell it to Bella, who cried with her arms around him. Her tears were of grief, for everything they'd all lost, and somehow offered him a measure of healing he'd never expected. Then he'd told it again to Jamie, who'd reacted with considerably less affection but absolutely no judgment.

Now he needed to tell Eva. Before they took their relationship to the next level, she had a right to know the truth about who he was. She needed the whole truth in order to decide if she really wanted to be with him.

"It's not a story with a happy ending," he warned.

"Tell me anyway."

So he did.

He led her to the sofa and sat beside her, then told her the whole sordid story of what happened the night his parents were killed—how he'd been drinking at an out-of-town bar with his friends and his brothers, because Bailey would never be served in Rust Creek Falls where everyone knew that he wasn't yet twenty-one. He'd been having a great time, dancing with some of the pretty girls in the bar that night and simply loving life.

"How old were you?" Eva asked.

"Twenty-one," he admitted. "Bailey was twenty, Danny only eighteen."

"You've been beating yourself up for almost twelve

years over a mistake that you made when you were twenty-one?"

"That mistake changed everything."

"Maybe you exercised poor judgment that night," she acknowledged. "But you're not responsible for what happened to your parents."

He continued as if she hadn't spoken. "I was drunk, so a lot of my memories of that night are hazy—but only up until the part where a county sheriff came into the bar and told us about the accident." He dropped his head into his hands. "The funeral was—" he paused, searching for a word that could somehow sum up the gut-wrenching experience of standing shoulder to shoulder with his brothers and sisters to say a final goodbye to their parents. No word was adequate so he settled on "—awful."

Truthfully, he didn't remember much about the funeral, except that his tie had been knotted too tight at his throat, and his heart had felt like a lead weight in his chest. He didn't hear anything the minister said, because the words were drowned out by the echo of *my fault, my fault, my fault* over and over again inside Luke's head.

"After the funeral, we all went back to my grandparents' place. Matthew and Agnes Baldwin were my mom's parents—and they weren't happy about having the responsibility of even their youngest grandchildren thrust upon them, after making it clear that me and Bailey and Danny couldn't stay with them."

"That's when you left Rust Creek Falls," she realized.

He nodded. "We told ourselves that we were doing what was best for our younger siblings, believing that the grandparents would be able to handle four kids more easily than seven. But the truth was, I was grateful for the excuse to get away—from my own grief and guilt."

Eva touched a hand to his arm in a wordless gesture of support. He glanced at her, saw that her beautiful blue eyes shimmered with tears. But there was no judgment in her gaze, only sympathy and compassion—neither of which he deserved.

"We headed south and ended up in Wyoming, where we got hired on as ranch hands. We stuck together for a while…then we didn't.

"Danny and Bailey were all I had left of my family, but I let them go, too…because I felt like I deserved to lose everything and everyone who mattered to me."

Listening to the anguish in his tone, seeing the devastation in his eyes, nearly broke Eva's heart. But concerned that he might misinterpret her tears, she determinedly held them in check.

"It wasn't your fault, Luke," she told him, her tone sympathetic but firm. "And maybe that chapter of your life didn't have a happy ending, but it's not the end of your story. There are a lot more chapters still to be written. You get to decide on the ending you want."

"I've never had a serious relationship with a woman," he confided. "Anytime someone starts to get too close, I back away."

"You've lost a lot of people that you cared about," she acknowledged. "It's understandable that you'd be wary about falling in love."

"Maybe I'm not just wary. Maybe I'm not capable of loving anyone."

She didn't believe that. She wouldn't believe it. Luke had suffered more loss than any one person should ever have to, but she was confident that his return to Rust Creek Falls was the beginning of his healing. His family's support and understanding were only one key to the process. Another key was finding a woman that he could trust enough to open up his heart to love again, and she believed that she was that woman. Because she was already in love with him.

Of course, it was far too early to tell him that, so she decided to show him instead. She lifted her arms to his shoulders and rose on her toes to press her lips to his. "What time do you expect your sister and brother-in-law to be home?"

"They're gone until Friday," he admitted. "Hudson flew Bella to New York City to go ice-skating at Rockefeller Center."

"That's a long way to go to strap on a pair of skates."

"There was also something about shopping on Fifth Avenue and taking in a Broadway show. He's pulling out all the stops for their first Christmas as husband and wife."

"She's a lucky girl."

"Yes, she is," he agreed. "Now."

She lifted her hands to his face. He had that look in his eye, the one that told her he was still haunted by events from the past. She didn't want him thinking about the past. She wanted him in the here and now, with her.

She brushed her lips against his again. "What do you say we get lucky, too?"

Any lingering sadness in his eyes was pushed aside by heat. "I'm realizing now that I got luckier than I ever imagined the day I walked into Daisy's for a cup of coffee."

"Large. Black. To go." She recited the first words he'd said to her that day.

His lips curved, but the smile didn't quite edge the worry from his eyes. "Are you sure about this?"

She responded by lifting her sweater over her head and tossing it aside, then reached back to unzip her skirt so that it puddled at her feet, leaving her standing before him in only a white lace bra, bikini panties and stay-up stockings.

He swallowed. "I don't think we're going to make it upstairs to my bed," he warned. "Not this time."

She smiled, pleased by his response and satisfied that he was no longer fighting what they both wanted. "I don't want to go upstairs. I want you here. Now."

He yanked a blanket off the back of the sofa and spread it out on the floor. Then he reached for a remote on the mantel, pressed a couple of buttons and flames flickered to life in the hearth.

"Nice," she said approvingly.

"Very nice," he agreed, his eyes never leaving her body.

The heat in his gaze warmed her all over, but she stepped closer to the fire, closer to Luke. She splayed her hands on his chest and, even through the thick flannel of his shirt, she felt his heart beating, strong and steady, beneath her palms.

"You're a little overdressed," she told him.

This time, when she reached for his button, he made no move to stop her. Her fingers worked quickly, and she parted the fabric and pushed it over his shoulders, eager to put her hands on his bare skin—only to discover that he was wearing a long-sleeved thermal shirt beneath the flannel.

"It's winter in Montana," he explained, but he tugged the shirt over his head and tossed it aside. She hummed her approval as she slid her hands over his bare torso, her fingers tracing the ridges and ripples of his muscles, her nails scraping lightly over his skin.

He took her mouth in another hot, hungry kiss as she reached for the buckle of his belt, eager to help him discard the rest of his clothing. When he was completely and gloriously naked, he peeled the last scraps of lace from her body before easing her down onto the blanket and stretching out over her.

"You smell like a sugar cookie," he murmured as his lips moved over her jaw and down her throat, the stubble on his jaw scraping erotically against her skin. "And you taste even sweeter."

She didn't—couldn't—respond, because his hands were stroking boldly and confidently over her body, sending delicious shivers of sensation to her core and wiping all rational thought from her mind.

His calloused thumbs scraped over her rigid nipples, making her gasp with shocked pleasure. Then his mouth was at her breast, his tongue exploring the ultra-sensitive flesh. "Much, much sweeter."

His lips fastened around the tight peak. He suckled gently, and she moaned softly. Her fingers threaded through his hair, holding him in place against her breast, wordlessly encouraging him to continue. He suckled harder, and she moaned louder. Then he shifted his focus to her other breast and gave it the same close attention.

She couldn't remember when she'd last been with a man, except that it had been a very long time. So long that she'd almost forgotten how good a man's hands could feel on her body. But Luke was reminding her now. So long that she'd almost forgotten how good a man's body could feel under her hands. But she was remembering now. While he continued to taste and tease her breasts, she reached a hand between their bodies and wrapped her fingers around his hard, velvety length. This time, he moaned.

She rocked her hips against his, wordlessly telling him what she wanted, what she needed. He rummaged around on the floor until he found his discarded jeans and pulled a condom out of his wallet.

"You must have been a boy scout," she said, partly teasing but mostly grateful that he was prepared for what was about to happen.

"I can tie you up in forty different ways, if that's your thing," he told her.

She laughed as she took the square packet from his hand and carefully tore it open. "Forty ways, huh?"

"Well, I used to know forty ways," he amended. "Now I probably only remember about half of them."

"Let's save that for another time, then," she suggested, carefully unrolling the prophylactic over his erection. "Right now, I don't want props or tricks. I only want you."

"And I want you," he said, rising over her and, finally, easing into her.

"Oh." She closed her eyes on a sigh of pure pleasure as he stretched and filled her, a glorious tension beginning to build deep inside her.

His lips brushed against hers. "Okay?"

She opened her eyes to find his on her.

"Okay," she confirmed.

He kissed her again, his tongue mirroring the intimate strokes of his body as he began to move.

Her hands glided over him, her fingers tracing the contours of his muscles, digging into his shoulders as, with each thrust, he pushed her closer and closer to the edge.

She held on to him, her anchor in the storm of sensations that battered at her from all directions.

She couldn't think; she couldn't speak; she could only feel. And the way he was moving inside her felt so good she never wanted him to stop. The pleasure continued to build with each stroke until it was an almost unbearable pressure inside her, almost more than she could stand.

Then…finally…release.

As her body shuddered with the aftershocks of pleasure, he groaned deeply and let his own climax take him.

Chapter Twelve

"Best. Christmas. Present. Ever."

Several minutes later, when Luke's brain was capable of functioning again, they were the first words that came to mind. They spilled out of his mouth uncensored, surprising a laugh out of Eva.

She lifted herself up on an elbow and smiled at him. "It was pretty spectacular, wasn't it?"

He stroked a hand leisurely down her torso, loving the softness of her skin—and the nakedness of her body. "I'm not ever going to be able to look at this tree without thinking about you and what we did here tonight."

"Good."

"And when my sister asks, on Christmas morning, why I've got a goofy smile on my face, I'll tell her to ask you."

She was still smiling, too, as she shifted away from him and began to gather up her clothes.

He found her panties before she did and held on when she tried to tug them from his grasp.

"I'm going to need those," she told him.

"Not just yet."

She lifted a brow. "When?"

"Later." He pulled her close and kissed her. "Much later."

But instead of easing her back onto the blanket, he lifted her into his arms.

"Where are you taking me?" she demanded.

"Upstairs."

"Why?"

"Because I want to make love to you in a bed...very slowly...and very thoroughly...and without worrying about bruises on your back or friction burns on my knees."

"That sounds like an incredibly appealing idea," she agreed as he effortlessly carried her up the stairs.

"I was hoping you'd think so." He tumbled with her onto the bed, straddling her hips with his knees and catching her lips in another mind-numbing kiss.

"You're really good at that," she said when he eased his lips away. "Which makes me wonder..."

He nuzzled the sweet spot below her ear. "What are you wondering?"

"How it is that..." She momentarily lost her train of thought when he nipped at her earlobe, then nibbled his way down the side of her throat, raising goose bumps on her skin and sending shivers of excitement coursing through her veins.

"You were saying?" he prompted.

"How is it that you can tie twenty different knots in a piece of rope—" she sucked in a breath when his hand slid down to the apex of her thighs and embarked on a lei- surely exploration, but she made a valiant effort to finish her thought "—but you can't wrap paper around a box?"

"Is that really what's on your mind right now?" he

asked, his tone colored with amusement as he continued his sensual exploration.

"Right now my mind is pretty much blank," she admitted. "But earlier... I was trying to make sense of the... dichotomy."

"We all have different talents," he told her.

"Apparently," she said as he zeroed in on the bull's-eye and, within minutes, sent her soaring.

"That was a pretty impressive display of talent," she commented when she'd finally managed to catch her breath and form a coherent thought again.

"That was just the warm-up," he said.

And he proceeded to prove it to her.

"What time is it?"

Luke opened one eye to glance at the glowing numbers of the clock on the bedside table. "Almost midnight," he said in answer to Eva's sleepy question.

"It feels so much later."

"We've had a busy day." And hers had been even busier, as she'd started the morning baking at Daisy's.

"But a good day," she said, a smile in her voice.

"A very good day," he confirmed.

After another few minutes, just as he was starting to think that she might have fallen asleep, she spoke again. "I should go."

"I wish you didn't have to," he said, surprised to realize it was true. While he wasn't ready to analyze his feelings too deeply, there was something about being with Eva that just felt...right.

And though their lovemaking had been beyond spectacular, he didn't just mean between the sheets. He truly enjoyed spending time with her—wherever they were and whatever they were doing.

He'd never enjoyed shopping. And, for the past dozen years, he hadn't enjoyed Christmas, either. The season that brought families together only served to remind him that his family had been torn apart—that he'd torn his family apart.

Now, with Eva, he actually felt as if he might be able to move past his grief and his guilt.

But even if he finally managed to dump the emotional baggage that had weighed him down for so long, he suspected that his heart would still bear the effects, like the bowed back of a pack horse never relieved of his burden. But when he was with Eva, he almost believed that she could fix whatever was broken inside him. In fact, he almost believed that, if she could love him, maybe he was worthy of being loved.

"I wish I didn't have to go, either," she said. "But I need at least a few hours' sleep before I have to be at work."

He wanted to suggest that she could sleep right where she was, but he knew that she couldn't. While her mom and dad seemed to respect that she was a grown woman, he was sure they wouldn't approve of her spending the whole night in a man's bed. And although he would prefer to stay exactly where he was, with Eva's naked body in his arms, he didn't want to cause any conflict in her relationship with her parents.

"And people think that ranchers work crazy hours," he noted.

"I don't mind the early mornings," she said. "In fact, I like being in the kitchen when it's quiet, watching the sun rise as I sip my first cup of coffee."

"I'd need *gallons* of coffee."

She smiled at that. "I'm well aware of your caffeine addiction."

"And even with gallons of coffee, I'm not sure I'd make it through the day," he admitted.

"I sometimes sneak a nap in the afternoon," she confided.

"Why don't you sneak over here so that we can have that *nap* together?"

She laughed. "When I say *nap*, it's not some kind of code. I actually mean *sleep*. Besides, aren't you supposed to be helping at Sunshine Farm tomorrow?"

"I'd much rather nap with you," he told her.

"I appreciate the thought," she said. "But right now, I'd really appreciate a ride home."

It was 12:39 a.m. when he pulled into the driveway of her house, and she exhaled a grateful sigh of relief when she saw that the porch light was on but the living room was dark—confirmation that her parents had already turned in for the night. Though her parents weren't thrilled about the amount of time she was spending with Luke, she knew that they wouldn't express any outward disapproval. But she also suspected that her mother would take one look at her and know she'd had sex, and Eva wanted to keep that joyous event to herself for just a little while longer.

So she unlocked the door, turned to wave goodbye to Luke, then tiptoed up the stairs to her bedroom.

When he got back to his sister's house, he sent her a text message to let her know, and she hugged the phone to her chest where her heart was beating in a crazy erratic rhythm, like some kind of cardiac Morse code that spelled out her feelings for him.

He'd been completely honest and up-front with her about his plans—and he didn't plan to stay in Rust Creek Falls. She'd known that before she kissed him the first time, but what she knew in her head didn't hold much sway over her heart. She'd fallen in love with him anyway. All the way, head over heels in love.

But even if she ended up with her heart broken, she wouldn't regret giving it to him. She still hoped that he might change his mind about leaving and decide to make Rust Creek Falls his home once again, but if he didn't, she hoped he would look back on the time he'd spent with her and smile at the memories they'd made together.

The bed that Luke had been sleeping in, comfortably and soundly, for the past two weeks, suddenly seemed cold and empty without Eva beside him. He wished she could have stayed the night—so that he could make love to her one more time before they fell asleep and again in the morning.

But he understood why she had to leave. Not just because she lived with her parents but because she was a part of the community. He couldn't blame her for not wanting everyone to know that she'd gotten naked with "the oldest Stockton boy"—as he was referred to by many residents.

Maybe it would be different if he planned to stay in Rust Creek Falls, but he didn't and it wasn't. So he would take whatever moments she would give him, enjoy whatever pleasures they found together. At some point last night, he'd decided to accede to his sister's request—and his own desire—to stay through the holidays. But after the New Year, he would go back to Cheyenne as he'd originally planned.

He fell asleep, refusing to admit—even to himself—that there was a part of him that wanted to change that plan.

And he dreamed of Eva.

Eva was seriously tempted to hit the snooze button when her alarm beeped only a few hours later. Unfortunately, the donuts and pastries wouldn't bake themselves, so she forced her weary body out of bed and stumbled to the shower. She closed her eyes as the hot water poured over her, easing the unfamiliar stiffness in her muscles.

Not that she was complaining. Not at all. Because aside from a few aches, she felt good. Better than good. For the first time in a long time, her body felt sated.

It was her heart that continued to yearn.

She'd promised Luke that she didn't want anything more than he was offering, because she'd wanted it to be true. But she'd lied, perhaps to herself as much as to him, though that had never been her intention. She hadn't known, maybe hadn't wanted to know, that her heart had already opened to him, wholly and completely.

Unfortunately, his heart was still intent on heading back to Wyoming after the holidays—and the New Year was now less than two weeks away. Which meant that she needed to make Luke fall in love with her before those two weeks were up. A daunting task, perhaps.

Or maybe—her lips curved as a plan began to take shape in her mind—a piece of cake.

Eva decided that cookies were more practical than cake, and she was carrying a tin when she walked into the barn where Danny and Annie were planning to get married. There had been a lot of volunteers at the property over the past few days as they raced against the clock to get the venue ready for the big event. Today, however, there were only a few vehicles parked by the barn, which suggested that either the work was almost done or the crew had given up.

When she muscled open the door and stepped inside the cavernous space, she knew that her first guess had been correct.

"Wow," Eva said. "This place looks great."

Luke stepped down off the ladder he'd been perched on and crossed the room to meet her. "*You* look great," he said. "This place looks like a barn."

"Because it is a barn," she reminded him.

"Uh-huh." He dipped his head and touched his lips to hers. "I thought you were going to nap this afternoon."

"I was, and then I thought that the bride and groom might need a couple of extra hands—"

"Always," Annie interjected.

"—and a snack to keep everyone going."

"Snack?" Danny echoed hopefully.

Eva pried the lid off the tin.

"You mentioned sugar cookies yesterday," she reminded Luke, and though her words were deliberately vague, the mischievous twinkle in her eye told him that she had a clear and specific memory about when and where he'd been thinking about the treats. "So when I was baking this morning, I made an extra batch to bring out here."

"That was incredibly thoughtful," Annie said, peering into the tin at the snowflake-shaped cookies decorated with glossy icing and colored sugars. "Oh, but they almost look too pretty to eat."

"No, they don't," her fiancé denied, reaching over her shoulder to pluck one from the tin. "But they taste as good as they look," he said around a mouthful of cookie.

Annie rolled her eyes, but she chose one and nibbled on a corner. "Oh, these are good," she said. "Maybe we should have opted for cookies rather than cake for the wedding."

"Cake is traditional," Danny noted as he reached for another cookie.

"It's about the only part of our wedding that is," Annie pointed out. "Well, that and the bride in a white dress."

"Speaking of which," her fiancé said, pulling his cell phone out of his pocket to check the time, "we're supposed to pick up your dress at the bridal shop in Kalispell this afternoon."

Annie cast a critical glance around the room. "Or *I* could go there while *you* string up the lights here."

"I could help Luke with the lights," Eva volunteered.

"It's a big job," Annie said worriedly.

"I think we can figure it out," Luke told her. "If not, I'm sure there are sketches in your wedding folder."

The bride-to-be's cheeks flushed, confirming the accuracy of his guess.

"Are you sure you don't mind?" Annie asked.

"They're sure," Danny said, taking her arm to steer her toward the door, eager to make his escape.

But he did pause long enough to grab a few more cookies from the tin on his way out.

"Wedding folder?" Eva asked when they'd gone.

Luke shook his head. "You don't want to know."

She helped herself to a cookie. "I thought there would

be more people here. I didn't realize the work was almost done."

"I guess that means more cookies for us."

She put the lid back on the tin. "*After* the lights are done."

"While I appreciate the offer of help, it's not really a difficult job so if you don't want to stay—"

"I do want to stay," she said.

A few hours later, the muscles in her shoulders and arms were protesting her decision as she reached up to catch the final coil of lights that Luke dropped from the top of the ladder. "It's been fun to watch this place transform from a livestock shelter to a wedding venue."

"All the twinkling lights in the world aren't going to make this place look like anything but a barn with twinkling lights," he said as he began his descent. "And why anyone would want to get married in a barn is beyond me."

"Maybe the location has some special significance to them," she suggested. "Perhaps the first time he kissed her was in this barn. Or maybe the first time they made love was in the hay loft."

Luke held up his hands. "Enough speculation. I don't really want to know."

She laughed as she looped the lights over a nail that had been hammered into the wall for that purpose. But the laugh cut off as she sucked in a breath.

He was immediately at her side. "What happened?"

"Splinter," she said.

He took her hand and gently unfolded the fingers that had instinctively curled into a fist. "That's a big one. And it seems to be in pretty deep."

"Are you talking about my hand or trying to evoke memories of last night?"

"It's not a good idea to distract me with dirty talk when you're wounded," he chastised.

"It's just a little wood."

His gaze narrowed. "Definitely *not* what you were saying last night."

She laughed. "Can you get it out? Please."

"Again, not words I've heard you say before." But his expression grew serious as he turned his attention back to her hand. "You should have been wearing gloves."

"I'm not a delicate flower," she told him.

He stroked his thumb along the side of her palm, sending tingles shooting up her arm and down her spine. "Your hands are soft."

Because she pampered them before bed every night, using a special scrub and lotion to ensure they didn't bear evidence of the arduous work they did in the kitchen. "And strong."

He nodded, acknowledging the fact. "I've seen you lift fifty-pound bags of flour as effortlessly as an angel food cake," he agreed. "But you should still be careful."

"It's a splinter," she reminded him. "Not a bullet wound."

Though it wasn't lodged completely under her skin, his fingers were too big and clumsy to be able to grasp the end and pull it free.

"There used to be a first-aid kit in the tack room," Luke remembered. "I might find a pair of tweezers in there."

"Let's take a look."

He continued to hold her hand as he led her toward the back of the barn.

She hadn't been in the tack room before, but someone had obviously done a thorough job sweeping the space free of dust and cobwebs. Eva might have grown up in town, but she was enough of a country girl to recognize the faint scents of saddle soap, beeswax and leather—with just a hint of wood smoke, courtesy of the old stove in the corner—that lingered in the air.

Beneath a row of bridle hooks, empty saddle racks hung on the wall. On another wall, there were benches and shelves. A row of wooden boxes was lined up on the lowest shelf, and Luke instinctively reached for the nearest one and pulled it down.

"Here we go," he said, lifting out a smaller white box with a familiar red cross on the cover.

"That doesn't look as if it's been in here for at least a dozen years," Eva noted with relief.

"Whoever cleaned up in here must have replaced the old one," Luke said.

"Probably Annie," she surmised. "Moms appreciate the importance of having antibacterial cream and Band-Aids on hand."

"Hopefully tweezers, too," he said, unsnapping the lid. He rifled through the contents. "Even better—individually wrapped sterile splinter removers."

He opened the package and lifted out the instrument, then reached for her hand again. She was aware of his palm—wide and calloused—beneath her hand, and she found herself remembering how those strong, hard hands felt sliding over her naked skin, skimming over her curves, caressing her—

"Did I hurt you?"

She blinked. "What?"

"You shivered," he said. "And I thought maybe I hurt you."

"No," she said, her cheeks flushing beneath his scrutiny. "I guess I just…um…got a chill."

"Well, it's out."

"Out?" she echoed, uncomprehending.

His lips twitched at the corners. "The splinter."

She looked down at her hand, still cradled gently in his, and saw that the sliver of wood had, indeed, been removed from her palm, leaving only a small red mark where it had been. She started to draw her hand away, but he held it still.

"You still need some antibiotic cream and a Band-Aid."

"It was just a splinter."

"It was a big splinter and it was wedged deep."

And yet, she hadn't even felt him pull it out of her skin, because her mind had been too busy spinning romantic fantasies.

Still holding her hand, he lowered his head and pressed his lips to her palm. Her breath hitched.

"A kiss to make it better," he said.

"Should I give you a list of all the other places that hurt?"

He smiled and released her hand to unwrap a Band-Aid and dab some cream on the pad, then carefully place it over her wound. "The first time I ever kissed a girl was in this room," he told her as he worked.

"Was it?"

"Charmaine Wilson. I was twelve, she was fourteen."

"An older woman," she mused aloud.

He nodded. "She wore her long, dark hair in a single braid down her back, skin-tight jeans and she had the most amazing br—" he cleared his throat "—brown eyes."

Eva chuckled. "And how long did your infatuation with Charmaine Wilson last?"

"Almost a whole week."

"You did tell me that long-term relationships aren't your thing," she acknowledged.

"So why are you still hanging around with me?"

"I happen to enjoy your company." She dropped her voice to a conspiratorial whisper. "And the off-the-charts sex."

"I think we're done here for today," he decided as he drew her into his embrace. "It's Thursday, isn't it?"

"All day," she confirmed.

"Does that mean your parents are bowling tonight?"

"It does," she said, impressed that he'd remembered.

"So what would you say if I suggested that we grab a bite before going back to my sister's place?"

"I'd say 'yes, please.'"

Over the past twelve years, Luke had almost forgotten what it meant to be part of a family. In only a few weeks, being around Bella and Hudson, Danny and Annie and Janie, and Jamie and Fallon and HJK—as his youngest brother fondly and collectively referred to his triplets—had reminded him and shown him how much better life was with people he cared about and who cared about him. Which made him think that maybe he should forget his promise to stay in Rust Creek Falls until after Danny's wedding, until after the New Year, and head back to Wyoming now, before he started to feel as if he belonged here.

That would be the smart thing to do, but it wasn't what he wanted to do.

In fact, the prospect of going back to Wyoming was surprisingly unappealing. He didn't want to walk away from the siblings he'd just started to reconnect with, and he didn't want to leave the woman who had already taken hold of his heart.

Chapter Thirteen

Eva couldn't remember a time in her life when she'd been happier than she was with Luke. Her euphoric mood was dimmed only by the fact that Luke hadn't said anything to her about his plans for the New Year. Or rather that he hadn't said anything that suggested he'd change his plans.

Because the truth was that he'd clearly—and repeatedly—told her of his intention to return to Cheyenne after the holidays, but Eva kept waiting for him to realize that he wanted a future with her and decide to stay in Rust Creek Falls so that they could build a life together. So far, he'd remained silent on the topic, so she'd pushed the questions and concerns aside and focused on preparing for the holidays—and spending every possible minute with the man she loved.

"Your dad and I are going to watch *White Christmas* tonight," Marion told Eva after dinner on Friday. "Do you and Luke want to join us?"

She appreciated that her mom had included Luke in the invitation, but she shook her head. "We're going to the Ace in the Hole. Rosey's hosting another viewing party to show the final episode of *The Great Roundup*. Practically the whole town is going to be there."

"That will be quite the crowd," Marion said. "Why don't you watch it here?"

"Aside from the fact that you want to watch *White Christmas*, Dad can't watch anything without the clicker in his hand, changing channels every few minutes to ensure he isn't missing something better on another station."

Her mother sighed, unable to deny the fact. "We're supposed to get another storm tonight. Please keep an eye on the weather and come home early if it gets bad."

"I'll keep an eye on the weather," she promised.

But the concerned expression remained on her mother's face as she continued to dry and put the dishes away.

"What are you really worried about, Mom?"

Marion folded the towel and hung it over the handle of the oven door. "That you'll marry Luke and move to Wyoming," she finally said.

Eva was stunned. "Why would you ever think something like that?"

"Because I know you're in love with him, and I'm beginning to suspect, considering the amount of time he's been spending with you, that he has some pretty deep feelings, too."

She hoped her mother was right about Luke's feelings, but right now she was more concerned about Marion's. "Where's this coming from, Mom?"

"I guess I was just thinking about how much has changed over the past few years—and how much more is going to change."

"What do you mean? Is Dad—"

"Your father's fine," Marion hastened to assure her.

"He's really, truly fine. I'm sorry—you know I always get emotional around the holidays."

Eva smiled. "I know. You don't only cry during holiday movies, you cry over the commercials."

"Some of them," her mother acknowledged. "But as I was digging through the holiday movies, looking for *White Christmas*, I was thinking about all the times we watched it together as a family. Then Calla got married and moved away, and Delphine got married and moved away, and…well, you're the only one I have left."

"I'm not going anywhere," Eva assured her.

But Marion shook her head. "I don't want you to make those kinds of promises. Don't get me wrong—I would miss you terribly if you went away, but you have to live your own life. Follow your heart."

"I will, but I'll always be here if you need me."

"I know." Her mother hugged her tight. "But right now, you need to get ready for your date."

"I still can't believe that Brenna and Travis are actually married," Eva remarked to Luke as they left the Ace later that night.

"That certainly seemed to be a big surprise ending to the season," he agreed.

She knew he hadn't really followed the series, insisting that the only reality TV he was interested in was live-action football. She also knew that, as a result of being in Rust Creek Falls over the past few weeks, he'd been caught up in the fervor.

"I'll bet it was a surprise to both their families, too. Although Travis is several years older than Brenna, they've known each other forever, and I don't think anyone ever suspected there were sparks between them."

"Sometimes there needs to be friction to generate sparks," Luke commented, opening the passenger door of his truck for her.

"I guess that's true," she acknowledged, still stunned by the revelation of the on-set wedding. But maybe she shouldn't have been surprised to learn that the gorgeous hairdresser and sexy cowboy had found love on the reality show. Over the past few months a lot of romances had blossomed in Rust Creek Falls.

Eva loved a happy ending as much as anyone, and while she was sincerely pleased for the newlyweds, she couldn't help but feel a little envious, too. She was grateful that she'd met Luke, and getting to know him had inevitably led to falling in love with him, but she was still waiting for some hint or indication that he felt the same way. Because as exciting as it was to be in love, she wanted to be loved, too.

Luke turned onto Cedar Street, then reached across the center console to take her hand. "Is everything okay?"

"Of course," she replied automatically.

"Are you sure? Because you've been quiet since we left the Ace."

"I'm just tired," she said.

And she was—physically and emotionally. The early mornings at Daisy's took a toll on her body, but it was her heart and spirit that were really feeling beaten down. Tired of being left out. Tired of helping other people plan their weddings—which reminded her, "And I still have to finish making the flowers for Danny and Annie's wedding cake."

"Speaking of their wedding," Luke said. "Annie's been stressing about making sure there are enough seats at the wedding and she wants to know if I'm going to have a 'plus one.'"

"Are you asking me to be your 'plus one'?"

"I know it's Christmas Eve and your sisters will be here with their families so you're probably busy…"

"Just ask the question, Luke," she interjected.

He smiled at the impatience in her tone, "Will you go to Danny and Annie's Christmas Eve wedding with me? I can't recommend the venue, but the cake should be good."

"I would love to," she said.

"This must be a director's cut," Eva commented when she walked into the house and found her parents snuggled together on the sofa watching the end of *White Christmas*.

"One of the benefits of watching a movie on Blu-ray is being able to pause it to make popcorn or take bathroom breaks," her dad commented, hitting the pause button again.

"Or to watch the final episode of *The Great Roundup* and the postshow reunion," Marion added.

Eva smiled. "I wondered if you would switch over."

"I wanted to find out if Brenna and Travis were still together," her mom admitted. "And your dad wanted to know who took the prize money."

"And now you know that Brenna was the big winner," Eva noted. "She got the money and her man."

"I'll bet there was a lot of buzz at the Ace when Travis and Brenna admitted they were married for real."

"There was, but that wasn't the only buzz," Eva said, then proceeded to tell them that Phil Dalton had bought a huge parcel of land on the outskirts of town.

"I knew he'd been looking for some property around here," Ray admitted.

"After losing his home and his wife in January, it's understandable that he'd want a fresh start," Marion noted.

"His sons, too," she said. "Apparently they're going to live on and work the land with him."

"That's wonderful news," her mother said. "During times of tragedy, it's more important than ever for families to stick together."

Eva agreed, and she knew that Luke was still feeling the effects of losing touch with his siblings after the deaths of their parents.

"There are rumors going around that some of Neal Dalton's kids are planning to move to Rust Creek Falls, too," she said.

"Phil could use the extra hands," Ray commented.

"And the support of more family close by," Marion added.

And because spending time with Luke had helped Eva recognize and appreciate the value of her family, she settled onto the sofa and watched the end of *White Christmas* with her parents.

All of the guests agreed that the newly refurbished barn at Sunshine Farm was a beautiful setting for a Christmas Eve wedding. Only those who had been involved with the intense rehab efforts over the past few weeks could truly appreciate the transformation that had been effected. Eva had pitched in a little herself, but even she was awed by the end result.

His two sisters that the groom had reconnected with stood up with the bride. Though Dana hadn't lived in Rust Creek Falls since she was a child, Annie knew how much his siblings meant to her soon-to-be husband, so she'd chosen to involve them in the ceremony as much as possible. Bella and Dana were dressed in long-sleeve, scoop-neck gowns of dark green velvet. The flower girl—Danny and Annie's daughter, Janie—was wearing a matching style in red. All three of the attendants carried bouquets of red roses with festive accents of evergreen, pinecones and berries.

The bride's dress was silk taffeta with a lace overlay. Annie had confided to Eva—who wanted to match the icing on the cake to the color of the bride's dress—that she had reservations about wearing white, and although her dress was technically ivory, she worried that tongues would wag. But when she took her first steps down the makeshift aisle, Eva didn't imagine anyone was thinking anything except that she was a truly beautiful bride.

The ceremony was an interesting mix of traditional and nontraditional elements. Instead of walking down the aisle on the arm of her father, the bride was given away by her ex-husband. Unorthodox, perhaps, but considering that Annie and Hank were both committed to continuing to co-parent the daughter they'd raised together from birth, it was a gesture that spoke to the bond of their family.

Dana had arrived in Rust Creek Falls the night before, taking up Bella's offer of a spare bedroom, and Luke had stayed up late with her, as if a few extra hours might somehow allow him to catch up on everything he'd missed over the past twelve years. At first it had been difficult to reconcile the little girl he remembered with the young woman who walked into Bella's living room. Then Dana smiled at him, and it was the smile he remembered. The sparkle in her eyes was the sparkle he remembered. And it felt so good to see her again, even if it hurt to think about all the years he'd lost, all the moments they'd never shared.

Now, as he stood between the groom and his youngest brother and watched the bride make her way down the aisle, he felt an array of emotions. Happiness for his brother, who was finally marrying the woman he'd always loved. Gratitude that Hudson's PI had found him and convinced him to make the long journey to Rust Creek Falls. And pride that the prettiest woman at the wedding—aside from the bride, of course—was his date.

The only disappointment was that the entire family wasn't there to witness the nuptials. He had long ago accepted that his parents were gone forever, but he keenly felt the absence of Bailey and Liza, and he was sure it was the same for each of his brothers and sisters in attendance. But no one was letting their absence put a damper on the occasion, and the smile on Danny's face as he watched his bride make her way toward him could have lit the whole barn without the hundreds of twinkling lights.

When the minister asked the assembled guests if there was any reason the bride and groom should not be joined together, a deep voice called out from the back. "Well, it just doesn't seem right for Danny to get married without all of his brothers as witnesses to the big event."

The bride sent a panicked glance toward her groom, obviously shocked that anyone would speak up in response to the question. Almost as quickly, the meaning of the words became clear, and her shocked surprise turned to pleasure.

It took Danny another half a second to put the pieces together after he turned from his bride to face the back of the barn. "Bailey?"

The latecomer took a few steps closer to the happy couple. "I think my invitation must have gotten lost in the mail."

"It must have," Danny agreed. Then he gave his bride's hands a light squeeze before releasing them and turning to embrace his brother. "Glad you could make it."

"Me, too."

Jamie was next in line to hug his long-lost brother, apparently not harboring any lingering animosity toward this particular sibling. "When did you get into town?"

"Just about half an hour ago," Bailey told him, turning to embrace Bella.

"Where are you staying?" she asked, wiping tears from her eyes. "Because we've got plenty of room at our place."

"I can attest to that," Dana said, edging forward to hug him next.

"But we can probably work out those details *after* the ceremony," Luke suggested. "Because there's a pretty girl in a white dress waiting patiently for the groom to put a ring on her finger."

"Not quite so patiently," Annie admitted.

"I've waited a lot of years to see you again," Danny said to Bailey. "But I've waited even longer to make Annie my wife, so it would be great if we could move forward with the ceremony now."

The guests laughed as the groom resumed his place beside the bride.

"Does anyone have anything else to say?" the minister asked the assembled guests.

This time there was no response, and the officiant resumed his duties.

And despite the whispers and speculation sparked by

Bailey's unexpected arrival, the focus of attention returned to the happy couple.

Eva watched through eyes blurred with tears as the bride and groom exchanged vows, promising to love, honor and cherish one another "till death do us part." The words were no different than those spoken by countless couples at countless weddings, but having at least a little bit of knowledge of what Annie and Danny had been through, the events that had torn them apart and, finally, brought them together again, made the promises that much more poignant.

It was an emotional day for all of the Stockton siblings—or at least all of those who were present. Having Bailey show up in time to witness the exchange of vows was undoubtedly sweeter than the icing on the wedding cake, but Eva suspected they were all aware of the absence of Liza, the little sister who had yet to be found.

After the ceremony, there was much eating and drinking and toasting the happy couple. Then the bride and groom cut the cake before taking to the makeshift dance floor for their first dance. As Eva listened to Dierks Bentley claim "there ain't nothing that love can't fix," she crossed her fingers that it was true. For Annie and Danny, of course, but also for her and Luke.

She knew that love couldn't magically obliterate the geographical distance between Cheyenne and Rust Creek Falls, but she had to hope and believe that Luke would acknowledge his feelings for her and reconsider his decision to leave after the New Year.

"What thoughts have you looking as if you're a hundred miles away?" Luke wondered.

She felt her cheeks flush, embarrassed to have been

caught daydreaming and unwilling to admit to Luke that he was the subject of those daydreams. "I was just thinking about Danny and Annie," she said. "They really are living proof that love can last."

His gaze shifted to the couple on the dance floor. "He never wanted to leave Rust Creek Falls—or Annie."

She reached up and touched a hand to his face, drawing his attention back to her. "That's not on you, Luke."

"Isn't it?" he asked, his tone heavy with regret.

"He made his own decision," she insisted.

"He was an eighteen-year-old kid who'd just lost his parents," Luke reminded her. "So he followed the lead of his oldest brother and left the only woman he'd ever loved."

"He was only eighteen—how could you possibly know that she was the only woman he'd ever love?" she challenged.

"Maybe I couldn't," he allowed.

"And you certainly couldn't have known that Annie was pregnant," she said, anticipating his next argument. "Not even Annie knew she was pregnant when you and Bailey and Danny left Rust Creek Falls."

"That's true," he acknowledged.

"So why don't you forget about the past and focus on the present—like they're doing," she suggested.

"I never used to believe in the mystical power of love," he told her. "Then I came back to Rust Creek Falls and I saw Bella with Hudson, Jamie with Fallon, and Danny with Annie." As he spoke, his gaze searched the room, finding each of his siblings and their partners in turn, before returning to meet Eva's eyes again. "And I met you."

With those words, she felt as if her heart actually

swelled inside her chest. "My life changed when you came back to Rust Creek Falls, too," she admitted.

"In a good way, I hope."

"In all the very best ways," she assured him.

Luke smiled. "I'm glad, because I've been thinking that—"

Chapter Fourteen

Before Luke could finish his thought, Bailey brought a hand down on his brother's shoulder, effectively cutting off the words Eva desperately wanted to hear.

"I had no idea, when I decided to make the trip to Rust Creek Falls, that I'd show up just in time for Danny's wedding," Bailey said.

She managed to keep the smile on her face, though what she really wanted to do was lift both her hands to Bailey's chest and shove him aside so that she and Luke could finish their private conversation.

"The best wedding present you could have given him," Luke told his brother.

Bailey glanced at Eva. "Was I interrupting something?"

Yes, she wanted to shout at him.

But she knew that Luke was thrilled to see his brother again, so she pushed aside her own disappointment and said, "Nothing that can't wait."

She hoped.

"In fact, I was just going to excuse myself to get a glass of punch."

"Let me get it for you," Luke suggested.

But she shook her head. "You stay and chat with your brother. I'm sure you have lots to catch up on."

"We do," Bailey responded before Luke could. "Thanks for understanding."

She nodded and slipped away.

Luke watched Eva go, admiring the mouthwatering display of shapely leg as she moved through the crowd toward the makeshift bar. In the few weeks that he'd known her, he'd rarely seen her in anything other than the long, flowing skirts she obviously favored. Today she was wearing a blue dress that deepened the color of her eyes and hugged her every curve, with shiny black platform heels that added several inches to her height.

He watched as she helped herself to a glass of punch, then turned to smile at something Hank said to her. He didn't blame the man for the way his gaze followed Eva as she turned away, but he didn't like it, either.

"Looks like I got here just in time," Bailey noted.

Luke forced his attention back to his brother. "It meant a lot to Danny that you were able to be here for his wedding."

"He seems happy enough—for now," Bailey said.

"What's that supposed to mean?"

"Just that the rose-colored glasses tend to get wiped clean after the honeymoon."

"I did notice that your wife doesn't seem to have made the trip with you," Luke commented.

"*Ex*-wife," Bailey said grimly.

He winced. "I'm sorry."

His brother shrugged. "It turned out that marriage wasn't quite what I expected."

"What did you expect?"

Bailey lifted his beer to his lips, took a long sip. "Till death do us part."

"What changed?"

"I couldn't be the kind of husband Emily wanted me to be—that I wanted to be." He swallowed another mouthful of beer. "Hell, Luke, you know as well as I do that the scars of the past never go away. Even when, on the surface, it looks like they've healed, the wounds still ache deep inside."

Luke frowned, not wanting to believe what his brother said, though the words closely echoed his own thoughts. "Danny seems to be doing okay," he noted.

"Maybe because he loved Annie before everything went to hell in a handbasket," Bailey suggested.

"What even is a handbasket?" Luke wondered aloud.

His brother chuckled, though the sound was without humor. "I have no clue."

"You really don't think they'll make it?"

Bailey looked out at the dance floor where the newly-weds swayed together to the music, oblivious to everyone and everything around them. "I hope they do, but I don't think the odds are in their favor."

"Don't tell that to the groom."

"I wouldn't," his brother promised. "But I felt it was important to tell you."

"Why?"

"Because I saw the way you were looking at the pretty blonde in the blue dress."

Luke scowled. "This is about Eva?"

"This is about wanting to prevent you from making the same mistakes that I made," Bailey told him.

"You really believe marrying Emily was a mistake?"

"I do," his brother said, and immediately grimaced. "And those are the words I never should have said the first time."

"When you left for New Mexico, you seemed so certain that it was what you wanted," Luke noted, troubled by the obvious disillusionment and bitterness in his brother's tone.

"If I've learned nothing else over the years, I've learned that I'm not certain about anything. Losing Mom and Dad, then being turned out by the grandparents, well, that kind of rejection can't help but screw up your mind and heart."

"You're right," Luke acknowledged. "But I believe that sometimes, if a man is very lucky, he might meet a woman who can help unscrew his mind and heart."

"And you think your blonde is that woman?" Bailey asked skeptically.

"Eva," he said again. "And yeah, I think she might be."

"How long have you known her?"

"A few weeks."

His brother's brows lifted. "You've known her a few weeks and you think she's the woman to fix everything that's broken inside you?"

"She's already made a start," he said.

"Or maybe you're looking for an excuse to stay in Rust Creek Falls and you're letting her be it."

Luke scowled. "That's not true. I have no intention of staying." Except that wasn't true, either. Not anymore.

"I know what it's like to feel alone, to miss family," Bailey told him. "Why do you think I finally went back to Wyoming?"

"You went back to Wyoming?"

His brother nodded. "I arrived early last week, but it

took me several days to track you down at Leaning Pines. It was your foreman who told me that you were in Rust Creek Falls for your brother's wedding. Of course, he didn't specify which brother, but my curiosity was piqued enough to follow your trail. I didn't expect to walk into a family reunion."

"An incomplete family reunion," Luke clarified.

"Yeah," Bailey acknowledged. "I guess no one knows where Liza is?"

"Bella's husband has been looking, but so far, no luck."

"That was a kicker, too," Bailey said. "Finding out that she was married—and to some rich guy from Oklahoma to boot."

"Hudson's a good guy," Luke told him.

"He seems to dote on our sister, that's for sure," Bailey agreed. "Of course, they haven't been married very long, either, have they? They're still in the honeymoon phase." He drained the last of his beer and held up the empty glass. "I'm going for a refill. Do you want anything?"

Luke shook his head. "No, thanks, I'm good."

But he wasn't.

His brother's words had put a damper on not just the evening but his whole outlook for the future, too.

He'd meant what he'd said to Eva. He'd never believed in the power of love, until he saw how it had changed his siblings. And while he couldn't deny that he had deep feelings for Eva, now he had to wonder if those feelings were deep enough.

Was he capable of loving her the way she deserved to be loved? Or was Bailey right? Had the death of his parents and subsequent rejection by his grandparents left him emotionally stunted?

* * *

Having finished her punch, Eva set the empty glass aside and walked over to where Luke was standing.

"Hey, cowboy." She nudged him playfully with her shoulder. "You promised me a dance."

His lips curved, but she noticed that the smile didn't reach his eyes.

"It's been a long time since I've danced," he warned. "And I can't promise I won't tread on those pretty shoes you're wearing."

"I'll take my chances," she assured him.

"In that case—" he offered his hand "—never let it be said that I'm not a man of my word."

He led her to the dance floor and turned her in his arms.

"Speaking of words," she said as they moved in rhythm with the music. "You started to say something earlier, before your brother interrupted us."

"Did I?" he hedged.

"Mmm-hmm," she confirmed. "Something about how your life has changed since you came home to Rust Creek Falls."

"It's been great to reconnect with my family," he said. "But Rust Creek Falls isn't my home. Not anymore."

"That's all you meant?" she asked, unable to hide the disappointment evident in her tone.

"That's why I came back," he reminded her.

"I know, but I thought—I hoped," she admitted, "you might find some other reasons to stay."

He looked away. "You know I can't."

But she didn't know any such thing. What she suspected was that Bailey had said something to cause

Luke's sudden withdrawal, because even while she was dancing with him, she could feel him pulling away.

"Do you really want to spend the rest of your life working as a ranch hand for somebody else?" she asked in a desperate attempt to open a dialogue with him.

"What other choice do I have?"

She lifted her hand from his shoulder and gestured to their surroundings. "You could put your time and energy into this place. Make Sunshine Farm a working ranch again."

She saw it then—a flicker of yearning in his eyes, there for only a second before it was shuttered away.

He shook his head. "That would be a lot more responsibility than I want to take on."

"Really?" she challenged.

"All I want is a paycheck, a six-pack and a willing woman at the end of the week."

The music continued to play but her feet stopped moving. "Is that all I was to you, Luke? A willing woman?"

He had the grace to look chagrined. "We had some good times together, Eva, but we both knew our relationship wasn't going to last."

In the past, whenever she'd been told the same or similar words, she'd quietly turned away rather than admit her heart was breaking. This time she lifted her chin and looked him straight in the eye.

"I disagree," she said. "I think that we had something pretty special together, but for some reason, you'd rather throw it away than give it a chance."

Then she turned away.

But she'd only taken a few steps when she pivoted on her heel to face him again. "As much as I'd like to storm out of here and leave you to contemplate my parting words, I need a ride home."

Under other circumstances, Eva's furious indignation might have made him smile, but Luke found it was impossible to smile while his heart was quietly bleeding. So he only reached into his pocket for his keys and said, "I'll take you."

"Thank you."

The cool primness of her tone didn't quite mask the hurt he'd caused, and he had to bite down on his tongue to prevent himself from offering excuses and explanations that wouldn't change anything in the end.

The ground outside was icy, and he automatically took her arm to help her navigate the treacherous terrain. She might have preferred to avoid his touch, but she was also practical enough to endure his assistance rather than end up on her butt.

She was quiet for the first several minutes of the drive back to her parents' house, and he wondered if she'd decided to never speak to him again. But then she broke the silence to ask, "What did he say to you?"

"Who?"

"Bailey," she said, somehow zeroing in on the topic that preoccupied his own mind.

He didn't deny that they'd talked—or that their conversation had changed the course of the evening for him. "He reminded me of some difficult truths I'd forgotten."

"What kind of truths?" she pressed.

He kept his gaze fixed on the road, not daring to look at her as he responded. "That the Stocktons are damaged."

"I don't believe it," she told him.

He pulled up in front of her parents' house, unable to squeeze into the driveway behind the two minivans that hadn't been there earlier—proof that her sisters and their families had arrived for the holiday.

He shifted into Park and turned off the ignition before he turned to face her. "I can't give you what you want, Eva. I don't have it within me."

"You can and you do," she insisted. "You're just afraid to admit your feelings."

"Feelings don't change anything. I told you in the beginning that I didn't want to get involved and I meant it."

"I love you, Luke."

He flinched as if she'd struck him. "Don't say that."

"Whether I speak the words or not, you know the feelings are true," she said. "You know how I feel about you."

He did. He'd told himself that her feelings were her own, that he wasn't responsible for her heart, but none of that helped him feel any better now.

"It's also true that I sometimes give my heart too easily," she told him. "I tried to hold back this time. I didn't want to fall in love with you, but I couldn't help myself. And I think you have some strong feelings for me, too."

She paused, as if giving him a chance to confirm or deny it. He didn't dare confirm it, and he couldn't honestly deny it, so he said nothing.

"But I'm not going to beg for scraps of affection," she continued when he remained silent. "Either you want to be with me or you don't. That's your choice to make and I'll accept whatever it is, but I'm going to suggest that you take some time to think about what you really want."

"Time isn't going to change anything," he said.

"Maybe not," she acknowledged, reaching for the handle of the door. "But I'm giving you a week anyway."

He hurried around to help her out of the vehicle. "Why a week?" he asked, curious about the arbitrary deadline she'd established even if it wouldn't change anything.

"Because there's a big party at Maverick Manor on New Year's Eve. If you decide that you feel the same way I do, you can meet me there. If you don't show up, I'll know that you don't, and I won't contact you again."

Then she slid her key into the lock of the front door.

"Eva."

She hesitated, for just a fraction of a second, before turning back.

But he didn't know what else to say. He only knew that he didn't want to leave her like this, with so much unspoken between them. Or maybe the problem was that too much had been spoken.

"Merry Christmas, Luke."

He dipped his head to touch his lips to her forehead. "Merry Christmas, Eva."

As Eva closed the door at her back, the click of the latch sounded loud in the quiet of the night. And final, like an exclamation mark at the end of a sentence—or the end of a relationship.

She felt the sting of tears behind her eyes, and stubbornly held them in check. She'd told Luke that she wasn't going to shed any tears over him and she meant it. The click of the latch notwithstanding, nothing was truly final yet. She'd given him a week to come to his senses and she had to trust that he would do so. If not, she would have plenty of time for tears in the New Year.

The house was dark and quiet, confirming that everyone had turned in early in anticipation of being awakened by the kids at the crack of dawn. But Eva knew that she was too unsettled to sleep right now, so she decided to make herself a cup of tea before heading up to bed.

Delphine wandered into the kitchen as Eva was pouring boiling water into a mug. Without needing to ask, she reached into the cupboard for a second mug, popped another tea bag into it and added water.

"Thanks," Del said, stifling a yawn as she accepted the mug her sister passed to her.

"I thought everyone was asleep already."

"I tried to wait up for you, but I snuggled with Freddy to help him settle down and fell asleep beside him."

"He's excited about Christmas," Eva guessed.

"They all are," her sister confirmed. "How was the wedding?"

She forced herself to push aside the painful memories of everything that had happened after and focus on the simple beauty of the ceremony. And remembering, she sighed wistfully. "It was beautiful."

"So why do you look so unhappy?"

"Because I did it again," she admitted.

"What did you do?"

"I fell in love with a man who doesn't love me back."

"The long-lost cowboy who recently returned to Rust Creek Falls?" Del guessed.

"Luke Stockton," Eva confirmed.

"The guy you went to the wedding with tonight?"

She nodded.

"How do you know he doesn't love you back?"

"Because he keeps reminding me of his plans to go back to Wyoming in the New Year."

"And you keep refusing to listen."

She sighed. "I was sure that when he had a chance

to see how good we were together, he would change his mind."

Del sighed. "Honey, you should know by now that it's a mistake to go into a relationship thinking you can change a man."

"I don't want to change *him*," she denied. "I just want him to change his geographical location."

"Asking a man to uproot himself from his job and his home and move eight hundred miles away is a big deal," her sister pointed out.

"I didn't ask him to move," she denied.

"But you want him to."

"I want it to be what he wants." She felt the sting of tears in her eyes. "*I* want to be what he wants."

Del reached across the table to squeeze her hand. "If you're not, then he's an idiot."

Eva managed a smile, but as she sipped her tea, she wondered why she always seemed to fall for the idiots.

Chapter Fifteen

In the usual chaos of Christmas morning, there was no time for self-indulgence or self-pity. After the mountain of presents had been opened and the debris cleared away, there were games to play and cars to race and LEGO cities to build. Through the course of the day, Eva barely had time to catch her breath much less feel sorry for herself. But through it all, she did realize something important.

She realized that, even if Luke didn't show up at Maverick Manor on New Year's Eve, even if she didn't yet have a partner to share her life, she was lucky to be surrounded by the love and support of her family.

And that, she knew, was a priceless gift—and one that Luke hadn't experienced in the past twelve years.

But this year would be different for him, because this year, he was with his family. She hoped he was having a good time with his siblings and their spouses and children. And she hoped that when he handed out the gifts they'd shopped for and wrapped together, he would think of her—for just a moment.

* * *

Luke was glad he'd decided to stay, not just for Danny and Annie's wedding but to celebrate Christmas with his siblings.

Because for the first time in a lot of years, it *was* a celebration.

Dana had to leave early in the morning to head back to Oregon because she had holiday traditions with her adoptive parents that she wanted to uphold, but she stayed long enough to have breakfast with Bella, Hudson, Luke and Bailey—who had spent the night in another one of the guest bedrooms. Jamie and Fallon showed up with Henry, Jared and Katie just as Dana was leaving, contributing to an even longer and more emotional goodbye scene. Then the rest of the family adjourned to the family room to open the presents that were under the tree.

He was grateful to Eva for her assistance with his shopping—and wrapping. Thinking back to that day, he couldn't help but remember the sparkle in her eyes, the warmth of her smile...and the expression of bliss on her face when their bodies joined together on the floor beneath this very Christmas tree.

Excusing himself from the gathering, he retreated to the kitchen to pour another cup of coffee. And steal another piece of the coffee cake that Bella had put out for breakfast and that he knew she'd picked up from Daisy's.

He was licking the crumbs off his fingers when his sister came in to refill her mug.

"Busted," she told him, softening the admonition with a smile.

He just shrugged. "What can I say? It's addictive."

"The cake or the baker?" she teased.

Instead of answering, he lifted his mug to his lips and sipped.

"You know, no one's going to mind if you want to slip away for a few hours," Bella told him.

"Why would I want to do that?"

She shook her head. "If I have to tell you, then you're not nearly as smart as I always thought you were."

"If you'd been in the truck when I took Eva home last night, you'd know that I'm an idiot."

"Were you a forgivable or unforgivable idiot?"

If you decide that you feel the same way I do, you can meet me there. If you don't show up, I'll know that you don't, and I won't contact you again.

He pushed the echo of Eva's words out of his mind. "It doesn't matter," he said. "Because I'm going back to Wyoming next week."

The teasing light in his sister's eyes immediately dimmed. "You're really leaving?"

"Isn't that what I've been saying all along?"

"It is," she admitted. "But I really thought you'd change your mind and decide to stay."

"I can't."

"You can," she insisted. "But you're stubborn and thick-headed and you're still punishing yourself for what happened to Mom and Dad. And, as a result, you're punishing the rest of us, too."

"You don't need me here, Bella."

She lifted her chin. "You're right. I don't need you in my life. I survived without you for almost twelve years and, if you leave, I'll continue to do so. But it's not what I want. I want you in my life."

"I'm not dropping off the face of the earth—I'm only going to Wyoming," he told her.

"What's so great about Wyoming?" Bella grumbled.

"It's where I live and work," he reminded her.

"You live in an apartment over a hardware store and you work on someone else's ranch."

He nodded his head in acknowledgment of those facts.

"If you stayed, you could live and work at Sunshine Farm."

"Bella—"

"I'm just putting it out there," she said. "Hudson told me not to pressure you, that you have to make your own choices about what's right for you. But I want to ensure you know what all your options are before you make that decision."

He slid an arm around her shoulders and drew her close. "The one thing I do know is that I'm going to miss my pain-in-the-butt sister when I'm gone."

She sniffled a little as she buried her face in his shirt. "I'll miss you, too, you big idiot."

While Eva and the other women were busy in the kitchen, preparing the big meal, the kids went out to play in the snow and the men were sent to supervise. A few minutes later, her brother-in-law Harrison came to the door asking for an extra hat and a scarf for the snowman they were building.

While Grandma went to the closet to see what she could find, Calla peeled potatoes, Del stirred her cranberry sauce and Eva worked on the relish trays for the table.

Marion came back with a hat and scarf and a square box wrapped in snowman paper with a big red bow on the top.

"I can't believe I forgot about this," she said, setting the box on the table beside Eva.

"What is it?" Calla asked.

"A present for Eva."

"For me?" she said, surprised.

Her mom nodded. "Luke dropped it off a few days ago and asked me to hide it until Christmas."

"It's from Luke?"

Marion nodded again.

"Well, go on," Del urged. "Open it."

She did so, tearing the paper at the end, then sliding the box out of the wrap.

"It's a cake stand," Calla said, clearly unimpressed.

Eva shook her head. "It's not a cake stand—it's a tilting turntable. You put the cake on top of it, then adjust the angle to make decorating easier."

"So…a cake stand," Calla said again.

But it was so much more than that to Eva. It was an extravagance that she hadn't been able to justify for herself, even when she'd noticed it was on sale the day she was shopping with Luke. And maybe she'd paused for a moment in front of it, but she'd never actually mentioned that she wanted one—and he hadn't asked.

But he'd clearly been paying attention.

And then he'd gone back to get it for her. But…why? Why would he do something so unexpectedly kind and thoughtful and then dump her a few days later?

"Well, that's…handy," her mother decided.

Eva laughed at the bafflement in her mother's tone. Maybe it wasn't flashy or extravagant, but that cake decorating tool proved that Luke knew her better than most of the other men she'd dated—and even most of her family.

While Marion took the snowman accessories to the

door and Calla resumed her peeling, Del leaned close and whispered in Eva's ear, "I'm starting to think that maybe he's not such an idiot, after all."

He was an idiot to even be considering this.

Luke had told Eva that he was going back to Wyoming and that was exactly what he should do.

Instead, he was putting a noose around his neck—literally.

"You'd be much more handsome if you'd stop scowling."

He glanced at his sister's reflection behind his own in the mirror. "I hate wearing a tie."

"You certainly don't know how to tie one," Bella noted.

"This was a bad idea anyway," he said, tugging at the knot.

"No, it's a good idea," she said. "It's just the execution that needs some work."

"I'm not just talking about the tie."

"Neither am I." She brushed his hands aside and pulled the ends, adjusting the length before she began making the knot.

He watched, fascinated, as she quickly and expertly completed the task that he'd struggled with unsuccessfully. "Where did you learn how to do that?"

"Watching Hudson," she admitted.

"He wears one of these every day, doesn't he?"

"Mmm-hmm," she agreed.

"Why?" he wondered.

"I'm not sure, but he looks good in a tie. And without a tie. And without—"

"TMI, little sister," he interjected.

She laughed softly. "And when a man who doesn't usually wear a tie puts one on for a woman, it tells her that she matters."

"Does it?" he asked dubiously.

"Of course, if you had a diamond ring in the pocket of that jacket, it would say the same thing much more effectively."

"If I had a diamond ring in my pocket, don't you think I should show it to Eva before I showed it to you?"

"I'm not asking to *see* it, I'm just asking if you *have* it," Bella pressed.

"Thanks for your help with the tie."

"Anytime." She tugged on the accessory in question. "And I mean that, Luke. I'm happy to help you with anything, anytime. Of course, it would be easier to lend a helping hand if you were living in Rust Creek Falls."

"You never quit, do you?"

"Perseverance is one of my many charms."

"Is that what your husband tells you?"

She grinned. "All the time."

"He's a smart man."

"Smart enough to put a ring on my finger," Bella agreed.

He took his sister by the shoulders and turned her gently toward the door. "Go find that smart husband of yours so that you can go out and celebrate the New Year together."

As she did so, he scooped his keys off the dresser and headed out to his truck. But the closer he got to his destination, the more questions and doubts that assailed him.

Was he doing the right thing?

He eased up on the gas as he approached the entrance

to Maverick Manor, but instead of turning in to the drive, he kept going.

Because there was still a part of him that believed Eva would be better off if he returned to Cheyenne. Then she would be free to fall in love with a man who wasn't burdened with the kind of baggage that weighed him down. And there was no doubt in his mind that Eva deserved better than him.

But in the few weeks that he'd known her, she'd already helped to lighten the load he carried. Of course, talking to his siblings had helped, too. Their support and acceptance had given him hope that he could finally move forward with his life, but it was Eva who had given him hope that he didn't have to move forward alone.

With her sweetness and kindness and patience, she had shown him that he wasn't only worthy of being loved, but that he was capable of loving in return. Because he knew now that he did love her—and he didn't ever want to leave her.

Unfortunately he came to that realization about an hour after he'd driven past Maverick Manor, which meant that it would be another hour before he could get back. And it was almost eleven o'clock already.

He checked his mirrors to confirm that there were no other vehicles around, then made a U-turn in the middle of the road and stepped on the accelerator.

Eva had practically floated through the day, buoyed by foolish hope that she'd walk into Maverick Manor and find Luke waiting for her. But he wasn't there.

Of course, she hadn't given him a specific time and, in retrospect, she could acknowledge that "New Year's Eve" was a little vague. Just because he wasn't there promptly at eight o'clock didn't mean he wasn't going to show up.

But eight o'clock had become nine o'clock, which was when Travis and Brenna were scheduled to renew their vows in front of their families and friends. As Eva watched them promise to love, honor and cherish one another, she couldn't help but wonder if she would ever find a man to look at her the way Travis looked at Brenna. For a very short while, she'd let herself believe that Luke Stockton might be that man, but his absence from the festivities tonight forced her to accept that she'd been wrong.

When the groom was instructed to kiss his bride, he did so with lavish enthusiasm and Eva lifted a tissue to dab at the moisture on her lower lashes. More than a few of the female guests were wiping their eyes, and she trusted that anyone who saw her tears would assume they were a response to the emotional ceremony. Only she knew the truth—that at least a few of those tears were for herself, for the weary heart that had been rejected yet again.

As she looked around the room, hoping for a quiet corner to escape to for a minute, she couldn't help but take note of all the happy couples and families in attendance. Newlyweds Autry Jones and Marissa Fuller were there with her daughters Abby, Kiera and Kaylee, the girls all sporting festive berets from their recent trip to Paris; and Abby's BFF, Janie Lattimore, who was staying with her dad, Hank, while her mom, Annie, was off on her honeymoon with her other dad, Danny, in celebration of their Christmas Eve wedding. Lydia Grant was cozied up in the corner with Zach Dalton, and Eva had heard rumors that a springtime wedding was being planned for the recently engaged couple. Hadley Strickland was wearing a ring on the third finger of her left hand now, too, and was in attendance with her doting fiancé Eli Dalton. Because everyone in town was pairing up and falling in love.

Everyone except Eva.

Well, she'd done the falling in love part.

Unfortunately, Luke hadn't fallen in love, too.

And now it was after eleven o'clock and, as each minute passed, she became more and more certain that he wasn't going to show up. How could she have misread the situation so badly? Was she so desperate for love that she only saw what she wanted to see?

She didn't believe it. The way Luke had looked at her, kissed her, touched her, she'd been certain that he had deep feelings for her.

But tonight was New Year's Eve and he wasn't anywhere around, forcing Eva to acknowledge the possibility that she might never see him again.

She glanced at the slender gold watch on her wrist—a gift from her parents when she graduated high school—and felt her heart sink a little deeper. It was almost eleven thirty now. She looked around the room again. There were so many people packed into the ballroom that she wasn't sure she would be able to pick him out of the crowd if he was there. But she felt confident that she would know it in her heart—and right now, her heart was empty.

"Can I have this dance?"

The voice was familiar, albeit not the voice she longed to hear. But she forced a smile and turned to Bobby Ray Ellis. She didn't want to dance with anyone but Luke, but she also didn't want to look like a pathetic wallflower. It was New Year's Eve and this was a party, so she would dance with anyone who asked and pretend that her heart wasn't shattered into a million pieces.

It was almost midnight by the time Luke pulled into the very full parking lot of Maverick Manor. He scanned for an empty space, certain that everyone in Rust Creek Falls had turned out for the New Year's Eve party. Or maybe they were here to watch the reality TV newlyweds renew their vows. Either way, the prospect of such a crowd had a bead of sweat sliding down his back.

He preferred intimate gatherings to boisterous parties, and there weren't a lot of women that he would venture near a fancy shindig like this for. In fact, he couldn't imagine doing it for anyone but Eva. Because he loved her.

He wasn't sure that he was worthy of her heart, but he wasn't foolish enough to let a woman like her slip through his fingers. Yeah, he had scars, and they went pretty deep. But Eva had seen them all and she loved him anyway.

The doors of the hotel opened up, spilling out light and music and a familiar figure in a black dress. A very little black dress. His mouth went dry and his heart, already racing, started to pound even harder and faster.

But Eva didn't see him. Nor did she seem to be looking for him. Instead, she ducked behind a support column, as if she wanted to be alone, and dropped her chin to her chest.

He'd started eagerly toward the entrance as soon as he saw her, but now his steps faltered.

Was she...crying?

Of course she was, and even an idiot could figure out why. Because she'd asked him to meet her tonight, to prove that he cared about her, and she thought he was a no-show.

The absolute last thing he'd ever want to do was hurt her, but the streaks of moisture on her cheeks confirmed the painful truth. The tears were his fault.

But he could fix this—he *would* fix this. And he would spend the rest of his life making it up to her, if she would let him.

"Eva?"

Her head came up fast and her eyes, swimming with tears, met his for only a brief moment before they slid away again.

"What—" the word sounded a little hoarse, and she paused to clear her throat before continuing "—what are you doing here?"

"Isn't this where you told me to be?" He took another step closer. His gaze roamed over her hungrily, taking in every detail from the spiraling curls piled on her head to the strapless figure-hugging dress that ended several inches above her knees and the ice-pick heels on her feet. "You look…wow."

And a little cold, he realized, noting the goose bumps on her arms. He unbuttoned his jacket and draped it over her shoulders.

"Thanks," she said, then gave him a casual once-over and offered a small smile. "You clean up pretty good yourself, cowboy."

"I hate wearing a tie," he admitted.

"Why did you?"

"Because—" he reached for her hands and linked their fingers together "—according to my sister, when a man who doesn't usually wear a tie puts one on for a woman, it tells her that she matters."

"Words could probably accomplish the same thing."

"I'm not always good with words," he confided. "But I'm here—and wearing a tie—because you matter."

She dropped her gaze to their joined hands. "I thought you weren't going to show up," she admitted.

"I'm sorry I'm late," he said.

"You're here," she said, and offered a tremulous smile. "That's the important thing."

"Do you remember telling me that my story wasn't over? That I could write a happy ending if I wanted it?"

She nodded.

"I want that happy ending—with you." He dropped his hands so that he could draw her into his embrace. "I love you, Eva."

"I love you, too," she said.

Inside the crowd began the countdown to midnight.

"Ten..."

"I didn't intend to cut it this close," he told her.

"...nine..."

"We still have nine seconds."

"...eight..."

"Eight," she amended.

"I want to kiss you at midnight, so I'll have to talk fast."

"...seven..."

"Or we could skip the talking and move—"

"...six..."

"—right to the kissing."

"...five..."

He reached for the box in his pocket—only to remember that she was now wearing his jacket. He patted his hands down her sides, searching.

"Or the awkward, fumbling foreplay," she teased.

"...four..."

He found the box and dropped to a knee in front of her. "Will you marry me, Eva?"

Her eyes went wide and she lifted a hand to press it to her heart. "Ohmygod—I feel like I'm dreaming."

"...three..."

"You're not dreaming," he assured her. "You're also not answering my question."

"...two..."

"You really want to marry me?"

"...one..."

"More than anything else in the world."

"Then yes," she said quickly. "My answer is yes."

He slid the ring on her finger.

"Happy New Year!"

He smiled. "Happy New Year, Eva."

"Happy New Year, Luke."

Then, finally, he was kissing her.

And Eva forgot that she was standing outside at midnight on New Year's Eve in twenty-degree weather because being in Luke's arms warmed everything inside her.

While he continued to kiss her, she became aware of something that sounded like...clapping?

Then someone said, "Now that gives a whole new meaning to the expression 'ring in the New Year.'"

Luke reluctantly eased his mouth from hers, but he kept his arms around her, holding her close. "While your enthusiasm is appreciated," he said dryly, "you're interrupting a private moment here."

"I didn't mean to intrude," the stranger said. "But that really was perfect. In fact, I don't think my producer could have scripted it any better."

"Producer?" Eva echoed warily, noting the camera propped casually on his shoulder.

"Of *The Great Roundup*. That's why I was here—to film Travis and Brenna's renewal of vows," the man explained. "I was on my way out when I caught a glimpse of something from the corner of my eye and started the camera rolling. I got the whole proposal—and that really hot kiss."

Luke didn't look happy to hear his admission. "You recorded us—without our knowledge or consent?"

"The candid stuff is always the best," the cameraman said. "Do you guys think you'd be interested in taking part in the show next season?"

Eva had enjoyed watching Travis and Brenna compete for the big prize—and Luke hadn't grumbled too much about it—but she didn't think either of them wanted that kind of fame or fortune. She looked at him now, and they both shook their heads.

The man pressed a card into Luke's hand. "In case you change your mind."

Then, finally, he took his camera and walked away.

"You're not going to change your mind, are you?" Luke asked.

"No," she said. "I don't want to be famous. I just want to be with you."

"Good." He brushed a sweet kiss on her lips. "Because that's everything I want, too."

Epilogue

"Are you sure you want to do this?" Eva asked, seeking reassurance before she slid the scraper under the seam of the wallpaper.

"I'm sure this paper is hideous," Luke told her. "Which means that it has to go."

She looked at the printed ivy that seemed to crawl up the walls, and though it wasn't anything she ever would have chosen, she didn't think it was ugly so much as dated. Which made sense, considering that his parents had papered the kitchen walls some twenty years earlier.

Even when Luke had decided that he wanted to stay in Rust Creek Falls with Eva, he'd balked at the idea of moving back to his childhood home. But over time she'd managed—with the encouragement and support of his siblings—to counter his objections.

They hadn't decided what they were going to do with the land, because they were still looking for Liza so that all of the siblings would have input into that decision, and Hudson's PI hadn't had much luck in tracking her down. But David Bradford had done some digging locally and discovered that Matthew Baldwin was the one who had paid the taxes on Sunshine Farm. The *why* was still unknown and the old man had rejected all efforts by his grandchildren to find out, but Eva was confident the truth would be revealed in short order.

For now, Luke and Eva were working toward making the house livable again, one room at a time. They'd tackled the master bedroom first, for obvious reasons; then Luke had wanted to redo the kitchen—for Eva.

"I was trying to decide what room to do after we're finished with the kitchen," Luke said as he scraped the paper on the wall next to where Eva was working.

"We've just started with the kitchen," she reminded him.

"I know," he admitted. "But when it's done, maybe we could do the bedroom across the hall from ours."

"Don't you think it makes more sense to focus on the main floor first?" she said.

"We could do what makes sense—" he said, holding his palms up as if they were scales and he was weighing the options "—or we could make a baby."

The scraper slipped from Eva's hand and clattered to the floor. She left it where it fell and turned to face him. "You want to have a baby?"

"Well, not before we're married," he said. "But yeah, in the not-too-distant future. As long as it's what you want, too."

"Yeah, it's definitely what I want, too."

Then she lifted her arms to link them behind his head and drew his mouth down to hers.

"In fact," she said, whispering the words against his lips, "I think we should go upstairs now and check out the bedroom you were talking about."

"You just want to get me upstairs so that you can seduce me."

"You don't know me as well as you think you do," she said, shaking her head in mock disapproval as she reached for the buckle of his belt. "Or you'd realize that I can seduce you anywhere."

"You've got me there," he admitted. "In fact, you've got me anywhere you want me."

She kissed him again. "Which is only one of the many reasons I love you."

"I love you, too," he said, and proceeded to show her how very much.

* * * * *

Can't get enough of those Mavericks?
Don't miss our bonus Montana Mavericks
summer special.

Vivienne Shuster is an expert wedding planner, but her
own love life is a disaster—and now she needs a fiancé
to impress her boss! Cole Dalton thinks
weddings are for the birds. Can he cowboy up and help
Viv—without falling for the
Rust Creek Falls marriage magic?

Look for
THE MAVERICK'S BRIDAL BARGAIN
by
Christy Jeffries

Available wherever Mills & Boon
books and ebooks are sold.

Euphoric that she had the freedom to touch and feel him, she pushed her fears aside and gave in to her desires.

They came together in an explosion of need that rocked her world.

"You don't know what meeting you has done to me." Luca kissed every centimeter of her face and throat. "I could eat you alive. Don't ask me to stop because I can't, *bellissima*."

"I don't want you to stop. Surely you know that by now? Why else do I keep finding excuses to stay?"

"I love you, Gabriella Parisi. I'm so in love with you I can't think about anything else. Don't say it's too soon, or that we barely know each other. None of that matters because we know how we feel."

THE MAGNATE'S HOLIDAY PROPOSAL

BY
REBECCA WINTERS

MILLS & BOON

First Published in Great Britain 2017
By Mills & Boon, an imprint of HarperCollins*Publishers*
1 London Bridge Street, London, SE1 9GF

© 2017 Rebecca Winters

ISBN: 978-0-263-92352-0

23-1217

MIX
Paper from
responsible sources
FSC™ C007454

This book is produced from independently certified FSC™ paper to ensure responsible forest management.

For more information visit: www.harpercollins.co.uk/green

Printed and bound in Spain
by CPI, Barcelona

Rebecca Winters lives in Salt Lake City, Utah. With canyons and high alpine meadows full of wildflowers, she never runs out of places to explore. They, plus her favourite vacation spots in Europe, often end up as backgrounds for her romance novels—because writing is her passion, along with her family and church. Rebecca loves to hear from readers. If you wish to email her, please visit her website at www.cleanromances.com.

CHAPTER ONE

November, two years earlier.
Piancavallo, the Italian Dolomites, Italy

"PAPÀ? IS THIS where you skied when you were my age?"

"Yes. I'd practice right here whenever my parents would let me."

"I want to be an Olympic champion like you."

"I have no doubts you will be one day, Dino," his *mamma* said. "But it's getting cold and time to go back to our chalet. We'll come again tomorrow, darling."

"Urra!"

Suddenly the three of them heard a loud crack higher up the mountain.

"What was that, Papà?"

"We have to get off the mountain, *now!*"

November 29, present day

On Thursday morning Luca Berettini left his villa for work later than usual and got in the car to drive to Spilimbergo in Northeast Italy. It took only a few minutes from Luca's home in Maniago, Italy, eleven miles away.

For the last year and a half, Luca had been acting CEO of Berettini Plastics, their hundred-year-old family business, while his father, Fabrizo Berettini, had been recovering from a heart attack. The position was one he'd never wanted or sought. But both the board and his mother had pressured him to do it. She'd done everything in the world for him all her life, and he couldn't turn her down.

Since the avalanche that had robbed Luca of his wife and Dino's mother, Luca had run a business of his own on the side, all to do with the manufacture of Italian skis and boots. His venture had proved lucrative. If the gods were kind, the day might come when Luca could say goodbye to the job of CEO and be fully involved with his interest in the ski industry.

The horrendous avalanche that had changed his world and had kept him away from the ski slopes hadn't altered his love for the sport. What a joy it would be to walk away and have the freedom to do what he really wanted, but he couldn't do that until he knew the outcome of his father's health.

As for Dino, until Luca knew what kind of life was in store for his son after the impending operation to remove a benign brain tumor, it was difficult to think about anything else. The boy meant more to him than life itself.

Luca parked his car and nodded to several of the employees before taking the private elevator to his suite on the third floor. As he entered, his secretary, Sofia, got up from her desk and hurried over to him. Something was going on. In a hushed voice she said,

"Before you go in, I wanted to warn you that your father is here. He's been waiting several hours for you."

Anger swamped Luca. The doctor had ordered his father to stay home and continue to work with his various therapists until he was given permission to put in part-time work again. But that hadn't stopped him from crossing the threshold today. It was so like him to intrude on Luca's private life without warning. In the past he'd tried to sabotage several of Luca's relationships with women by making demands and criticisms.

Today was all Luca needed after having to console Dino following one of his nightmares this morning, but he knew exactly why his father had shown up and shouldn't have been surprised. When he hadn't gotten satisfaction after a fiery exchange on the phone with Luca last night, he'd decided to barge in on him.

Being armed with that information, Luca thanked Sofia for the heads-up and walked in his inner sanctum. His silver-haired sixty-eight-year-old father sat at the large oak desk while he read some sensitive documents Luca had been working on.

He looked at Luca without getting up. "I asked Sofia to hold your calls so I could talk to you."

How like his father to come to the office without advance warning when the doctor hadn't given him permission to be at work yet. Throughout Luca's life his father had interfered, never approving of his sporting interests, always trying to stifle his career ambitions that had nothing to do with the family plastics business. No girl, no woman was good enough for Luca except the one they were fighting about right now.

"We said all there was to say last night on the phone."

His father slammed one hand on the desk. "I don't know why you continue to thwart me about Giselle."

"Frankly, I'll never understand why you hoped she and I would ever get together. I was never interested in her, which is why I married Catarina."

"But your wife has been dead for two years. Giselle is still very much alive and beautiful. Her father tells me it was you she always wanted. We're determined to get the two of you together. I told him I'd arrange it."

Luca shook his head. "Don't you understand I have more important things to think about at the moment? I'm dealing with my son's fears over his operation," he exploded. "Henri Fournier may be your best friend and the two of you are desperate to keep the fortunes of both our families sealed with a marriage, but I made it clear last night. I don't want to see his daughter and have no interest in any woman! Since you look settled in that chair where you once sat for years ruling the company, I'll leave it to you."

The older man's cheeks grew ruddy. He would never change. His father had been the same intransigent dictator for as long as Luca could remember. Nothing Luca had ever wanted or done had met with his father's approval, and Luca had given up hope for a transformation.

"Where are you going?"

"Home."

"Wait, Luca—"

But he walked back out and told Sofia to ring him if anything vital came up. Now would be a good time to do an on-site visit to the ski manufacturing plant he owned in nearby Tauriano before returning to Maniago. It might cool down his anger.

At three thirty that afternoon Luca returned home and found his son still in his pajamas watching TV in the family room.

"Hey—*piccolo*." He hugged him. "What's going on?"

"My favorite show."

Ines, the nanny, got up from the sofa and walked over to him. "It's the *Start with a Wish* program that's on every weekday afternoon." Luca had heard of it. "He's obsessed with it because they make a child's wish come true."

If only that were really possible.

"I take it his headache finally passed."

"Yes."

Every headache his son suffered caused Luca pain that crossed over the older lines of grief etched on his hard-boned features. "After we have dinner, I'll take him to watch a hockey game. Hopefully it will get his mind off the operation."

He left the kitchen and raced up the stairs, as ever feeling devastated by Dino's condition. Earlier that morning his son had cried to him. "I dreamed I was in the avalanche and couldn't find Mamma. I wish she didn't have to die."

How many times had Luca heard that? He'd kissed the top of his head. "We all wish she were here, but at least we have each other, don't we?"

"Yes," his boy whispered.

"Pretty soon you're not going to have headaches anymore."

"But I'm scared."

"I know, but the operation is going to take them away. Doesn't that make you happy?"

"Yes, but what if I never wake up?"

Luca clutched him harder. "Where did you get an idea like that?"

"On TV."

"What show?"

"That cartoon, *Angel's Friends*. Raf's mother never woke up."

Diavolo. A simple cartoon had played on his fears, doing more damage. "Listen to me, Dino. I've had four operations in my life, and I'm just fine."

"Was Nonna with you?"

He'd closed his eyes, praying for inspiration. "Yes." Luca's mother had always been there for him. "And *I'll* be with you. Don't you know I wouldn't let anything happen to you?"

"Yes." But Dino's voice was muffled against Luca's shoulder and he'd finally fallen asleep.

The heavy lids that covered blue eyes revealed his misery. In the last year, his headaches had grown more frequent as the doctor said they would. When the medication didn't stop them, sleep was the only thing that seemed to help, but that meant he stayed in bed until they subsided.

At his last checkup three months ago, the doctor had brought up the operation to remove it. But Dino fought the very thought of one, even if it would make him feel better.

Now Luca was frightened, too, because the neurosurgeon told him the tumor was in a dangerous place. Removing it wasn't without risk. But Luca knew it had to be done so his son could be relieved of pain.

His operation had been scheduled for December 21, less than a month away now. Dr. Meuller, the Swiss-

born doctor from Zurich who was doing some volun-
tary work in Africa, would fly in to the hospital in
Padova to perform the surgery. Luca had arranged
his business affairs so he'd be free during that time.

Luca and his mother had done everything to reassure Dino they'd be there for him during the surgery, but whenever it was mentioned, he would run
to his room and sob. He wanted his mother, and no
one could replace her. It broke his heart that Dino
dreaded it so much.

Something out of the ordinary had to happen to
help his son. Luca wished to heaven he knew what
it was…

Another Monday.

Gabi Parisi left the house in Limena and drove the
four miles under an overcast sky to the office of the
Start with a Wish foundation in Padova, Italy. In the
fifty-six-degree temperature, she didn't need a coat
to wear over her long-sleeved blue sweater and black
wool skirt.

After the weekend, Mondays meant tons of mail.
So many letters came in from children needing help.
Some required money for medical procedures or operations that parents or guardians couldn't provide.
Others were dying and the family or caregivers wanted
to grant them their greatest wish, which was beyond
their means.

Edda Romano, Gabi's boss, was a famous philanthropist who had been giving away her money for worthy causes ever since her husband's untimely death.
Being the heiress of the Romano manufacturing fortune had allowed her to establish the foundation that

would continue to give happiness to children for generations. There was no one Gabi admired more than Edda. She felt it a privilege to work for this remarkable seventy-five-year-old woman who was truly selfless.

Gabi maneuvered through the heavy traffic and drove around the back of the building to the private parking area. After touching up her lipstick, she ran a brush through tousled ash-blond hair and got out of the car. To her surprise she was met with several wolf whistles coming from some workmen doing renovations on the building to the west.

Men.

Her divorce two years ago had put her off getting involved again. She'd moved back home with her widowed mother, who still worked part-time at the hospital as a pediatric nurse.

Gabi had gotten her college degree in accounting and had worked in a bank. She'd even fallen in love and had married the bank manager, having faith in a wonderful future. But a miscarriage soon after their marriage had been devastating. And then she'd learned her husband had been having an affair.

In less than a year of being married, it was over and she'd filed for divorce. Once again she'd started looking for another job.

When the position with Edda had opened up, Gabi had grabbed at it, sensing it would be a healing kind of work. Edda's whole purpose was to make children happy. Still mourning the baby she'd lost at five weeks, Gabi could pour out her love on other people's children.

The foundation business filled three floors of the neoclassic building, depending on the department

where you were assigned. To Gabi's mind, she had
the best position. She, along with four other women,
had the exciting opportunity of opening and reading the letters. When they'd made their group decision about each child's letter, they took it to Edda in
the suite next door to make the final decisions about
what to do.

Once Gabi had gone inside the rear entrance and
had grabbed a cup of coffee in the open reception
room, she walked upstairs to the conference room on
the second floor to get started for the day. She and her
coworkers sat around a big oval table. Three of them
were married, one was single and Gabi was divorced.

Stefania, the woman Edda had put in charge of
their group, received the mail from the mail room and
passed around the new letters that came in every day.
Gabi marveled that so many children needed special
help and praised Edda for the service she rendered on
a continual basis. Such goodness put her in the cat-
egory of a saint.

"*Buongiorno*," she said to Angelina and Clara,
who'd already arrived. In a minute Stefania came in
with Luisa, the one who still wasn't married and had
become a good friend of Gabi's. They smiled at each
other before Luisa sat down next to her. "How was
your weekend?" she whispered to her friend.

"I spent it with my cousin. We did a lot of early
Christmas shopping. What about you, Gabi?"

"My mother and I drove to Venice for the fun of
it." Gabi had done a little sketching.

"How wonderful!"

Pretty soon everyone had settled down. Stefania
opened the mailbag and distributed a bundle to each

of them. Gabi opened her envelopes and pulled out the letters. Then they each took a turn to read a letter. In the afternoon they would form a consensus of what to turn over to Edda for final consideration. All the letters came from children who were deserving of blessings.

Just before lunch Gabi picked up her last letter. Most of them had been written in cursive by an adult. This one had been printed by a youngster and there was no greeting.

"My name is Dino Berettini." She didn't know of another Berettini except the international Berettini plastics conglomerate near Venice. The billion-dollar business helped keep the country afloat financially.

"I am seven years old. Every night I tell God I am afraid to have an operation because my *mamma* died and won't be with me. But if it will take away my headaches and make my *papà* happy again, I will do it. He is never happy and I love him more than anyone in the entire world."

The words *make my* papà *happy again* swam before Gabi's eyes. They took her back to her childhood when at the age of seven, her adored father was dying. She'd gone to the priest after Mass and begged him to ask God to make him better. The priest smiled kindly and told her she should ask God herself.

Hurt that he hadn't said he would do it, she still went home and said her prayers, begging God to save her *papà*. Within two days he rallied and got better. In Gabi's mind a miracle had happened.

Touched by the sweet, prayer-like missive from this boy, she was moved to tears.

"Gabi?"

She looked up. Everyone was staring at her, so she read them the letter.

"What else does the letter say?" Stefania asked her.

"There isn't anything else. This child wrote what was in his heart. Obviously an adult had to address the envelope and mail it to us, but I'm convinced no one helped him with the wording."

"I agree. Read it to us again."

Gabi looked at Stefania. "I don't think I can without breaking down."

"I'll do it." Luisa reached for it and read it aloud. After she'd finished, she said, "What a sweet little boy. But he hasn't asked for anything."

"Yes he has," Gabi murmured. "He wants the foundation to grant his wish not to be afraid for the operation that will help him feel better and make his father happy."

"But we can't do that," Clara exclaimed.

Stefania shook her head. "No. It's beyond our power, but this is one letter Edda has to read. Enjoy your lunch. I'll see you back here at one thirty."

They all got up and left the building. Luisa and Gabi walked around the corner to the trattoria where they usually ate. While they ate pasta and salad, Luisa asked her why the letter had touched her so deeply.

"I don't know exactly. A combination of things made me tear up. He mentioned losing his mother, and it reminded me of my miscarriage and how I would never raise my child. As I told you, Santos and I got pregnant on our honeymoon. But I lost it after carrying it five weeks, and nothing could comfort me."

Luisa eyed her compassionately. "I can only imagine how painful that would have been for you."

"That was over two years ago. But when I read Dino's words today, some of those feelings returned. Now *he's* the one suffering so terribly."

"The poor little thing has lost his mother. The pathos in that one line squeezed my heart."

"I know," Gabi murmured. "Especially the last line that said his father was never happy."

Luisa shook her head. "In the six months I've been working here, we've never had a letter like this one."

"I agree. Today I found myself wishing a miracle would happen for that boy. He wrote that letter as an act of faith because of Edda's program. The trouble is, she can give any child a tangible gift, but she can't move mountains."

"No." Luisa shook her head. "It needs a miracle."

"Do you remember me telling you about the time I wanted a miracle so my father wouldn't die? That did happen and he lived until three years ago when he finally passed away from heart failure. If only one could happen again for Dino…"

On that solemn note they left to walk back to work. A half hour later Stefania told Gabi to go in Edda's office. Since Gabi had been the one who'd opened the letter and had been affected by it, their boss wanted to talk it over with her.

Gabi and Luisa exchanged surprised glances before she walked down the hall and entered Edda's private domain. The trim, classily dressed philanthropist with titian-colored hair smiled at Gabi and asked her to sit down opposite her desk. She held the letter in her hand.

"Stefania told me about your reaction while you were reading this. I confess tears welled up in my throat, too. That adorable child's simple plea for help leaves us with a dilemma."

"Luisa and I were talking about that over lunch. How do you move a mountain?"

"Exactly." She picked up the envelope the letter had come in. "Someone mailed it from Maniago. I did research while you were at lunch. There are two Berettini families living in that town. Does the name Luca Berettini mean anything to you?"

"No, but I immediately thought of the Berettini Plastics Company near Venice."

She nodded. "It's the family business. Recently the elder Berettini stepped down as head and now Luca Berettini, his son, has been made CEO. Dino is his boy."

"How do you know that?"

"Because of a tragedy that happened to that family two years ago. It was all over the media and in the newspaper. You didn't hear about it or see it on TV?"

Gabi lowered her head. "That was a difficult time for me and I'm afraid I hadn't been paying much attention to the news."

It was two years ago that Gabi had discovered her husband had been unfaithful to her. She'd already had a miscarriage. With her marriage in shambles, she'd filed for divorce. It had been a horrific time for her and she'd been blinded to anything going on around her at the time.

"I'm sorry to hear that. You've been a wonderful employee."

"Thank you. I've been so much better since you hired me to come to work for you. It's so marvelous making children happy. I'm more grateful to you for this job than you could possibly know."

"I'm glad of it."

"Please tell me what happened to Dino."

"Luca Berettini was a downhill alpine skier who became a gold medalist in the Olympics in his early twenties."

"I remember something about that. I was probably around sixteen at the time," Gabi murmured. "But that was ten years ago. I haven't heard anything about him since."

"You wouldn't have. He could have gone on for more medals but was taken into the family business early because of his brilliant marketing acumen. He married, and he and his wife had a son. Two years ago the three of them were skiing near their chalet in Piancavallo when they were caught in an avalanche."

"Oh, no—"

"I don't recall the details, but his wife was killed. According to all the reports, Luca saved his son from certain death."

"The boy would have been five then. Old enough to have memories of his mother."

"Yes. According to this letter, he needs some kind of an operation to cure his headaches."

Gabi's head lifted. "But he's afraid because he wants his mother with him."

"Sadly no one can bring her back, and they don't need money for an operation. Our foundation can't help him, but I'll get you the unlisted phone numbers of the Berettini families, hopefully before the day is out. When I do, why don't you try to reach the person who mailed Dino's letter and set up a time to visit him? He needs a personal visit to know we received it."

"I think that would be wonderful."

"Would you like to be the one to go from our office?"

"I'd love to be the one to visit him. I know what it's like to want a wish to come true."

Gabi was reminded of another experience at Christmastime around twelve years of age. One of her best friends had almost died from a bad appendix. Their group of friends were so sad, and someone suggested they wish on a star for her so she'd get better.

None of them really believed it would do any good, but they'd grasped at any hope to pull their friend through. Wonder of wonders, she did recover. To Gabi it had been another miracle. This boy needed one, too.

"Good. However, the family may not allow it. But if they do, you can take him a gift to let him know we received his letter. Since it's getting close to Christmas, I'm thinking the latest building blocks game. It's a Christmas scene with trees and snowmen. Children that age love it. I'll ask our gift department to get it ready for him. But if it turns out the family doesn't want anyone to come, then we'll send him the gift."

"I knew you'd have a solution. You always do. Thank you for giving me this opportunity."

Gabi left her office and rejoined the others in the conference room. She told them what Edda had said. Near the end of the day Edda's secretary walked in and gave Gabi a sheet of paper with the telephone numbers of the Berettini families.

Stefania smiled at her. "Go ahead and make your call at the desk while we finish up."

"Thanks." She walked over to the corner of the room and sat down, wondering which number to choose first. But it didn't matter as long as she reached the person who sent the letter.

On the first call she was asked to leave a message. Gabi decided not to do that before trying the other number. On the third ring, someone picked up.

"Pronto?"

"Hello. My name is Signora Parisi. I'm calling from the Start with a Wish foundation in Padova. Today we received a letter from a boy named Dino Berettini. There was no address on the envelope, but we saw that it was postmarked from Maniago. Edda Romano, the founder, has asked me to speak to the person who knows about it."

Maybe Dino mailed it himself and no one in his family knew about it. If he'd wanted to keep it a secret, it was too late now.

"Signora Parisi? I'm Giustina Berettini, Dino's grandmother, the one who sent it for him." Her answer filled Gabi with relief. "I'm surprised you received it so quickly. I only mailed it on Friday."

"We try to be prompt with a reply when the letters come in because we know the desperate needs of these children."

"I was home with him on Friday when he said he wanted to watch your program," the older woman said. "I'd heard of the foundation, of course, but I'd never seen it on TV. Before long he asked me to help him with his letter and mail it. What he printed came straight from his heart."

Gabi nodded. "When I read the letter to my coworkers, we were all very touched. Once Edda read it, she suggested I contact your family. We realize he needs an operation, and we can't bring back his mother, but would it be possible for me to come and bring him a gift? Edda wants him to know all our prayers will be with him."

"That's very kind of you. He'll be so thrilled."

It would be a thrill for Gabi, too. "I'll bring it when it's the best time for you. I believe the sooner he receives it, the better."

"Would it be possible for you to come to my house in the morning? Say nine o'clock? Or is that too early? I don't have any idea about your hours of work."

"Nine o'clock would be no problem. What's the address?"

After writing it down, Gabi hung up and told Stefania what was planned. Then she headed for the gift department to pick up the Christmas-wrapped set and put it in her car.

Excited over her mission, she drove home to Limena and shared all that had happened with her mother. They talked until late and she slept poorly, waiting for morning to come.

CHAPTER TWO

THE DRIVE ON Tuesday morning took an hour and a half. Gabi was familiar with part of the route leading to Venice, but she'd never had a reason to take the turnoff going north to reach Maniago. The picturesque town filled a valley surrounded by the Italian pre-Alps.

Her car's sat-nav helped her drive to a lovely pale pink villa located in the foothills. Gabi found the property enchanting as she made her way along the tree-lined path to the front door carrying Dino's gift.

She rang the bell. Now that she was about to meet Dino, she was feeling nervous for fear she might say the wrong thing. At least his grandmother would be with him. Gabi would follow the older woman's lead.

Soon the door opened. A sober-faced woman in a maid's uniform appeared. She eyed the gift. "*Buongiorno!* You must be Signora Parisi from Padova. Signora Berettini is waiting for you. Come in."

Gabi followed her through a luxurious entrance hall to a set of opened French doors on the left. Her gaze traveled to the elegantly dressed older woman who was probably the same age as Gabi's mother. She detected traces of silver in the woman's black hair. The boy's grandmother was tall and very attractive, but there was such sadness in her eyes.

She asked the maid to take the package and put it on the damask love seat, then turned to Gabi. "Thank you for being on time."

"I enjoy getting up early. It was a beautiful drive and I'm anxious to meet Dino. Is he here?"

"No. He and his father live in a villa on an estate about two minutes away. Luca has already driven him to school. Come and sit down."

The news disappointed Gabi, who didn't understand why his grandmother had asked her to come if he was at school. And why not at Dino's home?

"Thank you." She found an upholstered chair opposite her and took her place.

"Allow me to explain. His father doesn't know about the letter. If he'd heard about it, he might have discouraged me from sending it in order not to get Dino's hopes up. What if there'd been no response? He adores that child and doesn't want anything to hurt him. That's why I preferred that you and I meet here first."

Gabi nodded. "I can understand that. Edda gave me some background about the avalanche where Dino lost his mother, but she didn't know specifics or why he needs an operation. I honestly don't know how you survive a tragedy like that."

"I'm not sure we're doing it very well," the older woman said in a sad, quiet voice. "But I don't want to dwell on it. What's important is that you've come. It will make him so happy."

"I'm glad Edda sent me."

She wiped her eyes. "I could never deny my grandson anything. He and my son are both in a fragile emotional state at the moment. As the time gets closer to the operation, I'm afraid Luca has grown as anxious as Dino. You see, when my grandson was brought in to the hospital after the avalanche, the scans revealed a benign brain tumor."

"Oh, no."

"The doctor says it's the reason for the headaches. But removing it could cause other complications, increasing our anxiety."

"Of course." Gabi clasped her hands together. "How soon does he have to have it?"

"December twenty-first. That's three weeks from now. The neurosurgeon will fly in to Padova and perform it at San Pietro Hospital."

"No wonder your son is so worried. How frightening for all of you."

"Exactly. But we can't afford to think about anything negative now. The family has videos of Dino with his mother at various ages, and he watches them whenever he misses her too much. I hope that your quick response to Dino's letter and the fact that you came in person will cheer him up even if it can't solve the problem. He's struggling so terribly over the loss of his mother you can't imagine."

Gabi's heart went out to her, to all of them. "The poor thing. Everyone at the foundation is praying for him. Edda sent a gift for him. It's a building blocks game he can put on a table."

Tears kept welling in her blue eyes. "What I'd give if that present and your kindness to come in person will help him face the operation! My son is absolutely desperate." The older woman clasped her hands under her chin. "Since I want it to be a surprise, this is what I'd like to do. If you'd be willing, I'd like you to follow me to my son's villa."

"Of course." Gabi had made her first phone call there apparently.

"When we get there, I'll go pick him up at school and tell him I have a surprise waiting for him at home. The cook will have our lunch prepared. He'll be delighted to get out early since his father doesn't normally bring him home until one. But not today! I'll leave a message at his office that I wanted to pick him up. That way my son can stay at work longer."

That made sense to Gabi, who was eager to meet Dino.

"When he comes running in the house, he'll see you and the gift. We'll go from there." She stood up and called to her maid.

"He sounded so sweet in his letter, I'm looking forward to meeting him, Signora Berettini."

"He's a combination of imp and angel. I'll get my car and ask Carla to take the present back to yours."

"Thank you."

In a few minutes she found herself following the black Mercedes sedan through the hills. When she rounded the next corner, she let out a quiet gasp at the sight of a sprawling two-story yellow villa set in the mountain greenery like it had grown there.

From the style, she imagined it had been built in the eighteenth century. Gabi had toured through many splendid villas from the past opened to the public. But she'd never seen anything more gorgeous than this one owned by the wealthy Berettini CEO. How sad his money couldn't fix what was wrong with Dino.

She drove through the gates and went all the way to the circular drive in front, where she parked the car behind Giustina's. After retrieving the gift, she joined her at the entrance, where another woman answered the door who was all smiles.

"Ines? Please meet Gabi Parisi from the Start with a Wish foundation. Gabi? This is the nanny who has looked after our precious Dino with unswerving devotion."

"I'm very happy to meet you, Ines."

"It's a privilege to meet someone from the program we see on TV. He loves it and watches it every time it's on. He won't believe you're here."

"I hope it will bring him some comfort."

"We're counting on it, aren't we, Ines? Will you take this gift into the family room?"

"Si, signora."

They followed her through the magnificent interior to the rear of the villa. It overlooked the breathtaking town with snow-covered summits beyond it in the far distance. Ines placed the present on the big table.

The first thing Gabi saw was the framed photograph of a young woman that hung above the fireplace. With her long dark hair, what a beauty she was! "Is this Dino's mother?"

"Yes. That's Catarina."

Gabi looked around at the warm, friendly room. It was made for a child's pleasure with books and games, comfortable furniture, a TV and several wonderful photographs of animals living in the wilds of Africa.

She turned to Giustina. "A room like this must be heaven for a little boy."

"Dino's mother decorated it. Naturally it's his favorite spot in the villa."

"It would be mine."

"Gabi? I'll leave now to get Dino and won't be long. His school is nearby. I'll ask the maid to bring you tea or coffee. Do you have a preference?"

"Tea would be lovely."

When she left, Gabi walked over to the floor-to-ceiling bookcase to look at them all. There were so many darling storybooks he'd probably been read over and over again.

Ines brought the tea. Now would be a good time to ask a few questions. "Tell me about what Dino is like."

"He's very bright and loves to play with friends. When he doesn't have a headache, you would never know he has a problem. But he still suffers from nightmares to do with the avalanche. It came upon them so fast. When he hears a really loud noise like thunder, he freezes and runs to hide under his bed."

"I can imagine. How horrible for him."

"His father is hoping that once the operation is over, he won't be so anxious about everything."

"The poor dear. What are some of the things he likes?"

"Swimming and comic books. His father won't let him look at *Diabolik* for fear it will give him nightmares, but he's allowed to read *Lupo Alberto*."

"I too loved the comics when I was young." While she was deep in thought, she heard the sound of footsteps running down the hall toward the family room.

Suddenly the boy raced inside but came to a halt when he saw Gabi.

She jumped to her feet, taking in the sight of Dino

Berettini in the blue smock all Italian children his age wore to school. He appeared on the taller side of seven with forget-me-not-blue eyes and black shiny hair like his mother's in the photograph. The handsome child didn't look like anything could be wrong with him.

"Hello, Dino."

"Hi! Who are you?"

His grandmother came in the room. "Dino? You should wait to be introduced."

"Sorry, Nonna," he murmured.

"I'd like you to meet Signora Gabi Parisi. She's come all the way from Padova to meet you."

"How do you do, *signora*?" What an adorable boy. "Why have you come to see me?"

Gabi took a deep breath. "Because you sent a letter to the Start with a Wish foundation, right?"

His eyes widened. "You got it already?"

"Yes. That's where I work. Yesterday the mail came and I opened it."

"You did?" He sounded utterly incredulous, then turned to his grandmother. "You said you mailed it, but—"

"You didn't believe me?" The older woman sounded surprised.

"Yes, but... I was afraid it wouldn't get there."

Gabi took a step closer. "Well, it did, and it was my lucky day because my boss said I could come to visit you and bring you a present." During their conversation Gabi had seen his eyes darting to the package on the table.

"You have a boss?"

"Yes. Her name is Edda."

"My *papà* is a boss, too."

She nodded. "He's such an important boss, every-one knows him, even Edda. She was the one who wanted me to bring his son a special surprise in person. Would you like to open it?"

"Yes, but it's wrapped for Christmas."

"That's true, but she said you could open it now if you want. I know if I were in your shoes, I'd run right over to the table and rip off the wrapping paper to see what she sent you."

A smile broke out on his face. No longer hesitating, he rushed toward the table. Gabi's eyes met Giustina's. They both walked over to watch the untidy unveiling.

"A building blocks set!" His happy exclamation told her a lot.

"It's a winter wonderland scene. I bet you can make it look like the one here in Maniago at Christmastime."

Those brilliant blue eyes darted to her. "Can you stay and help me put it together?"

"There's nothing I'd rather do, if it's all right with your grandmother."

"Is it, Nonna?"

"Of course. I'll have lunch served in here while you play."

"Can I call you Gabi?"

"Of course."

"Evviva!"

For the next two hours Gabi had the time of her life helping him put the project together while they ate. They talked about dinosaurs and his favorite emojis. Soon they got on the subject of another comic book character called Tex, from American television; the indomitable hero. Dino was so smart and a perfect delight. You'd never know anything was wrong with him.

Unfortunately, she'd overstayed her welcome and the time had come when she needed to leave for Padova. Edda would want a report in person before the day was out. "Guess what, Dino? I've had such a terrific time, but now I'm due back at the office."

"No—" he cried out and jumped to his feet. The abrupt change in his demeanor took her by surprise.

"I'm sorry."

Tears filled his eyes. "But I want you to stay."

"I would love to if I could."

"Will you come tomorrow?"

"She has to get back to work," Giustina spoke up. "Now thank her and say goodbye."

"But I don't want her to go." He was relentless. It was an indication of how difficult life could be for him at times. Her heart ached for him and his whole family. His grandmother looked absolutely crushed.

As Gabi turned to leave, he dashed past her and out of the family room.

The older woman seemed frantic. "I'm sorry. I've never seen him act quite like this before."

"He's going through a very difficult time in his life."

"I shouldn't have mailed his letter."

"Don't say that. He loves and trusts you. Now he knows our foundation received it. He believed in something and it happened. That has to have increased the faith he needs to face his operation."

Giustina followed her to the door. "About his letter... There's something I have to tell you before you go. As I told you, his father doesn't know about it. When he finds out, I don't want him to know everything Dino said. It would kill my son if he thought Dino saw him so unhappy all the time."

"I hear what you're saying and will let Edda know."

"Thank you, Gabi."

"Thank you for the delicious lunch. I'm happy to have met you."

Gabi hurried out of the villa to her car. As she started the engine, she looked up and saw Dino standing at an upstairs window staring down at her. *That precious boy.* There was so much sadness in that house, she could hardly bear it as she drove away.

Between the grandmother's pain and the worry in Ines's expression, Gabi couldn't see any happiness. She wished something else could be done, but she didn't know what.

At four o'clock, Luca ended the staff meeting and headed for home. His mother's earlier message that she'd be picking up Dino had allowed him to get a lot of work done today.

For the last two years Luca had trimmed his work schedule in order to put his traumatized boy first. Because he was no longer in kindergarten, their normal routine had changed.

Monday through Saturday they ate breakfast together first before he drove Dino to primary school at eight o'clock. Then Luca would leave his office in time to pick him up at one o'clock and they'd go home for lunch. After that, Luca would go back to work until five and Dino's nanny, Ines, would take over.

But today had been an exception from start to finish. Now he could enjoy the rest of the time with his son. Maybe they'd go to another hockey match. He liked watching it with Luca.

He got back in his car and drove to Tauriano. He was furious that his father, who'd always been cold and unyielding, seemed especially devoid of human feelings when it came to Dino. He'd always resented Luca's marriage to Catarina, and had passed on a feeling of dislike toward his grandson.

Thank heaven for Luca's mother and Catarina's aunt and uncle Maria and Tomaso, who'd raised her from a young age. They were like another set of grandparents to Dino, and he adored them.

For the next three weeks he needed to fill each day with activities for both of them in order to face the ordeal coming up. Once the tumor had been removed, who knew what other problems might ensue. But right now he needed to shelve that worry and handle the present.

He pulled up to the villa and hurried inside. Since his son was usually in the family room, he headed there first. "Dino? Papà is home!"

There was no answering cry, and nothing from Ines. Luca paused long enough to see a giant set of building blocks on the table. The box it came in showed a winter wonderland scene. A certain amount of work had been done on it already. He was impressed.

Apparently this was a surprise from Luca's mother and that was why she'd gone to pick up Dino today. Maybe he'd gone home with his grandmother for dinner.

Curious, he took the stairs two at a time to the next floor, passing Dino's bedroom on the way to his own suite for a shower. That's when he heard sobbing and opened the door to see Ines sitting on the side of the bed trying to comfort his son. Luca felt like he'd been kicked in the gut.

Ines got to her feet and hurried over to him. Sorrow was written all over her face. "He's had an upset today," she whispered, "but it's not because of a nightmare or a headache. He had a visit from a woman representing the Start with a Wish foundation. She brought him a gift, but when she had to leave, it upset Dino. I'm glad you're home. He'll be much better after talking to you." On that note, she left the bedroom.

Luca walked over to the side of the bed. Dino lay on top of the covers on his stomach, hugging a pillow. He was dressed in a T-shirt and jeans. Luca sat down and began to rub his back.

"Polpetto mio." The meatball endearment he'd used with him forever usually brought a laugh, but not this time. "Want to tell Papà what's wrong?"

He whirled around and sat up. His face was a study in misery. Luca hadn't seen a look like that in a long time. "My *nonna* is mad at me. Did she call you?"

His mother didn't have a mean bone in her body, but clearly something had disturbed Dino to the point of tears. "No. I just got home from work."

"She didn't say anything?"

Luca put up both hands. "I swear it."

"Well, she's going to." He slid off the bed. "And then you're going to be really mad at me."

Since when? What the devil had gone on here? "Why would I be mad?"

"Because… I was rude to Gabi."

Gabi? "Who's that?" he asked, though Ines had already informed him.

"She brought me a present from that *Start with a Wish* program on TV." Luca had heard of it, of course. Who hadn't? How had they known about Dino?

"We were having so much fun putting it together, and then she had to leave and I didn't want her to go. I got so mad I ran out of the room. After I went upstairs, I watched her drive away. And now I know she'll never come back."

He ran to Luca and wrapped his arms around him. "I'll never see her again."

Luca didn't have a clue what was going on, but with those words, he knew this had something to do with the loss of Dino's mother. Luca needed to stop the bleeding before there was a full-blown emotional hemorrhage.

Gabi arrived at work Wednesday morning, anxious to talk to Edda when she came in. She hadn't been in her office when Gabi returned yesterday. Today she needed to pass on Giustina's concerns about certain contents of the letter and tell her what had happened at the Berettini villa. Dino hadn't wanted her to leave, and heaven help her, she hadn't wanted to leave either.

His quick mind, his laughter, the funny things he said—everything about him tugged at her heart. She'd meant it when she'd told him she'd love a son just like him. It was true. What wasn't there to like? The fact that he was facing a serious operation only made her feelings more tender toward him.

An hour later, in the middle of opening more letters, Stefania told Gabi that Edda wanted to see her in her office. Gabi hadn't realized her boss had already come in.

She excused herself and walked down the hall. Edda welcomed her in and told her to sit down. "I'm happy to inform you that your visit yesterday made a deep impression on Dino Berettini. So much so in fact that he's downstairs in the reception area with his father, who took time off from his work to drive them here. They've come specifically to see you."

What? His father had brought him? Gabi couldn't credit any of it.

"There's more, Gabi. They've asked if you could spend the day with them while they're here in Padova. I told them it would have to be your decision. Of course you have my permission. How do you feel about that?"

How did she feel? "Do you think I should?"

Edda scrutinized her. "Is there a reason you wouldn't want to see him again?"

"No, but I haven't met his father."

"Ah. The idea makes you uncomfortable."

"Not at all, but I'm just surprised he's here. Did you show him Dino's letter?"

"The subject didn't come up. It appears he wants his son to apologize to you in person for the way he behaved toward you before you left their home. He's concerned that Dino ran out on you and didn't say goodbye or even thank you."

She shook her head. "That wasn't important. He was like all children who don't want something fun to end."

"Well, he's here now and waiting to see you. I've informed Stefania."

"Thank you." Gabi stood up. "I'll go down."

"Keep me informed."

"Of course."

Fortunately, Gabi had worn her navy suit with a lighter blue collared blouse to work and felt presentable. She stopped in the conference room for her purse and waved to Luisa, who knew about her visit to Dino. Once outside in the hall, she brushed her hair and put on a fresh coat of pink frost lipstick before she made her way downstairs to the reception room.

People doing business or needing information came to the foundation throughout the day. Gabi looked around at the half-dozen visitors until she saw Dino, who slid off the chair but didn't run to her.

Seated next to him had to be his father, who got to his feet. He was tall and fit, with black hair and blue eyes that matched his son's. The thirtyish male who'd once won an Olympic gold medal for Italy's ski team was beyond gorgeous despite the telltale lines of grief.

She took a quick breath and walked the short distance to them. "*Benvenuto*, Dino! What a wonderful surprise! Here I thought you were at school this morning."

He looked so solemn. "I asked Papà to drive me here. I'm sorry about yesterday."

Gabi smiled. "I'm not. I had such a great time and didn't want to go back to work. I felt just like you did."

A half smile broke out on his face. "So…you're not mad at me?"

"What do you think?"

A huge smile broke out on his face. Over his dark head her eyes fused with his father's.

"Dino?" the man asked in a deep voice that penetrated her body. "Aren't you going to introduce us?"

His son looked at both of them. "Gabi? This is my *papà*."

CHAPTER THREE

GABI CHUCKLED. "SINCE you two look like each other, I figured he has to be your father. I'm delighted to meet you, Signor Berettini."

The CEO of the Berettini empire had dressed in a charcoal-colored suit with a gray pullover and probably had to shave twice a day. No man's looks or masculine aura had ever given her such a visceral reaction.

Amusement lurked in his eyes fringed with sooty black lashes. He took her breath. "After hearing about Gabi this and Gabi that, I've been the one anxious to meet you," he said, shaking her hand.

She felt the contact zap through her like a bolt of lightning. His blue gaze traveled over her as if he were trying to piece everything together using his son's assessment of her. In truth she'd been doing the same thing to him and hoped to heaven it didn't show.

She looked down at Dino. "Edda told me you wanted to spend the day with me. Guess what? She gave me permission to leave."

"*Evviva!* Do you know where we should go?"

"Since I've lived here all my life, I have a lot of ideas. One of my favorite places is the insect museum in Brusegana."

"Insect—" His reaction was comical.

"That's right. When I was in school, we took a field trip there. I thought it would be stupid until we arrived on the bus. Was I ever wrong! It's a few kilometers from the center of the city."

"Does it have real insects in it?"

"Thousands! Of course, most of them are dead, thank goodness." His father laughed. "It's an amazing museum, Dino. Maybe we could eat lunch at Da-Pretta's first. It's only a few blocks away. They do fast food and make the most delicious bacon and potato *panzerottos.*

"Afterward we'll drive to Brusegana and spend part of the day there. If you want, we can watch a movie about insects while we're at the museum and buy something in the book shop to add to your collection of books in your family room. I never saw so many. You'll love visiting there!"

His face lit up with excitement. "Papà? Have you been there?"

He shook his dark head. "It'll be a new experience for me, too." His gaze focused on her again, and she felt an instant awareness of him that went deep beneath the surface. "Are you ready to leave?" She nodded. "Then let's go."

Gabi followed them out to the parking area, where he headed for a fabulous dark red Lancia luxury passenger car. While Dino climbed in the backseat and strapped himself in, his father helped Gabi in the front passenger seat. She felt his gaze on her legs as she swung them inside.

His interest was that of any normal male, but she hadn't been with a man in two years. If she was going to be this affected by his every look and touch, maybe she'd made a mistake in not accepting dates from guys since her divorce. But Luca Berettini wasn't just any man.

She'd heard of the expression *coup de foudre*, love at first sight. Gabi had never believed in such a thing, but if it existed she feared it had happened to her.

When they stopped to eat and find a table, she'd noticed every female in sight, young or old, staring at Dino's striking father and eyeing her with envy for being in his company. She needed to get herself in hand and concentrate on his son. Before long they were served and Dino seemed to like his food.

In a few minutes one of the male servers who was probably Gabi's age left the counter to walk over to them. He stood by Luca. "Excuse me for interrupting, but I know you're Luca Berettini. I saw you win the gold medal in the downhill when I was sixteen. I can't believe you just walked in here. Would you let me take a picture with my phone? My friends won't believe it."

Gabi saw a clouded expression enter Luca's eyes. "I'd rather you didn't."

The guy nodded. "Excuse me, then. But I have to tell you that seeing you has made my day."

When the man walked off, Gabi looked at Luca through shuttered eyes. "I imagine that must happen to you often."

"More than I'd like. If I were alone, it would be different, but not when I'm with my son."

"I would feel the same way," she said in a quiet voice. Every mention of skiing had to be a reminder of Dino's suffering and what his life had once been like before the avalanche. "Luckily he's enjoying his food and didn't seem to pick up on anything."

He darted a glance at Dino. "These *panzerottos* are a definite hit and have provided the needed distraction."

"I've loved them forever. What are your favorite dishes?" Gabi found herself wanting to know everything about him.

His eyes played over her with a definite gleam. "Pizza *patate*."

"Potatoes on pizza. I've never tried it."

"It's the specialty of a place near my work."

She smiled at him. "You mean you don't have your secretary bring in fabulous meals for you every day?"

"Afraid not. I can hardly wait to get out of there and go home to eat. But sometimes I have to stay longer, and a pizza *patate* helps get me through the rest of the long cruel hours."

"I see." Gabi drank the last of her coffee. "Are you telling me you don't like being the CEO of one of the most famous companies in Italy?"

"Would it shock you if I told you it's the last place I want to be?"

Gabi averted her eyes. "Actually it wouldn't, not when you've had something so serious on your mind for the last two years."

He shook his dark head. "That's not the only reason. Before I was forced to take over for my father, I'd been building my own skis and boots manufacturing business. I still run it on the side and have little interest in my family's company. I'm afraid I never will. One day soon when my father is able to take over again, I'll walk away and not look back."

That sounded final. Gabi wiped her mouth with a napkin. She couldn't help but wonder about the history behind it and how his father felt about that, but it was none of her business.

Luca put some bills on the table. "That was delicious."

"I want to come here again," Dino replied.

"Maybe we will. Shall we drive to Brusegana now?"

Dino got up from the table. Luca helped Gabi and they left for his car. It had been a long time since she'd been anywhere with a man, and never with one as appealing as Dino's striking father.

When she'd come to work this morning, she couldn't have imagined his driving to the foundation with his son in order to thank her and give Dino a chance to apologize, let alone spend the day with her. The whole situation had caught her completely off guard.

After a short drive, they pulled in the parking lot of the museum. Luca had a devastating smile. Her pulse raced when he used it on her. "This ought to be interesting."

"I hope so," she said in a slightly breathless voice.

From the moment they walked inside the doors, the three of them were mesmerized by the hundreds of insect displays. For the next hour Dino ran from one to another, marveling over the varieties and colors.

"Gabi—look at this big black one with the orange stripes! Ew. I'd hate to meet that in the forest."

"It's probably pretty harmless."

"How about the sculpture of this giant cicada standing upright?" his father called out. They hurried over to look at it. "He could be a soldier."

The large statues of insects were something new since the last time she'd been here. "I'm thankful they don't grow that huge in real life."

"Except in the movies," Luca murmured.

She chuckled. "I'm afraid I paid a lot of money to watch them in my youth."

"So has the whole world." Their eyes met in mutual amusement.

"You mean you liked them, too?"

The corner of his compelling mouth curved upward. "They were the best films to take a girl to."

His surprising sense of humor got to her. What girl wouldn't have wanted to go anywhere with him, even a scary show? Every time she looked at him now, her body quivered in reaction.

Dino hurried along to inspect the butterflies. There were hundreds of them.

"I like the black one with the green spokes from Africa. It's my favorite."

After Gabi had taken a picture with her phone, his father said, "Let's go in the theater now. They'll be starting a movie in a few minutes."

Somehow she ended up sitting next to Luca at the very back of the auditorium with his son on his other side. Judging by the oohs and aahs coming from the audience, the film engrossed everyone watching, but no one more so than Dino.

"First the food was a huge hit, now the museum," Luca whispered. She felt his warm breath against her cheek. More delicious sensations traveled through her body.

Though she agreed with his assessment, right now

she couldn't concentrate on anything except being next to this exciting man. "I thought he'd like it."

"You've made his day. Are you sure you weren't a schoolteacher instead of an employee working at a boring bank job in another life?"

Gabi laughed gently. "I'm going to have to be careful around Dino. He doesn't miss a trick."

"I figure I've heard about your whole life story already. At least the parts you chose to share with him. I guess you know you've made a big impression on him."

She smiled. "He's a very sweet boy. You're so lucky to have him."

"He's my life." The tone in his voice spoke volumes about the love he had for his son.

"Of course he is." But before she could say more, the lights went on because the show was over and Dino expressed a desire to visit the bookstore.

He wanted the big two-feet-by-two-feet colored picture book on insects. Who wouldn't? But Luca walked him around to look at other books just to make certain it was the best one so he wouldn't change his mind. Gabi admired his patience and thoughtful concern.

After they went out to the car, he climbed in back and started poring through the book that would give him hours of pleasure.

She glanced at his father. "See that *gelateria* on the corner? Let's stop and get one, shall we? I'd like to pay for it."

"You're reading my mind, but it will be my treat. For you to have come up with an outing like this means more to me than you know." Once again his voice penetrated to her insides. So did his words that touched her on a deeper level. He parked outside the shop. "Do you have a preference?"

"Any fruit gelato with *panna*." She loved whipping cream.

"I like *fondente* with *panna*, Papà."

Gabi grinned and looked over her shoulder at him. "You like chocolate, eh?"

"Si." He was still concentrating on the pictures.

She eyed his father, who smiled at her before he said, "I'll be right back."

"I wish we didn't have to go home," Dino admitted after Luca left the car. "I wish—" he began, then stopped.

"You wish what, *piccolo*?"

"That you could be with me when I have my operation."

With those heartfelt words, Gabi had trouble not falling apart. "It's funny about wishes. Sometimes they come true. When I was young, I had a group of friends and we wished on a star for a friend who was very sick. And guess what? She got well. You never know."

"How do you do that?"

"At night you look up in the sky, find a star and make a wish."

"I'm going to do that tonight."

Just then Luca returned and handed her a peach concoction.

Their fingers touched, igniting her senses. Could he tell how the contact affected her? What was wrong with her? "Thank you."

"Prego."

It seemed he was a chocolate lover like his son.

Soon they were all enjoying their treat. She eyed his father. "The *panna* on yours looks delicious."

"Papà loves *zabaglione*."

Gabi didn't realize Dino had been listening, and it took her by surprise.

His father darted her a lighthearted glance. "Marsala wine–flavored *panna* is a weakness of mine. You'll have to try it another time."

Maybe when she went out for lunch with Luisa. But she couldn't imagine there'd be another time with Luca Berettini or his son. She pondered that thought all the way back to the parking lot behind the foundation building.

Today's outing had proved that it wouldn't be wise to get any more involved with Dino's father. She'd enjoyed being with him too much. After Santos, she was afraid to get too close to another man again and be hurt. Luca was already an unforgettable man, bigger than life. Something told her that if she were to fall in love with a man like him, she'd never get over it. The possibility of that happening shook her.

Again something had to be wrong with her to even be thinking this way when the Berettini family was facing a huge ordeal in a few weeks. Luca's fear for his son was all that mattered to him.

Gabi had done her part and knew for a fact Luca would never have come to Padova if it hadn't been for her visit on behalf of the foundation. How foolish of her to believe Luca could be romantically interested in her that way. The sooner she got out of the car, the better.

Edda had asked Gabi to follow through on the foundation's commitment to Dino. She'd done everything possible she could. Now she needed to walk away before the attraction to his father and his boy became so great, she couldn't.

After he turned off the engine, she undid her seat belt and looked around at Dino, who had a hold on her emotions. "I'm so glad you came to my work today. I had the best time with you."

"Me, too," he said, but he didn't look up and continued to turn the pages of the book.

"You're the smartest boy I know, and I bet you'll finish your building blocks game by the end of the week."

No response.

"I'll keep you in my prayers. I want you to know you'll always have a friend at the Start with a Wish foundation. Now I have to go in."

She grabbed her purse. In that fleeting moment her gaze met his father's. For the first time all day they were filled with undeniable pain, all of it because of his son. She knew her pain for Dino was reflected in hers, too.

Today had been a lovely moment out of time, but it was over. She opened the door and hurried to the building entrance, but she'd left her heart behind with that child and...heaven forbid, Luca Berettini.

The day had been heavenly for Dino, but unsettling for Luca, who'd been far too aware of Gabi while they'd walked around the museum...connecting. With Catarina's death he'd buried his heart, or so he'd thought. Yet everything about Gabi had brought out feelings he didn't want to experience again. To care for a woman after all this time, to fall in love and then lose her would be too terrible to contemplate. Luca couldn't deal with that.

But as he'd watched Gabi disappear into the building after they'd dropped her off, he'd felt a strange sense of loss that had nothing to do with his son's pain. Luca had been out to dinner with several women since his wife's death, trying to get back to some kind of normal existence. But the nightmare that had taken Catarina's life had left him empty.

Until today...

While he tried to put Gabi out of his mind, the journey back to his villa in Maniago turned out to be the drive from hell. Pure silence accompanied him all the way home. Dino had kept his promise to his father not to cry or protest when they had to say goodbye to her. He'd been a model of obedience. No pleading. No tantrums. That had been the bargain they'd made before they'd ever left the villa.

She lived in another city and had an important job to do. She'd brought his son a gift from the foundation and had shown him unparalleled kindness in answer to his letter, but that was all Dino could expect. That's what he'd told him.

Now his son wasn't talking to him, causing Luca to relive the events of the day in his mind. To his astonishment, he'd found himself enjoying the outing with the beautiful blonde Signora Parisi more than he would have imagined. Her engaging personality had a seductive power that had ensnared his son from the moment he'd first met her. Luca had seen him reach for Gabi's hand several times throughout the day.

But it was in the movie at the museum he'd felt a pull on his emotions that had shocked him. It had been a long time since he'd shared one of those moments that had made him wish he'd known a woman like Gabi in his teens. She had a unique sense of fun, yet showed amazing compassion for his son's fears.

Edda Romano knew what she was doing when she'd hired Gabi to work for her. Gabi had a vivacious quality. When she walked in a room, a light went on, something he hadn't thought could possibly be ignited inside his soul again. Now it seemed Luca himself hadn't escaped the special magic that was as natural to her as breathing.

When they arrived at the villa, Dino carried his book into the family room and put it on the table, ignoring Luca. Ines came in to announce dinner, but his son wanted to show her the book first.

"What amazing pictures! Where did you get it?"

With that question, all the information you could ever want came pouring out of Dino. "Gabi took us to the insect museum in Padova."

"I didn't know there was one."

"Gabi went to it when she was in school. We even saw insects and blue butterflies from Africa!" It had been another connection to Catarina, who'd promised that one day the three of them would go on safari. Dino talked all the way through their meal. Then it was time for his bath and bed.

Tonight Luca took over the duties. But after Dino had said his prayers, he darted over to the window and looked out at the night sky.

"What are you doing, *figlio*?"

"Nothing."

"Then come get in bed."

Dino ran back and climbed under the covers. He

looked up at Luca. "Thanks for taking me to see Gabi. I had the best time of my whole life."

More than everything else in his whole life?

Luca swallowed hard. "I enjoyed it, too."

"I wish she lived in Maniago so I could see her every day," he said with tears in his voice. "When I'm with her, I have so much fun and… I'm not as afraid to have the operation. But I know she can't come every day." He half moaned the words.

Oh, Dino. Luca's heart lurched. His son's attachment for Gabi went beyond the superficial. Dino was crazy about her.

"*Buona notte*, Papà." The last was smothered as Dino turned away and buried his face in the pillow.

After turning off the light, Luca disappeared down the hall to his own suite of rooms, aware of a new burden weighing him down. Dino's mother wouldn't be coming back, but Gabi Parisi was alive and living in a city not that far away. No one was more aware of that than Luca, who would like nothing more than to see her again tomorrow.

The woman was beautiful, feminine. During the film in the darkened room, he'd found himself wanting to taste her mouth. They'd sat close enough that it would have been so easy for him to move close enough to kiss her. It had been over two years since Luca had made love to his wife. Today it stunned him that his feelings for Gabi were so strong.

Luca had sensed she was aware of him, too. There were certain signs he'd noticed when their bodies or fingers had brushed against each other by accident, or when she'd thanked him, sounding a little breathless.

There was no doubt she'd made an impact on Dino

that wasn't going to go away. Judging from the way she reacted to his son, Gabi had showed him genuine interest and attention. So much so that by the weekend, Dino had become more taciturn than Luca had ever seen him.

He showed no excitement at the hockey match and had stopped working on the project left on the table. The impending operation had to be responsible for part of that behavior, but not all of it. His son wanted to see Gabi again. So did Luca, who was pained by the effort Dino made not to mention her name.

When Luca's mother came over on Sunday for dinner, he didn't want to talk about the outing to Padova. It was too painful for his son. The weekend had been hard on Luca, too.

After he drove his son to school on Monday morning, he had every intention of going to work. But when he reached the highway, something made him turn around and head for Padova. En route he phoned and made an appointment to talk to Edda Romano. As soon as he arrived at the foundation, he was shown upstairs to her office.

"Thank you for seeing me so quickly. I know how busy you are."

She smiled. "Never too busy when this involves your son, who is facing a difficult ordeal. How soon is his operation?"

"December twenty-first."

"I see. What can I do for you?"

"You've already done everything humanly possible, and I'm deeply grateful. Since you hired Signora Parisi, you have to know she brought sunshine into Dino's life. He had a wonderful time with her last

Wednesday and wants to see her again. I realize that wasn't something any of us could have predicted."

"Are you asking my permission for her to spend more time with Dino?"

"After hours, yes. But only if it doesn't break your rules."

"Of course it doesn't! The person you need to ask is Signora Parisi herself."

"But I don't want to make her uncomfortable. Would you be willing to ask her to meet me in the reception room downstairs?"

"Of course."

"Bene, signor. Arrivederci."

Luca left her office with trepidation and went downstairs to wait. Gabi might not want any more contact with him for her own personal reasons. He didn't want her to feel obligated. If she wasn't interested in getting to know him better, that would be the end of it.

CHAPTER FOUR

"GABI?" STEFANIA HAD just returned from Edda's office. "Signor Berettini is downstairs in the reception area waiting for you."

She almost fell off her chair in shock. He was here? Gabi knew she wasn't dreaming. Just the mention of the man's name caused a small gasp to escape her throat. "Do you know what it's about?"

"I have no idea."

"I'll go now. Thanks."

She reached for her purse and hurried downstairs, embarrassingly breathless when he saw her coming and walked toward her. Darn if her heart didn't leap at the sight of him. "Signor Berettini—" Her hand went to her throat. "Has something happened to Dino?"

"Only that he's missing you and wishes he could see you again."

"You mean it?" she cried softly, giving herself away. "I'd love to see him again, too. He's a wonderful boy!" And so was his father.

"He feels the same way about you. Why don't we go out for a cappuccino and plan something? I've already checked with Edda."

"I'd like that."

"If you're ready."

She nodded and he walked her out to his car. He was wearing navy trousers and a crew neck matching sweater. With his hard-muscled physique, he looked magnificent in anything.

She really couldn't believe this was happening. Adrenaline kept her pulse racing. "Where are we going?"

"I thought we'd visit the James Bond Bar at the Abano Grand Hotel for the fun of it."

Fun. When had she ever had fun like this? "I've heard about it but have never been there."

Gabi felt like she was floating. For the rest of last week, she'd wondered if there was something wrong with her because she'd been reliving the day with Dino and his father to the exclusion of all else.

She'd wanted to do something like it again, but had given up hope such a thing would happen. In fact, there'd been moments when she'd wanted to call Dino's grandmother and find out how he was doing, but she hadn't dared. Now because of his father's visit to the foundation, Gabi was going to see him again and spend this beautiful morning with Luca.

Her heart pounded crazily while he walked her into the bar, famous for the selection of cocktails created as a tribute to the famous 007. But when the waiter came over to their table, Luca ordered cappuccinos and croissants. "Unless you'd like a martini, shaken but not stirred."

Gabi laughed gently. "Not this early, in fact hardly ever."

"My feelings exactly."

"Not even while you were winning medals at ski races?"

"Especially not then. You have to keep your wits."

She studied his arresting features. "I admire you for that."

He winked at her. "The nondrinking, or the racing?"

"Both, if you want to know."

"Would it surprise you to know that if you hadn't agreed to come with me this morning, I was virtually at my wit's end?"

All of a sudden their conversation had taken a downturn. She took a bite of croissant. "Why is that?"

"Dino hasn't been the same since our outing. I'm afraid that's my fault. I told him that when we said goodbye to you at the museum, I didn't want there to be any tantrums."

"That's why he was so quiet on the drive home."

"Dino only speaks when spoken to now and has suffered another headache."

"Oh, no!"

"It's all right. He would have had the headache no matter what had happened. But he's so unhappy, I had to see you again. I figured that if you turned me down this morning, I wouldn't be able to cope any longer."

The honesty of this father gave her insight into his torment. Gabi was thrilled, not only because his son missed her so much, which was very touching, but to realize that Luca had driven all this way to be with her in person when a phone call would have sufficed. Her instincts told her Luca wanted her company, and not just for Dino's sake.

"I have an idea. I could get off early from work

tomorrow and drive to Maniago. Depending on the traffic I could be there close to six."

She heard his sharp intake of breath. "We'll be waiting for you when you drive up to the house, and we'll go out for a meal. How does that sound to you?"

"I'll love it."

"Do you have a preference?"

"No. I like surprises, just like this one."

"So do I, and you're one of them. *Grazie, signora*," he said with what sounded like heartfelt sincerity. She knew Dino's father was relieved. Since their outing, she'd dreamed about being with him to the point she'd been thinking about him all day long, too. Gabi had even wished on a star in order to see him again.

"My name is Gabi."

She heard his low chuckle. It sent curls of warmth through her. "Don't I know it! When you came to our home last week, Dino never stopped saying it."

"The joys of fatherhood."

"It has its moments."

Gabi envied him, no matter how much pain he was in. "I'll see you tomorrow. In case I haven't said so before now, I'm glad you talked to Edda this morning. She's very understanding of Dino. I can't wait to see him again. Now I'd better get back to work, *signor*."

"Luca, please."

"Luca it is."

He put some bills on the table, and they left the hotel to reach his car. Christmas decorations were everywhere. For a minute, as she walked with the man who had a stranglehold on her heart, she could dream she was in the middle of the winter season Dino was building. When they reached her office and said goodbye, Gabi was so excited for the next day, she knew she wouldn't close her eyes all night.

After work that evening, she walked over to the worktable in her bedroom and pulled down her four-teen-by-eighteen sketch pad from the shelf. Since the visit to the museum, Gabi had been making a draw-ing of the black-and-green butterfly Dino had loved from her phone photo, not knowing when there'd be an opportunity to give it to him.

Now she needed to color it with the pastels to make it come to life. She'd already signed it "Gabi," and had written the date they'd gone to the museum beneath it. Tomorrow she'd buy a frame with clear glass on her lunch hour and mount the drawing. When she saw Dino later, this would be her personal gift to him. She couldn't wait to surprise him!

In truth, Gabi couldn't wait to be with Luca again either.

Luca told Ines and their cook, Pia, that he and Dino would be eating out. He'd debated whether to tell his son the news early. In the end he decided it would be much more exciting for him to walk out the front door and discover Gabi parked in the drive.

At ten to six Luca went to the family room and shut off the TV. "Come on, Dino. We're leaving. Grab your jacket."

"Where are we going?"

"Out to dinner."

"I don't want to go anywhere."

"You'll change your mind when you find out who's going with us." He left the room and started down the hall to the foyer.

"But we were with my *nonni* last night. Is it Signorina Gilbert? I heard them talking about her. I don't want you to marry her."

Luca was furious at his father for talking about it in front of Dino, who picked up on everything. "I'd never marry her."

"Promise?"

"I swear it. This is a happy surprise. Now let's go." He opened the front door and headed for his car in the dark. Dino followed him and climbed in the back, fastening his seat belt. Luca got behind the wheel and backed out to the street, where he pulled the car to the side. "Why are we stopping?"

"You'll see."

A minute later he saw headlights in his rearview mirror and waited for Gabi to park behind him. That's when he turned to Dino. "Why don't you get out and see who pulled up? She's come to have dinner with us."

Dino got out of the car. Luca followed.

"Gabi?" Even in the dark he could tell his son's countenance had completely changed. *"Evviva!"*

Luca watched his son hug Gabi around the waist. In that revealing moment she hugged him back. Her feelings for his son were just as strong. He knew he'd done the right thing to bring them together.

"Look, Papà! She's brought me another present."

Another Christmas-wrapped package. "I can see that." There were too many of them. "I'll put it in the car."

Before long they were settled in the Lancia and Luca drove them down to the town. Dino talked his head off answering her questions. When they stopped for pizza and salad, Luca carried her gift inside so Dino could open it.

His son had told him that Gabi had wanted to go to art school. But he had no idea how talented she was until Dino pulled the wrapping away and the butterfly from Africa appeared in all its glory. While an astonished Luca stared at it, Dino went into ecstasy.

"I love it, Gabi. I'm going to hang it over my bed."

"I'm glad you like it, *tesoro*." Gabi had used the endearment so naturally, she sounded like any mother with her child. Luca was so deeply touched, he couldn't say anything for a minute, but it didn't matter. The two of them were engrossed talking about what he'd learned in school earlier in the day.

While Dino left the table long enough to use the restroom, Luca eyed the gorgeous woman who had been on his mind day and night. "Quick, before he comes back, would you be willing to spend the coming weekend with us?

"We have a guest bedroom that will be yours while you're there. I realize you probably have other plans, but I confess that I don't want to try and get through another weekend without you." After being with Gabi at the bar and again tonight, Luca couldn't wait to get to know her better. In fact, he needed to be with her so badly he could taste it.

A stillness surrounded her. He could tell he'd taken her by surprise. Before she could answer him, Dino came running back. "Can we go home and play a game now?"

Luca put some bills on the table. "I'm afraid Gabi has to get back home."

The time had passed too fast.

As they walked out of the pizzeria and left for home, Luca's frustration grew because he was aware she still faced the hour-and-a-half drive back to Padova. It wasn't fair to her to come such a long way for such a short period of time. Worse, she hadn't answered his question.

After pulling behind her car, he kept his headlights on and started to get out of the car to help her. But she'd undone her seat belt and had turned to Dino.

"Guess what? Your *papà* has invited me to come spend this weekend with you."

Dino undid his seat belt and sat forward. "He did?"

Gabi shot Luca a glance before she said, "Yes! I think it would be fun. On Saturday we could go get a Christmas tree and decorate it. I saw some for sale in the town while I was driving through. What do you think?"

"A real tree?"

"How about it, Papà?" she asked Luca. "Maybe after we're through, we can go Christmas shopping and walk around the town eating our heads off."

"Can you stay at our house all night?"

"Yes, she can," Luca spoke up before she could answer Dino. "On Sunday we'll put a new puzzle together and work on your Christmas scene."

"Do we have to wait until Saturday?"

She leaned over the seat and ruffled his hair. "I have to work, but we can talk to each other on the computer. You're supposed to be learning your computer skills for school, right? Tomorrow you can send me an email and tell me what you learned in class. When I get home, I'll write you back. How does that sound?"

"I'll send you a whole bunch of stuff."

"Wonderful! Now I'd better get going."

They walked her to her car. Luca opened the door for her. "Thank you for driving all this way. Be careful going home."

Her eyes lifted to his. "I promise I will. We've got Saturday to look forward to."

Indeed they did. She wouldn't have agreed to come if she didn't want to. Luca would be counting the hours. The next time they were together, he intended to get her alone. He could hardly think about anything else.

They waved goodbye.

Life would be different this week now that his son knew he'd be seeing Gabi again. The rest of Luca's workweek would be different, too. He'd manage to get through it now because in the next few days she'd be with them.

Dino carried his framed butterfly inside. After his bath and prayers, he got in his bed. Luca gathered what he needed to hang it above him. Trust his son to put his pillow on the other end so he could look up at her artwork. "She's *molto bello*, Papà."

Yes, Gabi was awesome. "Don't forget to get under your covers."

"I won't. Tomorrow will you help me send her an email? I want to surprise her."

"Si, figlio mio. Dormi bene."

As he walked out of the bedroom he heard him say, "I wish she lived in Maniago."

Luca smiled. His son would beat a daily trail to Gabi's door no matter how he had to do it.

As for himself, Luca didn't dare say what he wished for, but it was a given he wouldn't be far behind his son. If he could have his heart's desire, he'd hold her in his arms and kiss her senseless. Gabi was in his blood.

Emails flew back and forth for the rest of the week. Dino mentioned his friend Paolo many times. With his father's permission, he'd talked Gabi into coming on Friday evening and staying until Sunday afternoon. That would give them more time to do all the plans he had in mind.

But Gabi suffered an emotional panic attack when she realized how strongly attached she was to Dino. In her love for him and the ordeal he was facing, it had made her vulnerable. Though she refused to believe that anything could go wrong during the operation, a part of her wondered how she would handle it if she had to suffer another loss in her life.

And what about his father? She could hardly breathe when she was around him now. It frightened her that Luca had become so important to her in such a short amount of time. What if he wasn't interested in her? What in heaven's name was she doing allowing herself to get close to him?

On Friday after work, Gabi's mother walked her out to the car. "What's wrong, honey?"

"The truth is, I'm concerned because Dino is growing more dependent on me, but I can't help it."

"Of course you can't. This goes deep with you. The divorce so early in your marriage didn't give you time to try and have another baby. I certainly understand the appeal of this boy who has opened up his heart to you. He's responding to you like you're his *mamma*."

Gabi nodded. "I know you must be worried, too.

I'm wondering what's going to happen after he has the operation, but I don't have an answer."

"I know you love him."

"Anyone would," she murmured.

"I think you're crazy about his father, too."

She hid her face in her hands. Her mother knew her through and through.

"Signor Berettini is a pretty irresistible force. I know of his reputation and have seen pictures of him in the media."

"There's no one like him and… I'm hugely attracted to him. That's my dilemma. I know he's doing whatever it takes to help his son get through this frightening time. The letter Dino sent wanting a miracle brought the three of us together, but after the operation I have no idea what things will be like. Any interest Luca has in me is connected with Dino. I wish I knew how to distance myself from his father."

"No one knows that. You're going to have to take all this on faith."

"You're right," she whispered.

"Go and enjoy this special time. Remember you're helping Dino and his father prepare for the operation. Be part of the miracle."

She nodded, not wanting to risk more pain in her life, but no human could avoid it. She hugged her mother through the open window. "Love you to pieces. Stay safe. We'll keep in touch throughout the weekend."

On the trip to Maniago, Gabi went over their conversation in her mind. She had witnessed several miracles in her life. By the time she reached the house, she'd made up her mind to take her mother's advice.

Be part of the miracle. One of the ways Gabi could do it was to be as happy and upbeat as possible to get rid of the sadness pervading the villa.

When she pulled up in front of the entrance, Dino came running out the doors. "Gabi—" he called to her and opened the rear door to reach for her suitcase. "I've been waiting for you!"

She smiled. "Hi, *piccolino*! I came as fast as I could."

While getting out, she noticed Luca's powerful silhouette outlined by the foyer lights. The sight of him caused a fluttery feeling in her chest. He caught up with Dino. Together the three of them went inside.

"Dino? Will you take my suitcase in the family room?"

"Yup." He took off.

Luca's blue eyes played over her. "We're glad you arrived here safely."

"So am I. Thank you."

Everything he said and did excited her. It wasn't something she could prevent. In the letter, Dino had talked about his father never being happy. Gabi would do whatever she could to erase those grief lines.

"Why didn't you let me take your suitcase upstairs?"

"Because I have a couple of presents to give out first."

"For me?" Dino had reappeared.

"What do you think?" Gabi teased. She walked to the family room and opened the suitcase. Inside she reached for two gaily wrapped gifts. "You'll have to open these at your own peril."

He eyed Luca, who stood nearby with his hands on

his hips in a totally striking masculine stance. "What does she mean?" Dino was so cute.

His father's lips twitched. "I think she's brought something that will surprise you. Why don't you open the package with the Christmas elves first?"

Dino reached for it and took off the paper. He held up the box with the cellophane top. When he realized what it was, he stared at Gabi in shock. "These are chocolate-covered *insects*!"

"That's right. Worms and crickets. They're nummy. Did you know one cricket gives you more protein and amino acids than a serving of fish or beef?"

Luca's head reared and he let out a deep, rich laugh that resonated in the whole room.

"Have you ever eaten one?" came Dino's earnest question.

"Sure. I'll eat one of your crickets now." He handed Gabi the box. She lifted off the lid and put one in her mouth.

Dino looked horrified. "What does it taste like?"

"Chocolate."

He giggled nervously before looking at his father. "Are you going to eat one, too?"

Luca flashed her a smile before he reached for a worm. He put it in his mouth and munched. "Gabi is right. It tastes like chocolate."

"Did you know that two billion people in the world eat insects as part of their diet? The most common are beetles, wasps, bees and caterpillars."

He frowned. "I don't think I want to try one."

"That's all right. Why don't you open your other gift?"

"Okay." But he wasn't nearly as enthusiastic.

"I brought you a pack of twenty treats in blueberry, grape, orange and strawberry flavors so you can give one to every student in your class."

"Um… *Suckers!*" He pulled one out. "What's that in the center?"

"A cricket."

Once again his father roared with laughter.

"Oh." Dino thought about it and put it back in the box.

"Aren't you going to thank her for the gifts?"

"*Si*, Papà."

Gabi decided to take pity on Dino. She drew one more present out of her suitcase and handed it to him. Luca just shook his head. She grinned. "I think you'll like this better."

After removing the paper, he took off the lid and smelled the contents. "Chocolate *bocci* balls! *Evviva!*" In the next minute he'd eaten two of them before hugging her. "Thanks for everything."

"You're welcome."

"I promise I'll try an insect pretty soon."

"You don't have to eat one if you don't want to, but you can have a lot of fun with your friends at school. You could give one to your teacher and see if she'll eat it in front of the class."

He thought about it. "I bet she won't."

"What about Paolo?"

"I don't think he'll want to eat one."

"You never know," his father said, winking at Gabi. "Shall we go upstairs and show you where you're going to sleep?"

"That would be lovely."

Dino grabbed her hand while Luca carried her suitcase. The stunning guest bedroom in peach colors was an absolute dream. They agreed to meet downstairs in ten minutes to play a game before Dino had to go to bed.

Gabi took advantage of the time to freshen up. From the bedroom window the lights of the town looked like fairyland. Dino had been born into a very special household. But rich or poor, he had a father who doted on him, and there was no greater blessing. She applied more lipstick and ran a brush through her hair before going back down to the family room.

"Come over to the table, Gabi. We're going to play *guardie e lardri.*"

She'd loved cops and robbers when she'd been little.

"I haven't played that in years. Is Ines going to play with us?"

Luca shook his head. "She and Pia have the next two days off."

A delicious shiver ran down Gabi's spine. The three of them would be alone.

"We'll guard the treasure and fight Papà."

Gabi made a face. "How sad for him because we're not going to let him get near it!"

Her comment brought a gleam to Luca's eye while Dino laughed. They played for an hour, but in the end his father proved to be an indomitable opponent. She smiled at Dino. "Even if your *papà* beat us this time, we'll do a rematch tomorrow night and win!"

Luca eyed her with a devilish grin. "We'll see about that. Now it's time for bed."

"Not yet," Dino protested.

"Afraid so, but we'll have all day tomorrow to have fun."

"I know. Gabi? Will you come up while I go to bed?"

"Of course."

"Leave all your chocolates down here, son."

"*Si*, Papà."

She followed Dino out of the room and up the stairs to his bedroom. Hers was farther down the hall. The first thing she saw when she walked in was her butterfly hanging over his headboard.

"Papà put your picture right there."

"So I see."

"I look at it every night."

She couldn't believe the thrill it gave her. Dino lived in a room made for a boy with signs of hockey equipment and several large posters of hockey and soccer heroes. "I'll brush my teeth and be right back."

"I'll be waiting." While he was in the bathroom she studied the small framed photos of his family. The consequences of that avalanche had changed their lives forever. Through unimagined circumstances, it was changing hers, too.

Dino came out a minute later wearing Harry Potter pajamas and knelt down at the side of the bed. "I love my *papà* and my *nonna*, and Maria and Tomaso. Please bless Ines and Pia."

Gabi noticed Dino didn't ask for a blessing on his grandfather. Something was wrong there. She'd sensed there was a problem when Luca had told her about taking over for his father at work.

"Please bless me not to be scared of my operation. Please bless Gabi that she'll never leave. Amen."

CHAPTER FIVE

NEVER LEAVE. ONE OF the wishes that lay at the heart of Gabi's turmoil.

"Amen," sounded the vibrant voice of Dino's father, who'd walked over to the other side of the bed to hug him.

Gabi waited until Dino had climbed under the covers, fighting the instinct not to kiss him. "Get a good night's sleep, Dino. We have a big day planned tomorrow. *Buona notte*," she said to both of them. Without looking at Luca, she exited the room.

Once past the door, she hurried to the guest bedroom to get ready for bed. But before getting out a nightgown and toiletries from her suitcase, she was drawn to the huge window to look up at the sky. It had been a glorious day, and an even more magnificent night. The cold made the canopy of stars twinkle, creating a magical scene. While she stood there mesmerized, she heard a knock on the door. "Dino?"

"No. It's Luca. I need to talk to you for a moment."

Her pulse suddenly sped up. "Come in."

Dino's virile father walked in and approached her, still wearing the white pullover and gray trousers from earlier. This close to him, she could smell the soap he'd used in the shower.

Yes, she'd been married to a good-looking man, but it was no use pretending Luca wasn't the most attractive male she'd ever seen or known in her life, physically and otherwise. With the contrast of his black hair and brilliant blue eyes, Luisa would call him the hunkiest man alive, and she'd be right.

For days now Gabi had been telling herself it was Dino she was crazy about. But as she studied his father's hard-boned features and the five o'clock shadow on his chiseled jaw, she couldn't lie to herself any longer. The two men, one young and one in the prime of his life, had pulled her into their gravity field. There was no escape because she knew she was desperately in love.

"Is everything all right?"

"Yes, but I couldn't talk to you the way I wanted around Dino."

"You think he's asleep now?"

"I'm sure of it. He had a big day."

She nodded and looked up at the sky again. "The view from this window is incredible."

"You're right."

"The stars are so bright, you feel like you could reach up and pull one down. It's a Christmas sky. As you're here, how would you like to wish on a star with me for Dino?"

He studied her features. "I've never tried it."

"When I was around twelve, one of my close friends almost died from a burst appendix. Our group decided to get together and wish on a star to make her better. Within twenty-four hours, we heard from her mother that she'd started to get well. It was like a miracle. I want one for Dino."

"Let's do it," he said in a husky voice.

Gabi took a moment to say a silent prayer, the kind she'd uttered years ago with a child's faith.

Star light, star bright. First star I see tonight. Send your light to help Dino not be afraid of his operation.

When she'd finished and looked at Luca, he was still making his wish. What a gorgeous man he was.

When he opened his eyes, the two of them stared at each other for a long moment. Luca rubbed the back of his neck, as if he didn't know what to say next. She knew it was very unlike the charismatic man who ran a business empire. His rare show of vulnerability tugged at her emotions.

"There's no way to tell you how thankful I am that you're here," he began. "Losing his mother changed Dino. I can't get him back, yet he's a different child when you're with us. I know you didn't expect anything like this to happen when you answered his letter with a personal visit and gift. I guess that's what I wanted to say before you went to bed."

Gabi had to silence a moan. When she'd heard him say that he couldn't get his son back, she'd detected his pain. "Surely you know your son worships the ground you walk on, Luca."

He folded his arms across his chest. "I know he loves me, but there are times when I don't seem to be able to reach him."

She took a quick breath. "Maybe it's a case that he feels he can't reach you."

A frown marred his striking features. "What do you mean?"

Gabi couldn't let him go on thinking he'd lost touch with his son even if she'd promised Giustina she wouldn't say anything.

"I wouldn't have missed this experience for anything in the world, Luca. Dino is a dear boy with that childlike faith that makes the world a better place for simply being around him. Now I'm going to tell you something you don't know about the letter he sent to the foundation. I've decided you need to hear everything right now."

He blinked. "I don't understand."

"Then I'll explain. Your mother didn't tell you the whole content of the letter. In fact, she decided she wouldn't tell you until after the operation was over. Maybe not even then because she was afraid it might hurt you too much to know what has been in Dino's heart."

A haunted look crept into his eyes. "Why? Don't keep me in suspense."

"I memorized Dino's letter. He wrote, 'Every night I tell God I'm afraid to have the operation because my *mamma* died and won't be with me. But if it will take away my headaches and make my *papà* happy again, I'll do it. He's never happy and I love him more than anyone in the entire world."

With those words, there was silence followed by a transformation that came over Luca. Tears entered his fabulous blue eyes. She put a hand on his arm.

"Yes, he loved his mother and will miss her forever. But you've always had your son. Don't you see? He's praying for a miracle that will make *you* happy again. That's more important to him than anything else. I don't know of a child who could love his father more than Dino loves you. You needed to know that."

He shook his head. "All this time he's been worried about *my* unhappiness?"

She nodded. "He's your son and has your kind of compassion. That makes you both unique in this world."

A sigh sounded deep in his throat. "You always manage to say the right thing at the right time with a touching sensitivity that speaks to me."

In the next breath he cupped her face in his hands and lowered his mouth to hers. Gabi moaned as their bodies came together and they began kissing each other, one after another until she stopped counting.

Soon she lost track of time and got lost in his arms, never wanting to be anywhere else. The things his mouth was doing to her filled her with the kind of rapture she'd never known or imagined. When he finally lifted his head for air, she didn't want to let him go. But he had more willpower than she did and removed his hands. His breathing had grown shallow.

"The last thing I want to do is walk away from you tonight, but you're a guest in my home and it's time to say good-night. You'll never know what the revelation about that letter has done for me. *Dormi bene, bellissima.*"

The way he'd said *bellissima* melted her bones. Gabi felt new energy radiate from him as he strode to the other wing of the villa on his long, powerful legs. She shut the door and got ready for bed. Once she'd pulled the covers over her, she buried her face in the pillow. This time tears of joy trickled out of the corners of her eyes. Being part of the miracle was a wonderful thing.

* * *

Luca got up early Saturday morning a new man, but he didn't know how he'd had the strength of will not to take Gabi to bed last night. Her breathtaking response to his lovemaking had swept him away.

He stood under the shower reliving those moments in her arms. Before the day was out, he'd get her to himself again because he needed her like he needed the sun on his face.

After pulling on jeans and a sweater, he hurried downstairs to fix breakfast for the three of them. Last night he'd slept better than he'd done since the avalanche. Like an omen, the sun had come out.

He checked the calendar on his watch. Two weeks from today Dino would undergo his operation. *Grazie a Dio* that time would be here before they knew it. Throughout the lead-up, Gabi would be here for his son to cling to.

When Dino walked in the kitchen wearing pants and a pullover, Luca plucked him from the floor and gave him a huge hug.

"*Whoa.* Papà."

Luca chuckled. "Sorry. I was just happy to see you." No sign of a headache or nightmare with Gabi here.

His son smiled at him. "Me, too." He kissed his cheek before Luca put him down. "I thought Gabi would be down, but I guess she's still in bed."

"I'm sure she is, *polpetto mio.* She works long, hard hours every day, and last night she had to drive all this way after work."

"How soon can I go up and get her?"

"Give me time to cook the frittatas first, then you

can knock on her door and tell her we're ready to eat. Why don't you set the table?"

Dino got busy. "Do you think she likes apple juice?" He pulled the bottle out of the fridge and put it on the table with three glasses.

"I don't know. Maybe at home she likes beetle juice."

"She wouldn't drink that!" He made a gagging sound.

"What wouldn't I drink?" sounded a familiar female voice. Gabi walked in the kitchen wearing a Christmas-red sweater and black wool pants. Between the feminine mold of her body and her tousled ash-blond hair, Luca could hardly take his eyes off her.

Dino ran over to her and gave her a hug around the waist. "Beetle juice."

"That's one of my favorites, but only on picnics," she teased him. "In the mornings I love apple juice." Her gaze flew to Luca. "I didn't know you were a chef as well as a boss."

His son giggled. "He's not a chef. You're funny, Gabi."

"He looks like one to me."

"Let's hope you approve of my efforts. Breakfast is ready," he announced and put their plates of food on the table.

"Mmm. It smells wonderful." They all sat down. "Does your *papà* cook like this for you every morning?"

"Hardly ever. That's because you're happy today, huh, Papà?"

"You'd better believe it."

Luca trapped her gaze while silent words passed between them. Clearly she'd identified the key to keep Dino on an even keel while they got through the countdown. His son ate with a big appetite. Things couldn't be better. "What do you want to do first today?"

"Can we go get a tree, Papà, and lots of lights?"

"We'll do it. After that we'll have lunch and go to a movie."

"And tonight we'll set it up in the living room! This is going to be the best day of my life!"

He smiled to himself. Whenever the three of them were together, his son said it was the best day of his life. What was even more true was that every day she was with him and Dino, it was the best day of Luca's.

"Since your father made such a delicious breakfast, what do you say we do the dishes? Come on. While you clear the table, I'll put everything in the dishwasher."

Dino jumped up and started to help.

Luca darted her a speaking glance. "I can see I'm superfluous around here, so I'll make sure everything is locked up tight."

Before long they walked out to the car and left for town like any family out for a fun Saturday together. But they needed to bundle up because the temperature had fallen during the night. Before the day was out, Luca predicted snow.

For the moment it felt like they were a real family. Which was a huge problem for Luca, who was having trouble remembering Gabi wasn't his wife or Dino's mother.

Last night after wishing on a star, Gabi had told him everything that had been in his son's letter. The truth of it had helped him see the situation through clear eyes. Being with her last night had also aroused the kind of desire he hadn't felt since before the avalanche. After losing Catarina, he hadn't thought it possible to feel it again.

Gabi had to know he wanted her. There'd been no doubt about it last night. But only time would reveal where both their feelings were leading. She'd brought happiness to his son for the first time in two years, and Dino's needs had to come first right now. It meant Luca had to show some restraint around her. He hadn't mistaken emotions of gratitude for desire, but he needed to take a step back.

In two weeks Dino would have his operation. No one knew how it was all going to turn out. Luca couldn't allow anything to upset the balance of a precarious situation. The only solution for now was to show some discretion with Gabi.

"Look up the street, Papà! There are the Christmas trees Gabi saw."

Luca had seen them among all the holiday decorations and noticed a sign that said the trees could be delivered. Since Dino wanted a big tree, that would solve a problem for taking one home with them. Once they'd picked out the Noble fir they all loved, his son was disappointed they would have to wait until five in the evening for the tree to arrive at the house.

Gabi squeezed his shoulder. "That tree is so big, it would stick out on both ends of your father's car and bump into the ones in front and behind it." Dino's giggle made Luca laugh. "But if you want, we could buy a baby tree instead that would fit right on top. What do you think?"

His son pondered her question. "No. I want the big one. I guess I'll have to wait."

She kissed his cheek. "Hey—we'll be gone most

of the day. When we get home, the tree will arrive. Right?"

"Right!"

Crisis averted, all because of Gabi, who was an original and handled his son with all the clever inspiration of a mother. Luca had never planned to replace Catarina. And then this amazing woman had come along...

They walked around buying Christmas presents at the Christmas market with all the wooden huts selling their crafts. There was a life-size nativity scene with real animals Dino loved. After a while they went to a children's Christmas movie and then headed home just as snow started to fall. Dino put his head back and let the flakes melt on his tongue. They all did the same thing during an outing of pure joy.

By the time the tree arrived and the deliverymen had set it up in a corner of the living room, the Berettini villa looked like Christmas had already come.

While they'd been in town, Gabi had never had so much fun and had picked out half a dozen pots of red flowers to decorate the house. With Luca's help, they draped garlands of greenery over the fireplace, the doorways of the main floor, even the magnificent grandfather clock in another corner of the living room.

After he'd strung the lights and put the glittering star at the top of the tree, Luca went out to the kitchen to make them sandwiches and hot chocolate.

Gabi in turn started putting on the ornaments while Dino hung the elves he'd personally picked out with their funny faces. "Where are your old ornaments, *piccolino*? Do you want to get some of them out?"

"We never had a tree before."

"Oh! I didn't realize."

"I'm glad Papà got us one."

"So am I." Gabi knew a lot of families who didn't put up a tree, but she'd always wanted one and her parents had gone along with her wishes. When she'd mentioned getting a tree in front of Dino, Luca hadn't said a word against it.

He eventually came in the room and put on some Christmas music while they ate and wrapped the nutcrackers Dino had picked out to give for his Christmas presents to everyone. After they'd placed the gifts under the tree, they put the crèche together.

Gabi had spent her own money buying them a nativity scene for an early Christmas present. She wanted to help Dino put it together on the coffee table before he went to bed. He seemed delighted over it.

"It's funny to think of Jesus being a baby."

Gabi smiled at Dino's down-bent head as he lay it in the manger. "I agree it's hard to realize he started out his life just like all of us. When I think of my father, I can't imagine him a baby," she murmured as she put a lamb near the crèche.

"Nonna has a picture of Papà when he was a day old. He had a dress on."

How Gabi would love to see it! "My grandmother had a baby picture of my father. He was in a dress, too."

They both laughed.

"Mamma didn't put one on *me*, huh, Papà."

"No. You were wearing a hospital gown in the nursery."

Gabi wanted to see everything, but stopped short

of saying as much in case it was too sensitive a subject. Needing to change the direction of conversation, she rose to her feet. "What a mess we've made!" She started cleaning up and took the tray out to the kitchen.

Luca went for the vacuum, and soon the room looked perfect. Gabi stood behind Dino with her arms around his neck while they admired their surroundings. "In one day we've transformed this room into Babbo Natale's workshop. I think we're pretty good elves."

"Me, too. I can't wait for Paolo to come over so I can give him the skinny Red King wooden nutcracker. He'll laugh his head off."

"I'm sure he will." Gabi leaned over and kissed the top of his head. "Do you know I'm anxious to meet him? Maybe he can visit some time and help us finish your building blocks project. You can offer him a treat."

Dino turned around and looked up at her with shining eyes. "Do you think he'll eat one of my chocolate-covered insects?"

"Hmm." She cocked her head. "He's your friend. You know him better than I do."

Luca walked over and picked him up. "Why don't you dare him, and see what happens? While you're thinking about that, it's time to get ready for bed."

"I don't want to go up yet."

"But *we* do. We're exhausted."

Dino jerked his head toward Gabi. "Are you tired?"

"I'm afraid I'm very tired," she lied. Luca's blue eyes thanked her.

"Tutto bene." He'd caved, but he didn't sound happy about it.

Together they headed upstairs and went through Dino's nightly ritual until he'd said his prayers and had climbed under the covers. "How long are you going to stay tomorrow?"

Gabi had known that question was coming. "For as long as I can before I have to drive back. How does that sound?"

"Why do you have to work?"

She eyed Luca, feeling helpless. "Why does your father work?"

"He says it's so we can eat."

"Your *papà* is right. How else could I have bought those nummy insects for you? Just remember that one day you'll have to work so *you* can eat."

After a silence, "Gabi? I love you."

"I love you, too. Now go to sleep. I'll see you in the morning."

"I love you, too, Papà."

She watched Luca lean down and kiss his son before they left the bedroom and went back downstairs to the living room. The scent of the pine tree had already filled the air. Between all the decorations, Gabi felt like they'd walked into a Christmas wonderland. She sat down on the couch while he rearranged a couple of the elves that were too close together.

"Why did you buy a tree when you've never done it before?"

He turned around. "Dino lit up when you suggested it. Before the avalanche, we always spent our Christmas holidays at the chalet in Piancavallo so we could ski. With trees all around in the mountains, we didn't need one.

"As for the last two years, Dino and I have spent

Christmas at my parents' villa and have gone to mass with them. Naturally on the fifth and sixth of January we've celebrated Epiphany. Dino has put out his stocking for La Befana to fill with candy. He hasn't known anything different, but thanks to you a new tradition has been started."

"Because of me?"

"Yes. You answered his letter, and a whole new world of hope has opened up for him. Dino is like any child who will keep taking more and more. But this experience hasn't been fair to you because you know what's involved and I can see that it's almost impossible for you to say no to him about anything. That's my fault. I'm just as bad and I've selfishly allowed and urged it."

"No, Luca. Not selfishly. You've lived for the last two years not wanting to say no to him. I don't know how you've handled everything. In the short time I've known him, I can tell you I've wanted to be here for him every bit as much. When Edda asked me if I would like to take him a gift, I leaped at the chance."

"I'm thankful you did. Dino's not the only one happy that you've come into his life, but you already know that."

"The feeling's mutual." She could hear her voice throb. "Would it be possible for me to see a video of Dino's famous *papà* winning the gold medal? Dino says it's in the family room. I'd love to see you doing the sport you love so much. I know I heard about you winning when I was around sixteen."

"You don't want to see that."

"I do. Please—" She stared into his eyes.

"Then come with me."

Filled with excitement, she followed him through the villa to the family room and sat down on the couch while he found the disc and put it in the machine.

Then he joined her and put his arm around her shoulders. For the next fifteen minutes she watched in utter disbelief to see him in the start house waiting for the signal. Then he flew down that mountain with unmatchable skill and beat every other competitor's time.

He'd been drop-dead gorgeous at twenty-two, but ten years later he was even more attractive. His white devastating smile combined with his bronzed olive complexion melted her to the core. As he accepted the gold medal to the accompaniment of the Italian national anthem, tears came to her eyes and melted her to the core of her being.

She turned to him. "How absolutely fabulous, Luca. I'm so proud of you. Don't tell me it wasn't the most exciting moment of your entire life!"

"One of them," he confessed.

"I saw your mother hugging you after. Where was your father?"

"He didn't come because he hated my love of skiing."

Her eyes closed tightly for a moment. "I can't comprehend that."

"It doesn't matter."

Oh, Luca. "Of course it does. When I think of my father… He was so wonderful to me. Last night I told you about one miracle that happened to my friend after we wished on a star. But I experienced an even greater miracle when I was seven. My father was going to die, so I talked to the priest and asked him to ask God to make him better. The priest told me to go home and ask God myself.

"I was very upset by this, but I did what he said. Only two days after I prayed to God to help my dying father, he started to get better and lived until three years ago. It was a great miracle."

"Those are experiences you'll never forget in your whole life. As far as I'm concerned, your coming to the villa to see Dino has constituted another one. Especially being here with me tonight."

He lowered his head and started kissing her again. Gabi feared getting more involved with this unforgettable man. The awful possibility that his feelings for her might not last caused her to pull away from him. "I can't do this, Luca."

She stood up, afraid to look him in the eyes. "On the drive here yesterday, I determined to help any way I can. Until he's had the operation, I'll avail myself as much as possible to help make him secure. Edda knows the situation and will give me the time off I need. But to get any more involved with you right now—"

"We *are* involved," he said in a grating voice and got to his feet. "But for the time being, we'll concentrate on Dino. To know you'll be there for him through the surgery will help him and save my sanity."

"You can count on me, Luca. I wouldn't be anywhere else. What I'm going to do is have a talk with Edda when I get back to work on Monday morning. Maybe midweek, say Wednesday, I could be here when Dino gets home from school."

"He'll be thrilled."

"If you made arrangements for Paolo to come home

with him, we could have a fun day and evening. It would give Dino something to look forward to. How would you feel about that?"

"I'll contact Paolo's parents as soon as you get permission from Edda. Even if he can't come, Dino will be overjoyed to see you before next weekend."

"As soon as I know on Monday, I'll call you."

He stood there with his powerful legs slightly apart. "There are no words to thank you, Gabi."

She got to her feet. "You don't have to thank me. Dino is a blessing in my life, too. If I can play any part in answering your son's prayer, nothing could make me happier."

"Where did you come from?" he asked quietly.

"I've found myself asking the same question about you. One day I'd love to hear how Luca Berettini became all the things he is, but not tonight. I can see you're exhausted. *Buona notte.*"

CHAPTER SIX

LUCA WONDERED IF he was dreaming when he heard, "Papà?" He turned over and opened his eyes. No. He hadn't been dreaming. Had Dino awakened with a nightmare? Here he'd just told Gabi his son had been free of them for the last few days.

He shot up in bed. "What's wrong?"

"Nothing. I just wanted you to get up and show me how to stuff a *corneto* with jam for Gabi's breakfast and serve her in bed. I'm afraid I'll make a mess. Can you fix her cappuccino, too?"

Relief washed over him in waves. "You want to bring it upstairs to her room?"

"*Si.* Paolo's *mamma* is going to have a baby and his *papà* took her breakfast in bed."

"I see." Luca chuckled. "What kind of jam did you have in mind?"

"*Frutti di bosco.*"

"Tell you what. Let's both get dressed, then we'll hurry down to the kitchen and get busy."

"*Fantastico!*"

Within a half hour, they arrived at her door with a tray. Luca held it while Dino knocked. "Gabi? Are you awake?"

"Yes."

"Can I come in?"

"Of course!"

"My *papà* is with me."

"Oh—"

Luca smiled.

"Just a second, Dino."

His son looked up at him while they waited.

"You can come in now."

Dino opened the door. Luca's gaze focused on the gorgeous woman who'd just come out of the bathroom in bare feet wearing a knee-length pale blue robe. She didn't need makeup. He loved her tousled hair.

"*Buongiorno, signora.* We've brought your breakfast I made myself. I mean… I made part of it."

"You did all this for me?" Dino nodded. "Well, aren't I the luckiest person on the planet. *Grazie.*"

"*Prego.* Where would you like us to put it?"

"Right over there on the table in front of the window. We can all eat together and enjoy the view. I'll pull up the dressing table chair so there are seats for the three of us."

Luca couldn't stop staring at her. "Dino wanted to surprise you."

"It's the best surprise I ever had. This *corneto* is superb. You say you made it yourself?"

"I didn't cook it. Papà showed me how to put the jam in the middle."

"Well, you did a perfect job and it's absolutely delicious. I'm totally impressed. What did I do to deserve having breakfast served in my room?"

Luca could tell his son had something specific on his mind, but he had no idea what it was.

"I think we should talk about a new job for you."

Both she and Luca choked on their coffee and reached for a napkin from the tray. "A *new* one?" she murmured.

"*Si.* I know you have to work, so I wish you could be my new *mamma.*"

Luca wasn't at all surprised. Out of the mouths of babes...

Gabi said, "You already have Ines. But I can come to see you whenever possible."

"But if you were my *mamma*, you'd live right here."

"True, but Edda has hired me to work for her. I couldn't just leave her."

His expression sobered. "Wouldn't you rather be my *mamma* than work for her?"

Before Luca could try to salvage the situation, she said, "I tell you what. I'll have a talk with her about taking a vacation so I can be with you more."

"You will?"

"Yes."

"*Evviva.*"

Gabi was a master psychologist. Without promising Dino anything, she'd bought some time. But knowing his son, Dino would plague her for an answer every time he was with her. While they were finishing their breakfast, Luca's cell phone rang. It was his mother, wanting to know if she and his father could come over. Luca told her he'd call her back in a few minutes and hung up. His son had just finished the last of his *corneto.*

"Dino? Your *nonni* wants to drop by for a visit."

He frowned. "You mean today?"

With that one word Luca already had his answer. "Yes."

"But Gabi's here and we're going to play. They'll probably stay a long time and she has to go back to Padova later."

His son had a point and Luca had no desire to see his father, who probably wouldn't be impressed by Dino's attachment to Gabi. "All right. We'll make it for another day. Right now, why don't we go downstairs so she can get dressed."

Dino brightened and stood up. "Don't take too long, Gabi. We'll be in the family room."

"I promise I'll hurry."

Luca put their plates and cups back on the tray and carried it out the door. Dino followed him after giving Gabi a hug, and they walked down to the kitchen. His son darted to the family room, giving Luca time to phone his mother and tell her that Dino wanted Gabi all to himself for the day.

"I never thought I'd see the day he'd become this close to another woman. Maria and Tomaso can't believe it either. When they call him, Gabi is all he talks about. It's like it happened overnight!" his mother exclaimed.

"She has a special way with her. It's why she works for the foundation."

"Your father's not pleased. He still wants you to meet up with Giselle."

"That's too bad. I have never been interested in Giselle. He needs to give up that fiction."

"I know you wanted nothing to do with her, but he can't seem to let it go and is upset about Gabi spending so much time with Dino."

"Well, I'm not. *Grazie al cielo* you sent his letter. Dino is so happy right now, Gabi is exactly what he needs leading up to the operation."

"But what's going to happen afterward? She has her own life to lead."

Luca closed his eyes for a moment. He knew what he wanted but kept his thoughts to himself. "I can't answer that. No one can. It's all I can do to hold it together for the next two weeks."

"I realize that. Let me know how I can help."

"You do it all the time, and I love you for it. I'll talk to you later." They hung up.

Luca especially couldn't control Dino, who had a strong mind and will of his own. His son was determined to keep Gabi close no matter how he manipulated to get his way. Luca's mother would be shocked if she'd heard Dino say he wanted Gabi for his mother. But he couldn't blame Dino for anything, not when Luca was already imagining Gabi in his life on a permanent basis.

On his way to the family room, Luca heard laughter. Gabi had kept her promise to get dressed fast. Already they were involved in some game. When he walked in, Dino ran up to him.

"Look what Gabi brought me! She has a collection of her favorite *Tex* comic books and says I can keep them for as long as I want. Come and read with us."

Luca hadn't thought Gabi could do anything else to enchant his son, but he'd been wrong. Their connection really was uncanny. His eyes shot to hers. They were a beautiful green with flecks of gold. Right now they revealed the depth of her emotions brought out by desires they were both having to hold in check.

The next time Luca got her alone…

After he took a deep breath, he said, "I think if we're going to read them, we should go in the living room. I'll light a fire and we'll get comfortable."

"I'll bring the snacks." Gabi picked up the box of chocolate insects.

Dino's expression crumpled, causing Luca's laughter to echo all the way through the villa. While his son lay on the floor poring over some of the comics for a little while, Gabi sat back on one end of the couch. Luca chose the other.

"Would you be willing to show me the new ski boots and skis you've designed?"

Luca flashed Gabi a wicked grin, reminding her of last night when they couldn't get enough of each other. "I'd rather see some more of your sketches. I know Edda needs you, but wouldn't it be exciting if you had a chance to go to art school and carve out a new career for yourself?"

"Of course it would."

Luca would have explored the possibility more, but then Dino wanted to put a puzzle together. Afterward they ate, then played another round of cops and robbers. Until the grandfather clock chimed the half hour, Luca forgot what it was like not to have a worry in the world.

Gabi lifted her head. "I can't believe it's three thirty already. I'm afraid I'm going to have to leave for Padova."

"Not yet," Dino protested.

"It's a long drive," Luca reminded him, hating for this to happen after such a glorious day.

"I don't want to go either, Dino, but it'll be dark

before I get home and I have a lot to do to get ready for work in the morning."

He jumped up. "You said you would talk to your boss."

She tousled his hair. "I will."

Luca groaned silently before darting her a glance. "Are you packed?"

"Yes."

"Then I'll bring your case down. Come and help me, Dino."

"While you do that, I'll clean up the living room and put everything back in the family room."

Anyone watching them would describe it as a scene of domestic bliss set on the cover of a Christmas card. But that would be without seeing the turmoil going on inside Luca, who couldn't bear to be parted from Gabi.

Gabi put on her coat while Dino insisted on carrying her case out to the car and putting it in the backseat. Some of the snow had melted, but not all. There'd be more coming in the next few days. Luca would give anything for Gabi not to have to drive in it.

She got inside behind the wheel and lowered the window when Luca and Dino walked around. "Thank you for the loveliest weekend I've ever had. Be good in school, Dino, and send me an email telling me what project you're working on this next week."

"I will. Let me know when you've talked to Edda."

Her eyes sent Luca a silent message. "I promise."

"Drive safely," he whispered. Suddenly the thought of anything happening to her filled him with such terror he could hardly breathe. A car accident on the black ice of the highway could end her life as fast as the avalanche that had buried Catarina. Even thinking about that possibility made him realize he'd fallen in love with Gabi.

After losing Catarina, the pain had been so terrible, he'd never wanted to care like that about another woman again. Yet here he was, frightened to lose this woman who'd become of vital importance to him in every way. He simply couldn't go through that kind of pain again.

"Text me when you get home so we can stop worrying."

She nodded.

"When you're on vacation, you won't have to drive from Padova." Dino never gave up. "You've got your own room at our villa and Pia will make all your food. Can your *mamma* drive?" Luca wasn't surprised at the question. His enterprising son worked all the angles.

"Si." She smiled at Luca.

"Then she can come and visit, can't she, Papà?"

"Of course."

"A piu' tardi," Gabi said before she started down the drive to the road leading into town.

Dino left his side on a run and dashed inside the villa. The only thing saving Luca was Gabi's promise to come midweek. He was already living for it.

Before Gabi had driven away, she'd seen anxiety in Luca's eyes. It matched hers. She knew he didn't like it that she had to drive so far, especially after it had snowed. The thought of an accident haunted her, too. Worse, they were both suffering from a new burden Dino had placed on her.

To her relief she got home safely. The second she

turned off the engine, she texted Luca. Almost immediately he texted back, thrilling her.

We miss you. I'm going to be as bad as Dino and remind you to get back to me when you can about plans for midweek.

She pressed a hand to her heart. That was all she'd been thinking about.

I'll text you tomorrow after my talk with Edda.

Don't write anything else, Gabi, or he's going to know you're head over heels in love with him.

Gabi dashed in the house. "Mamma?"

"Oh, good. You're home. I take it you had a wonderful time."

"You can't imagine."

"I think I can."

"I want to hear about your weekend with Angelina."

"Since you've been with Dino's dashing father for the weekend, I'm afraid anything I have to say isn't worth mentioning."

"That's not true!"

Her mother's laughter followed Gabi, who carried her suitcase down the hall to her bedroom. Before she did anything else, she sat down at her computer to send an email to Dino. She'd promised.

Wednesday morning Luca drove Dino to school and dropped him off. "I'll see you at one o'clock."

"Do you promise Gabi is coming this afternoon?"

"Do I have to? You read her email. She's excited to meet Paolo."

"But—"

"But what?"

"I don't know."

"Dino—she's coming! See you in a little while." His son climbed out of the rear seat and hurried inside the building with his backpack.

Luca sped to work, grateful there hadn't been fresh snow yet to become a hazard for Gabi. He would put in a few hours, needing to keep busy until he went back to the villa to welcome Gabi. She planned to be there by one thirty.

'Around eleven that morning, while he was dictating some letters to his secretary, he got a text from Gabi. At first his heart almost failed him. Until he read it.

I left Padova early. Will be at the villa by twelve thirty.

From that point on he was out of breath. After clearing his desk of work, he told his secretary he was leaving for the day and took off for Maniago. He'd planned for Gabi to stay overnight and drive back to Padova early Thursday morning for work. The cook had instructions to fix meals the boys would love.

Luca walked out the front entrance when he saw Gabi's car pull up the drive. She slid from the driver's seat wearing another long-sleeved sweater, this time in a bright blue with a navy skirt. With the fifty-eight-degree temperature, she obviously didn't feel the need to wear a coat. The silvery ash of her blond hair combined with her curvaceous figure robbed him of breath.

"You got here early!"

Her smile knocked him sideways. "Edda told me to leave. I was hoping I would be on time so I could go with you to pick up the boys. I'd love to see Dino's school."

"He'll be ecstatic when he finds out you're with me. Do you want to freshen up before we leave?"

"I'm fine."

"Then come and get in my car."

After she locked her car with the remote, he cupped her elbow and helped her in the Lancia. Before he started the engine, his gaze wandered over her. He loved the strawberry fragrance drifting from her hair. "I've read your emails with Dino, but I want to know how you've really been."

"Probably the same as you. Thank goodness we only have to hold out nine more days until he goes in the hospital."

He nodded. "Having Paolo come over has given him something new to think about."

"That's good."

"Paolo's parents will come and get him after dinner. Dino's happy about that because he doesn't want to share you with Paolo into the night." She let out a gentle laugh. "You think I'm kidding, but I'm not. I can't say I blame him. There's no act to follow you."

"Luca..."

"It's true. My whole household has undergone a distinct shift since Gabi Parisi arrived bearing gifts in answer to a certain letter."

Gabi's eyes filmed over. "My life has changed, too. You have to know that. He's the sweetest boy in the world. How lucky he is to have you for his father."

"Thank you," he whispered before pulling her to him. "I've missed you, Gabi."

"I've missed you, too."

He kissed her long and hard, unable to wait another second to feel her in his arms. But it was time to leave for the school before he forgot where they were and he started to devour her where anyone could see them. After letting her go, he turned on the engine and drove down to the road.

"You live in a virtual garden even though its winter."

"I love it and run along here most mornings at six."

"Does Dino ever join you?"

"He'll need the doctor's permission first because he doesn't want his head jarred. When that happens he'll probably keep up for about a block and then quit."

"He loves you so much. One day he'll be well again."

"I need to believe that." Needing more contact, Luca reached over and grasped her hand. "You give me hope anything is possible."

"That's because it is. Try not to dwell on what will happen after the tumor is removed." She squeezed his hand before letting it go, leaving him bereft.

Before long they entered the town. Luca drove to the piazza with the fountain and parked on the east side. Dino's school building was one of several surrounding it.

"This must be a fun place for the children to enjoy."

"The school uses it for parades and plays. The rest of the time it's a playground." He shut off the engine and turned toward her. They still had a few minutes before Dino came out. Luca craved every second he could be alone with her and studied her profile.

Her gaze darted to him. She couldn't keep his eyes off him either. "Have you always lived in Maniago?"

"I was born and raised here."

"What about Dino's mother?"

Oddly enough any questions about her didn't bother him anymore. Naturally Gabi wanted, needed, to know about her in order to have normal conversations with Dino.

"Sorry, Luca. I—"

"Don't be sorry," he broke in on her. "Ask me anything you want. It doesn't hurt me to talk about her. In fact, I think it's good that we do. We both know Dino is afraid to have the operation because Catarina isn't here. But if he wants to talk about her, he should feel free to do so and so should you."

She nodded. "Was Catarina from Maniago, too?"

"No. Venice."

"That city is one of my favorite places to explore and sketch. I drive there when I can, often with my mother. Does Dino love it, too?"

"I haven't taken him there since the avalanche. In the beginning, it pained me too much to consider making the trip."

"Of course it would." Gabi eyed him intently. "Does Dino have grandparents there on his mother's side?"

"No. Catarina's parents died when she was in her teens, so her aunt and uncle Maria and Tomaso Guardino raised her along with their own two children. He works for our company and commutes from Venice. That's how I met Catarina. They've come to visit Dino many times. He enjoys them both."

"So *they're* the couple I've seen in some of the little photos in Dino's room."

He nodded.

"I can't imagine losing Dino's mother the way you did," she said.

"It was horrific, but what would have made it worse was to lose Dino, too."

She shook her head. "Was there no warning?"

"Yes. A crack, like the loudest thunder you've ever heard in your life. It shook the ground and reverberated throughout the entire valley. I knew what it meant because I'd lived through several avalanches both in France and Austria.

"In an instant I picked up Dino and shouted to Catarina that we had to get off the mountain now. But we still couldn't move out of the way fast enough. This one came shooting down with the speed of sound and swallowed everything before you could even think. We were buried alive and I had to swim through it, trying to hold on to Dino.

"The ski patrol had to dig down through ten feet to find my wife's body. I'd swum near the top of the cascading snow with Dino in order to ride it out. There was no way I could have found her."

Gabi shuddered. "No wonder he has nightmares."

"He's not the only one."

She reached out to touch his arm. "Edda heard about it on the news and said Dino got injured."

"That's right. Somehow the tip of my ski pole punctured his scalp."

"Oh, Luca—I can't believe it."

"Neither could I. You probably know the rest. The wound healed, but the X-rays they took showed a tumor of all things and another nightmare began. The doctor felt it best to wait for an operation until he turned seven."

She shook her head. "I don't know why some people are forced to live through so much tragedy. I can't comprehend it. Edda told me it made the world news for days, but that was at the time when I was going through a divorce and wasn't aware of anything else."

"Which is understandable."

"There are degrees of pain, Luca. Yours has to be the worst. I'm so sorry for what happened to you. Your poor families. All the agony and suffering you've gone through while you've been waiting for Dino to have the operation."

He covered her hand still touching his arm. "You've been through agony, too. My friend Giles, a ski buddy, got divorced recently. He said it's worse than death."

"It felt that way to me, too, at first, but no longer."

"Ever since Dino told me you'd been married, I've wanted to ask you about it, but we haven't had time alone to talk like this before now. My son would monopolize your time every second if he could. Half the time I have to fight to get a word in."

She laughed.

"He said you'd wanted children."

"I did. What I didn't tell him was that I had a miscarriage before I learned Santos had been unfaithful to me."

"*Gabi*—" He reached across the seat to cup her neck. "I had no idea."

"We'd only been married ten months, but it didn't matter. I filed for divorce and moved back with my mother."

"You've had so much pain with his betrayal, I don't know how you've survived it. I want to hear more, but if you look out the window right now, you'll see our time is up because it appears school has ended."

Luca had been so involved in their conversation, the boys had almost reached them without his being aware of anything. Quickly he levered himself from the driver's seat. But Dino only had eyes for their visitor.

"Gabi—"

She got out and was almost knocked over by the hug he gave her. "I thought I'd come and surprise you. This must be Paolo."

"Buongiorno, signora."

Dino's friend, who was an inch shorter with chestnut-colored hair, was on his best behavior for the moment, but he could get rambunctious. His mother must have had a talk with him. Luca could only wonder how long it would last.

"It's so nice to meet you, Paolo. I've heard you're a good swimmer. I can't wait to watch both of you in the water one day."

Trust Gabi to say something to make everyone feel better. There was no one like her.

"Papà says I swim like a tadpole."

"That wouldn't surprise me, Dino."

Luca put a hand on their shoulders. "What do you say we get in the car and go home for lunch."

"Cook is making us pizza!" Dino announced as they drove home.

Gabi looked over her shoulder. "We have some special snacks for Paolo, don't we, Dino?"

Luca started to chuckle. He couldn't help it.

Nonstop commentary continued from the backseat

to the villa. Once Dino dragged Gabi's suitcase into the house, they all headed for the bathroom to wash up. Then they sat down at the table to eat.

Halfway through the meal Luca's phone rang. He'd told his secretary not to call unless it was an emergency. Maybe it was his mother. When he checked the caller ID, it surprised him to see that Dr. Meuller was phoning. For some reason it unnerved him. The neurosurgeon was supposed to be in Kenya right now.

Luca looked at Gabi, who eyed him with concern. "Excuse me. I've got to take this call, but I'll be right back."

After getting up from the table, he hurried into the living room and clicked On. "Dr. Meuller?"

"Hello, Luca. How is my patient?"

"Remarkably well all things considered." All of it due to Gabi.

"That's good news. I have some, too. My work here in Nairobi finished up sooner than I'd anticipated. What I'd like to do is move up Dino's operation a week. Would that be possible for you?"

His hand tightened on the phone. "You mean *this* coming Saturday?"

"This Friday actually. You'll have to be at the hospital by six in the morning."

That was the day after tomorrow!

CHAPTER SEVEN

"If that won't work for you, I understand. I haven't given you much notice."

"No, no. I'm thrilled with this news. The sooner you remove that tumor, the sooner my son won't get those headaches anymore. We'll be there Friday morning on the dot."

"Excellent. I'll make all the arrangements so the staff is ready for you when you check in."

"Thank you, Doctor. See you soon."

Luca hung up in a daze. After two years, the operation they'd been waiting for was really going to happen! He needed to inform his work that he was going to be out of the office for an unknown period of time. Before the day was out, Dino's teacher would have to be told he might not be back to school until after the new year. The doctor couldn't give him a timetable for a full recovery. Luca refused to believe Dino wouldn't be cured.

But most important of all, he had to tell Gabi what was happening and ask—beg her if necessary—to take the time off to be with them. Luca would call Edda Romano and explain why it was so vital Gabi had to be there for Dino. Luca couldn't imagine getting through this experience without her.

He knew it was a lot to ask. Too much. Luca realized it depended on how much she loved Dino. She *did* love him. Luca had seen it and felt it in a dozen ways.

After calling his mother, who would alert Maria and Tomaso that the timetable for the operation had changed, he phoned the school to leave a message with Dino's teacher. Once he'd hung up, he followed the children's excited voices to the family room. Gabi was playing charades with them, acting out a movie or book title. She exchanged a secret glance with Luca while he stood there and watched for a few minutes.

What would life be like a week from today? A month? He didn't have an answer for that. What he did know was that there would be a huge change and he had to be ready for it no matter what. If Gabi only knew she was the magic dust to help them navigate through the uncharted section of their universe.

They played a few more charades before she said, "You're both tied for first place! Dino? If you'll bring my suitcase in here, I have prizes to give out."

"Evviva!" He was off and back like a shot.

"Put it here on the couch."

The boys clustered around her as she opened the lid and pulled out two Christmas-wrapped boxes the size of a big game. They took up most of the suitcase. At this point, Luca's excitement to see what she'd brought them was greater than theirs.

Within seconds they'd ripped off the paper and out flew twin Roman gladiator outfits: brown tunics, arm shields, armor, swords, daggers, axes and helmets with red gladiator feathers on top. But there was more. Each box contained a bag of fifty small Roman soldiers so they could play war.

No doubt about it. She'd broken the bank with these gifts. Luca didn't need to remind his son to thank her.

Dino flung himself at her and clung. "*Ti amo*, Gabi." The love in his voice was so tangible, you could pick it up where it had dripped onto the area rug covering the slate tiles. Paolo lifted a beaming face to her. "*Grazie mille*, Gabi."

She gave them both a hug. "I want you to get dressed up so I can take your pictures." While they hustled to do her bidding, she pulled the phone out of her pocket and started snapping photos.

"Woo-hoo!" she cried out. "You guys look terrific. Why don't you run to the kitchen? Pia and Ines won't know who you are."

"Come on!" Dino called to Paolo, and they ran out of the family room holding their weapons.

She turned to Luca. "Now that they're gone for a minute, tell me what caused that sudden dark expression to break out on your face earlier."

Gabi didn't miss much. "It was Dr. Meuller."

Her eyes grew anxious. "Is something wrong?"

"No. But he has come home sooner than planned and is going to do the operation on Friday morning."

"*This* Friday?" she murmured, visibly shocked.

"It means he has to be there by six in the morning." He had trouble swallowing. "Gabi—"

"I know what you're going to say," she interrupted him. "For the operation to happen this soon instead of a week from now, naturally you're facing this moment you've been worrying sick over and now it's become real."

Grim lines broke out on his face. "Anything could go wrong. Dino's life could be altered. He might not be able to have the normal life I've wanted for him, or worse."

"Don't go there, Luca."

Without thinking what he was doing, he reached for her and pulled her into his arms, burying his face in her hair. "I can't do this without you."

She lifted her head and stared into his eyes. "You won't have to. Don't worry. I'll talk to Edda. She'll understand I have to be here for him. I want to be here for him and you. I love him."

"There's no doubt how he feels about you. His declaration moments ago said it all."

"He's so precious."

"So are you," Luca whispered against her lips before urging them apart. He needed this more than he needed air to breathe and started drinking from her mouth. He'd been waiting to know this kind of rapture again. Her passionate response only fueled his hunger. His world reeled as her body melted into his like she was made for him. He couldn't resist caressing her back and womanly hips, unable to get enough of this marvelous, giving woman.

Gabi must have heard the patter of feet before he did. By the time the boys burst into the family room, she'd eased herself away from him. But her breath was coming in short spurts and her lips looked swollen.

She could tell the shape he was in and had the presence of mind to start cleaning up the wrapping paper strewn over the rug. "Did you scare Ines?"

"No, but Pia screamed."

Both Luca and Gabi laughed. "Come on over to

the table and set up your army, *ragazzi*. Then we'll have a great war."

"*Sì!*" they shouted in a collective voice.

Luca decided she could have been the original Pied Piper. When they were all ready to play, she eyed Dino. "Why don't you give Paolo a snack."

Dino flashed her an impish grin that caught at Luca's heart. His son hurried over to the bookcase with the red feathers bobbing on the top of his helmet. Then he put the open box of chocolate insects next to his friend. A few were missing.

"*Cioccolato!*" Paolo bit into one of the worms. "Mmm. It's pretty good."

When he'd eaten it, Dino broke down laughing. "Look what he did, Papà."

Luca nodded. "Don't you think it's time you had one, too? Gabi was so nice to bring them."

"I know."

"Gladiators loved them," she teased. "But it doesn't matter if you don't want one."

To his surprise her gentle goading forced Dino to reach for a worm and eat it. There was nothing like a little peer pressure, too.

Gabi clapped. "*Bravo!*"

"Hey—that wasn't bad."

Thanks to Gabi, this was a great victory for Dino. Luca was proud of him and hoped it was a good omen to overcome his fear for the operation.

The boys settled down to a game of war, then everyone got busy finishing the building blocks project. This was followed by a game of cops and robbers. By then dinner was ready. After they'd eaten, Paolo's parents came to get him. Already it was dark out.

Everyone assembled at the front door. "I had the best time of my life!" he told his mother, still dressed in his costume.

No surprise there. He sounded just like Dino.

Paolo looked at Gabi. "Are you going to be here again?"

"Yes!" Dino answered for her. "*Ciao*, Paolo."

"*Ciao*, Dino. Thanks for the gladiator game, Gabi."

"You're so welcome. See you again soon."

"*Ciao*, Signor Berettini."

After Luca shut the door, they went back to the family room to clean up everything. Luca eyed his happy son, who was still dressed in his costume. It had been another perfect day. "Guess what?"

"I know. I have to get ready for bed." They started up the stairs. "I wish you didn't have to go back to Padova in the morning."

"We've had this discussion before, *figlio mio*. Come on. I'll run your bath."

Gabi took advantage of the time to freshen up in the guest bedroom. Then she called her mother to tell her about the change in plans for Dino.

"I need to phone Edda and tell her what's happened, but I think I'm just going to stay here until the operation is over. I've packed enough things to last me for a few days. It seems ridiculous to drive all the way home for more clothes just to come back again."

"I agree. While you're in Padova for the operation, you can drop by the house for anything else you need. If you want my opinion, this time change for the operation is a good thing."

"I know it is. Luca has been on a countdown for too long."

"The situation has been hard on you, too, darling."

"You can hardly compare two weeks of worry to two years." She let out a deep sigh. "Today he told me about the avalanche. It was so horrific, I don't know how he has functioned since. He's a remarkable man, Mamma."

She shared some of things she'd learned with her mother. "I'd love to talk longer, but I need to get in touch with Edda."

"Go ahead and call her. We'll stay in close touch."

"I love you. Thank you for always being there."

She hung up and phoned her boss. Edda answered and was absolutely wonderful about everything. "That child needs you to cling to. Your presence will represent all of us from the foundation. You know our prayers will be with him, his doctor, his father and everyone who loves him."

"Thank you, Edda. I'll say it again. You're a saint. *Buona notte.* I'll keep you posted around the clock."

Gabi got off the phone and was reduced to tears. The relief of knowing the operation was coming a week sooner had opened the floodgates. She loved Dino like he was her own son.

For so long she felt like she'd been walking on eggshells, trying to do the right thing, hoping she didn't say or do the wrong thing. And all the time she'd been falling hopelessly in love with Luca, who was facing an uncertain future once the operation was over. Gabi's future was uncertain, too. The fear of losing Luca once everything was over had grabbed hold of her.

After forcing herself to calm down, she went into

the bathroom once more to wash her face and brush her hair. Then she hurried down the hall to Dino's bedroom. The door was open. Luca sat on the side of the bed while his son knelt to finish saying his prayers. "…and please bless Edda that she'll let Gabi have a vacation."

After hearing his heartfelt plea, Gabi tiptoed in the room and sat down next to Luca, who put his arm around her waist, filling her with warmth. When Dino lifted his head, she said, "I just talked to Edda."

"You did?"

"Yes. She's giving me time off so I can spend it with you."

"When?"

"Starting right now."

He blinked. "For how long?"

Luca squeezed her side. "For as long as you need me."

"So you don't have to leave?"

"No. How does that sound?"

She could tell it was a lot for him to take in. He looked at his father. "What do you think, Papà?"

"I think it sounds wonderful."

"So do I!" He leaped to his feet and threw his arms around her neck.

Luca stood up. "You still have to go to school in the morning," he reminded him. "Come on. Climb under the covers."

Gabi smiled down at him. "I liked Paolo."

"More than me?"

"What do you mean, more than you?" She tickled him until he was laughing. "I couldn't love any boy the way I love you. Now it's time to go to sleep. See you in the morning."

"Promise you'll be here?"

She was beginning to realize what Luca had been living through for the last two years. Everything you said and did with Dino meant life and death to him because he'd seen his mother vanish before his very eyes, never to come back. It was not hard to understand Luca's burden. He had no idea what was going to happen once Dino came back from that operating room.

"I promise." She kissed his forehead and left the room.

Gabi knew she couldn't sleep yet, so she went downstairs to the living room. Luca followed her and stoked up the fire. Then he sat down on the couch next to her where they could feel its warmth.

She turned to him. "What kind of tumor does he have?"

"It's called an astrocytoma, a slow-growing, noncancerous tumor that is usually found in children from five to eight."

"I see. If there'd been no avalanche, how would you have known about the tumor?"

"He would have eventually manifested several symptoms, with headaches being the most obvious."

"What will his surgery be like?"

"The doctor said he'll perform a keyhole craniotomy. In other words, it's a minimally invasive surgical procedure. Dino is a good candidate for it because his skull-based tumor is in a good location.

"They go in behind the ear where there's little scarring. The doctor said there's less pain and a faster recovery time. The downside, of course, is the danger of disturbing tissue around it. The more precise he can be in removing it, the better."

"Has he given you an idea of how long Dino will be in the hospital?"

Luca rubbed the back of his neck, a gesture she'd seen once before at his most vulnerable. "If all goes well, he could be home in three days. Some children go right back to school if there are no complications. Others have to be watched for several weeks or months. The doctor said every case is different, but most children bounce back faster than adults."

"Then we'll just have to pray that happens. I'm not going to think about what could go wrong. That doesn't help any of us."

He stared at her. "One of these days Edda will know my gratitude for sharing you."

She smiled at him. "I talked to my mother, too. She's a nurse and will do anything she can to help. So—" Gabi put her hands on her knees, "I'm here to stay for as long as you believe Dino needs me around."

"How about for as long as *I* need you? When you're with me, I feel like I can cope."

"That's a very touching compliment, but it's also a huge responsibility. Will it help if I assure you I'm not going anywhere?"

"I'll take you any way I can get you."

She laughed, but with those words her heart had started to thud. He hadn't told her he loved her. What if he never did? How would she be able to bear it?

"In case you were wondering, I've enjoyed kissing you at every chance possible," he inserted, knowing exactly what was on her mind. "To be honest, I never wanted to stop. As for tonight, it was a good thing you heard the children beating a path back to the family room. So I'm giving you fair warning. You're in big trouble if you get too close to me."

Luca didn't know it, but he was in danger from her. "I'm not worried."

"For all the reasons that my son is crazy about you, it seems I, too, have developed a crush on this amazing woman from Padova. To think she has a fascination for chocolate-covered insects and an addiction to cartoon heroes like Tex Willer! Who would have thought?"

Loving this man as she did, there were things she wanted desperately to know about him. "For Dino to have loved his mother so much, she had to be a very remarkable woman. Was Catarina your first love?"

"My first *real* love? Yes. First attraction, no. From the age of twenty to twenty-five, I competed on the Italian national ski team and met a lot of women. After placing first and second at the Olympic trials, I made the Italian Olympic team. It wasn't until after I gave it up and went into the family business that I met Catarina."

"Was she a skier, too?"

"No. I tried to teach her, but she wasn't crazy about it. What about you? Have you ever done any skiing?"

"No. None at all. That probably sounds crazy to you, but I never had an opportunity. My friends didn't ski either. How many medals have you actually won?"

"I was only in the Olympics one year and brought home the gold medal for the downhill. But if you're talking about awards, I won a lot during the years I was on the Italian ski team."

"Where are they?"

"In storage."

"Your gold medal, too?"

"Yes." That explained why his son hadn't shown the medal to her by now. "I already sold the family chalet in Piancavallo so he never has to be reminded of what happened there."

Gabi could understand Luca avoiding the place where disaster had struck. Skiing hadn't been a part of life with his son since the avalanche. Maybe he'd train his son to be an Olympic swimmer.

While she was deep in thought, he got up from the couch and turned to her. "Do you know we never talk about you and your life? It's always about me. Are you still in so much pain over your divorce, you can't talk about it? Do you still love the man you married? Where is your ex-husband now? Is Parisi your married name, or your family name?"

She stood up. "Luca—we'll talk about me another time."

His eyes never left hers. "In ways, I feel I know you through Dino. He's dropped little pieces of information here and there. Just enough to tease me. Why didn't you pursue a career in art? Is that why you love Venice so much? Did you only own one dog? I'm planning to get Dino a dog after his operation.

"The more we're together, the more I realize I don't really know you at all or how you ended up working for Edda Romano. But what is evident is that my son has bonded with you, and I thank God you relieved him of a great worry tonight after he said his prayers. It also relieved me because I'm going to need you tomorrow when I tell him he has to go to the hospital on Friday."

Gabi nodded. "I've been thinking about that, too."

"Shall I bring it up tomorrow night at bedtime, or earlier? What does your intuition tell you?"

She paced the floor for a minute. "I should think the less time he has to worry about it, the better."

"Then we'll do it together before he says his prayers."

She wanted to wrap her arms around him and tell him everything was going to be all right, but a drawn expression had broken out on his handsome features, causing an ache in her heart. Now wasn't the right time.

"I'll go on up and see you in the morning. I hope you'll be able to get some sleep tonight."

"I doubt there'll be much sleep for either of us," his voice grated.

Gabi hurried out of the living room to the family room to get her suitcase and take it upstairs. She passed Dino's room but didn't hear a sound. It had to be a good sign he was asleep.

In a few minutes she climbed into bed, but her mind was reeling from all the questions Luca had raised about her, questions she never knew he wanted answered. He hadn't brought them up until tonight, but he was so distressed and preoccupied, she imagined he was on the phone right now, needing to talk to his mother. Gabi realized that Giustina had been the one he'd turned to in order to cope all this time.

She tossed and turned during the night. When morning came, she was glad to get up and dressed. After putting on jeans and a cream-colored crew neck sweater with push-up sleeves to the elbow, she reached for her purse and hurried downstairs. Gabi heard Dino's voice coming from the kitchen and headed there.

As soon as he saw her, he ran over to hug her. He was dressed for school in his smock. "*Buongiorno*, Dino!" She hugged him hard. By this time tomorrow, he'd be in the hospital having the operation.

He put his head back and looked up at her with shining eyes. "I'm so glad you're here."

"So am I." This was a moment she needed to remember.

After lifting her head, she smiled at the cook and Ines before sitting down. "What a beautiful day! From my bedroom window I saw that the sun is out with no clouds. I can't believe it."

"I wish I didn't have to go to school."

"But think about all your friends who will be excited to see you. Especially Paolo."

"Gabi's right," his father's deep voice filled the kitchen.

"I guess."

Luca had been out running and was still wearing his navy sweats. There ought to be a law against a man who looked like a black-haired god from Olympus running around this early in the morning. It could give a woman a heart attack.

He sat down next to Dino. "Pia has made us a feast in Gabi's honor. You need to finish your breakfast so we can drive you to school."

Luca started eating as if there wasn't anything in the world troubling him. That helped Gabi, who ate another roll with her cappuccino before they headed out to the car. Dino brought his backpack and got in the backseat. She could get used to this life so fast it was scary. That's what was worrying her.

"Will you both pick me up right after school?"

They'd stopped near the entrance. Gabi climbed out with Luca.

"What do you think?" He rubbed Dino's head. Gabi gave him another hug. "Where else would we be but right here?" Other kids were going inside. One of the girls waved to him.

"Who's that?" Gabi wanted to know.

"Filomena."

"Ah. She's cute. Maybe you should offer her one of the suckers in your backpack." Her suggestion produced a laugh that made his frown disappear.

"*A presto!*" Luca called to him.

When Dino had disappeared inside, they got back in the car. "Your son appears to be a normal Italian male. Already he's attracting the *ragazze*."

Luca laughed as they drove away from the piazza. To hear it warmed her heart. She noticed he hadn't taken the road back to the villa. "Where are we going?"

"Since you haven't been here before, I thought we'd take a drive through the hills to Tauriano. I'll show you my manufacturing plant where the skis and boots are made. It will give me time to hear more about your life. I want to know what the world was like for you in the beginning. We've got until one o'clock with nothing else to do."

"The beginning?"

"Yes. What was your legal name before you were married?"

"I was born Gabriella Russo. My childhood was idyllic. We lived in a small house in Limena on the outskirts of Padova. My father, Enrico, worked in business for the Constantini paper company."

"I know of it."

"My mother, Nadia, grew up in Padova and went to nursing school. Afterward she started work at a doctor's office where they met when Papà had to see the doctor."

"Was it love at first sight?"

She chuckled. "I think so. They got married fairly soon and moved into a little house. Before long I came along. There were lots of children in our neighborhood. We played all the time. I remember when one of my friends had some guinea pigs and we planned a marriage ceremony for them."

Luca laughed again and kept laughing as she told him her various antics. "As I told you earlier, when I was seven my father got sick with pneumonia and couldn't get better. I heard my mother tell her friend he might die. I loved him so much I was in agony. You know the rest. The priest told me to go home and ask for help myself. I got mad."

By now they'd reached the small town of Tauriano. Luca pulled in a lay-by that opened up into a fabulous view of the valley. He turned to her. "Why did you get mad?"

"Because I was afraid to do it myself, but somehow I found the courage."

"And history was written," he said in a soft voice.

Her eyes swam with tears. They always did that when she remembered what had transpired.

Luca pulled her over so she half lay against him. "I need to kiss you again, Gabi. You've become my addiction."

She responded with a hunger that surprised her because she'd been trying hard not to give in to her longings. But it was ridiculous to hold back, and he wouldn't let her anyway. They clung to each other, full of desire and the underlying emotions driving them.

"You're so beautiful," he murmured against her neck and throat. "You don't know what you do to me, what you mean to me."

"I feel the same way about you," she admitted. "In this whole world there's no one else like you."

Just as she'd said it, a car pulled into the lay-by behind them and some people got out. Luca groaned. "Wouldn't you know we couldn't have a moment's peace?"

Gabi straightened up and moved back on her side of the car. Luca started the engine, then grasped her hand and gave her a tour of the town. He drove them past the large two-story building with a sign that said Giulia.

"That's *your* trade name? I've seen it everywhere!"

He nodded. "I needed one unique word that would sell my product. It's identifiable as coming from the northeastern province of Italy, but I shortened the full name by cutting off Friuli-Venezia."

"I love it. Italian and original, just like you."

In the next breath he leaned over and kissed her even though people could see them. When he lifted his mouth, he said, "I'm not going to apologize for giving in to the impulse. I find myself wanting to do it constantly."

Heat filled her cheeks before he sat back and started driving again.

"Can we drive to Spilimbergo? I'd like to see where the big boss works."

"That's a good idea. When we get there I'll buy you

a pizza *patate*. And en route I want to hear why you didn't pursue a career in art."

She shook her head. "That Dino has a lot to answer for."

"He absorbs information like a sponge, *if* he's interested."

Gabi chuckled. "Even though I had a part-time job, I'm afraid art school was too expensive and my father didn't make enough money to pay for it all. That was a disappointment because I liked to draw."

"That butterfly is a masterpiece."

"Hardly. But art school was out, and Papà urged me to try for a grant and go for something practical like an accounting degree. Businesses needed accountants, and it wouldn't cost so much."

"That was excellent advice."

"Needless to say I took it and ended up getting my degree. My father was very happy for me, but by then he'd developed heart problems and died of a fatal heart attack."

"Another difficult time for you."

She nodded. "I'm ashamed to say my faith wasn't very strong at that point."

"I hear you," Luca murmured. "Mine has been stretched many times. No one can measure the pain of another person's trial."

"That's true in theory. My mother helped me out until I could get an accounting job. I didn't know what I wanted to do and scanned the want ads. Nothing appealed because I was in a dark place.

"About then I found a temporary job at a bank working as a teller while I waited for an accounting job to materialize. It was there I met Santos Parisi, manager of the bank. I fell hard for him. We got married four months later."

"That was fast."

"Too fast, and my happiness didn't last long once I'd suffered a miscarriage. One of the girls at the bank had seen Santos at a local club with another woman while he was supposed to be in Florence on business. She felt sorry for me because I was so recently married and thought I should know.

"When he got home I confronted him and found out he'd been with the woman he'd been having an affair with for a long time. He said it didn't mean anything and that he would give her up. But that was it for me. I'd been a fool."

"*He* was the fool, Gabi."

"Thank you for saying that. I moved out of our apartment and filed for divorce using any money I'd saved to pay the attorney fees."

"You've been through hell."

"That was a time when I thought the world was over for me. Then I saw there was an opening at the Start with a Wish foundation that helped children with problems realize a dream. I felt like a child myself, one who needed a dream to come true, so I applied. Since then life has been so much better."

"For Dino, too." Luca parked around the side of a café in Spilimbergo and kissed her again. "Thank you for confiding in me. Now I'm not quite so jealous of my son, who knows so many things about you I still have to learn. Wait here. I'll be right back."

A few minutes later he returned with the food he loved and gave her a piece. "I'm still full from breakfast and don't think I can eat all of it." But she was wrong and had finished it by the time Luca drove them by the Berettini Plastics Company, an enormous building.

"Even if you don't enjoy your work there, I'm impressed you can run two entirely different companies at the same time."

He sat back. "It's just work and I don't want to talk about me. Let's head back to the villa. I need a shower, then we'll pick up the new puzzle I ordered for Dino at the store before we reach his school. They only had one left."

"What kind of puzzle?"

"It's a thousand-piece cartoon version of building the Roman coliseum. I thought we'd set it up in the living room in front of the fire. He'll love it, particularly since you bought him and Paolo those gladiator outfits. It has little figures of gladiators, soldiers, horses, plus workers and slaves. It's fascinating."

"*I* can't wait to get my hands on it!" If Luca only knew she needed a distraction to keep her hands off him.

CHAPTER EIGHT

EIGHT HOURS LATER, the three of them had eaten dinner and they'd gone back to the living room to work on the puzzle a little longer. It had been a hit and Dino couldn't wait to do more on it before bed.

Luca decided now would be the time to bring up what he'd been dreading most. There was no way to do this but be up-front. He looked at Gabi, who was keyed in to his radar. Then he glanced at his boy's bent head as he was trying to find matching pieces.

"I had some good news today, Dino. Dr. Meuller is back from Africa early, so he's going to meet us at the hospital in the morning and operate on you."

His head reared. "In the morning? I thought it wasn't going to be yet!"

"He had a change in plans. Once it's over, you'll never have to think about it again."

Luca had braced himself for a reaction, and Dino didn't disappoint him. His son almost knocked over the chair running out of the living room. By tacit agreement, Luca and Gabi hurried after him.

Dino had thrown himself on his bed facedown with his sandals still on. Luca removed them and lay down on one side of him. Gabi settled in on his other side.

"We're both here for you, *figlio mio*. You don't have to go through any of this alone."

He started sobbing, the kind that tore your heart out.

"Dino?" Gabi rubbed his back. "Did you know your *mamma* is watching and protecting you? She's been waiting and waiting for you to have the operation so you won't get any more headaches. Think how happy she's going to be when it's over. She'll stop crying and shout *evviva*."

Luca wasn't sure if she was getting through to him until Dino slowly turned over. "You think she's been crying?"

"Yes, darling. You're her dear, dear son. She's had to wait until Dr. Meuller said it was the right time. I know she's thrilled he came back from Africa sooner so he could make you well sooner. Tomorrow is going to be a happy day for all of us, especially Dr. Meuller."

"Dr. Meuller—" Dino sounded astonished.

"Yes. He has the skill to take your headache away. Isn't that marvelous? Do you have any idea how happy he is every time he takes a child's pain away?"

"Has he done it a lot?"

Gabi had him now. "He's taken away hundreds of headaches," Luca told his son. "Everyone wants him for their doctor, even the people in Africa who don't have enough money to pay him. But he operates for free because he's been blessed with a special gift."

"Just like your *papà* when he won the gold medal in the downhill for our country," Gabi explained. "It brought happiness to millions of people who can't do what he does and wish they could. Not everyone can ski like that and bring joy. Only a few people in the world have that gift. Only a few doctors like Dr. Meuller have *his* gift.

"Only a few people like Gabi have her gift for drawing," Luca interjected. "Think of that butterfly picture above your bed."

"I don't know anyone who can draw like that," Dino said.

"You see? One day you'll find out what *your* gift is, Dino. As soon as your headaches go away, you can start doing all the things you want to do. I bet you want to run with your father in the mornings."

"Yup, and play hockey and soccer!"

"I would love to see you play everything! All you have to do is have that operation in the morning and then we're going to have so much fun!"

Luca held his breath while he waited for Dino's next comment. "Will you two sleep with me tonight?"

"Yes," they both said at once.

Gabi kissed his forehead and got up off the bed. "While you and your dad get ready, I'll run to my room and change into my robe. Then I'll come back and bring a pillow."

"Hurry!"

Luca realized he'd just watched an angel in human form leave the bedroom.

She'd become his rock as well as the woman he wanted in his life forever. Just when he thought he couldn't go on another second, her beautiful, smiling face was there to give him a recharge. He loved her desperately and needed her with every fiber of his being.

The staff at San Pietro Hospital couldn't have been more wonderful. Gabi followed Dino and his father to the third floor, where he had a large private room. She carried his overnight case, while Luca brought in their overnight bags. She was thankful they'd made it this far without his son breaking down.

The nurse asked Dino to go in the bathroom with her for a minute. When he'd disappeared behind the door, Gabi grasped Luca's hand. "I can only imagine what's going through your mind right now, but I know everything's going to be all right. It has to be."

"You're right." He kissed her swiftly. "What would I do if you weren't here with me?"

"You'd handle it like you've been handling everything all your life. You're a warrior and your son is your greatest success. I've been frightened about the operation, too, but no longer. You know why?

"You brought a son full of confidence into this hospital. He's at the top of the mountain ready to race down the piste after his own medal. You wait and see. In a few hours he'll come out of this with the gold because he has your physical and mental DNA."

Luca drew her into his arms, hugging her so hard she had trouble breathing. He let her go when they heard the bathroom door open.

Dino ran over to them. "What's that?"

Luca grinned at him. "Your hospital gown."

"I have to wear that?"

"I know it's not as exciting as your Star Wars pajamas," Gabi spoke up, "but you only have to keep it on until tomorrow."

Silver-haired Dr. Meuller came in the room and walked right over to Dino with a smile. "Do you remember me?"

"Yes."

"Do you trust me?"

"Yes. This morning we prayed for God to guide your hands."

The doctor looked taken back. "I said the same prayer before I left my house. While my staff takes you to the operating room, your family will stay in the waiting room down the hall. Is that all right?"

Dino nodded. "How long will it take?"

"Maybe two hours. When it's over, I'll tell them how you are, and then they can come visit you in another hour or two after you wake up. How does that sound?"

"Do...other children get scared?"

"I know they do, but I've never seen a boy as brave as you."

"Do doctors get scared?"

One of Dino's gifts was an inquiring mind. Gabi wondered what Dr. Meuller would say. She looked at Luca while she waited.

"Not now that I've said my prayers."

"Me neither."

The doctor squeezed Dino's shoulder and left the room. Luca kissed him. "I'm so proud of you."

"Papà? Are you scared?"

"No. Not at all. We've got Gabi with us. Remember?"

In a minute, two members of the staff walked in. They put Dino on the gurney. *"A presto, mio figlio prediletto."* All the love in the world poured from Luca's broken voice.

Gabi reached for Luca's hand and clung to it while they watched the most precious child in the world being wheeled away to surgery. Alone in the room for a minute, she couldn't help but put her arms around him, wanting to comfort him in the only way she knew how.

He held her tighter until one of the nurses came in with a paper she put on the bed, causing them to pull apart. "Let's go to the cafeteria for a bite to eat," he murmured, "then we'll head for the waiting room."

Gabi wasn't hungry, but they needed energy to keep going. "That's a good idea. I'd like to tell Mamma what's happening."

He brought the paper with them. They walked out to the elevator and rode down to the main floor. Once they reached the cafeteria and went through the line, they found an empty table. While they ate, they both made phone calls. Luca talked with his parents and his secretary at work.

After Gabi hung up, she drank her coffee and read over the instructions that the nurse had brought in to them. Together they discussed the instructions for what to expect post-op. It all depended on how well Dino survived his operation. That was anyone's guess.

She saw the anguish on Luca's face and knew how terrified he was. If only she could relieve him a little. "Dino told me you've had a few operations."

He nodded. "Tonsils and appendix. But the other two were for a broken arm and later a broken hand while I was skiing."

"Your hand?"

"Yes. I skidded on ice down the piste and bashed into the barricade. My hand took the biggest hit."

"That's terrible. Which arm did you break?"

"My lower left. That time I careened into a tree."

"How fast were you going?"

"Probably a hundred and thirty kilometers an hour. It was a vertical drop."

She groaned. "You were out of your mind."

He smiled. It was the first she'd seen for hours. "You lied to Dino when you said I had a gift. Some would say a downhiller has a death wish."

"Well, I know that's not true of you. I have to tell you I'm very impressed. I've never known an Olympic champion before. One of these days I'd like to watch those hundreds of videos of you in storage. But I won't watch them while Dino is around."

"You'd be wasting your time. If you're ready, shall we go up to the waiting room?"

"Yes." Luca was so restless, but she couldn't blame him. One hour had already passed. Now they had to survive another one before they got any news.

Once upstairs, they counted the minutes. But already it had been two and a half hours since the operation and there was no sign of staff, let alone the doctor. Luca had to be jumping out of his skin.

Sure enough he eventually got up to bring them fresh coffee and some biscotti from the vending machine. By the time three hours had passed, alarm bells had been going off inside her, but she refused to show any fear in front of Luca.

"Something has gone wrong." Luca's pallor had become pronounced. He lowered his head, clasping his hands between his legs, a picture of abject pain. "Dino is probably going to have problems and he'll need health care for the rest of his life. I'm thankful I have the money, but it could mean breaking in someone who will have to live in. That will be hard on Dino at first."

"I don't believe anything's wrong. We just have to hang on a little longer. Remember the sheet said every operation was different. It means the doctor is being careful."

He lifted his head. Lines of anxiety stood out on his handsome face. "Do you have any idea how much your support has meant to me?" His brilliant blue eyes had moistened. "Every time it seemed like I couldn't find the strength to help my son take the next step, *you* were there to point the way along this torturous path. You always turned things around, making it better. My debt to you is beyond my ability to repay."

She put a hand on his arm in response.

Darling, Luca. I don't want repayment. I just want your love.

Another half hour passed. Gabi was ready to run to the nursing station for an update when Dr. Meuller appeared in the waiting room. He was still garbed in his gown and mask.

He pulled it down to reveal a smile on his face. "I didn't intend to keep you in suspense so long, but Dino was a unique case. I wanted to observe him when he first woke up in the event there were any signs of muscle weakness or breathing problems."

She felt Luca's body stiffen.

"There weren't, Signor Berettini. Your son has come out of this operation perfectly normal in every way."

"*La loda spetta a Dio,*" Luca whispered.

Gabi grabbed Luca's arm, praising heaven, too. Once again she'd witnessed another miracle.

The doctor smiled at him. "I'm happy to inform you that the surgery was a complete success! Dino will be able to go home on Monday morning and probably won't need anything more than an over-the-counter painkiller for a few days."

Luca shook his head like he was in a daze. "It's really over? I can't believe it."

The older man patted his shoulder. "There'll be no more headaches. What's important now is that Dino recovers now and after the new year he can go back to school and his activities."

"So he doesn't have to lie low for months and months?" Luca sounded incredulous. Gabi could see he was still in shock over the news.

"No, no. No more limitations. I'll ask you to bring him in after the new year for a checkup. If you have any questions, call me. You can go back to his room now. They'll be wheeling him in shortly. He's awake and doing remarkably well."

Tears streamed down Gabi's face. "There are no words to thank you, Doctor."

"I got my thanks when Dino woke up and said, 'When are you going to do the operation, Dr. Meuller?'"

Luca burst into the happiest laughter she'd ever heard in her life before he crushed Gabi against him. They both felt reborn. The doctor waved to them before leaving the waiting room.

"He's going to be fine now, Gabi!" Luca cried, rocking her for a long time before he grabbed her hand. They hurried through the hallway to Dino's room. Since he still hadn't come in yet, they both got on their phones to send out the joyous news that the operation had been a total success.

Gabi called her mother, then Edda. The older woman broke down in tears. She said she would tell

the whole building. As they hung up, there was an or-
derly at the door and here came Dino on the gurney
with part of his head wrapped.

"Papà. I'm all well!"

"I know. Dr. Meuller told us."

How could he sound this wonderful after what he'd
been through? Gabi couldn't get over it.

Once Dino was helped into the bed, Gabi watched
Luca embrace his son and saw his shoulders heave.

"Why are you crying, Papà?"

"I only cry when I'm happy."

"You must be really happy! I bet Mamma is really
crying hard, too."

"I know she is."

"So is Dr. Meuller. So am I!" Gabi exclaimed. She
hurried over to his other side, careful not to disturb
the IV drip, and kissed his forehead.

Then Dino's grandparents came in the room. While
Luca talked with his son, this was Gabi's first chance
to meet his father. She moved away from the bed toward them.

The physical resemblance between the two men
was extraordinary, both in coloring and build. They
were a beautiful family. Giustina made the introduc-
tions before hurrying over to Dino.

"Signora Parisi?" his father said. "Our family is in
your debt for making these last few weeks more bear-
able for little Dino. My wife told me about the letter
he printed. I understand he really loves that television
program. Now I know why."

"Thank you, Signor Berettini."

"Please tell Signora Romano we're grateful for her
foundation. She does a great service for children. I'm

sure you've been missed and she's anxious to have you back."

On that note he nodded to the other couple that had just walked in the room with another gift. "Tomaso and Maria? Come over here and meet one of the employees from the Start with a Wish foundation."

Gabi recognized the dark-haired couple from the photos. "I'm so pleased to meet you. Dino has talked about you a lot while we've put puzzles and building blocks together."

Tomaso smiled. "He says you like to eat chocolate-covered insects."

That made her laugh. "Then don't tell him the truth. Please. He loves chocolate *bocci* balls."

"We would have brought him some but know they're not good for him. They were Catarina's favorite candy, too. We brought him a game instead."

"He loves games."

"You've made a real hit with him, indulging him as you have," Maria said. "So many gifts we've heard about when we talk to him on the phone. Even a framed drawing from you hanging over his bed. Do you visit every child who writes to you?"

"No. There are different departments in place to make a child's wish come true. I work with a group of women who read the letters when they first come in. We screen them before turning them over to Edda Romano, who heads the program. She determines what will happen next. But Dino was a special case.

"Edda wanted someone from the foundation to take him a gift in person. She asked me to take him a building blocks game since she couldn't grant him the wish he really wanted."

"What was that?"

"He wanted his mother to be there for the operation."

"Of course he did." Maria put a hand to her throat and tears came to her eyes.

"Everyone at the foundation had the same reaction to his letter as you, Signora Guardino. A mother is irreplaceable."

Tomaso nodded. "There was no one like Catarina. We loved her so much. She was the perfect mother and wife. There'll never be anyone like her. Thank heaven Dino has come through this to help Luca go on living. Now he can really dig into his work, eh, Fabrizo?"

"Amen to that," Luca's father added and focused his gaze on Gabi. "Since we won't be seeing you again, Signora Parisi, we thank you for your time."

He didn't expect to see her again? How odd that sounded.

While she stood there trying to understand him, everyone clustered around Dino. Gabi feared it was too much excitement for him, and wondered why a nurse hadn't come in yet. But she also recognized that she'd been in protective mode around him since knowing him and needed to stop worrying. Luca hadn't seemed to notice, so why should she be concerned?

She watched Catarina's aunt and uncle. Dino was like a grandchild to them. They were all very close-knit, especially after such a tragedy. But Luca's father had given off a different aura to her.

Dino acted thrilled to see everyone and kept talking. Gabi had been so used to him seeking her out, she felt…she didn't know exactly how or what she felt... Oh, yes, she did. Whom was she kidding? She felt like an outsider.

That's what she was, a woman from the foundation who'd brought him a gift in response to his letter. Deep down she felt Luca's father resented her for some reason. She didn't want to be unkind about him, but there was no mistaking a certain tension he'd given off just now.

While they were all talking, she picked up that they were staying at a hotel in town. They would be coming over to the hospital for the next few days to keep Dino company until he went home.

The only thing she could see to do was be with her mom for the night. That way Luca would be free to visit with everyone for as long as he wanted and spend private time with his son. This would be the perfect time to bow out.

She slipped out of the room and walked around the corner to use the restroom and freshen up. When she came back out with the intention of telling Luca her plan, she rounded the corner again and saw him in the corridor with his father. Their backs were turned toward her. She had the impression they were arguing. All she heard was, "Now that Dino is better, you have to marry Giselle, do you hear me?"

CHAPTER NINE

MARRY GISELLE? Who was she?

Gabi felt like she'd been stabbed and hurried back to the restroom in agony. Luca had never mentioned that woman to her. But apparently he'd been involved with her before Gabi had come on the scene because Signor Berettini knew all about her. What on earth did any of it mean?

His remarks to Gabi no longer puzzled her. It made sense that he thought he'd seen the last of her. The older man would be shocked if he knew she and Luca had kissed passionately, let alone that Dino had asked her to be his *mamma*.

Gabi sank down on the couch and called her mother again. The moment she heard her voice, she broke down.

"Darling—whatever is wrong? This should be the happiest night of your life!"

"For a little while it was."

"You said Dino's going to be fine."

"He is, and he won't have to go through a long recovery period. I guess I thought I might be needed for a lot longer, but that isn't the case."

"I see."

"The doctor wants him in school after the new year. He's in amazing health now. All the trauma is over."

"Isn't that wonderful!"

"It is."

"But it means your life is going to get back to normal, too."

Her mother understood. "Yes. Tonight as I watched him laughing and talking with his family, I realized Dino has faced his fear and overcome it. He doesn't need me any longer."

"Darling—you're always going to be his friend."

"I know, but it won't be the same. All I've done is tell you my problems since I married Santos. It's not fair to you. I'm going to hang up now. In a little while I'll get a taxi and come home for the night. See you soon."

After hanging up, she left the restroom. When she looked around the corner, Luca was still there, but he was alone. He walked toward her, his expression glowing with happiness.

Already a transformation had taken place. Those deep grief lines on his unforgettably handsome face were receding. There was a new light in his eyes she'd never seen before. "I've been waiting for you." No mention of his father.

"Sorry I was so long. I called my mother to tell her about Dino and let her know I'll be home in a little while."

What had she said about those receding tension lines on his face? They came back with a vengeance. "I couldn't have heard you right. You promised Dino you'd stay here with him."

"I'll be back first thing in the morning. Your family is here tonight to be with him."

Luca's black brows met in a frown. "They'll be leaving soon to go to their hotel. Dino expects you and me to be here until we all go home on Monday. He's just had surgery. I don't want him upset by anything. If he found out you weren't here, I don't even want to think about it."

"Luca—you don't have to be afraid for him anymore. He knows he's fine. Everything is different now."

"The hell it is." For the first time since she'd known him, his response gave her a glimpse of the tough CEO he could be when necessary. "The operation has changed nothing for him where his feelings for you are concerned. You don't honestly think this has been some kind of an act for him—"

"No. Of course not, but given time—"

"Given time he'll what?" Luca cut her off. "Now that the danger is over, you imagine he'll just switch back to the way he was before you came into his life? What's happened to you since Dr. Meuller gave us the incredible news?"

Oh, Luca. If only she dared tell him what she'd overheard. Gabi had no idea what it had all meant, but she could see that tonight was not the time to have this discussion.

"I just didn't want to be in the way."

His expression looked like thunder. "What are you talking about? If Dino had his way, he wouldn't have anyone else around."

"That's not true."

"Whom are you trying to convince? The families

will be leaving any minute now, and I've ordered cots to be brought in for both of us."

"Please don't be upset, Luca. I never meant to cause you this much concern."

His chest rose and fell visibly. "As long as there's no more talk of you going anywhere, I can handle anything. This is a night for celebration."

She nodded. So be it for now. Gabi would have to text her mother that plans had changed once again. "It is! Now you can be happy. All our prayers have been answered."

His fierce gaze played over her, as if he were still having trouble settling down after she'd said she was leaving. "Dino's expecting us to come back in the room." He really was upset. She'd never seen Luca this formidable before. "Gabi—"

She could hardly breathe for the intense way he was looking at her. "What is it?"

His compelling mouth tightened. "Nothing. Are you ready?"

"Of course."

They walked back to the room together. It killed her to think that she'd upset him on this night of all nights. Everyone was still there. Luca's father watched them come inside. After what she'd overheard, it was hard to pretend everything was fine, that she wasn't in pain.

Maria kissed Dino, who was finally winding down. He'd closed his eyes. Gabi loved him so much she could hardly stand it.

"I think we should go, Tomaso." Dino's grand-mother followed suit. Everyone hugged and smiled at Gabi. "We'll see you in the morning."

Signor Berettini left last. He nodded to Gabi and

took his son aside to talk to him in private for a moment as they walked toward the door. Gabi turned away from them and walked over to the side of the bed. To her surprise Dino's eyelids fluttered open.

"Are you going to stay with me tonight?"

Guilt washed over her that she'd contemplated leaving him tonight. Whatever was going on in Luca's personal life, she'd made a commitment to this boy. "As if I'd be anywhere else."

"Good. *Ti amo*, Gabi."

"*Ti amo*, darling. Sweet dreams." She kissed his cheek before he fell asleep.

Out of the corner of her eye she saw Luca's father leave. The three of them were finally alone. A second later an employee from housekeeping wheeled in two cots.

She watched as Luca set them up and placed them side by side at the end of the bed. After sleeping on either side of Dino last night, the dynamics of the situation weren't anything new, but the stakes had changed because with one operation Dino had been cured.

"He looks so peaceful," she remarked.

Luca walked over and whispered, "I'd like to keep him that way."

"You haven't forgiven me yet, have you?"

She heard a deep sigh escape. "There's nothing to forgive. I'm afraid I've lived in fear so long, I can't quite believe the nightmare is over. If anything, I need to beg your forgiveness. The support from family has been vital, but you and I have been a team. The thought of that changing tonight threw me."

It threw me, too, Luca.

But he didn't know what she'd heard his father say out in the hall.

Gabi stood by as an attractive nurse came in to check Dino's drip and make notations on the computer. She smiled at Luca. Gabi recognized that look. She bet the nurse had never seen a more gorgeous man in her life. "Your son is doing great. I'll be in later."

After she left, Gabi removed her shoes and lay down on one of the cots. "The news just keeps getting better and better."

He leaned over and brushed his lips against hers. "Thank heaven. I don't know about you, but I'm suddenly exhausted."

"I honestly don't know how you've survived these last two years. I'm so happy it's over for you and Dino."

She turned on her side to watch as he removed his shoes and stretched out on his cot. His long, rock-hard body was too big. He'd never be able to sleep on it. She'd never get to sleep while she could still feel his mouth on hers.

"Incredible to believe he's fine now." Luca put his hands behind his head. "But we wouldn't have made it these last few weeks without you," he said in a quiet tone. "I'll never forget the moment this beautiful blonde woman walked into the foundation reception room.

"When you told Dino you weren't mad at him, he ran to you as if you were the most important person in his universe. I'll never forget it because I hadn't seen that kind of emotion since he lost his mother."

"Meeting Dino was a life-changing moment for me, too, Luca. When I was first married, I wanted a baby so badly. My parents could only have one child, and I always wanted brothers and sisters. So I hoped to have a big family, maybe three or four children.

"But as you know, that dream was dashed. Then I met Dino, the epitome of my idea of the perfect boy. I thought, how could any parent be so lucky to have such a cute, fun-loving, charming son like him. To realize he'd lost his mother just killed me.

"I know I've gone overboard with him, but I haven't been able to help myself. When he asked me if I liked Paolo more than I liked him, I wanted to shout, 'Can't you tell? Can't you see I'm crazy about you?'"

"I believe it was meant to be, Gabi," he said in a smoky voice. "Last night you were able to calm Dino's fears in a way I never could. I was too close to it. He actually slept until we woke him up to drive him here."

"The cute thing was so good and brave. Just think, tomorrow he wakes up to a brand-new world where everything and anything is possible. Go to sleep now, Luca. No one deserves it more than you do. *Buona notte.*"

She turned away from him and closed her eyes. Gabi needed to get undressed, take a shower, wash her hair and sob her heart out. But she couldn't do any of it. For the next little while she lay there reliving every second of her life since she'd first met Dino and his father.

You goose, Gabi. You've been living in a fantasy world.

She'd thought she'd learned her lesson after getting married to the wrong man. There'd been warning signs all over the place, but she'd refused to pick up on them because it had been so wonderful to be in love like her friends. Too late she realized it hadn't been love everlasting or anything close to it.

Now that she'd met the most marvelous, incredible man in existence and knew she would never love like this again, his father had sent out another warning sign. Tonight in this hospital room she'd seen and heard it loud and clear.

Saturday and Sunday turned out to be constantly busy days helping Dino get back to some kind of normal. He had to take walks and get another X-ray. Luca and Gabi kept him entertained between the routine tests, checks from Dr. Meuller and short visits by the family.

Luca had warned his father to stay off the subject of Giselle or he wasn't welcome at the hospital. For once his father left him alone about it, but he knew it wouldn't be over after they got home.

When Monday morning rolled around, he felt like they'd all been let out of prison. While the nurse pushed Dino's wheelchair out to the hospital loading area with Gabi at his side, Luca brought the car around. Dr. Meuller had unwrapped the roll of gauze from Dino's head and replaced it with a small patch behind his ear that wasn't noticeable.

A fresh snowstorm had blanketed the town. With all the Christmas decorations along the streets, there was a festive nature in the air. Dino loved being out in it. They all loved it. The second Dino climbed in the backseat, he bounced for joy.

"*Evviva!* I'm going home!" Luca no longer had to worry that his son was moving around too much. "Can we stop and get a *fondente gelato* with *panna* on the way?"

Gabi rolled her eyes at Luca. "That sounds good to me, too. I want the same thing, but with *zabaglione*."

He flashed her a smile that curled her toes. "You remembered."

"That was a very special day."

Once they'd found a *gelateria*, they enjoyed their treats and took off for Maniago. "Do I have to go to bed when I get home?"

"Only if you feel like lying down."

"When do you have to go to work, Papà?"

Luca chuckled. "After Christmas, but I'll put in a few hours at the office here and there."

"What about you, Gabi?"

"I'm still on vacation," she spoke up, relieving Luca's mind.

His car ate up the miles. Gabi started a game and got them counting how many blue cars they saw, then they switched to black cars. It kept his son busy because she knew how to make everything exciting.

When the three of them ran out of cars to count, it seemed to be the best time for the announcement. If Luca didn't make it, his son was going to drive them all crazy before they reached Maniago.

"*Ehi, figlio mio?* I thought we'd stop and pick up a friend for you to play with on our way home."

"What? A friend—Paolo's my friend, but he's at school."

"You can always use another one at home."

Four months ago Luca had planned on getting Dino a dog once his operation was over. He'd been in touch with the owner of a litter of twelve-week-old pups. Depending on how successful the operation was, he'd been planning to spring the good news on Dino later in the week. But necessity dictated that today had to be the day.

Gabi shot him a glance. He hadn't told her his plan, but with that razor-sharp brain of hers, she'd probably figured it out.

"I don't want to play with anyone else. Can't we just go home, Papà?"

"I think you'll change your mind when you meet her."

"Her—?"

Gentle laughter escaped Gabi's lips.

"Or him. Tell you what. I'll let you decide after we get to this lady's house."

"Where is it?"

"Here in Maniago, not far from our villa. We're almost there."

Luca shared another glance with Gabi, who was smiling. He felt her excitement as he followed the curving road and drove into an estate where the snow was a little deeper. After winding around to the rear entrance, he came to a stop and turned off the engine.

"Shall we get out?"

On cue an older woman came out the door in slacks and an apron.

"Signora Borelli? Please meet my son, Dino, and our friend Signora Parisi."

His son looked bewildered.

"I understand you just got out of the hospital, Dino. Would you like to come in on my back porch for a minute?"

Dino walked over to grasp Luca's hand before they walked through the snow and went inside. There they discovered half a dozen black-and-white border collie puppies running around their mother.

"Oh, Dino—" Gabi cried in delight as the puppies scrambled over to them. "Aren't these dogs adorable!" She reached down to pick up one of them and carefully handed it Dino, who looked so happy, Luca thought he was going to cry. The dog squirmed and licked his son, who couldn't stop giggling.

"We have four males and two females."

A pair of blue eyes looked up at Luca. "Can I have a boy dog?"

The woman lifted the dog out of his arms and picked up another one. "Now you can pick out one of the boys. They're twelve weeks old, close to being trained, have had their shots and are ready to go home."

Dino stared at Luca. "I don't know which one to pick."

"I have an idea," Gabi said. "Why don't you play with all of them and see which one seems to appeal to you the most. Maybe one of them will want to go home with you and let you know."

Luca's heart melted while he watched his son have the time of his life calling to each pup and running around with them. He wasn't the only one having a marvelous time. Gabi's eyes shone with a joy she couldn't hide because he knew she was a dog lover and had owned one. These pups were irresistible.

After a few minutes it became apparent his son couldn't make up his mind. He kept holding one, then another one. "I wish we could take them all home, Papà."

That produced laughter from everyone.

Gabi knelt down by him. "Their faces are all different."

"I know. Which one do you like?"

"It's hard to choose. I guess I kind of like the one where the black covers up one eye, like a mask. Once when I worked at a pet store, I watched people pick out their favorite dog or cat. No one wanted this one little beagle who was small and whiny. But I loved him and the owner let me take him home."

"You named him Tex, huh?"

"I did. I guess you have to decide which dog touches your heart."

"The one with the mask looks the funniest. Do you think people would laugh at him?"

"Probably, but he won't know why. He doesn't look in a mirror. He thinks he's just like his brothers and sisters."

"Yeah."

Even Signora Borelli laughed at Gabi's comment.

"Why don't you pick up each dog again and have a talk with him. Maybe then you'll be able to make up your mind."

Gabi could get Luca's son to do anything. He watched him catch each one and walk over in a corner to have a private conversation between licks. When he'd finished, he came over to Luca. "I can't decide."

"Then we'll come back tomorrow and take another look."

"But what if one of them is gone?"

"That's a possibility," Gabi remarked. "They're all so darling."

While they stood there, the puppy Luca now thought of as the masked puppy kept jumping around Dino.

"Do you know what I think?" They all looked at the owner. "That dog has picked you, Dino. He won't leave you alone."

"I know. He keeps running around me. I think he likes me."

"I know he does. They choose the master they want."

"They do?"

The owner nodded. "I see it happen over and over again. Someone comes in, and one of the litter chooses them. Nature is an amazing thing."

A huge smile broke out on Dino's face. He picked up the pup and was rewarded with half a dozen licks. He broke down laughing and looked at him. "How come he loves me so much?"

Luca glanced at Gabi, who was beaming. "That's just how it happens, with animals and people. No one can explain love at first sight, but it's a fact of life."

Do you hear me, Gabi?

It was love at first sight with them, but they'd both had to get past their own painful pasts to recognize it for what it was.

"Can we take him home now?"

"What do you think?"

"I have a dog crate you can buy," the owner said.

In a few minutes the transaction had been made and they left for the villa. The dog sat in the crate on the backseat next to Dino, who was entranced. Luca would set up a box to keep in the family room until the dog was fully trained.

After they got home, he carried the crate into the family room and everyone, including the staff, gathered round. They could see Dino was in great shape and hugged him.

"Guess what? I got a dog!" Everyone laughed.

Luca said, "After lunch I'll run to the pet shop and get the things we need. Then we'll let him out."

Ines stood there with her hands on her hips. "What's his name?"

"Nero," Dino announced. "He has a black eye. I love him!"

Luca patted his shoulder. "That's a good name for him, just like the emperor in your Coliseum puzzle. Now why don't you wash your hands and we'll eat the special pizza lunch Pia has prepared for you."

"Yum. *Grazie*, Pia. They didn't give me pizza in the hospital."

"I shouldn't think so."

The dog whimpered as they started to leave the room. "Don't cry, Nero. I'll be right back."

The dog wouldn't take the place of Gabi, but Dino would be so busy taking care of him, he wouldn't miss her so horribly when she did have to go back to work. However, Luca knew that would only be for a very short period while he made future plans for the three of them.

Before long Nero had a collar, a leash, puppy dog food and two bowls for meat and water. They kept the dog on the leash to take him outside, and to keep him near Dino in case the door was open to the other rooms. The training would take time, but with luck Nero would be fully trained in sixteen weeks.

A boy and his dog.

Gabi watched him run around the house with Nero getting in the way, running ahead and then behind him. Dino was free to do whatever he wanted. She loved Luca for thinking of this gift for him. Nothing could be more perfect than to start off his whole new life with a constant companion.

Gabi was so happy for him she felt like she could burst, but nothing could erase the pain when she remembered what she'd heard Luca's father say to him in private.

By late afternoon Luca insisted Dino stop for a while and take a nap on his bed. He'd had a huge day. They went upstairs and Luca carried the crate.

"Gabi? How soon do you have to leave?"

"Day after tomorrow. Since there's more snow forecast, I'll have to get up really early so I won't be too late for work. But you know I'll be back."

"But you're going to sleep here tonight and tomorrow night?"

"Yes."

"Will you and Papà take me when I go back to school?"

Pain, pain. "I'm sure I will."

"Will you sleep with me?"

"No, Dino," Luca spoke for her. "She has to stay in her own bed. We all do because we need a good night's sleep. But she'll be down the hall. And don't forget—Nero will be next to your bed in his crate like he is right now. You can talk to him and make him feel better because he'll be missing his mother and will cry during the night."

"He will?"

"Yes. All he's ever known are his mom and his brothers and sisters. You're going to be his new family."

"Don't worry. I'll take care of him."

The love in Dino's voice finished Gabi off. She excused herself to go to the guest bedroom. This had been a day like no other. She'd been storing up memories because starting day after tomorrow she needed to make new ones that had nothing to do with Dino or Luca.

Luisa had texted her, wondering if they could go to dinner and a movie soon. She texted her back and made a date for Friday after work. Then she got in the shower and washed her hair. After drying it, she slipped on a blouse and skirt. Before she went downstairs, she lay down on top of the bed just to close her eyes for a minute.

When she heard Luca call to her, at first she thought she was dreaming until he said her name again. "Gabi?"

She sat up. How long had she been sleeping? It was dark outside. "Luca?"

"We need to talk. Can I come in?"

"Please do. Is Dino all right?"

"I gave him a painkiller. Now he's out like a light and will probably stay that way until morning. I've already taken Nero out again."

"Have you had any rest yet?" He had to be utterly exhausted.

"Don't worry about me." Her door was still open, so they could hear Dino if he called out.

Luca moved over to the bed and stretched out on it next to her. "I need to hold you for a little while." In the next breath he pulled her into his arms and buried his face in her hair.

Gabi couldn't believe this was happening. The mention of another woman in his life had been eating away at her emotions, but this was what she'd been wanting for so long, she could deny him nothing.

Euphoric that she had the freedom to touch and feel him, she pushed her fears aside and gave in to her desires. They came together in an explosion of need that rocked her world.

"You don't know what meeting you has done to me." He kissed every centimeter of her face and throat. "I could eat you alive. Don't ask me to stop because I can't, *bellissima*."

"I don't want you to stop. Surely you know that by now. Why else do I keep finding excuses to stay?"

"I love you, Gabriella Russo. I'm so in love with you, I can't think about anything else. Don't say it's too soon, or that we barely know each other. None of that matters because we know how we feel."

So how did he feel about the woman named Giselle? What was the truth of that situation? She could ask him but didn't want Luca to think that she'd been eavesdropping earlier.

"I knew I wanted you the moment I saw you at the foundation. If you can deny that you didn't feel the same way, then you're lying to yourself and to me."

"I'm not denying anything, Luca. Over the last few weeks I've learned to love you more than life itself. You know I have. In truth I didn't think it possible to love any man like I do you. I didn't know a man like you existed, but here you are. And you're the father to the most perfect boy in the world. Half the time I feel I must be dreaming."

"Then we're both in the same dream. Love me, Gabi," he cried, before he started devouring her.

Being in his arms like this, being swept away by his

kisses that grew longer and deeper had her spinning out of control. She could hold nothing back. Their desire for each other was reaching flashpoint. He rolled her on top of him, trapping her legs. She gasped as he molded her to his hard, male body. This kind of rapture was indescribable.

"*Ti amo*," she cried, witless and breathless.

But in the next breath she heard whimpering sounds at the side of the bed that caused her to lift her head.

"Good grief. It's Nero," Luca muttered.

Before she had the presence of mind to move off him, the overhead light went on.

There stood Dino. "Papà! Are you and Gabi making a baby?"

Caught like rats in a trap as they old saying went. Another minute and they wouldn't have been wearing their clothes. She was on the verge of hysteria.

Luca rolled her over and got up from the bed. "What do you know about making babies?" Calm and collected. That was the man she adored.

"Paolo told me."

"That Paolo has a lot to answer for." He picked up the puppy. "How come you let Nero out of his crate?"

"He was whining and it woke me up. I thought I'd put him up on the bed, but he ran away from me."

"Now you know why you have to keep him on a leash."

"I'm sorry."

"That's okay. This is how you learn. Come on. We'll go downstairs and take him outside. Are you hungry?"

"No. I just want some water."

"Are you going to come, too, Gabi?"

"Let's leave her alone until she's ready."

"I'll be downstairs in a minute, Dino."

"Are you going to have a baby?"

"We'll let you know when we know."

She couldn't believe Luca had just said that and shut her eyes tightly, hardly daring to breathe. Gabi ran in the bathroom to fix her makeup and brush her hair. After straightening her clothes, she hurried downstairs. The grandfather clock chimed 9:30 p.m. She assumed the staff had gone to bed in the other wing of the villa.

Gabi went to the kitchen to wait for them. Pretty soon the two of them came in. "Where's Nero?"

"Papà put him in the crate in the family room for the rest of the night."

"I think that's a good idea. It's time for everyone to get to bed."

Dino pulled a bottle of water from the fridge. He hurried over to her and gave her a hug. "I know you said you'd stay until the day after tomorrow, but I wish you didn't have to go."

"I promise I'll be back. Have I ever broken one?"

"No."

"All right then. *Buona notte*, Dino."

He acted like he wanted to say more, but Luca gave him a look and that was enough to silence him. "I'll meet you in the living room," Luca mouthed on the way out of the kitchen.

A few minutes ago they'd been interrupted before a huge mistake had been made. Now Luca wanted to talk about it. She trembled like a leaf while she curled up on one end of the couch waiting for him.

* * *

At ten after ten Luca entered the living room and found Gabi right where he wanted her. He reached for her and pulled her onto his lap. "How about that son of mine?" he said against her lips. "I'm sorry I left your bedroom door open so the dog could get in."

She took a quick breath. "I'm glad you did. It woke me up to reality."

"The only reality is that I'm in love with you and want to marry you right away. After tonight it's obvious we need to be man and wife as soon as possible."

He tried to prolong their kiss, but she had to get away from him. Calling on every shred of self-discipline, Gabi slid off his lap so she could stand.

"We can't. *You* can't."

"What's to stop us?"

"For one thing, common sense."

Luca looked up at her in amazement. "We're both mature adults who've experienced marriage before. We know what we feel now. I want you to be my wife. I want to give you children we'll raise together with Dino. With you at my side, I see the chance for a lifetime of happiness for all of us. I know you do, too."

"I thought I did until the day Dino was operated on."

He got to his feet. His jaw had hardened. "What do you mean?"

She shook her head. "I hadn't intended to say anything, but at this point I can't keep this from you any longer."

"I'm afraid you've lost me."

Gabi kneaded her hands. "When your father entered the room and we were introduced, he thanked me for coming in response to Dino's letter. Later, when everyone was leaving he said something that gave me pause."

Luca's mouth had become a straight line of what she could only interpret as anger. "Tell me exactly," he whipped out.

She swallowed hard. "Tomaso had just made the comment that now that Dino was going to be fine, you could get back to work full-time. He smiled at your father when he said it. Your father in turn looked me straight in the eyes and said, 'Since we won't be seeing you again, Signora Parisi, we thank you for your time.'"

A harsh epithet escaped Luca's lips. "How dare he speak to you like that—as if you were a servant no longer needed. It's so like him," his voice grated. "No wonder you disappeared from the room for so long." He reached out to grip her shoulders. "I swear I'll never let him get near you again. He'll have nothing to do with us or our plans."

She eased away from him. "From the beginning I've sensed you and your father had some kind of a problem. I wondered if that was the reason you didn't want to be the CEO in the first place, but I never wanted to ask."

"I should have explained about him before now, but I've been so worried about Dino, I put it off. Please don't worry about him."

"I can't help it. You haven't heard everything yet."

His dark brows furrowed. "What more is there?"

"Luca—you didn't hear the conversation when everyone had assembled in Dino's room. Catarina's aunt and uncle, along with your father, painted a picture of life with your wife I'll never forget."

Lines marred his handsome features. He put his hands on his hips. "What picture?"

"Don't pretend you don't know what I mean."

"*What picture?*" he ground out.

Gabi moistened her lips nervously. "You and Catarina had the perfect marriage."

"No," he protested. "We had a good marriage despite a lot of differences between us. Like all marriages, it had its ups and downs. Dino was the best part of it. So it's already started," he muttered.

"What do you mean?"

"My father knows something monumental has gone on between you and me. He sensed it when Dino didn't want them to come over for a visit that day. The truth is, he's had a woman picked out for me since I was twenty years old and had almost finished college."

"You're talking about Giselle."

His head reared. "How did you hear about her?"

She took a deep breath. "After I came out of the restroom, I saw you and your father talking in the hall and overheard part of your conversation."

Those blue eyes had narrowed to slits. "What part?"

"He said you had to marry Giselle."

Luca paced the floor before coming to a stop. "Her name is Giselle Fournier. She's the daughter from a wealthy French industrialist family that made their money in plastics. Her father is my father's best friend. I was never interested in her, never could be. She's still available. My father is hopeful I'll marry her to seal the family fortunes."

"You're kidding—"

"He hopes you'll go back to Padova where you came from. That's why he said what he did at the hospital." Luca groaned. "You have no idea what depths my father will sink to in order to get his own way."

"I can't comprehend it. My father was so kind."

"You were lucky. From the time I was born, I'm afraid mine had an agenda where I was concerned. But when he tried to coerce me into marriage, I rebelled openly against him.

"After getting my business degree, I joined the ski team without his knowledge, and there wasn't anything he could do about it. From the age of twenty-one to twenty-five, I lived the life of a racer with my ski buddies all over Europe, even trained in the US and South America. As you pointed out, he didn't even come to watch me race for the gold medal.

"He threatened to cut me off, but I financed myself with racing money and endorsements so he didn't have to pay for anything."

"That's a horror story."

"In a way, it was. About that time, he had a heart attack and blamed me."

"Oh, no—"

"It wasn't a bad one. The doctor said to look at it as a warning. Wouldn't you know the chairman of the board of the company asked me to come in and take over my father's position while he recovered? I saw it as a ploy on my father's part to get me under his thumb. I refused.

"But Mamma begged me to reconsider for her sake. I adore her and since she'd always supported me in everything I did, I knew she was relying on me so I joined the company in an official capacity. Soon after that, I met Catarina and married her. This took my father by complete surprise. *I* was surprised it didn't bring on another heart attack."

He was feeding her so much information, Gabi couldn't believe it. She had so many questions. "Where were you married?"

"In Venice at her family church. I'll show you pictures."

"Did your father attend?"

"No. He pretended that he couldn't come because of his heart condition. Everyone who knew the truth was scandalized by his behavior, but I had my mother, plus lots of ski friends and members of the board who supported us."

"How hard all that must have been for you."

"He's always been a hard man and his own worst enemy. I knew he'd been waiting for me to cave in and get together with Giselle. My marriage to Catarina infuriated him, particularly because the Guardino family had no money or influence. It inflamed him more when I offered Tomaso a better position in the company because I knew it would make Catarina happy."

Gabi was absolutely stunned over what she was hearing now.

"The most important thing you need to know is that my father only tolerated Dino after he was born. My son doesn't know the reason, but he's aware he doesn't have a loving grandfather."

"That I *can't* believe, not when he's the dearest boy on earth."

"Be thankful you haven't ever known anyone like him. After Catarina was killed, he started in again talking about a marriage to Giselle."

"There's something wrong with him."

"Agreed. Mamma finally admitted something to me recently that I'd never known. She said that he and Giselle's father had a business together after the war years, but they couldn't sustain it between their two countries. So they made a pact to get their two children together. My father swore her to secrecy, but she wanted me to know the truth when she could see I would never bend to my father's will."

Gabi folded her arms to her waist. "It sounds like the story of two kings arranging affairs of state and treating their own children like chattel."

Luca smiled without mirth. "Exactly. He missed his calling as one. Now he's worried about *you*, with good reason."

Gabi averted her eyes. "This puts a different complexion on everything."

"I had no idea you'd been holding all of this in since the hospital."

She buried her face in her hands, incredulous over what she'd heard.

"The rest of the family can see how I feel about you, and I know for a fact they approve. You're the best thing that has happened to Dino and me since the avalanche, and they know it. They love him."

"Who wouldn't—?" she said.

"Gabi—" He put his arms around her neck. "You and I were meant to be together. I know it in my DNA. So do you. I don't care how long we've known each other. I want to marry you.

"My *mamma* considers you an angel from heaven. The staff never want you to leave the villa, and Nero came straight to your room. They say a dog follows a gentle heart."

"Luca—" she whispered in tears.

"So I'm not letting you out of my arms until you say yes, that you'll marry me."

She cradled his face in her hands. "You make it sound so simple, so easy."

"Why isn't it? I'll come to Padova. We'll call the priest and make arrangements for the wedding. I want to marry you right away. My father might try to cause more trouble, but he'll be powerless to get away with anything."

Gabi shook her head. "You don't know what you're saying! You haven't even met my mother yet, or my friends. I've been divorced, and it was ugly. I have a position with Edda, who depends on all of us at the foundation."

"She's a tycoon, Gabi, a woman who understands life. When you tell her we're going to be married, do you honestly think she would stand in your way?"

"No," she admitted. "Of course not."

"Then what are you afraid of? Forget my father."

"Y-you wouldn't understand," her voice faltered.

"Try me."

She eased away from him. "You're not thinking clearly right now. Too much has been going on to confuse the issue for both of us. Given time you'll—"

"I'll what?" he cut her off. "There's no other woman for me."

She flinched.

"Have you looked at yourself in the mirror lately? Have you noticed every man on the street practically having an accident as you walk by because they're so taken by your beauty? How about Paolo? Do you remember the excitement on his face when he asked if you'd be at the villa again and Dino said yes?

"Have you seen into my son's eyes and noticed anything but genuine love? Have you forgotten you're the reason he found the courage to have the operation? Talk about the perfect woman…"

Gabi could hear what he was saying. He believed what he was saying. *She* wanted to believe it. But how long would his feelings for her last?

"Tell me what's wrong, Gabi!"

She took a deep breath. "I thought Santos would love me forever. He said and did all the right things and swept naive little me off my feet. I was flattered that the bank manager who had a solid position had fallen for me. When I conceived so fast, I was in heaven.

"But then I miscarried and when I needed to talk about it, Santos always seemed to be preoccupied or working late. He didn't comfort me. It was a terrible time for me. It wasn't long before my friend at the bank told me about his long-term affair with another woman. I thought it was true that a man couldn't be satisfied with one woman.

"I'd married forever, or so I'd thought. If I marry you, I want it to be forever, but what if something happens and your feelings change for me? It terrifies me to think of being married to you, then lose you. Luca—I can't answer you right now, but I promise I'll go home and think about it."

"For how long?" he demanded. Just then he sounded like Dino. They were both so much alike that way. Once their minds were made up, they acted swiftly with no regrets.

"Trust me. Not long. Now I need to get to bed. Please don't follow me. Morning will be here before we know it and we'll be busy helping Dino learn how to take care of his new dog."

Gabi raced out of the living room and up the stairs. She cried herself to sleep, which was the last thing she should be doing. Luca wanted to marry her. Dino had survived his operation and had been given a clean bill of health. There shouldn't be a dark cloud in her sky. But Santos's betrayal after losing their baby had come back to haunt her.

Morning came when Dino brought Nero to her bedroom door on a leash. His barking woke her up. She lifted her head. "Come on in!"

"He's already minding me, Gabi!"

She was amazed that Dino acted as if he hadn't undergone brain surgery. "That doesn't surprise me." He'd dressed in jeans and a T-shirt and loved his dog so much it did her heart good.

Gabi hurried in the bathroom to get dressed. Then they went downstairs to the kitchen, where Pia had fixed breakfast. Luca walked in a minute later looking rugged and gorgeous in jeans and a navy crew neck sweater. He hadn't shaved yet, making him more attractive than ever. He hunkered down in front of Nero and scratched his head.

"Are you being a good dog?"

"He's the best, Papà!"

"While you eat, I'll take him outside, then we'll settle down and work on that puzzle. Tomaso phoned a minute ago. They stayed at your grandparents' last night. He and Maria will be over with Nonna to spend part of the day with you."

"I hope they don't stay a long time."

Oh, Dino…

Luca darted Gabi a speaking glance, letting her know that Dino adored her and wanted her to himself forever. She got the message. There was nothing she wanted more, too.

The day turned out to be a hard one to get through when it shouldn't have been. Luca's family stayed all day and enjoyed playing with the dog, too. At one point, she went upstairs to get her packing done so she could leave early in the morning.

They all ate dinner in front of the fire in the living room and listened to Christmas carols. Dino and Luca stretched out on the floor and played with Nero, who stayed by them, soaking up the warmth. This was bliss, except for the fact that Gabi had to go home and make the most important decision of her life.

She finally said good-night to everyone and went upstairs with Dino to put him to bed. Luca said he'd come up later. His son asked her to read *How the Grinch Stole Christmas* to him after he'd said his prayers.

When she'd finished she said, "Don't you love it when the Grinch realized Christmas didn't come from a store? Christmas was in a person's heart, and his grew three sizes that day."

"Can a heart really do that?" Just as Dino asked the question, her telephone rang.

"Yes," his father answered it from the doorway. He'd brought Nero in the crate with him.

She glanced at both of them. "Excuse me. It's my mother. I need to get it. *Buona notte, piccolino.*"

After giving him a kiss on the forehead, Gabi rushed past Luca and hurried to the guest bedroom. For the first time since staying in the villa, she locked the door. It wasn't to keep Luca out, but to keep her from giving in to temptation when she hadn't made any decision yet.

She called her mother back and said she'd be at the house in the morning before going to work. They'd talk then.

By four o'clock she still hadn't fallen asleep and gave up trying. After getting dressed, she reached for her suitcase and purse and left the villa for her car. This was for the best. Another prolonged good-bye would kill her.

Two and a half hours later after driving on parts of the highway with black ice, she arrived in Padova. Thank heaven her mother was an early riser. After Gabi got home, she didn't have to wait long to hear her mother making coffee in the kitchen.

Gabi ran to her and they hugged.

"What on earth is going on?"

"You won't believe what happened after we took Dino home from the hospital." For the next little while she told her about the events that led up to Dino's entry into her bedroom following his dog. "I about died when he asked if Luca and I were making a baby."

"Oh, no!" Her mother laughed till the tears trickled out of her eyes." Then silence filled the room for a minute. Her mother had sobered. "Tell me what's going on with you."

"Luca has asked me to marry him, but I'm afraid I can't."

"Because Santos proved to be what your father would have called poor protoplasm?"

"He was worse than that, Mamma, but even being the womanizer he was, I couldn't keep him interested."

"Santos married you to make himself look good, but you couldn't have known that at the time. It didn't take long before you found out he'd never intended to be faithful. Apparently he'd had that woman on the side for years, but she wasn't the kind you married."

"But what does that say about me?"

"That the moment you found out he'd been betraying you, my courageous daughter moved out that very day and filed for divorce. Do you know how many thousands, probably millions of women, would have stayed and put up with that in order to have a man take care of her? I was so proud of you, I could have burst!"

Gabi blinked. "I didn't know you felt that way. If you only knew how terrible I felt to intrude on you when you thought I was happily married."

"I was thrilled beyond words you had the gumption and the strength to walk away even if your heart had been ripped out and you felt humiliated. Not every woman is lucky enough to be married to the right man the first time."

"*You* were."

"Your *papà* was a special man. When we lost him, I know you missed him so terribly, it's the reason Santos's interest in you filled the void he left. But only temporarily. I'm glad you found him out so fast. The person who told you about Santos's activities did you the greatest favor of your life."

"I agree."

"Gabi—I know you were very bitter in the beginning, with reason. Since the day you moved back in with me, I've prayed the right man would come along when the time was right. Who would have dreamed it would happen through a precious child needing an operation? I think you were guided to work for Edda."

"That's a beautiful story."

"You need to believe it."

"Last night Luca told me a lot of things about his life I never knew that aren't beautiful. He has a dominating father who has tried to run his life." Gabi told her about Giselle. "Luca said he wouldn't let his father interfere with us, but nothing's that simple."

"I think you're using that as an excuse."

Gabi grabbed hold of a chair back. "Maybe I am. But what if we got married and he finds me lacking once the bloom of the marriage has worn off? There will always be women attracted to him, and some who'll want to do something about it."

Her mother cocked her head. "Santos did a lot more damage to you than I thought. Have you told Luca everything about your marriage?"

"Yes."

"But he has no idea how afraid you are to trust a man again. This is where faith comes into the picture. If you helped Dino believe in a miracle to get through his operation, don't you think you should show the same faith and trust in Luca?

"That little boy's father molded him, and he adores you. So does his father, who needs you to help him raise that child. Do you know if he wants more children?"

She nodded. "He said he did."

They looked at each other for a minute. "Are you going to say anything to Edda when you go to work this morning?"

"How can I? I don't know my own mind yet."

Her mother finished her coffee. "Don't take too long. There's a child and his father waiting for your answer."

A sad-looking child stared at Luca as they sat having breakfast together. Not even getting a new dog could make a dent in what was wrong. This wasn't the way things were supposed to go after Dino's operation.

"How come Gabi didn't come and say goodbye to me before she left for Padova this morning?"

Luca had to think fast. "She was worried she'd get caught in traffic if she didn't leave early."

"She promised she'd come back. But what if she doesn't?"

His son had just brought up Luca's greatest fear. "We have to give her time to get her work done."

"I want her to help us train Nero."

Luca took a deep breath. "She'll be back soon." While they were in the family room playing with the dog, Ines came in. "Your father is in the living room."

Luca patted Dino's shoulder. "I have to talk to your *nonno* for a minute. I'll be right back."

He walked through the house to the front room, where his father stood in front of the fire. Naturally he hadn't come to see Dino. "Papà?"

"Good. You're here. Now that Dino is out of the woods, I thought we'd make our announcement together."

"What announcement? I thought you were supposed to be taking things easy."

"I'm much better. The doctor says I can go back to work full-time now as long as you and I share the CEO job."

That was news to Luca, who couldn't imagine anything worse. He didn't have to guess why this had happened the minute the operation was over. Luca hadn't been wrong when he'd told Gabi that his father wasn't through running his life.

"Before you say anything, I want you to know that Giselle and her father will be having dinner with your mother and me at home this evening. I expect you to be there. Leave Dino at home with Ines. This is for business."

More than ever he understood why Gabi had been so alarmed after having been left to deal with his father in the hospital room.

Luca fought down his anger. "You'll have to have dinner without me. End of discussion. Please leave, Papà. You know the way out." He stared at him until the older man left the room and slammed the front door on his way out.

CHAPTER TEN

"HERE'S THE FRIDAY bundle of letters." Stefania passed them around the conference table at the foundation. The whole place was lit up like a Christmas tree. But Gabi had been in such a bad way since returning to Padova, she couldn't get into the spirit of the holiday.

There'd been no word from Luca, or emails from Dino. Why would there be when she'd told Luca she wasn't ready to give him an answer yet?

Work should be saving her life, but nothing was helping her. She started opening the letters, but for once she couldn't concentrate. Before long the women took turns reading. When it came to Clara's turn, she read, "My name is Dino Berettini and I'm seven years old."

Gabi gasped out loud and almost fell out of the chair.

"I'm all better from my operation."

She'd already told her coworkers the marvelous news on Wednesday morning when she'd reported for work. Everyone smiled and looked at Gabi.

"Now I wish Gabi would be my new *mamma*. I love and miss her. So does my new dog, Nero, and my *papà*. He still isn't happy."

Gabi shot to her feet. She remembered what Giustina had said about Dino. He was an angel and an imp.

The little imp in him had found a way to get to her heart. Was it Luca or his *nonna* who'd mailed the letter? It had to have been mailed the very day she'd come back to Padova. Realizing Dino had printed those words himself, she knew *her* heart had already grown three sizes, big enough to blot out past fears forever.

"Forgive me, everyone, but I need to talk to Edda."

Clara got up and handed her the letter. After giving her a hug, they all clapped and wished her *buon Natale*.

Edda read the letter and asked Gabi what she was waiting for. "I expect to be invited to the wedding!"

Gabi flew home, threw some clothes in her suitcase and drove to Maniago at full speed beneath a semi-sunny sky. On the way, she phoned her mother, who was at work, and told her another miracle had happened. She'd be in touch.

After reaching the villa, she hurried up to the front door and knocked. Her heart was pounding so hard, she was almost ill with excitement.

"Ah," Ines cried when she opened the door and saw her.

Gabi put her finger to her own lips. "Is Dino here? I want to surprise him." The older woman nodded. "He's in the family room with his *papà*."

"Thank you."

When she dashed through the house and entered the room, the first thing she saw was Dino seated at the table putting a puzzle together. As she got closer, the dog yapped. Dino raised his dark head.

"*Gabi*—" In the next instant he'd reached her and flung his arms around her waist. She hugged him hard.

"We got your letter this morning at the Start with a Wish foundation."

He threw his head back. "You did?"

"Yes, and as soon as I read it, I said goodbye to Edda and drove straight here to tell you I want to be your new *mamma* more than anything in the world."

She felt a pair of strong male arms enfold both of them. "What took you so long, *bellissima*?" Luca whispered against her neck. He must have been over in the corner taking care of Nero. "Don't ever do this to me again. I couldn't take it."

Christmas Eve had finally arrived. Their wedding day.

"Dino? We need to leave for Padova. What are you doing?"

"I'm coming. I had to go to the bathroom." He came running to the foyer. "I hope Nero will be okay at Paolo's house."

"For one night he'll be fine."

Ines had helped him dress in a new navy blue suit. Luca had also purchased a formal midnight-blue suit for the wedding. They both wore spotless white shirts and lighter blue ties.

"You both look splendid," Giustina commented.

Luca thought his mother looked lovely in a champagne-colored suit and told her so. The three of them hurried out to the car for the drive to Limena.

Maria and Tomaso were bringing Ines and Pia in their car. They would be congregating at the elegant, private, nineteenth-century villa located in the heart of Limena for the 10:00 p.m. ceremony. Once the priest married them, they'd proceed to the Valbrenta hotel for dinner and an overnight. Christmas morning they'd drive back to Maniago and spend all day at the villa celebrating.

Luca promised Gabi to get there in plenty of time while she dealt with the final arrangements. They'd both wanted something small and private with only immediate family. All their friends would celebrate with them at the hotel.

When he reached the villa, he drove around the side to park. They went inside to the foyer, where Luca kissed his mother and left Dino with her. Between the red flowers and Christmas candles, plus the greenery, everything looked out of this world.

"I'll see you in a few minutes, *figlio mio*."

His son beamed before he hurried to a room that would lead into the living room for the ceremony. In a minute Tomaso joined him. The absence of Luca's father was glaringly obvious, but Luca had known he wouldn't be coming.

Tomaso smiled at him as they pinned the red flowers Maria had brought in to attach to their lapels. "My wife and I have fallen in love with Gabi. We know she's going to make you very happy."

"Thanks, Tomaso. Coming from you that means a lot."

"I couldn't imagine happiness two years ago. Now I can't remember what it was like to feel terrible. Dino is a different child. He adores her."

Luca nodded. "She has a way that hooked me within five minutes of meeting her."

A moment later, a villa staff worker summoned them into the living room, where Father Giovanni stood in front of a beautiful stained glass window resplendent in his vestments. Luca couldn't believe the time had finally come. In ways he felt like he'd been marking time forever. Yet it had only been a month.

From the doorway leading in from the foyer he saw Gabi enter. She walked slowly in a cream-colored lace suit and met him in front of the priest. One creamy rose had been tucked in her blond hair. Could a heart fail you? Luca didn't know, but for a moment he couldn't catch his breath at the gorgeous sight of her.

They clasped hands to face the priest.

"Dearly beloved, what a special time this is to repeat vows of love in this holy place filled with the love of our Lord. Tonight we celebrate the time of his birth and rejoice that two hearts are being joined as one. Tonight a third heart also joins us. If Dino Berettini will come forward, please."

Luca was as stunned as Gabi to hear his name said. They both turned to watch his son walk up to them wearing a red flower in his lapel, too. "Dino, if you'll stand at your father's other side."

Dino did his bidding.

"Dino talked to me in private and expressed his desire to be part of this wedding ceremony because he is so happy. Certainly our Lord is happy on this sacred night. Let us pray."

The rest of the ceremony was a blur to Luca, whose heart was so filled with love for this woman and his son, it didn't seem real. They shared a sweet kiss. It had been arranged that Tomaso would hand Luca the simple gold wedding band to put on her finger. But it was Dino who performed the service in a princely manner with a face that glowed.

"…and now I pronounce you Luca Berettini, and you Gabriella Russo, man and wife."

Luca gave Gabi a loving kiss before Dino came around to hug her. The three of them embraced with the man and the boy on either side of her. This was Christmas joy beyond measure for her.

As she looked into Luca's blue eyes, she thought she'd never seen anything so beautiful. They were a real family now. She could feel his love.

Then she turned her head and stared down into Dino's blue eyes, alive with light. Gabi felt overwhelmed by love for her own little boy who had the most amazing personality. When he wanted something with all his heart, he didn't let anything stop him. Who else but Dino would have asked for such a favor from the priest? This wedding ceremony would be remembered forever.

Once they reached the foyer, Gabi was hugged by her mother, then Luca's mother and the Guardinos. Luca finally caught her around the waist and ushered her through the villa to the car. They left for the hotel and the celebrating.

"Ooh," Dino said while his blue eyes took in everything.

"It's so beautiful," Gabi exclaimed!

"Not as exquisite as my new wife." Luca gave her a husband's kiss in front of everyone.

The hotel had gone all out for their wedding. Besides dozens of Christmas trees with white lights, they'd twined glittering white wedding bells among the Christmas greenery. With white candles lighting every table in the dining room, Gabi couldn't believe it was real.

Besides fish, they were served *agnolotti* and gnocchi, more pasta stuffed with ricotta and spinach, potatoes and pumpkin covered in butter and sage sauce. For dessert, panettone, Dino's favorite Christmas bread. The eating didn't stop until Luca slid a possessive arm around her hip, reminding her of the wedding night to come.

Outside the hotel, church bells were ringing all over the city. "It's the midnight hour. *Buon Natale*, Signora Berettini."

Christmas *had* come, and with it a new life for the three of them.

Gabi kissed Dino good-night, then her mother, who was keeping him with her for the night.

"Everyone has been taken care of," Luca whispered against her ear. "Now it's time to take you to bed, something I've been wanting to do forever."

"You think I haven't wanted the same thing?" Her legs shook like jelly as he helped her out of the dining room to the elevator of the hotel. Luca had booked the bridal suite, but she hardly noticed it because he carried her over the threshold to the bedroom.

They fell into each other's arms, consumed by the need to pour out their love and forget the world. "*Ti adoro, mia moglie.* Love me, Gabi," he cried. "Love me and never, ever let me go."

CHAPTER ELEVEN

DINO'S EIGHTH BIRTHDAY party fell on December twenty-third. The festivities were in full gear in the family room of the villa when Gabi started to feel pains in her lower back.

At first she thought it was because she'd been doing a lot of work and was just tired. But no matter how she moved or sat, the pain wouldn't go away, and it was getting worse with stinging sensations. These had to be labor pains.

They'd invited Dino's school class. Paolo's mother, Bianca, had been helping her along with Ines and Luca's mother. Bianca's baby was now six months old, and Bianca looked in fabulous shape already.

Gabi felt like a walrus even though Luca told her she'd never been more beautiful. She walked over to Bianca to tell her she needed to visit the bathroom and got there barely in time before her water broke.

In another minute she reached the kitchen. The clock said four thirty. "Pia? Will you call my husband? He's in the study. I'm in labor. He needs to drive me to the hospital."

"Aiee!" She picked up the phone while Gabi stood there in shock, clinging to the counter. Their baby was

coming. They'd found out it was a girl, and no one had been more excited and attentive than Luca.

"Tesoro?"

She could hear her husband's voice as he ran down the hall and burst into the kitchen.

"It's really coming?"

"Yes! My water just broke. Will you grab my overnight bag in the bedroom? I'll meet you at the car."

What a far cry from the last time she was in a hospital with Dino. This time Luca helped her inside the ER, and she was immediately wheeled up to the maternity ward. She was taken into her own labor room where Luca could be with her the whole time.

His face had a slight pallor. It had been so long since he'd been worried about anything, she felt terrible for him. But there wasn't anything she could do about it. Her pains were coming hard and consistently.

She was checked several times but told that a first baby took its time. When she saw that it had gotten to be 10:00 p.m., the anesthesiologist came in and gave her an epidural. It helped the pain, but the baby still wasn't ready.

Luca held her hand, looking like death. He finally got up and said he was going to find a doctor. In a way she was glad he left the room. When he came back gowned with a mask, another doctor was with him. He did a check.

"It's still going to be a while. Your obstetrician will be here when you're ready, so don't worry."

"He should be here now," Luca muttered after the resident left. "I wish I could do something for you. I've never felt so helpless in my life."

"You've done enough by getting me in this condition," she teased him, but her joke didn't go over. "Now it's up to me."

Finally, her obstetrician came in at five after twelve, gowned and masked. "Let's have a baby, shall we, Signora Berettini?"

"Please," Gabi half cried. She was exhausted.

"Do you realize it's December twenty-fourth? This little one is a Christmas Eve baby. That's a special blessing. Luca? You sit by her head while I do the rest. Now that you've put on gloves, don't touch anything."

"Can you believe it's finally happening?" she cried to her husband.

The pediatrician and two medical staff members came in to get things ready. She kept her eyes on Luca. He was her rock, her lover, her life! "Remember where we were a year ago tonight?"

"As if I could ever forget our wedding, *innamorata*."

"The head is coming. Bear down again, Gabi. Everything looks good." Before long they both heard a gurgle and the baby emerged. "That's a fine, lusty cry," the doctor said.

"Our baby girl—" Tears trickled from her eyes.

"Here she is, Mamma." The doctor put her on Gabi's stomach. "Luca? Come around to this side and you can cut the cord. Your first job as her *papà*."

Gabi started crying as she looked at the baby. "She's gorgeous!"

"She's just like you with a dusting of golden hair," Luca exclaimed.

After he'd cut the cord, the pediatrician took the baby to weigh and check. "Three point one-eight kilograms, fifty point eight centimeters," he called out.

"Her breathing is excellent. She looks perfect. *Complimenti!*"

The nurse cleaned her and wrapped her up before bringing her over to Gabi, who was dying to hold her.

"Oh, darling—can you stand it? We've got our little girl."

Luca's color had returned. He took his time examining every inch of her. First he'd kiss her, then he'd kiss Gabi.

The doctor smiled at them. "She's a beauty. What are you going to name her?"

"We're still debating. We all have a favorite, but it's going to be a family decision as soon as our son gets here."

No sooner had the doctor left than the room started to fill with all the relatives, including Gabi's mother. But it was Dino who beat everyone and came running over to them.

"Here's your new sister, Dino. What do you think of her?"

He got up close to her and studied her for a long time. "She looks kind of funny."

Luca put his arm around him. "You should have seen what you looked like when you were first born."

Dino giggled. "Where's her hair?"

"There's a little bit there, *figlio mio*. It'll all come in soon."

"Her eyes look kind of muddy."

"They'll probably turn green or blue," Luca explained. "We'll have to wait and see."

How she loved this son of theirs. "Do you think she looks like an Alessandra?"

He made a face. "No."

"How about Elana?" Luca said.

"Hmm, no. Can we call her Daniela?"

Gabi eyed her husband. "What do you think about that name?"

"I like it. What made you think of it?"

"She's in one of my favorite cartoons."

"It's a good thing she's not a boy or you'd probably want to name him *Diabolik*," Gabi teased.

Everyone laughed, Luca loudest of all. He turned around to talk to the family. "It's official. Meet the latest addition to our family. Daniela Berettini."

Carefully he passed the baby around so everyone could hold her. While they were all engrossed, someone else entered the room. *Luca's father.* Gabi couldn't believe it.

He looked at Luca. "Please may I come in, son? I missed Dino's delivery. I didn't want to miss this one."

Gabi locked eyes with Giustina. The two of them realized this was a turning point for better relations between Luca and his father. "Why don't you hand the baby to him?" she whispered.

Giustina lifted the precious bundle and showed him their new granddaughter. He studied her for a moment before kissing her head. "She's beautiful, just like her *mamma*."

With those words Gabi knew this was the closest thing to an olive branch they'd ever receive from the older man. She smiled up at the misty-eyed husband she adored. "Our Christmas Eve baby really is a blessing."

While everyone continued to marvel over Daniela, Luca leaned over to hug her to him the best way he could. He didn't have to say a word, but she knew. No matter how terribly his father had hurt him, he'd never wanted their estrangement. Thank heaven it was over.

"*Ti amo*, Luca. I love our new baby. I love Dino. I love you."

She felt his tears drip down her neck. Nothing could have felt more wonderful or healing.

* * * * *

If you enjoyed this story, check out these other great reads from Rebecca Winters

WHISKED AWAY BY HER SICILIAN BOSS
BOUND TO HER GREEK BILLIONAIRE
RETURN OF HER ITALIAN DUKE
THE BILLIONAIRE'S PRIZE

All available now!

MILLS & BOON®

Cherish™

EXPERIENCE THE ULTIMATE RUSH OF FALLING IN LOVE

A sneak peek at next month's titles...

In stores from 14th December 2017:

- **The Italian Billionaire's New Year Bride** – Scarlet Wilson *and* **Her Soldier of Fortune** – Michelle Majo
- **The Prince's Fake Fiancée** – Leah Ashton *and* **The Arizona Lawman** – Stella Bagwell

In stores from 28th December 2017:

- **Tempted by Her Greek Tycoon** – Katrina Cudmor *and* **Just What the Cowboy Needed** – Teresa Southwick
- **United by Their Royal Baby** – Therese Beharrie *ar* **Claiming the Captain's Baby** – Rochelle Alers

---

Just can't wait?
Buy our books online before they hit the shops!
www.millsandboon.co.uk

Also available as eBooks.

1217/23

MILLS & BOON®

EXCLUSIVE EXTRACT

Snowed in together on New Year's Eve, their
attraction explodes…! Leaving Italian billionaire
Matteo Bianchi to wonder if he could finally open his
heart and make Phoebe Gates his bride.

Read on for a sneak preview of
THE ITALIAN BILLIONAIRE'S
NEW YEAR BRIDE

He could still taste her, and he'd never felt so hungry
for more. Every part of his body urged him to continue.

But he took a deep breath and rested his forehead
against hers, his hand still tangled in her hair. Phoebe's
breathing was labored and heavy, just like his. But she
didn't push for anything else. She seemed happy to take
a moment too. Her chest was rising and falling in his
eye line as they stayed for a few minutes with their
heads together.

Everything felt too new. Too raw. Did he even know
what he was doing here?

"Happy New Year," he said softly. "At least I'm
guessing that's why we can still hear fireworks."

"There are fireworks outside? I thought they were
inside." Her sparkling dark eyes met his gaze and she
smiled. "Wow," she said huskily.

He let out a laugh. "Wow," he repeated.

Her hand was hesitant, reaching up, then stopping, then

reaching up again. She finally rested it against his chest, the fingertips pausing on one of the buttons of his shirt.

His mind was willing her to unfasten it. But she just let it sit there. The warmth of her fingertips permeating through his designer shirt. He could sense she wanted to say something, and it made him want to stumble and fill the silence.

For the first time in his life, Matteo Bianchi was out of his depth. It was a completely alien feeling for him. In matters of the opposite sex he was always in charge, always the one to initiate things, or, more likely, finish them. He'd never been unsure of himself, never uncomfortable.

But from the minute he'd met this woman with a warm smile and thoughtful heart, he just hadn't known how to deal with her. She had a way of looking at him as he answered a question that let him know his blasé, offhand remarks didn't wash with her. She didn't push. She didn't need to. He was quite sure that, if she wanted to, Phoebe Gates would take no prisoners. But the overwhelming aura from Phoebe was one of warmth, of kindness and sincerity. And it was making his heart beat quicker every minute.

Don't miss
THE ITALIAN BILLIONAIRE'S
NEW YEAR BRIDE
by Scarlet Wilson

Available January 2018

www.millsandboon.co.uk

YOU LOVE
ROMANCE?

WE LOVE
ROMANCE!

For exclusive extracts, competitions
and special offers, find us online: